I0772335

BRAND OF BLUE

MICHAEL WOODRUFF

BRAND OF BLUE

To that irreverent passenger within you:
The one which disregards your internal governance of effort,
who ignores your opinion of what is 'acceptable',
and which can find a pound of gumption where you believe an
ounce might reside.
To the one who burns the boats.

For Millie...
...again.
Who would have thought that a September morning
and a trip on the road less traveled
would lead to the sun, sails, and a salty liquid blue horizon?

Contents

1

With Good Reason

She was running late. The Monday morning nine o'clock pipeline meeting had been pushed up by an hour. With little regard for the attendees, her Director of Sales was well known for moving start dates forward and back depending upon his busy schedule, including the recurring meetings and calls. The line at the coffee shop was extensive. Four deep in the line, with an order for eight on the face of her shiny phone, she looked at the three baristas behind the counter scrambling to meet their customer's demands. The addictive aroma filled the air in the coffee house.

He was on time - with a minute to spare. Checking the pockets of his black pants, checking them again, and once more – he realized that he had forgotten his name tag. Punching into a wall-mounted tablet computer in the office, he reached for an available co-worker's name badge. Today, he'd need to be someone else. The handsome young black man pinned the borrowed moniker on his khaki apron which was emblazoned with the company's bold green and white logo. Freckles speckled his cheeks. If he were to be wearing a suit and tie, he could have passed for one of the Financial District and down the avenue Wall Street types.

The company's service statement declaration was embossed on the top of a cork board in the backroom: 'We serve our customers best through exceptional products, superior service, and timely delivery.' He read it and brushed his fingertips down across the word *timely*.

Her silver phone buzzed in her hand. The incoming text requested two more orders. *Oh, that's just great*, she thought. *How will I carry ten cups? Never. Never volunteering for this crap again. We have Admins for this crap.* Her thoughts fell to her friend, the Admin. Ashamed slightly, she bit her lip while looking at the stagnant line. A host of warm and cold beverage choices were neatly arranged on the menu behind the service area.

The late-December Manhattan morning air was moist and cold, but not yet freezing. Clouds, deep and battleship gray, hung low in the sky, and appeared to be filled with buckets of rain or perhaps a rain and snow mix.

The barista saw the growing line of customers building, each wearing a dark colored coat, as he walked into the serving area. He quickly moved to step into the bullpen to help. Mixing, blending, garnishing, and capping the lineup of caffeinated beverages. Two cups here, one cup there, and an order for ten. He worked rigorously to move through the order quickly making little small-talk with his coworkers.

One more barista walked into the service side of the counter and quickly jumped in to provide speedy and *timely* service. Eight cups into the order, yet another java-jamming teammate jumped in and offered to double bag the beverages for the attractive young woman at the checkout counter.

He looked at her from the corner of his eye. She was shaking her head and mouthing the word 'yes', while holding another conversation with someone on her cell phone. When she shook her head, her tendrils swayed against the currents of her movement. A bright blue repeating flash appeared from an earpiece she was wearing.

She was an attractive petite blond with long hair. A seductive and crooked smile radiated on her face as a result of the conversation she was having. She was hearing something either she agreed to or was slightly skeptical of listening to. Under her black wool jacket, she wore a sleek gray dress with a dotted black design, and a long lapis blue scarf hung around her neck. A small corporate logo was found on the tail. She looked down at her shoes while the staff were completing the order. *Size 7 and a half*, she thought. *I never wear 7 and a half. But they're so cute.* Her heel lifted slightly from the shoe. She was thinking she'd get a blister on each heel from the rub, but it was worth it.

"I'm barely going to make it," she was heard saying. "We're still on the forty-second, right? I mean he doesn't have us in the war room on the forty third, I hope. We won't fit." Her voice was raspy, and it was apparent that she was speaking to a co-worker about a meeting location. The one-sided conversation continued with the mystery person on the other end of the call, "Meanwhile...hello...and more importantly...how did it go last night?" She listened intently to what was being said on the phone, and with wide eyes, became animated with what she had just heard, "Did you say it too?" It was said quietly and teasingly as her chin lowered to her chest. Flecks of emerald greens were shining brightly in her hazel eyes. Several seconds passed, and with a wide teasing smile she asked, "And did you mean it?" Several more seconds passed and she offered, "Well, you and Chris have only been together, what, a hundred times. So, you were in Chris's arms when you said it. Awe...so sweet."

She was fidgeting with her shoes, heels in, heels out, heels in, heels out. First it was the left foot, then the right. "You know what I'm going to say...just make sure you make him love you more than you love him!" It was a declaration shared with her from her grandmother. She returned to listening while watching the baristas quickly fulfill the manifest of the order.

Seizing the poly bag containing the coffees in varieties of sizes from the counter she paid by waving her phone above a tiny device on the counter and returned to the call. The ten cups were much easier to carry than she thought as she dodged new patrons in another building line toward the door.

Her unknown problem was that the order was not complete.

A middle-aged manager approached him. "Hey man. I apologize. Uh..." Hesitating and shrugging his thin shoulders, "You're not supposed to be here this morning."

"Oh? The schedule..." the young black barista pointed a couple fingers in the direction of the office.

"Yeah, someone accidentally replicated last week's and you're off today. I'm sorry. We have too many baristas this morning."

"Uh...alright...no problem. I'll clock out and...have a look at the schedule for my next shift." There was something other than coffee stirring behind the pick-up counter. Two teammates could be heard debating over an order.

"Thanks dude. I've got it right here." The curly haired scrawny manager was holding onto a tablet with the correct schedule, and squinting, handed it to him.

He observed the calendar and was handing it back to the manager when another younger coworker with short dark hair approached him, "Hey – that woman that just paid – the cute blond – she left two drinks behind. Do you remember her? She said something about the forty second or forty third."

The neighboring building was the technology tower. Many of the high-tech giants which occupied the skyscraper had their teammates run for the specialty coffees that didn't churn out of the glass carafes. The floors were well known to the coffee house staff. The 7th, the 9th, 16, 26 and 29. Skip the thirties - and the 41st, 42nd, 43rd, and 44th floors. He thought of the bright blue scarf. "I do. Hard to forget."

"Quick, see if you can catch her. Here..." The barista slipped the two remaining drinks in a pressed cardboard four cup holder. Their names were written on the sides of the drinks in black marker, steam billowing from the mouth of one of the lids.

The manager smiled and nodded at the handsome young black man, "Thanks. Sign out when you get back. Go, go, go!"

He grabbed the corrugated cup holder cradling the beverages, and without a jacket to brace against the cold morning, moved quickly to the exit to look for her. Once outside, the wind whipped and felt like it bit his face and at once his eyes watered. He noticed her crossing Barclay at Broadway. Horns honked and delivery truck engines revved as reds turned green, and brakes squealed as greens turned yellow briefly followed by red. He looked at one of the names on the beverages, and thought to shout out her name, but was certain there was too much ground transportation noise to be heard at this distance. Walking quicker did no good as he was held up at the corner traffic light. He could see her entering the glass and copper marble tower, with the blue scarf's tail waving slightly as she walked.

Once inside, he noticed her approaching the bank of elevators, but had to clear security to join her. Passing quickly through the metal detector after reaching into his wallet to show his delivery badge credentials, he saw her leap out of one of her shoes as she jumped into a closing elevator door.

"Oh shit, that did not just happen!" An elevator filled with mostly businessmen dressed in fine suits giggled as she said it. One of her new shoes, slightly too big, was left behind as the elevator door closed and immediately began its high-speed accent to the next floor. They were on three, heading to nine. She tried to balance. With her purse, a computer bag, and the beverages, it was difficult. One of the businessmen closest to her reached out his leather gloved hand to steady her. "Thanks," she whispered.

"No problem," he whispered back to her, adding, "Cinderella."

She looked in his direction, noticing he was wearing glasses, holding a cane. How could she not have noticed him before? *What is he...? Blind? No, dipshit. He saw the shoe thing just happen.*

Leaning against the elevator door since she was the last in, looking around the elevator for anyone she might know, she recognized no one. *I can still make it. Drop off the coffees and deal with the wrath, or just show up with one shoe? Ugh. We all manage trade-offs. What to do?* She hated the idea of the two-hundred-dollar shoe sacrifice. *They sure were cute for the two hours I wore them,* she thought. *Not the most expensive one-day wardrobe departure from my closet.*

A curly blond-haired small boy with bright blue eyes, perhaps five or six years old looked up to her. She smiled at him. *So cute,* she thought. He smiled back at her and in slow motion, reached to light all of the buttons he could reach. Thirty-three and down. "You've got to be kidding me!" She said it out loud drawing attention to each floor's button being lit in what would deliver a slow accent. "*You little monster*", she said under her breath. Anyone noticing what had just happened groaned - and subtle passenger explanation took place for those that did not. The mother of the little boy apologized, then began explaining to the child why the buttons could not be pushed.

The black barista picked up the shiny black pump in front of the closed door and deliberately moved to the next elevator bank and jumped in, punching 42 along with an already lit 12, 19, 23 and 37. He nodded to the half-dozen other passengers. With no chit-chat on the ride, he disembarked at the 42nd floor seeking the attractive blond. At first, he moved toward the electric blue logo glass lobby door then hesitating, thought differently. Perhaps he arrived before she did and moved to the elevator she'd arrive on.

A hazel-eyed, dishwater blonde with soft curls hanging to her shoulders, woman approached the same elevator and said to him, "You need to make a selection for anything to happen. Up or down. One or the other," she smiled in a playful way nodding her head to the arrows on the wall plate. She too, was pretty, but not like the customer he was waiting for.

"Oh, um yes, I'm waiting for someone."

"Hmm. Me too." She gave him an obvious second glance head to shoes, sizing up that this handsome black man must be a delivery barista. She didn't notice the shoe in his right hand, only the two coffees held in his left, "Hey, that's me!" she referred to the venti latte with *Maggie* printed on the side of the cup.

"Dave?" she asked. Referring to his name badge, she nodded her head toward his nameplate oh his chest.

He reached for the warm beverage, handing it to her, and she cradled it with both hands. "Oh, uh...no. It's borrowed, someone else's badge. Charlie. I'm Charlie."

"Dave is your stage name?" She smiled and took a tiny slurpy sip of the coffee while looking at him. Her pink lipstick marked the white plastic lid.

The elevator pinged, and out hobbled Allegra Sinclair. The stunning blond looked at both, offering a small smile of anticipation. There was her best friend Maggie in the accompaniment of a familiar looking man wearing an apron from the local coffee house.

"Hello beautiful," her friend loudly greeted her. "We have coffee, a bridge plan to speak to – which you're going to kill...and we're late!"

Allegra stared at the barista with her black shoe in one hand, and her coffee in his other. She did recognize him. It was a déjà vu moment. She wasn't sure how to interpret it.

Maggie grabbed Allegra's bag of beverages and said, "I'll take that for you. Meet Dave...or Charlie." She didn't notice Charlie handing the shoe to Allegra.

Allegra quickly slipped it on, bracing herself against his forearm, she whispered while looking into his eyes, *"Timely."* Then, slightly louder she spoke, "Thank you, Dave...or Charlie." She steadied herself, looked down at the shiny new shoes and then her glance came back up to Charlie with a small smile on her face. Allegra and Maggie took a few steps toward the company entrance, guiding his exit.

Attempting to piece together the puzzle of just how it happened that the barista turned up on the 42nd floor with the shoe, Allegra turned to the bank of brass elevators to express her appreciation once more and to ask him a question. The doors were closing, and she saw his face looking back at her.

She shook her head back and forth slightly in a form of wonderment, looked at Maggie and asked, "That was pretty strange, right?"

"Whatever girl. Don't make Vendemer wait. It's go-time, you pitch in five." To keep Allegra on task, with the coffee lineup in one hand she grabbed at her computer bag and together they hustled into the brilliant blue entrance. The blue circular logo on the door swung open easily and closed slowly.

Allegra turned one more time before the door sank closed to glance back at the closed elevator doors of the 42nd floor. *Something just happened*, she thought.

*****

"Miss it?" Ruby sat with his back to the door of the coffee shop. He swirled his index finger in the air, indicating the buzz of New York. His dark red suspenders loosely slung over his shoulders and a beige checkered shirt dangled from under his black wool coat. This is how he was dressed when they first met several years ago. It was not unintentional attire for this casual meeting. Disregarded by the crowd as a standout was his normal modus operandi.

Jacob was squinting from the glare of the outside light. He was maneuvering the paper cups of 'just joe' as his friend called it. No fancy shots-of-whatnot, boosters, dairy or non-dairy creams, or Italian jargon for size mattered. Just joe – black and medium. It worked. One for each side of the table.

"Want me to move?" the black man asked a second question.

"Like you'd miss a finger or a toe," Jacob replied, answering the first.

They had just sat down. Ruby froze, while tucking his gloves in his coat pocket, not understanding the reply. He stared at his handsome friend who was having some difficulty with the intrusive bright light streaming in from the storefront.

Jacob Paisley moved seats to be next to Ruby opposed to sitting across from him. The small maple table wobbled a little as he steadied the piping hot cup of coffee in his hands. Removing the white plastic lid, a plume of steam slowly lofted between them, then disappeared as another customer opened a door to the morning streets outside. He wasn't dressed like the rich fat cat that he once was. The expensive clothing was replaced with sensible business casual attire. An open collar dress shirt, jacket, slacks which may or may not match, and comfortable shoes which didn't cost a thousand dollars per foot. The overcoat depended upon the New York weather which changed often.

"I know you were speaking of Manhattan. What I miss is Oahu. I think I left my heart..."

"Well, you never know." Ruby made sure that they were looking at each other when he winked.

"Say when," Jacob encouraged, "I'm in..."

"Might be another three-hour tour." Ruby joked, chuckling to himself.

"I'm out."

Ruby watched the line continue to add patrons. The baristas weren't keeping up with the demand. When he and Jacob placed their order, the employees were speedy and efficient. The online order queue was two to one. He kept looking at the counter and the teammates behind the cash register, squinting himself to see better.
"And how's the kid?"

Jacob paused for a second, then answered slowly, "The other Gabiel Hollins?"

Ruby showed no teeth when he smiled this time, "Yeah, that one. You liked it how I influenced my name there, right?"

The money manager answered the second question first this time, "Yeah, that was smooth," he sipped at the paper cup and immediately decided that it was too hot. "Adele is heading back to Kapolei after Christmas. I don't think she booked a flight yet, but she's looking. And..." he trailed.

"And?" Ruby wrinkled his forehead as he repeated Jacob.

"And...whatever we might discuss may change things."

"Small steps Captain Paisley," he hesitated, then continued, "There are two people I want you to meet first. The first is..."

"Go on," Jacob coaxed, nodding his head toward Ruby.

"My son." Ruby glared at Jacob seeking a response.

Jacob frowned, "Your son...as in your boy?"

Even though they were sitting next to each other, a small amount of silence sat between the two of them. It lingered there for longer than Jacob would have liked it to while Ruby's direction was elsewhere in the coffee house.

"Heading out?"

Knowing how to reply and when it was acceptable to, the young barista turned delivery boy had his navy parka on and stopped at their table near the entrance. He looked at Jacob, then back to his father, seeking permission to speak freely.

Ruby, without words, looked up at the young man standing while the two men continue to sit. The father looked fondly up to his boy.

Jacob gazed at the two of them, seeing the resemblance. "There was a snafu in the schedule. I'm off today, on tomorrow."

"Charlie, I'd like you to meet a friend of mine." He looked at Jacob and added, "a new friend. This is Mr. Jacob Paisley."

Charlie looked at his dad for reassurance. "Pleased to meet you Mr. Pailey." He held out his hand.

Jacob reached out, with his hand that had shaken a million other hands in Manhattan, accepting the handshake, "It's nice to meet you, Charlie." Paisley didn't remember the last time he shook a hand in New York without the thought of making money attached to the grasp.

The young black man who looked like Ruby broke the clutched palms first and returned to looking at his father for direction.

There was none. Ruby just smiled at his boy and added, "I'll see you at home."

"Okay pops." He placed the hand that shook Jacobs on Ruby's shoulder, "Love you." Charlie departed as soon as he could knowing that there was a discussion of some kind in play and he wasn't invited to attend, nor could he. This was his place of business. The door opened with Charlie's exit, bringing with it the chilly street air and a grey skyscraper breeze, and exchanging it for a warm comforting coffee smelled air.

Jacob watched the family dynamics. There was more to the story, and he was curious. "Your son...he works for, he works with the..."

"Not here." Ruby glared at Jacob. He leaned in toward Jacob and spoke softly. "I know, I know it's a learn as you go thing here, but no text messaging, no email, no mention of it in public spaces." Leaning back, he added while still speaking quietly," It's getting difficult, with AI, to communicate and will continue to..."

Jacob leaned forward, narrowing the gap in distance between them, and spoke quietly too, "Artificial Intelligence is making things more difficult to..."

"Cameras. Fucking things - are everywhere. I mean...it's good and it's bad. But...the algorithms, the data, the facial recognition."

"Got it. Enough said," Jacob sat back and pondered. "But you texted me to meet you..." He was about to say 'here' before Ruby added in a non-clandestine way.

"Encrypted server." Ruby looked off into the distance and toward the line of customers that had again begun to shrink. In the course of doing so, he saw two cameras pointing into the coffee shop from the ceiling which allowed the headquarter location know when to add staff, when to cut staff, when to brew more, when to brew less, how to manage the retail items better based upon interest, which items were prone to shrink, where to position stanchions to manage the customer waiting, and a dozen other metrics which improved profitability or client satisfaction.

He paid no attention to cameras and instead thought of the next introduction as Jacob simultaneously asked the question.

"The first was your son, Charlie. Handsome young man. Looks nothing like you," Jacob grinned like George Clooney would have.

Then he smiled like Patrick Dempsey would have, showing off his perfect teeth, perhaps an Orthodontists finest work or just lucky to have such a smile. "Who's the second person? Your daughter?"

Ruby reached for a cell phone buried deep in his pant pocket and began toggling through pages of a social media site.

"Here she is. Meet Allegra Sinclair."

Grabbing the phone from his friend, Jacob paused when looking at her. He scrolled through several images of her. Handing the phone back to Ruby, he said it, then asked it: "Stunning. Not your daughter, for sure. Who is she?"

"A rising star in tech. We've had our eyes on her for a while. She's on the watch list. Want you to help me size her up, but only when I say so. Works there." Ruby used his thumb to point to a building out in the city somewhere.

"On the watch list? Like a stock?" Jacob asked the recruiter.

"Sort of. Enough said - for here, for now. No contact - whatsoever." Ruby shook his head some. He crumpled up the receipt still on the table, tucking it inside his coat pocket, and muttered toward Jacob, "Sit. Relax a minute. Enjoy your six-dollar bean juice."

Jacob pumped his head in understanding, as he grasped the warm white paper cup between his hands. It reminded him of her. Of Victoria. Her silence and departure ate at him. An unexplained curiosity was gnawing at him, and he decided to broach the topic. The cup of coffee was symbolic of their first date, not far from this location. She could appear at any given moment. *Where did you go girl?* Jacob thought about her playfulness, the teasing, his longing – back then, not now exactly. The memories ran deep, wild, and far from the professional well-kept image he held publicly. Their twist was a screw through his soul. It was gone, and only scar tissue remained.

"Will I ever see her again?"

There was a small pause, "Allegra Sinclair? We just..."

"Victoria. Sorry, I jumped topics on you there." Jacob was thinking of many things, one of which was his former seductress, his Aphrodite – the Greek goddess of physical pleasure, sexual lust, and beauty.

Ruby looked at him. He looked into Jacob's eyes which were fixated on the paper cup. Saying nothing, a deep breath was taken and slowly exhaled. He continued to study the listlessness of his table mate. "You're with Adele now..." Another small pause ensued, "Right?"

Jacob eventually looked up from the tabletop. With no conviction he answered, "You know the answer to that. I'm with Adele now, correct."

"Well, who knows anything about Victoria..."

"You know. You do." Jacob found his assurance in how he said it but wasn't certain that he wanted an answer that he didn't want to hear.

"Rikers." Ruby looked at his friend, sitting across from him with a blank stare becoming a furled brow. "Awaiting trial."

"For...what? For what...exactly?"

A calculated response was overdue. Ruby owed it to Jacob. He divulged what he knew. "For what she did with her money."

"The money I paid her?"

"Perhaps. Some of the money you paid her may have been used. She was in debt. She lived a rich life. Richer than she was. You know it and I know it. You know this too, when you're underwater – you come up for air. Somehow, some way. But there were sharks in the water..."

"Tell me, Ruby." Jacob used his finger on the maple table signifying and pointing with a few nudges on the surface that he wanted some facts.

"Alright. But you can't un-hear it. So, it goes – she's been held at Riker's for a while now. Every time her trial date or parole hearing or whatever it might be comes up, every five or six months or so, it seems that new information is revealed."

Jacob jutted his chin toward Ruby, "You?"

"Not me. She was investing in triple X schemes. X, X, X. Not exactly sure what that means but it had something to do with what they called apex, exotic, and toxic investing."

Jacob looked to the back of his hands, now clutched in fists in front of him. He slowly looked back up to meet Ruby's inquisitiveness and slowly replied, "I told her about that..."

"I tried to find something on the internet, but nothing came back."

"It's dark. You won't find anything online. *Apex.* Apex is pump and dump. Through penny stocks usually, sometimes options or micro caps. You fund an illegitimate account and have an influencer hype something of little to no value and then cut and run when the momentum builds. It's slap on the wrist stuff from the SEC, not usually jailhouse material."

"That wasn't the one. But it came up when the investigation began. The exotic one? Which is that?"

"Exotic investing is art and spirits and sovereign debt and the unusual instruments which may or may not lead to tax evasion."

"That's it – that's the one that started the investigation. She didn't declare some sort of a windfall or capital gains or something..."

"So quickly?" Jacob sat puzzled, "It would usually take years for an IRS or SEC trigger."

Ruby shrugged his shoulders.

"Toxic. Toxic investing is all sorts of salacious stuff. Fronting drug money, stolen cars, human trafficking logistics costs, the worst of the worst. You invest a hundred thousand, you get two..."

"Guns." Ruby divulged the remainder of what he knew about Jacob's former vixen. "She invested in illegal gun trade. It unraveled quickly and supposedly she was wearing shiny stainless-steel bracelets squatting into an NYPD cruiser after someone wearing a wire ratted her out."

"Again. I must ask. Did you or did someone you know do... Did anything happen here? To distract her or keep her busy? Was there any?" He didn't finish asking questions as he watched Ruby slowly shake his head from side to side.

"I must ask you, are we exposed in any of those strategies? We're not doing any of that to juice our returns, are we?" Ruby asked.

"No, I never have and won't." Jacob answered honestly, "There are too many other means, too many other opportunities that aren't worth the risks. Only someone who doesn't have patience or know that there's incredulous inspection around questionable schemes would pursue such a foolish end run."

Only the grinding of dry beans, the gurgling sound from the espresso machines, the clatter and the bustling sounds of the coffee shop filled the next minute.

"She lived left of center, Jacob. In the margins. Her life wasn't, *nothing* in her life *was* normal, I should say. You know that more than anyone." Ruby was simply the messenger, sharing what had been shared with him. Quite often, he knew a little something about almost everything or much about anything. Here he was without the growing network of good intentions in his ear. Ellipsis didn't have a seat at the table.

Jacob sat in silence reminiscing about her purple underwear in the white paper cup from their second encounter. His parting gift...her naughty secrets and irresistible smile as they departed. She knew shock value. It was her lurid product. Her playful flirting with the former CEO of PPCM was as far away from the present moment as his innocence was.

The influence of one individual upon another was commonly undetectable and beyond comprehension. Often, in a lifetime of actions, consequential and inconsequential, the impact might reveal itself. But more than not, influence was hidden and secretive in its wake.

Jacob was drawn to what American Author, H. Jackson Brown, Jr. reminded us of: *"Kind words and good deeds are eternal. You just never know where their influence may lead. "* He assumed that it was true of the other side of human interaction as well. The darkness and the evil lived within us because the light and radiance of goodness was not always lit.

Ruby reached into his jacket pocket and withdrew a tangerine. Bright, orange, shiny from the wax rubbed onto the citrus skin – he set it on the table between them.

Jacob reached for it, smiling, remembering his heart attack in the middle of an intersection south of where they were at the present. The cold pavement provided a runway for another tangerine to roll under a town car sitting idle, waiting. The bright tiger colored fruit rolled until it didn't. Clutching his chest in pain with one hand while ineffectively trying to grab the produce which Adele had told him he needed to eat more of, because it was heart healthy, he recalled the moment with clarity. Even in the shadow of the black shiny car above it, the tangerine had a cheery shine within a gloomy moment.

He reached inside his jacket and in between the buttons of his shirt to feel the remnants of the scar tissue as Ruby spoke next. The small incision was no more than eight inches running down the center of his chest.

"Got someplace I need to be. I'll call you tomorrow."

"What if I need to reach you? If I have something pressing?" Jacob didn't. This new pace was less than he was accustomed to. He thought that this meeting up with Ruby several times a week and talking little about how the trust was advancing and much about nothing was not only the slow lane but might be likened to a sleepy country road drive stuck in second gear. The scenery was pretty, but he wanted to go fast.

"Just call the 646 exchange, not the other. Never the other."

"The 212? That's what you call me with…" Jacob stopped speaking when Ruby held his finger to his lips, indicating silence about the topic. "Right," he continued, "Thanks." He held the shiny fruit up before he tucked it away.

Ruby stood and nearly turned to leave, hesitated, and looked back to Jacob, "Oh…you do Podcasts?"

"Everyone does, don't they?"

"Uh, well no, but I just started listening to them. Fascinating. There's one I'd like you to listen to." Ruby looked at Jacob reaching for his phone.

"What' it called?"

"I'll send you the link. It's right up your alley. It's about data."

"Sure. You're going to what?" Jacob looked at Ruby, "text it to me?"

"Right. I'll send you a link,"

"Okay – I'll try to listen to it right away," Jacob replied.

'Aloha." Ruby smiled slightly as rose again and turned away.

Before Jacob looked up and replied, his friend who lived shrouded in or hidden by secrecy had already taken steps toward the exit, to faint away into the busy city outside.

With good reason, Ruby was taking his time in onboarding Jacob into the secret society. He knew he was a work in progress, as this obscure mission statement of their clandestine organization, Ellipsis, was not the Manhattan-like prominence which he was accustomed to as the former PPCM CEO. That was then, this was not now – but was to be. It was soon, and it was mysterious, and it was somewhat void of meticulous and logical developmental steps which Jacob was accustomed to. He thought *with good reason, perhaps, they're...he's taking small steps with me.*

Jacob was more than just their rainmaker for money now. It wasn't a seat at the table. It was, however, as if he were suited up again and in the situation room, yet unable to hear what was being constructed or said.

✳ ✳ ✳ ✳ ✳

"Ninety-seven, ninety-eight...ninety-nine..." he counted out loud as the final few push ups from his knuckles were felt the most. "One hundred." The final rep was a whisper. There would be one more set. In between the chest, arms and abs in the evening's workout was stretching. He grunted as he bent over on the floor, feeling the burn in his thighs from the day before. The lactic acid buildup was intensifying.

Aiden Ashford, web-designer by day, personal investigator by day and by evening and by night, was on a journey. The 'personal' in personal investigator was his personal agenda - alone. The former software engineer had recently shifted careers to accommodate his more important mission. His freelance work funded his interests and afforded him the opportunity to work when he wanted to.

He chose to go by his last name, instead of his first. There was a reason behind it that didn't always share. Ashford's muscle tone had defined dramatically over the past several months. His strength, upper body, core torso, and leg strength was twice what it had been when she left him. Forty push ups were once the stretch. The extreme workouts helped relieve the mental anguish and had been prescribed by the doctor to help him keep his wits during this dire time of healing. The obsession in physical fitness extended from the conclusion of the last job to this new work-from-anywhere flexible position. The Covid-19 pandemic had created hybrid work environments and new gig positions abounded.

She. He couldn't stop thinking of her. If he did, she might slowly disappear. If he wasn't as occupied with her as he always had been, then maybe she would diminish. Then, hope would be lost, and he might as well not live on. She, she was his reason to live. She had to remain the centerpiece of his purpose, his desire, his reason for the physical transition. She – the apple of Ashford's eye – couldn't be gone. She was still out there. Others told him that it was maybe, just maybe, time to move on. Ashford didn't think that it was – far from it - and asked them not to give up their faith that they could be reunited.

Ashley's smoky eyes looked back at him as he studied her picture taped to the mirror in the bathroom. It was his favorite picture of her looking into the camera, directly into his eyes. She said his eyes were the color of the world, her world. Greens and blues and peace from above. Her silky hair, chestnut with golden highlights cascaded in layers to the sides of her high cheekbones. Her winsome nose, probably from her mother's side, was petite like the rest of her. She had a slight smile on her face as her champagne-brown eyes in her picture looked back at him.

Neither of them imagined something like this might happen. Knowing that this unbearable moment of separation would come wasn't what they dreamed about. It wasn't a consideration. It certainly wasn't what they planned to have happen. But it did.

As a coastal bachelor, the beach scene in Tampa had many eye-candy offerings. The Big Guava had been his home since Ashford moved there as a small child and from New Mexico, the Land of Enchantment. That was a long time ago. He couldn't remember it.

Ashford loved the opposite sex - when he was once available to love multitudes of the opposite sex. He just hadn't met the right girl. There was a half dozen serious relationships which fizzled because of something which he or she or they did or didn't do. There was more than a dozen 'friends with benefits' in his orbit since turning twenty.

Then, at a corporate event, he met her: Ashley. It was then that he loved the opposite sex in a monogamous way. It was her, only her.

Ashford was eleven years older than her when they first met. He was a lively thirty-five-years young beach-loving single, and she was an old soul with just twenty-four years behind her when they first met. He towered above her in height. Rising to six foot, three inches, Ashford was a foot taller than Ashley's five foot, three inches tall frame. His hair color was the same as hers. The sunlight worked its magic in highlighting it. The chemistry between the two of them was intense. They could not, not be with each other their first year together. Sex-on-the-beach was more than a drink shared. Physically, emotionally, intellectually, they were in sync in all that they did. They shared their deepest secrets, which neither of them really had any of. In between the sheets, they vowed to love each other eternally as they fell asleep holding each other nightly.

She kept him a secret from her parents that first year though. Ashley shared with Ashford that after they finally met her parents, her mother pulled her aside and said, "He's lovely. I see what you see in him." Then she asked, "But, well...isn't he...isn't he just a little bit old for you?"

"I think I love him, Mom. If he asks me to marry him, I'll say yes – absolutely."

Her mother and father blessed the arrangement of the age differences and offered to support them and their evolving relationship in any way they could. That was the beginning of another good thing. Ashford's gallivanting around the beaches of Tampa ended after he met Ashley. He proposed. She said 'yes – absolutely', and the wedding planning began.

Ashley Ellsworth looked a lot like Kate Mara. Some said she resembled Anna Kendrick. Ashford thought she was more Kate and less Anna as he stared at her long eyelashes in the picture. They flicked against his lips as she tiptoed to kiss him goodbye.

Her position as a first-grade teacher had taken off. She loved her students, and they adored her, Miss Ellsworth. She told the class that she would change her name after she became married, and she would be Mrs. Ashford. When asked '*why*' from a small child, she answered "Because I love my future husband, and I want to take his name." The small child asked, '*what will his name be if you take his name?*' Ashley thought about it, and simply replied, "Mine." The child contemplated the name exchange, shrugged their small shoulders, and picked their nose as they returned to recess.

Ashford was in the trap. Thinking about her while standing there, doing nothing. *Keep moving*, he told himself. Picking himself up from the floor, he reached for the dumbbells and began alternatively curling the forty-five-pound steel blue weights. His grunts grew louder as the reps increased in number.

They had friends together that thought they were great together. Mr. and Mrs. Happy, they described them. He was well established in the software industry as a premier engineer. She was a fun-loving and Ashford-loving schoolteacher who completed his restless spirit. The silver-bullet chugging weekends with other partner-less guys was replaced with wine parties, friends' dinners for couples, movies and road trips. They enjoyed streaming a plethora of for-him action flicks, for-her documentaries, and for-them rom-coms.

Ashley had a way of changing Ashford's mind. At ten-thirty on a Saturday night, he would ask her, "Ash, you ready for sheets?"

She'd answer, let's stay up until tomorrow.

He'd pop some corn, cut Honeycrisp apples and fetch them a diet coke to share, and they would find the energy within each other to make it until two or three in the morning.

Ashford left Ashley looking seductively back at him and returned to the floor for another set of pushups. "One...two...three...four...five...six..." The counting paused at fifty for a hold. He could smell his own stink of perspiration. Then began again, only stuttering for gasps in the nineties. "Ninety-seven...ninety-eight...ninety-nine..." he held it. "You can do this. Do it for Ashley. One hundred." He gasped, sometimes surprised at the new strength he was finding.'

✳ ✳ ✳ ✳ ✳

She was a Bravado Surf girl. A former Bravado Surf girl really – an alumnus representative of the Pacific rim brand. Her photo, taken twelve years earlier, along with a half dozen other model spokespersons, was still featured in their flagship store in the Ala Moana Center in Honolulu and in thirteen other Hawaii locations. Leaning against each other, smiling under the shade of coconut trees, wearing well-coordinated Bravado Surf clothing, the curling overhead waves on Oahu's North Shore was the backdrop for the iconic picture which was wallpaper behind the cash registers in their stores.

Tamsen Makua walked along the railroad tracks by Electric Beach with the young, eighteen-year-old named Kate – the new addition to their team. It was common practice by the curators of the brand to nurture the young talent joining their team. "What made you want to become a Bravado girl?"

"What it will do for me. The springboard into other modeling. Or surfing – see how that develops," the short platinum blond-haired girl replied.

"Hmm. How about this...*what you can do to influence other young women*. How would that sound through your lips?" Tamsen asked her, but really coached her on the reply that a Bravado teammate should respond with when asked.

"Yeah, that's what I meant to say," she smiled at Tamsen while carefully watching each step they were taking on the gravel, next to the railroad ties and the steel tracks. "I wanted to be a Bravado girl because of what I might be able to do to influence other young people..." She repeated it aloud. "And it's better than being one of those Roxy bitches..."

Tamsen spun around, "Let me stop you right there..."

"I was teasing! OMG," interrupting and offended, she held one hand lightly over her chest, touching the slight space between her small breasts. "When did you become so pro-Roxy anyway?"

"Since forever. If Roxy wanted you, you might not be a Bravado girl. They're a great brand and they stand for great things. Besides, we're all friends of the industry."

"We're friends? With our competition?"

"Just like out in the lineup," Tamsen referred to surfing, awaiting the sets out on the water, "we coexist, complimenting each other when we can."

"But I thought..."

"Co-ompetition. They are our frenemies." Tamsen cut in with a brand-to-brand explanation of the bridge between the two well-known fashion companies. "Everything in the Liberated Brands portfolio is like that. Volcom, Billabong, RVCA, Quiksilver – great companies with awesome messaging. No disrespect, but they have pick of the litter. They go after the best surf girls with platform-building personalities often and early."

"Platform-building personalities," she repeated.

"Besides, when we go to the marketing conventions, the fashion shows, we're all drinking buddies," Tamsen continued.

"Drinking buddies," the girl repeated, carefully watching her step across the larger rocks.

Tamsen found her a little odd. "Huntington Beach is home, right?"

"Yeah, that's where Mom and Dad and Andy, my feisty little terrier – named after Andy Irons – all live. I grew up there learning to surf along the SoCal beaches, but mostly Huntington, Newport and Laguna."

Tamsen's long chestnut colored hair, healthy yet drenched by the sun, had highlights of a lighter brunette, almost gold. At thirty-five, she was one of the originals and helped define the culture behind the beloved brand. *Sea the Change for Good* – the company's tagline, was intended to represent respect, integrity, and human kindness.

They both wore short denim shorts, tight fitting Bravado branded tank tops, and Keds for the short hike along Oahu's leeward coast.

"We had a store in Newport..."

"I know, I shopped there all the time," the young girl interrupted. "I was surprised to see it close. It was always busy, like...so busy."

"About that - the rent went into the stratosphere, so we closed it to open two other locations nearby. Retail can be tricky like that. With developers it's often a two-fer." Tamsen recalled the real estate transaction while looking up at the olive-green stacks of the electric company, painted to blend into the nearby hills and cliffs of the Nanakuli Reserve.

"Two-fer?"

"Commercial real estate developers. They say something like, *'We'll let you into this location for two years if you agree to occupy over there for three. And we can jack rent based upon foot traffic, or revenue, or whatever other cock-a-doodle-doo metric.'* As an up-and-coming brand, we made some bad choices in our frenzy for recognition and growth, but many good choices too. That's why we grew so fast. Then we got picked up by some of the national mall-based chains, and things really scaled quickly."

"And I just thought you just surfed and looked pretty, posing for ocean-side photo shoots," the girl added jokingly.

They came out to a rocky shoreline bluff. The water's surface was twenty feet below them.

"This is it," Tamsen stopped and held her hands on her hips. This is one of my first swim and snorkel spots as a kid. Out there where those catamarans are sitting, rocking. There's an eddy out there, from HECO," her thumb pointed toward the industrial facility across Farrington Highway. "Hawaiian Electric," she added, knowing only the kamaaina would know what HECO stood for.

"Wow...unreal. Beautiful. It's nothing like Huntington. So much blue. Turquoise, azure, lapis, sapphire, deep navy way out there, and where the arc of the earth meets the sky, more of a Dodger blue."

"Listen to yourself, you already sound like one of our buyers working with the suppliers on the color pallets." Tamsen was a little surprised that the girl had that many shades of blue lined up in her mouth.

"I could look at this all day, like...every day."

"If you were selling the color blue, this is where you'd come for a brand assortment, right?" Tamsen looked out at the familiar cobalt coast she was accustomed to, and while it wasn't virgin to her eyes as it was her young companion, it never got old.

"My brand of blue would be this, right here," the girl pointed nearby, adding, "where the sandy bottom meets the coral formations. Absolute Blue – I'm calling it."

They stood there, hands on their hips, staring out to the gentle surf. Sets from a swell curled off to the left toward the condos and hotels nearby. In this spot, between the mesmerizing blues and Tracks Beach, was the tall dry grasses and brush which was more gold than green, blowing gently in the trade winds.

Kate took a deep breath. "I love the way the ocean smells." She continued to gaze at the Pacific's basin of brazen blues.

"Up those white sandy beaches a little way, that's Nanakuli. That's where my parents first taught me to surf." She pointed. Tamsen squinted and looked at the small wave breaks on the deep sands, coconut trees dotting the shoreline, fronds blowing in the breeze.

The girl was still fixated on the blue waters, "I thought Makaha..." she said without looking to the right.

"Makaha came later. It can be rough, not for novices. Maybe not for you and me when the big swells roll in." She touched the shoulder of her new young acquaintance with the back of her hand, her brown skin nudging the girl to follow her.
"I've got something for you."

"Oh yeah?"

Tamsen reached into her tight pocket and pulled a two-foot weathered leather lace. She unraveled it as they approached the steel railroad tracks. There was a metal punch within the carefully wound small bundle of leather lace. "There." A penny had been laying on the metal tracks, flattened by the tourist train that ran along the coastline several times a day on the weekends and a couple times throughout the week.

The girl picked it up from the tracks squinting to make out President Abraham Lincoln's likeness.

"What's this..."

"Here, please." Tamsen held out her empty and open hand. The other contained the metal punch and the old leather lace. Once she had it in her hand she bent over and reached for the heaviest stone she could find near the railroad ties. She beat the punch with the stone onto the surface of the penny six times to get a hole next to the word LIBERTY on the thinned penny. Its copper was brightened from the train smashing it. After beating the coin lightly several more times she was able to push the thin leather through the hole.

"What's this for?"

Tamsen tied a square knot into the ends of the leather, creating a necklace. "Even an old penny, with the right amount of pressure, just like us - can be changed." She slipped it over the head of the blond-haired girl.

Immediately, she looked at the date on the shiny coin. A smudged date was detectable. "It isn't that old. That's the year I was born," she said, realizing that she was only mastering the obvious as the words spilled across her tongue.

"Yeah, I know. That's the point." Tamsen smiled.

"Of course," the little blondie named Kate nodded her head. "You were here days ago laying this penny on the tracks just waiting for me and this moment."

"That's the way it works out sometimes." Tamsen looked at the wide and bright blue eyes staring back at her with amazement. "And if not, well then..." Tamsen pulled another flattened penny with the same mintage out of her pocket, "there's a backup plan." She handed the duplicate to the girl and turned her back walking toward where they came from.

The girl followed, peppering Tamsen with more questions. "Are you Japanese?"

"I'm Hawaiian, mostly. My mom's side has some Japanese," Tamsen replied.

Curious about Tamsen's nationalities, Kate asked, "Can you speak Japanese?"

"*Nihongo wo hanasemasen,*" Tamsen quickly responded.

"Well, that sounded authentic!" Kate said. "What does it..."

"That means, '*Sorry – I don't speak Japanese*' – in Japanese," Tamsen lied. She spoke it fluently.

Moving on, Kate complimented her, "You're so pretty."

"Thanks." Tamsen knew that being a surfer on the west side of Oahu, having a certain diverse and demographic look could lead to many things. She didn't want beauty to define her. It was impact she sought – not appearances, even though her attractive qualities were a catalyst for the change she was seeking.

"Like really pretty. You're beautiful."

Tamsen said no more about the compliment, picking up the pace back to her Wrangler parked a quarter mile away.

The girl continued, "So, you're divorced, right?"

"I am. I met him when I went to school at Berkeley. He was a tech guru. Developed an algorithm for AI before any of us really knew about artificial intelligence, and founded a company, which got bought out – making him a gazillionaire. Money changes people. He started chasing skirts and became someone he wasn't when I first met him and fell in love with him. So, I stopped loving the new guy he became. Still loved the old guy but he wanted the fast lane - and with a need for stability and change, I wanted to pick up where I left off with Bravado Surf - and we ended it. Mutually. I got our dog, Kona, and a small house on the North Shore. He got everything else. I didn't want it, the shit ton of money, because it was what ended our four-year thing." Tamsen wasn't completely telling the truth, but it was convincing.

"If he begged you to come back, would you?"

Tamsen shook her head, ponytail whipping in the breeze as they hiked back, "Not a chance. Too much damage done."

"I had a boy once. The one that got away. We were a thing, then we weren't, then we were, then we weren't – but went our different directions. I ended it mostly but want him back. We just started talking again." Their shoes crunched the gravel beneath their feet. "Did you ever have *the one that got away*?"

Tamsen calibrated sharing too much information. She answered with some of the truth. "I wouldn't' say one that got away, but there was a guy that I had a huge crush on. High school. I was a Junior. He was a Senior. Neither of us had a boyfriend or girlfriend at the time. We were friends, had a couple classes together. It was a time in the year approaching the height of prom-asking season. When I worked up the courage to ask him, he shot me down and said that he was going to ask Julie Tucker – some new girl to our school that year from the mainland that all the boys were gaga over. She was exotic, looked like you, fairer skin though. Not a surfer. Pretty. Blue round eyes, long blond hair, big tits, you know." Tamsen remembered the crush. Brian. "He gently turned me down. If I had to pick a dude - that was probably the one that got away."

"What was his name?"

Tamsen thought of the first name she could think of without saying Brian, "Tony," she lied. Her deepest secrets were uncommon, needed to be well-kept, not for the inquisitive Bravado rookie.

"I bet he was good looking. I knew a Tony once. Super-hot. It seems all Tony's are hot..." The girl rambled on as they trekked back along the tracks, but Tamsen's thoughts drifted - like the currents on the surface of the blue Pacific waters. They were surrounded by the hot and dry grasses, yellowing from the lack of rain on the leeward side of the island. Kate's *Tony's* were noise, competing with the gravel's crunch beneath their shoes. Occasional bursts of a breeze only cooled them slightly. Tamsen Makua wasn't thinking of the hotness of *all Tony's*. Her thoughts were of growing up in this area – and of Brian Kekahanamanui.

2

Randomness

Betsy Murphy was now a seamstress. She was laid off as an administrative assistant at a holding company in Midtown and was a month late on rent. Moving money from her high-yield savings to checking was coming to an end because there were no more savings to move. The gold button didn't match, and she had to search the couch cushions for change to buy a matching button at the fabric store. For Betsy, everything had to be just right. Appearances mattered. Her sister worked at the same firm and was not impacted by the headcount cuts. Her sister who was prettier, funnier, smarter, and had a handsome husband. Her sister who had the brownstone in Queens. *Envy* was the resentful and covetous thoughts and in some cases actions which led her to wanting what was her sister's in

Kenny Testa liked to get high. He smoked pot daily, usually right before work. His weed was supplied by a dealer from Hell's Kitchen who didn't want to deal marijuana any longer – graduating to the hard stuff. Kenny shoplifted Visine from Duane Reade, the local drug store, on occasion to hide his red eyes. He bounced from job to job but settled in at the department store as a stocking person in the shoe department. *Gluttony* is often associated with the over-consumption of food or alcohol. It can include an insatiable desire to smoke too.

And smoking dope was all that Kenny wanted to do – consuming him morning, noon, evening, and night.

Matt Becker sold shoes...lots of shoes. He almost always hit his commission target and had earned a nickname from his district manager, *Million Dollar Matt*. He won the trip to the Bahamas in his district as a sales incentive. The Regional Vice President asked him if he was interested in moving up within the ranks of the company. It made him move faster and want to do better. He was inspired to exceed. When he asked if it paid more money, the answer was that it was a lateral move. In short, 'no'. Matt said that he was loyal to the company, honored to be considered and would work harder to sell even more shoes as an individual contributor. And that was that. A *greed* for the almighty dollar without the vision to see beyond it defined Matt. The only thing which Matt liked more than the smell of new shoe leather, was the smell of a dollar bill.

Phil Donnelly was not paranoid – far from it. He knew that people were talking about him. It didn't bother him to ask for dollars at street corners even though panhandling was illegal. It was better than work. He'd rather be the recipient of socialism than a contributor to capitalism. Occasionally, he'd position himself outside of the local Olive Garden at Times Square and attempt to meet someone eye-to-eye as they came out of the restaurant with leftovers. If he was provided their remaining meal, he could preserve his dollars and buy booze. Sometimes, he'd tell a stranger who was handing him their warm leftovers that Jesus was watching, and that they were blessed. Sometimes that might cause the stranger to pull out a few dollars from their pants pockets. The scope of *sloth* is wide. Taking no care to make something of himself, he allowed others to provide – instead wallowing in his imprudence and heedless approach to nearly anything.

Gordon Elrod hated Democrats. He was in the wrong city for it. New York was filled with them. They were everywhere. And they were responsible for the reprehensible situation the country was in. Fox News and Newsmax said so. The notifications that pinged his phone constantly pointed toward another Democratic mistake. The hatred seethed through him. Something had to be done. *Wrath*. It was ripe. It was time to pay. Now, not when the election came around again. It was time for the radical leftists to pay for their pathetic choices now. But first, hot chicks. He sought them out whenever he got the chance. Women were drawn to him. He was sure of it. It wasn't his title as the regional real estate Vice President. Although he loved the power he felt from it. It must be his good looks, he thought. The women, they were irresistible. He had to have them and as many as he could. He kept track of how many he'd slept with. *Lust* – pure fornication in any sense. Anything goes, he mused. Married, single, young, not-so-young, attractive, almost-attractive, he was unbridled in sexual desire – hosting not one, but two of the seven deadly sins. *Wrath* for the fucking progressives and *lust* – for any pretty woman, perhaps even a Democrat.

Mary Gordon owned a soup kitchen on the Lower East Side. On a cold December night, once upon a time she was given three-hundred dollars and a million-dollar trust from a former wealth management manager while on the street begging for a handout. She spent the night in a Marriott at the request and arrangement from the rich guy. Her daughter, Marcy was with her always. It was just the two of them. The arrangement was beyond her wildest imagination. The wealthy money manager was leaving his company and had his former Executive Admin named Adele establish a trust fund. She invested the million dollars in seed money into a hedge fund that blew up. One became two, two became four, four became eight, and eight was enough. She worked with Adele to structure with debt and leverage at the request of the wealthy man which she had only met once, in the cold December night at Battery Park. This was when she was most desperate. She placed the shelters into a non-profit, a 501c3 he coached Adele to arrange. *Sometimes things just don't turn out how they were supposed to...*she smiled as she thought about the cardboard sign which was a moniker of her low point. Mary's rags-to-riches story may have been short lived, but tall with *pride*. She told it to anyone who might listen. She also told it to anyone who might not be listening. While her intentions were good, her publicity was growing, and she was *proud* of what she had accomplished in such a short amount of time. So much *pride*. Her purpose had swelled to the point where she wanted everyone to know of her influence and scale. Everyone in greater New York needed to have a sandwich and hear about her story – even if they weren't hungry for it.

What makes any of this matter or weave together is a series of consequential reasons. The human condition stitched together a variety of deadly sins which combined for consequential actions. Betsy Murphy bought the size seven shoes that Allegra Sinclair would have purchased. Enter vanity. This caused Allegra to buy the size seven and a half. Betsy broke her ankle while falling from a curb into a street drainage grate. She couldn't afford them in the first place but used some money from the next month's rent to pay for them. Were they essential? No. They did, however, match what she was going to wear to an interview for a bougee Executive Administrator's position in Manhattan.

Since Matt Becker was eager to sell more shoes, he decided that he'd limit store swaps which was the process of requesting sizing from other metro department stores. Instead, he'd lie that the manufacturer was changing the style and when the size requested wasn't available, he'd bring out a half size or full size too big or too small. Vanity was not necessarily one of the seven deadly sins – but it was a great sales aid.

And since Kenny Testa was always high when stocking shoes, he'd often use the boxes out of the cardboard cases to plug open holes in the shelves in the back room. Even when a size was listed in stock and Matt would check the online inventory system, he'd resort to his tactic of selling up and down the size stack to achieve a greater commission.

Mary Gordon had just given Phil Donnelly a brownbag lunch. Since he was drunk, it spilled out of the bag and onto the sidewalk. He bumped into Betsy, knocking the spare change out of her hand. As she bent over to pick up two quarters, she felt a stranger's elbow land on her hip. It was the encroachment from the falling man who smelled bad which caused her to lose her balance and land awkwardly - hearing a crack in her left ankle.

Where was Gordon Elrod in all of this? He was on the side of the corner away from the Democrats which he hated and near a hot looking woman near the street sign. Maybe their eyes would meet, and it would lead to something beyond his wildest imagination. She could be his number twenty-seven. The psychopath was working the corner for a female squeeze on his way to get a haircut. He noticed the disturbance and did nothing.

There's always more to the story. What it was that caused Mary to provide Phil a sandwich, bag of chips and an apple in his brownbag lunch was the harbinger for the coincidences to come together.

The instance could have included the best of human intentions too. However, on this day, at this moment, the Greco-Roman antecedents came together for a small and random tragedy - a random and misunderstood action upon an action upon another action. The capital vices were at work and thriving within as the bases of other sins.

*****

Jacob listened to the man's voice in the podcast which Ruby sent him immediately after they had coffee. He was walking Kolohe on the sidewalk heading toward Central Park. His ear buds were black. The

The unknown voice actor, sounding much like James Earl Jones, described a situation...

"Don Richard "Richie", and later "Whitie", Ashburn was a speedy Hall of Fame outfielder who played for Philadelphia. In fact, he was wanted and signed by three teams. The Cleveland Indians, at his age of 16, and soon after, the Chicago Cubs, signed Richie for their farm teams for his speed. When the Commissioner voided the contracts because he was prohibiting signing high school students. The two voided agreements soured his opinion of Major League Baseball, and he went on to college, even though 13 of 16 teams were expressing an interest in him. The year was 1944. After just one semester at college, it was a Phillies scout, Ed Krajnick which convinced Richie's family to sign him to the ballclub. He reported to the developmental Class A Eastern Club League for the team.

However, early in the season, the US Army drafted him and deployed him to Alaska. He spent 1946 there, missing a season of baseball. He returned to the farm team a year later, in 1947, and attended his second semester of college where he met his future wife, Herberta Cox.

It was the 1948 season where he was brought up from the farm club to play for the Philadelphia Phillies, starting as a left fielder. After just 12 games he was re-positioned to center field. His light blond hair earned him another nickname, "Whitie". Piercing blue eyes, only 5' 10" tall, weighing 170 pounds, boasting broad shoulders – he was a handsome man.

Whitie went on to a successful career with the Phillies organization, was traded at the end of his career to the Cubs, then the Mets, and hung up his cleats in 1962 while with the New York ball club. He accepted a broadcasting job following the successful career as a player. The broadcasting gig spanned a 35-year period.

Married to his wife Herberta "Herbie" Cox Ashburn, and while still playing the game, they had six children together. But unfortunately, Whitie missed all their births due to being away for baseball. He would go on to say that he was a miserable 0-for-6. He made it up to his wife and children by being a good dad.

His durability as a player was quite strong. Missing only 20 games from 1948 through 1960. The Phillies organization later, in 1979 retired his number, 1, the second number given the honor. A plaque is featured in Ashburn Alley on the Phillies' Wall of Fame. Richie "Whitie" Ashburn passed away in September of 1997.

Alice grew up in England. At the age of 17 she moved to the United States to care for her sister. Later in life she married Earl Roth, the sports editor of the Philadelphia Bulletin. Philadelphia Phillies baseball was a passion they shared, enjoying many games in choice seats, close to the action. Stadiums were smaller back then. By comparison, Los Angeles Dodger stadium today can hold 56,000 fans. Throughout their marriage they had children, and those children had children.

On a Saturday afternoon in August of 1957, just 7,929 fans filled Connie Mack Stadium, north of Philadelphia. Alice Roth was among them. She, Earl, and two of their grandsons watched the game from their seats on the third base line side of the stadium. Raving fans of the game, they enjoyed watching their struggling Phillies – attempting to break above .500 territory baseball. One bright spot was always the play and bat of the Phillies leadoff hitter and left-hander, Richie "Whitie" Ashburn.

The game of baseball can sometimes be considered slow. This is why a timer was established between pitches, to move the game along. On the other hand, when a pitch is thrown, the speed at which it crosses home plate can clock faster than 100 miles per hour. Equally speedy is the m.p.h. at which a hit ball comes off the bat. Called "exit speed", home runs are clocked at exit speeds of up to 120 miles per hour.

And so it goes, as Alice Roth and her husband and grandsons watched the game, fast balls pitched, fast balls hit – they enjoyed the game. Until one foul ball coming off the bat of lefty Whitie Ashburn struck Alice Roth – on the nose, breaking it. As the medics rushed to her aid, the game was temporarily paused. When Alice was placed on a stretcher and being carried away, bloody mess and all, play resumed. On the very next pitch, another foul ball left the bat of Ashburn, striking Roth again. This time, on her knee, breaking another bone.

The odds of catching, or getting hit by, a foul ball is 1 in 1,189. Depending upon one's seat location, the use of protective netting, the combination between the pitcher and batter's dominant hand, and an undeterminable number of other factors – the odds increase and decrease depending upon the components of data. Perhaps the odds were against Alice Roth, that Saturday afternoon. She was rushed to Temple Hospital. It was on Sunday, and repeatedly during her stay, that Ashburn visited Roth, autographing balls for her grandsons, inviting the family back to another game (from the press box), and for the royal treatment. Ashburn and Roth became long-term friends, remembering birthdays and Christmas cards until she passed away in the mid-1980's.

In something as, both simple and complex, the game of baseball there are countless elements, particulars, and facets which cause an outcome. There were the aspects which brought Alice to the United States. The process of the assignment of Whitie to the Phillies. His degree of play – including statistics from the pitcher delivering pitch count and velocity. The sub-components and fragments of the known and unknown actions created the event. But the human kindness between the two individuals shaped their friendship which lasted another thirty years.

The randomness of their fellowship can be outlined as well as enigmatic. Accompanying a greater and master plan for reasoning – as well as data explaining the visible or hidden side of everything – randomness was at work. Randomness, producing different results from definitive patterns and predictability in information, did not always follow intelligible combinations of outcomes. An oddness for explanation was as in control as it was not."

That was it.

The voice-over stopped. There was no more context on the Podcast other than pointing out randomness.

Jacob found it odd that Ruby would want him to listen to it.

A small boy of five or six years old and his young mother approached Jacob and Kolohe walking on the grassy side of the sidewalk. Sometimes, a child would reach out their hand to touch the yellow lab and the parent would ask permission. On other occasions, the child might be frightened and cower from the dog. This was that situation. Jacob held Kolohe tightly when a small child expressed fear or uncertainty. As Jacob watched the little boy duck behind his mother's leg and hide behind her overcoat, a blue mitten fell from his available hand. They continued walking past him and Kolohe, not knowing that the mitten was left behind, lying on the concrete.

Jacob called out, "Hey! Hey! Excuse me...You dropped this." He reached down to pick it up and extended it for the mother.

"Oh, thank you," she said, as she reached for the small navy-blue mitten. The woman glanced at Jacob, paused, then looked at the child, "This nice man helped us with your mitten. Can you say, 'thank you'?" The boy ducked further behind the mom. "Well...he's shy. Thanks." She glanced at Jacob again and turned to walk in the direction they were originally heading, now past Jacob.

As Jacob Paisley turned, returning to walk in the direction he and Kolohe walked less than half a city block. Central Park was quiet. He could see Gapstow Bridge in the distance.

In an odd bout of Deja Vu, the same woman and the same child approached them, from the same direction – the direction Jacob and Kolohe were approaching. *How could that be?* Jacob thought. *There's no way they could have circled around.* They continued walking toward each other, moments away from passing one another. The child appeared less aware of the two, and nearly disinterested in them, being tugged by his mother. She made no eye contact with Jacob. He kept walking with Kolohe, anticipating something. Nothing. They walked past them. Jacob thought it was strange. As he stopped and turned, the woman appeared to be picking something up from the ground. It wasn't a blue mitten.

She turned to Jacob and said, "Here. You dropped this." He didn't see what it was at first, tucked behind the hand she was reaching out. As she turned her hand, with the palm up, he saw it. A baseball. There were a few scuffs, but it was more new than worn. The red stitching was tightly woven over the leather cover.

The woman stood there, poker faced, holding out the ball for Jacob to take from her.

He said nothing, gripping Kolohe in his left hand reaching for the out of season ball with his right. She made little eye contact, unlike what she did a few minutes earlier. The child had both of his hands in his mittens and curiously now looked at Kolohe, who sat at Jacob's feet, panting. Jacob gripped the baseball, felt the weight of it in his hand, looked at it, and glanced back at the same woman with the same child.

"Thanks," he said, watching her turn back to the sidewalk and coax the child to continue walking. Jacob could hear her say something to the small boy as they kept walking away.

Standing there, wondering what had just happened, Jacob turned his attention to the ball. Rolling it over in his hand, there was an autograph. It was cursive, a signature. Under the Rawlings manufacturer label moniker and in between the red stitching he could make it out. Just legible enough to read, it was autographed by *Richie Ashburn.*

Jacob turned to find her for explanation, the mother with her child. They were nowhere to be found, having slipped into a small gathering of people or perhaps a cab.

Of course. The weirdness begins again, Jacob said to himself.

*****

Jacob replayed a conversation he had with Ruby earlier, recanting the message.

"There are several categories," his friend's discourse was explained with a groveling tone as he tried to keep his voice low. They were sitting with the sun at their back on an emerald-green park bench surrounded by Castleton green holly bushes. "Several categories which play alongside our efforts. I don't expect you to remember all of this. Some of it is a discipline, some of it is autonomous, some of it is connected, and then some of it is...well, random."

"Random?" Jacob asked. His thick black P-coat was unbuttoned. The dress shirt he was wearing once donned an expensive necktie, would have complimented his custom and tailored suit. Thousand-dollar shoes would strike a cadence of confidence as he would stride the cement sidewalk walking to the offices of Paisley, Pierce Capital Management. PPCM's logo, etched on the heavy glass door of the co-founder of the firm would whisper whisk open as he would arrive on any given morning. Those were no longer these types of mornings or days. It was much simpler – and yet becoming intriguing as Ruby explained the structure and workings of Ellipsis – the clandestine organization which made things happen.

"Random indeed. Like Team Hope – things happening for a reason, and Team Logic – things happening because of reasons, there are the most random damn things which drive results, favorably and unfavorably. We work with them and against them for the outcome we seek."

"Go on," Jacob encouraged the data-dump, knowing that the Team Hope and Logic reference which Ruby referred to came from how Jacob previously described himself and Adele as a balanced team to Ruby.

"Those powers which I spoke of: Suggestion, Persuasion, Connectivity...they're met with intelligence at the edge."

"What – in – the – hell you are talking about?" Jacob made a familiar face. The kind he would have made when one of his Wall Street traders spoke gibberish to hide incompetency. But it wasn't incompetence at all coming from Ruby. His explanation of Ellipsis was being spoon fed to Jacob, earning bite size chunks of trust from Ruby explaining their organization further and further, meeting after meeting, but not completely.

"Those principles we spoke of back when we first met: Beliefs, Perspectives, Feelings, Thoughts, Behaviors, Actions – they all feed into the outcomes we coax. It's distributed technology that was an accelerant. It was guys like you, taking the money which was granted and growing it. That has allowed our organization's growth."

"How many of me are there?"

"I don't know, a dozen maybe. Let me finish." Ruby rubbed the backs of his old, weathered, dark brown hands, and rolled them over to observe the lighter olive palms as if admiring something.

"Please...do." Jacob always asked too many questions about Ellipsis which were left unanswered. *Unsaid* was Ruby's modus operandi.

"The tech at the edge, the data leveraging, the elasticity of our ever-growing ledgers, the interface with our recipient's momentum – these things have contributed to the efficiencies we seek." He leaned forward with his elbows lodging on his thighs. Ruby looked at Jacob, hanging his head while he spoke some more.

"When you say tech at the edge...that's the wiretapping, the bugging...monitoring...spying...right?" Jacob sought confirmation. Receiving none, he heard plenty within the silence.

Finally, to meet Jacob's countering silence with some conviction, Ruby only added, "Our use of technology has done *so much* more good than harm."

"I'm just...guarded, I guess is the right word. If big brother, Ellipsis, is taking my privacy especially with Adele within my home...then, where does it stop?'

"There's no surveillance within your home, trust me."

"Can I? Can we?" Jacob shot back. "You're still bringing us in, tryout after tryout. It's like we're on the god-damned JV team, trying to earn our way to varsity."

"Star players. I want you on my team. As I transition from a recruiter to operating a pod, I want the two of you. Others too. But you have my trust and the trust of the organization. There may be another gig or two to see just how far we can go with Adele – but I trust you –

both of you, really." Ruby pointed to himself, then Jacob, and added, "You should trust me too. The last thing you want is to have to whisper to each other in your living room and scratch notes on a notepad."

"We've done that several times," Jacob added quickly.

"I know you have," Ruby snuck in a crooked smile looking at Jacob from the corner of his eye, "Just kidding."

Jacob reached into his pocket for a small bag of peanuts he picked up from a street vendor on the way. He shook his head, returning the slight smile, "Yeah, right." He cracked open a peanut, tossing the shell over his shoulder into the bushes. "Peanut?"

Ruby reached for the brown paper bag, withdrawing a few of the nuts. "Say...what do you make of all this AI stuff? Artificial intelligence. Is it the real deal, or a bunch of hype?'

"Game changer. It's the internet circa 1995. Jump on it. Sure, there are going to be some shenanigans along the way, but it'll end up being one of the single greatest advancements in our lifetime. Ellipsis needs to get in front of it. Understand its implications."

Ruby slowly nodded his head with what Jacob said, looking off into the business of Manhattan as he cracked the nut lodged between his thumbs, "Working on that."

A minute passed by with neither of them speaking. They were merely observing the city life, buzzing, and beeping, and humming as late morning paved its way to the noon rush hour. Jacob smiled, rubbed his chin, and looked up at the clouds. "Got a quick and slightly relevant story for you."

"I've got time, storyteller, go ahead," Ruby encouraged.

"It may have been late '99 or early 2000. I was traveling with one of our pitchmen in the Bay Area. He arranged a meeting with a man named Larry and another man named Sergei. The company was called Google, but it was misspelled."

"G, O, O, G, L, E?"

"It's actually a mathematical term spelled G, O, O, G, O, L – but it was taken. Their original name was BackRub."

"No kidding?"

"No kidding. So, we're walking down the hallway to pitch managing their portfolio because we see search as a big deal. There's this drawing that looks like a stick-figure two-dimensional spider taped to the wall. On each of the eight legs coming from the body of the spider there are these codes. Hyperlinks or something – and I ask one of the engineers what they signify. He says one is for education, another is for government, and another is for commerce, and so on. Then, there are three that are circled with a red crayon. *'And these?',* I asked him. And he says, *'Oh – that's porn. If we're going to make money from the internet, clicks or whatever, we've got to know where the human imagination leads.'"*

Ruby smiled broadly, "Borderline insider trading right there, wouldn't you say?"

"That's when I knew we had to go as deep as we could with some of the Silicon Valley moonshots. When you connect making money with burgeoning interest – it's a bit of a no-brainer."

"A rising tide floats all boats."

"Something like that. Rest in peace, The Final Trade." Jacob looked off into the warm lobby of a nearby hotel. The illumination of bright lighting showcased the well-appointed amenities inside. He was thinking of his Aicon yacht, being cut into pieces on a Hawaiian shipyard. *Easy come, easy go.* Ruby was there, before the stress fracture became an incurable leak which led to the luxury vessel's sinking. Ruby wasn't there for the pirate's takeover. He also wasn't there when Kolohe and the child were surrounded by sharks. He also wasn't there as Kito rescued them in the small fishing boat which was slightly larger than a dinghy. But Jacob was sure that with Ruby's sophistication with Ellipsis – that he and the yellow lab and the infant weren't as in danger as he once thought. As he was lost in thought, he didn't notice Ruby staring at him. "It's as if you're in my head," Jacob said – finally noticing the stare.

"Projection," Ruby said. It was just one word.

From their original meeting, Ruby acting as a mock hospital volunteer, to his staged death, to his stint as a bartender at Bobby Van's, to a victim of cancer accepting a charity sunset cruise – Jacob was certain that their interactions were intentional. The circumstances played to Ruby's advantages. And so, too, he saw the outcomes of Ellipsis acting as deliberate, purpose-filled, wittingly planned, and executed through a host of actors, each playing their part. *Where was the randomness in that?* Jacob thought to himself.

"Are these little tests of yours really necessary?" Jacob squinted as the light was beginning to make its way higher into the sky and beginning to reflect its rays from a turquoise glass facing tower above them. "It's like we're on the proving grounds, or something," he shrugged his shoulders, questioning the validation he and Adele were trudging through.

"I don't know what to...protocol, substantiation, justification...you aren't alone. Anyone which is introduced to the level you're going to play is validated. If you just want to be the money man, so be it. If you want a position which you've asked for – there's going to be several tests. Yeah – the proving grounds is a fair description for it. Can you handle the heat? What scares you? How many vulnerabilities do you truly have? Do you black out at Mach 10? Can you operate under the surface of the ocean's open waters at 300 feet deep? Dorothy did. Are you capable of modifying your behaviors and your personal preferences to play your position and can you even play a position? A leader's heart shows some pain, suffering and scars – where are yours? Small tests over time reveal what you can leap and reach for."

"Her name wasn't really Dorothy, was it?" Jacob was referring to their sunset cruise again, at the Ko Olina on Oahu – where she wasn't really his caretaker, helping the old blind man onto the vessel.

"No, it was not, that was random. She wanted to play the part in her high school drama club, you know The Wizard of Oz. But I believe she was given the part of a flying monkey instead of Dorothy." Ruby slowly shook his head.

"Well, vindication then," Jacob held the paper bag which was becoming crumpled toward his friend.

Ruby held his hand up, signaling he'd had enough. "Funny...funny that you'd choose to use that word."

"What...vindication?"

"Vindication." They listened to the city sounds around them. In the distance a siren, down an alley a delivery door slamming, up the streets, wheels screeching and a short honk. "Maybe another time for...for vindication."

He shrugged, knowing a free sermon or perhaps an intriguing story was coming at some point. Jacob's thoughts meandered to the team which Ruby was building within Ellipsis. He wondered what the hole in the lineup looked like. Whatever quantum component which might be missing from their roster would be conditional and leveraged to their tasks. Not completely knowing of the provenance of Ruby's leadership was a bridge of faith he was blindly extending. His and Adele's core belief that this man and this organization that they were getting to know was earnest and devoted to noble and magnanimous causes. Baked into the recipe for Ellipsis' good intention was meticulously planned teams, the use of technology to extrapolate human behaviors, and an unorthodox execution to deliver a difference. It also involved a healthy dose of randomness.

*****

Aiden Ashford's key-clicking was frenzied. As soon as he finished with the code for the web-page which he had been at work on over the past two hours, he could return to research a lead. *It might be nothing, but it may be something,* he thought. Any clue might turn out to be helpful. It was another fifteen minutes of writing, copying, posting and publishing before he opened the dark website he had been baiting. There was no reply to his query. Unanswered, he returned to the kitchen for a protein shake. The blender sounded like a jet engine on the tarmac, mixing the organic super-foods powder with the icy water, blueberries, and bananas.

It was cardio and leg-day, which meant running in deep sand on the beach and on the strand for three miles. The sun was intense today. He buttered up with the SPF to avoid the rays beating. Waiting until sunset wasn't the conditioning Ashford wanted. He intentionally wanted the challenge from the heat and humidity. As much grind as Mother Nature could drill him with was what he wished.

He wanted the strength to stop a truck. This is what he asked of his personal trainer. The physical fitness guru thought he was joking. He wasn't. Ashford followed the coaching with ceremonial adherence, pushing himself to a brink. His body was responding. The trainer called him a *freak of nature.* He said that if everyone received the results which Ashford was commanding, business would be unmanageable – too much of it. Clientele would line up, out the doors of the gym, for results like Ashfords. It wasn't a random thing, though, results such as his. The ritual and discipline which Ashford was exerting was equal to an Olympic athletes training protocol.

His size twelve running shoes looked like small boats. They'd be filled with sand after the run. Ashley would have said that one was large enough for two of her feet to fit in, and then she would have tried it. They'd giggle together at her silliness. He logged off the laptop and checked his phone for messages. There she was, filling his screen saver, looking at him with the Gulf of Mexico behind her. It was a Sunday morning. Ashford remembered taking the picture. It was the last one.

Their time on the sandy shores was filled with introspect. Ashley would discuss child development and how it was much different than adult learning. Ashford discussed building algorithms to calculate, behave, and potentially think for themselves. Their passions about their work, the world, its current affairs and all-things environmental were common ground for the two. But laughing – laughter was a medicine, an essential adhesive which tended to bring things together. Like the movies, or music or even viral trending posts on social media, it was laughter which was their special binding agent. They were competitive in trying to find a giggle within each other.

Their competitiveness was far more than making each other happy in a silly sense. Sports were sometimes intense. Especially during the NFL season. Ashley, intentionally or not, found herself on the opposite side of the ball. Bears-Packers. Cowboys-Eagles. Ravens-Steelers. Ashford was one team; Ashley was the other. This friendly fire led to a host of bets. The wagers ended in household chore payoffs. Who washed and who dried the dishes. Who had to take out the trash. Who's turn it was to vacuum and whose turn it was to dust was settled by who lost the over/under in the score. From total points to the number of field goals to discrepancies in dinner choices, their sportive competitiveness was rollicking in a fun way. It led to sexual preferences too. Uninhibited desires were revealed, drawing them yet closer. The bedroom Olympics challenges acted as another course to cling them together.

Sitting there, ready to go, Ashford remembered them in Clearwater one weekend morning, lying there on the beach. Ashley leaned over lifting a floppy straw hat from her face, "Hey babe."

"Yeah...?"

"A turkey was chatting with a bull," she reached for the Sun Bum, squeezing the tan tube. Beige liquid filled her palm. She began lathering in on herself, over-applying it to her cleavage and the insides of her thighs.

"Here we go," he was beginning to doze off in the warmth of the sun but was more interested in what happened between the turkey and the bull.

"So, this turkey and bull were talking about the turkey's strength. The turkey said, "I'd love to be able to get to the top branch of that tree. But I just don't have the energy."

"Uh-huh," Ashford propped himself up on one elbow to face her as she spread the creamy lather over her shoulders.

"Well, why don't you eat some of my droppings. It has all kinds of nutrients in it."

"Gross." Ashford asked, "Want me to do the back of your arms?"

"Please," she laid down continuing with the joke. "And wouldn't you know it, after the turkey pecked at the lump of dung, he found out that he did feel stronger and had just enough strength to make it to the lower branch of the tree."

"Protein." He finished rubbing and gave her perky butt a quick pat.

"Yes. Maybe. Wait, my butt or the dung?"

"Both."

She smiled and continued with the joke, "The next day, that turkey ate more dung and found himself a little stronger. And the next day, even stronger. The turkey was able to get to the next branch and the one after that and the one after that as he ate the bull's dung. Finally, that turkey made it to the top branch. As soon as the farmer saw that, he went and got his rifle and shot the turkey."

"Ha!"

"Moral of the story. Bullshit might get you to the top, but it won't keep you there."

"You're a dork, did you know that?" Ashford lay back down on his stomach facing her – admiring how beautiful she was and how lucky he was.

"I know. You are too."

"I'm good with it. You – you're the one that tries to be cool." He spoke with half of his face smashed against the towel on the sand.

"Punk." Lying next to him, she flipped a Cheeto at him with her fingers, it's mystery-orange cheddar dust remaining on his bowling ball sized shoulder as the snack bounced away. Ashley smoothed the over-sized cotton towel between them.

Ashford did the same. "I love you."

Quickly, she added, "I love you too. But…"

"Yeah…"

"It is Sunday," she giggled, followed by him chuckling too.

"And the Bengals are playing the Browns," Ashford added.

"I've got the Browns." Ashley chimed in first.

"The battle of Ohio. Then, I've got the Bengals." It was on. Someone would end up on top, and someone would end up on bottom. It didn't really matter.

"That's the NFC, right?"

"Ash, do you even know of one player on the Browns?"

"Cleveland? Uh...yeah...what's his name...Leroy." She'd hold both of her breasts in her hands and alternate lifting them to distract him and sing the limited lyrics she knew of Jim Croce's song attempting to explain how bad Leroy was.

Ashford remembered her silly attempts to draw goofy and giddy innocence in what she understood as well as what she didn't. *The world was already serious enough*, she would have said.

He laced the trainers tightly and walked toward the front door for a run in the serious world outside.

*****

She had questions.

Ruby combed through several of them but not all. Instead, he got to the point of his call to her. "Hey, Tamsen, I need a favor."

"Sure, what is it?"

He hesitated slightly, "Uh just a second, there's another call...and...I don't know that number. Okay – need to have you reach out to someone I've been closely working with here in New York." Ruby was seasoning his crew. The veteran and financiers -with the newbies and money makers. Tamsen described the first.

"Do I know him?"

"Ever heard of a Jacob Paisley?"

"The money man? Older, salty colored hair, good-looking guy, a bit smug – maybe even full of himself at times?" She was blunt in calling it as she saw it. Like the waves rolling in, either you take it and ride it in, or you pass and wait for the next one. "Runs or ran JPMorgan Chase?"

"Uh, no. Maybe you're thinking of Jamie Dimon."

"Jacob Paisley."

"Still good looking?"

"Something like that," he smiled. "I've been working with him for a few years off and on. A new team member is what he is. He's not only running point on investments, but we have him as a tertiary field agent too."

"Interesting combo. Is he competent at either?"

"He squeezes quarters from dollars quite nicely. Can't really answer if he's a field agent just yet. We're assessing that."

Tamsen squinted listening to Ruby as the sun filtered in through dirty windshield which caused additional glare. The traffic on the Kamehameha Highway was hit or miss. Mostly miss since the construction started. She pumped the wiper fluid toggle on the steering wheel causing the stream to flood the glass and the wipers to come to attention, smearing a little more than cleaning.

"Well, my grant will only go so far in this..."

"We have him managing two hundred now."

"Good Lord, two hundred is a lot," Tamsen knew the financing complexities of running a vigilante organization like Ellipsis. 'Who else is managing that much?"

"He turned fifty into eighty quickly."

"Legally?"

"Yeah, he's not betting on the ponies or running up a tab at Caesar's like someone else."

"Too soon, Ruby." Tamsen thought of her ex and the secret life he held from her as the money multiplied exponentially. There was the drugs and the hookers, the gambling and the favors, the lobbying and politics, the endless list of lies that accompanied one found truth after another.

"I couldn't help myself. Sorry" He thought she could take the tease. The brazing sun and the pounding surf made her tough. The competitor she was compared to any athlete in nearly any sport.

"What do we talk about?"

"Keep it coy. But you talk about Hawaii. Oahu. Work with our organization that you have yet to do – you know, the shit you're good at, inspiring people and revealing what should be done to cure the ills that aren't being solved. Talk about your aspirations for a better world."

"You want me to be a kitten?"

"No, no, not at all...just maybe don't leave it all on the battlefield. He's to be trusted, but he wants all it. Like you. It's his personality. Hell, maybe he can handle it. I like the guy. Maybe I'm protecting him. He's got a woman he used to work with, Adele, and we like her too. I temper his ego by telling him the reason we selected him is because of her. Perhaps that's true. They're a team. Two people here and we want more but only so much. Be a little recessive, please. Toes in. No cannonballs.

"You're talking to a surfer, we're all in," she replied, fidgeting with the wipers again as the traffic crawled along the North Shore roadway. A man on a light blue cruiser biked past her.

"Huh, how 'bout that..." she said it out loud.

"What?"

"Nothing. I think that was Jack Johnson." The reception crackled in her handset. Ruby. Ruby." She said his name louder each time. Then finally Tamsen heard him speak. Ten seconds passed by, "Ruby! Can you hear me? Shit." Another ten seconds elapsed.

"...But only when I say to..."

"You broke up."

Ruby repeated himself, "But only when I say to."

"Say what?"

"Call the number," Ruby repeated.

"What number are you talking about, you broke up. Bad reception. I didn't hear the last thing you said."

"The Hawaiian number. The message we need you to text. It's a prompt." Ruby was difficult to hear but not as bad as before.

"Are you recruiting again. For your team or another? Your crew is filling up, isn't it."

"Just send the message to the 808-exchange number. It should do the trick."

"Text me what you want to have happen. And send me Jacob Paisley's number. We'll connect. I can play the submissive part if need be. And the other thing, an 808 number... Well, that's...that's just a bit random."

"In this line of work, nothing's really random, is it?" Ruby's intentionality accompanying a playfulness was his royal flush beating anyone's four aces. He hung up and Tamsen heard four long beeps signaling the call's end.

"I want to be you when I grow up," she said to herself with no one listening as she pulled up to stop at the sole traffic light in Pupukea. Tamsen smelled the lotion she was quickly lathering up with, taking a deep breath. The coconut scented skin care product was local. Her love for the organic Bubble Shack soaps and reef friendly concoctions was free advertising for the rainbow-colored brand. The pikake and tuberose smells returned to her memories of lei-making with her family on the west side of Oahu. She could talk with Jacob Paisley about whatever, as Ruby had asked, especially about surf life on the North Shore and Hawaii in general. There was much to say. There was also much not to say.

*****

Adele read the last paragraph in the article about randomness again. She then had another look at the headline in bold print: Maryland Man Wins $580,000 Lottery Jackpot After Clerk Gives Him

Wrong Ticket. She smelled the newsprint. *Is it the print, or the paper?* She asked herself about the scent. They didn't even subscribe to the newspaper any longer, but it was lying at their doorstep. Looking at the date – it was yesterday's news, being two weeks old.

Kolohe sat at her feet, cocking his head to the side, wondering what she was doing and if there was something in it for him.

"Oh no. You're going to get fat," she said looking at his willful eyebrows. "Okay, one little bite. Just because Jacob isn't here. It'll be our little secret." She folded and tossed the lifestyle section she was reading on top of Business, Classifieds, Sports, and the cover page.

The Maryland Lottery was protecting the identity of the winner. A Prince George's County resident and frequent shopper at a gas station in Upper Marlboro attempted to buy Cash4Life tickets for a recent drawing. However, the attendant misheard and distributed Multi-Match tickets. When the customer called attention to the mistake, the clerk who was new tried to fix the error. Both unfortunately and fortunately – he was unable to void the ticket. Instead of arguing or making a situation more complex, the customer shrugged his shoulders and accepted the clerk's apology, leaving the convenience store with a $10 Multi-Match ticket.

Several days later, the customer checked his numbers online. He couldn't believe what he saw. In a state of concealed disbelief, he stopped by the store on his way home from work and scanned the ticket – taking a picture of the screen's message for proof – to prove it was true.

His wife thought he was pulling one over on her and called it a prank. After it was confirmed that the $580,000 was a legitimate win, she later referred to it as 'divine intervention'.

Like Team Hope, and in Adele's affection for "things happening for a reason" – there were multitudes of people believing in a master plan which they played a part in. These hopeless romantics rallied around the possibilities of potential. Similarly, Team Logic, which Jacob was admittedly a member of, believed that things happened because of reasons, such as mathematics, science, circumstance, human behavior, and similar explained equations. Randomness found a place either between the two or on a pillar of its own. Generally explained by "shit happens", randomness was a mix of the unexplained and the explained.

The timing of life - the old and slow – as well as the sprightly, adaptable and agile – at times had a clock of its own, owing an explanation to no one. The timelines of relationships complicated the timepiece of an existence. *What's taking him so long to propose? Why's she pressuring me for an engagement ring so quickly?*

Randomness, the minute-by-minute master of loathing and liking, was a mystery.

3

Engagements

Allegra was fidgeting. Vendemer, the Director, was delivering a long-drawn-out soliloquy following his usual Monday morning preamble. *Just get to the fucking point,* she thought, *save us an hour or give us quota relief for time served...*

Maggie sent a text. *How's it going in there?* Allegra inconspicuously texted back: *dragging ass – no drubbing yet.* She knew her "recovery plan", regardless of the prep hours she'd spent on it over the weekend, would be in the cross-hairs for intense scrutiny. Her long sequential run of crushing her numbers had been met with exceedingly growing budgets and the inspection that accompanied sub-par performing.

Benjamin Vendemer pounced upon weakness and was relentless in his attack. The thing she hated was that he was usually right, and she found benefit within his tough demeanor. The thing she hated most was that he, in several ways, was one of the best leaders she followed. And there were many within her young career.

From Epson to Dell Technologies, to HP, to Intel, to IBM, to Vimeo, and on...to her current employer – her leap to reach new positions within new brands came with ever-increasing knowledge, experience and with each transition...more money. But the channel and client line level positions lacked people leadership, and this was her next quest within the industry.

Maggie was a "Sales Enablement Operations Specialist". She seldom attended the sales meetings and only when she was summoned. By the meaning of summoned – it meant when everyone needed to know something. The title was fake. It was created to keep her from a reduction in force, a layoff. Allegra lobbied hard on that one.

"You don't know how valued you're becoming," Maggie would say.

Allegra would respond with a smile and a reply, "Okay, ego stroker."

"No, I'm serious. Like...no one knows more about the next platform or AI than you. You cannot tell..."

"I just listen to podcasts when everyone else is jamming out to Taylor Swift, or enjoying The Bachelorette, or scrolling social media, or...hooking up with hot guys."

"Ooo...so many handsome men in the FinDis here in Manhattan. You're probably right though. You are a geek." The financial district of Manhattan, sometimes dubbed 'FinDis' was a smorgasbord of well-to-do, up-and-coming and eligible bachelors. To Allegra, this also represented a throng of immaturity. She had no time for dating sites, casual happy hour tryouts, or the crucibles of intelligence rehearsals. It wasn't that she wasn't interested. It was that that was for another time.

Allegra would roll her eyes and attempt to change the subject.

Maggie would press, "You know, maybe take some of those corporate ladder moves to the dance floor. That would do it."

"Yeah? You think the robot would do the trick?"

"I think if you put yourself out there, you wouldn't need to do much. I'd give you a go, and I'm a girl. But I know you're not into that sort of thing."

"What you have, Maggie Latch, is a mighty fine thing. When it happens, it happens. You don't force it."

"Says the woman who can force anything into happening. C'mon. Get back on the horse. You're smoking hot. Hotter than hot. Why you denying all the good looking men of Manhattan your hotness?"

"Ugh! The Manics. Juniors. I...well, you know what I like." Allegra looked at Maggie from the corner of her eye, "Nothing wrong with a little rough and tumble. You know, tease me by tugging my hair and throwing me on the mattress for a good time. Strength. Confidence. Experience. But not the ponies, the thoroughbreds."

"Age." Maggie ran the mouse trap with one word.

Allegra didn't answer. "Girl, you know I think you're a mega-hot-tie. You even smell like it. Is that new?" Maggie asked, referring to a new perfume.

"Love, Don't Be Shy – by Kilian." Allegra thought she knew what was coming next.

"See...don't be shy, love..." Maggie replied. "It smells delicious. Just makes me want to eat you up. But not that way," she reaffirmed, "Not into that. I'm into dudes."

Allegra tipped her head in a recalibration. Maybe she didn't know exactly what was coming next. She diverted their attention to one of several photos in Maggie's cubicle. She looked at Maggie in the picture, healthy, smiling, a summer's glow, wearing a cute yellow sundress. Standing next to Maggie was her sister, Kerri. Sullen, with half of the smile, dark circles below her eyes, head tilted away from Maggie, Kerri looked hungry. Hungry for love or attention or a happy moment or something else. Maggie didn't like to talk about her sister.

As much as Allegra tried to, Maggie's interest in saving Kerri from her wayward course toward drug abuse had set sail. Allegra met Maggie's eyes and the two didn't need to revisit the topic.

"You should try again," Allegra coaxed, pursing her lips after she said it.

"What do you know, it's time for email." Maggie strayed from the sermon. Her fingers began clicking on silent keys of a black aluminum laptop, eyes fixed on tiny font filling the screen. She moved her chin down to her chest to conceal her eyes as Allegra slowly departed, wearing both size seven and one-halves.

*****

"Booth," He answered the question from the voice on the other end of the call.

"Thdeve." The questions continued. He held the credit card in his hand. It was grubby from engine grease. His fingernails, what little there were left, were blacked from the diesel work. This was as clean as his hands were. "Eth, TEE, EE, VEE, EE." The knuckles were scared from cranking and grinding and turning wrenches in tight places. "No, no EN." The pinky from his left hand was missing and healing was as complete as it would ever become. That unfortunate lesson was learned nine months ago. He was faithful now.

Steve Booth used what fingers he had remaining to fix, restore, rebuild, dismantle and replace the motors powering the airboats and swamp buggy boats for the tour operators in the tine Everglades City area.

Hidden away in Florida's southwest coastline and 35 miles south of Naples was the Gulf-Coast community where visitors could claim they went to get away from it all. It's backward ways in some respects were fitting for *"Thdeve"* with the speech pediment. Accompanied by four dis-formed short stubs for front teeth, causing his C, S, T, and Z sounds to resemble that of a two-year-old leaning English, a stammering joined his slight disability when he was troubled. The loner wasn't apprehensive or nervous often. He worked alone at his pace, as the jobs came, and if necessary, for the side-hustle. Steve would refer to it as a "thide-huthle" – and the side-hustle was how he was missing the pinky. Mechanics needed their fingers to get work done. It would be best if they had them all: eight fingers, two thumbs. Again, in Thdeve-speak, not *theven fingerth, two thumbth.*

"When you get caught with your hand in the cookie jar, you know what happens, right?" The cutter of the finger wasn't a surgeon. There was no pain reliever given. Just an intimidating practice snip from the steel blade shears. The Fiskars handles were black and orange. Steve was duct taped to a lawn chair behind the shanty he lived in, which was on land his mother once lived on as well. The pain was excruciating, and he had hoped he would faint from the devastation of losing a valued member of one's hand. He did not. He cried out in pain, eyes wide and bulging, as the blood spurt from the missing digit. Where there was once a small finger, the throbbing at the knuckle pounded, keeping beat with his heart.

A nearby blowtorch was lit with a flint lighter. The ferrocerium was struck in his face, sending fiery sparks onto his cheeks. The blowlamp was used under normal conditions for Steve to apply heat and flame to a surface for soldering or brazing metals. In this instance, it was used to cauterize where the pinky once was.

Breathing wildly, bound tightly to the chair by the silver-colored tape, he wiggled uselessly. The aluminum chair with missing mesh strips nearly rocked over as he revolted from the torment and anguish.

"There, that should help...some." The cutter of the finger was much bigger than Steve. He was overpowered. Man against man, one big, one not so – there was an unfortunate lesson, more like a message, being delivered. Steve made the mistake of looking at the cutter crossly.

"Oh no. you're not going to look at me like that you shit!" The cutter picked up the pinky from the floor, dripping with blood, and proceeded to place Steve in a headlock. With his mouth open, gasping for air, Steve's own detached pinky was shoved into his mouth. He tasted the metallic blood gushing through his mouth, dripping down his chin onto his chest. Spitting it out was worse. The cutter picked it up and drew a gun. Steve felt the barrel from a Glock lodge into the socket of one of his eyes. Eat your dirty little finger you Shit. Steve opened his mouth, again tasting his own blood. "Now swallow, don't spit." Steve's eyes were as wide as when the pinky was removed. Only the pain from his hand where the tiny finger once was, was worse. He couldn't. The Glock clicked and began trying to swallow it. Crying out, he mustered to say between cries and with a mouthful of his own digit, "Can't, can't." With his tongue pushing the finger into his cheek, he added, "Too big, too big!"

The cutter pulled the finger from his cheek and shoved it in his jeans pocket.

Breathing in a manic panic from the pang and throes of loss, he felt tears fall where sparks were moments ago. The baptism of what not obeying the demands of the organization meant, was not a lesson or even a message, it was a permanent reminder and intense threat. "Don't fuck up like that again! Don't fuck with the product. Do not fuck with the product. Th-th-th-thdeve!" With a brown hunting knife used to filet small alligators, he was unbound from the tipsy chair and the torture. The sounds of the tape made a swift ripping sound as the blade sliced the binds. He held his hand with the missing finger to his chest, focused on the throbbing at the remaining knuckle, blood streaming down his forearm and pooling on the floor. Then, he was kicked in the scrotum before the sadist departed.

Lying there alone, on the surface of the car port where most of his tools were, he cried, finally mumbling, "Momma," in a whimper. She was long gone. He called her 'momma' because that's what she wanted. Perhaps because it didn't have the letter S in it. She passed away nearly six years ago. Her name was Sara, or in Steve speak: *Thara*. He was on his own now, which led to an abundance of disturbing and dark choices. Becoming a surrogate in the organization had evolved into something more than expected. *Or less,* he thought as he looked at the missing pinky.

That was then. Now, he needed a starter from his parts supplier for the diesel engine sprawled out on the worktable. He read the credit card number and an expiration date. "Tuethday, okie dokie," Steve spoke, confirming when he would need to pick it up at the Postal Express in town. It wouldn't be delivered here, out in the swamp, where Alligator Alley earned its name. He would need to make a short drive from Everglades City, population 400, up the Tamiami Trail to the southernmost part of Naples – where his pickup location was for most of the heavier parts from the supplier.

This was also where Steve would pick up groceries for the product. The product was inside a 53' container, painted a celadon green to blend with the canopy of cypress trees it sat under. Brush, old branches and artificial Spanish moss was scattered across the top of the steel container. It sat three hundred yards from Route 29, well out of sight from the few tourists driving by. A chain link fence, locked like the container holding the product, was just one of the deterrents from anyone brave enough to venture into the brush and scrub of South Florida in the grassy waters which the Seminole once called Pahokee.

Here, in the rivers of grass, the product was away from curiosities. The tourists en route to Chokoloskee would cruise by the gated and guarded drive without distinguishing marks. It was hidden away and secluded from contact with the modern world. The smell was musty. Sitting water, pooled and allowing rot and decay from the foliage gave occasional earthy, meaty smells of sulfur, burnt matches and rotten eggs.

The product was contained by the steel walls, a soundproof layer of insulation, regulated with two small vents which did not cool, but merely circulated fresh air into the compartment. A wet season and a dry season meant that the months of May through October were especially soggy. High temperatures were in the mid-nineties and the humidity was unbearable. Record highs reached one hundred five Fahrenheit. To prevent the product from dehydrating, a small spigot was installed by Steve. The winter months of December through January were much drier and cooler.

The organization had installed cameras throughout Steve's land. Six were facing east, toward the road access. Others were attached to small trees and posts within the brush pointing in each direction of potential access.

Further south from Everglades City, where Smallwood Drive ventured out the small community on Chokoloskee Island, fishing boat charters offered to take anglers out to the sprawling Ten Thousand Islands wildlife. Some crassly designed business websites, raffish hand-painted signs, and budget-minded fliers laid out in lobbies of local businesses led the hustle for smalltime and would-be captains of the bay boats and skiffs to venture out into the waters with their souls on board, seeking the notorious *big one*. The small aluminum-bottomed flats boats and airboats with their large propellers were what kept Steve busy. That and tending to the side hustle.

He hung up the phone with the parts supplier. It was time to feed the product. Steve Booth reached for the door to the refrigerator. He removed nine chicken breasts and dumped them into the dingy and yellowed, shallow plastic serving container. Nine scoops of white rice from a gallon bucket were arranged in the same bin as the cold chicken. Nine biscuits were pulled from a brown wicker basket on a cluttered putty colored laminate countertop. It was once white. The water faucet he welded would serve as a drink. He gathered this assembly of the larger meal of the day together and approached the green container. As he unlocked the padlock latch box, Steve heard the rumbling inside. Swiftly, he slid the grungy plastic box into the gateway passage into the side of steel sided box, containing the product. He slammed it shut, hearing the echoing sound of metal against metal within a big fifty-three-foot metal box.

One word was spoken by Steve into the threshold of the container, as he served the meal: "Thupper."

* * * * *

"I know, I know," Ruby said. "Me first this time, if you don't mind, because I keep meaning to ask you this and continue to get interrupted – and then forget."

"Sure, what is it?" Jacob asked.

"Your health. You good there? Seeing the cardiologists and primary care doctors?"

"They don't," Jacob shrugged, "have much to add. Still on the baby aspirin, low blood pressure medicine and a statin, but that's that. Did a stress test a couple months ago and aced it. They even did a scan about six months ago and were amazed at how everything looked."

Ruby held out his hand to shake Jacobs. It wasn't a handshake as much as it was Ruby holding on to Jacob's hand deliberately and uncomfortably long, "That it so good to hear. It kept wondering and not only have a responsibility to ask you, but I genuinely was concerned and have been thinking about your physical wellness."

Jacob winced, "It is amazing to me that a dietitian isn't the primary focus of health care. Eighty percent is diet, twenty percent is exercise. You are what you eat. Most of us need to figure it out on our own. We're left to the internet and whatever to do that. Hell, in the hospital they served me a cheese omelet, sausage and a biscuit. I washed that down with three cups of coffee. Supposedly that was the heart healthy option..."

"Maybe they were counting that as your cheat meal of the week." Ruby scoffed at the thought of Jacob's hospital dietary regime.

"Well, Adele...Commander Kirby...she has me on high fiber, vegetables, fruits, whole grains, vitamins, protein-this, protein-that..."

Ruby summarized, "The good stuff. Adele, has you eating what you're supposed to eat, right?"

"Right – " Jacob rolled his head to the side, "you could say that"

"What did you eat when you were with the other one?" Ruby wasn't afraid of bold statements, asking matter-of-factly.

"What I wanted." Jacob turned to look at his friend. "With Victoria, there wasn't a daily count for milligrams of sodium. No cholesterol unfriendly food lists. The caffeine consumption was as much as one could consume without having your heart beat out of its chest. I think I was addicted to bacon. The booze...it was free flowing. I mean, like, it was an every single day thing. And Victoria... Well, she...she was friendly with coke – not the soft drink – leading to all sorts of shenanigans."

"So, a bit reckless, you'd say. Maybe that didn't go so well if diet is eighty percent of health and wellness."

"Yeah. Something like that." Jacob pondered in silence, remembering a time of irresponsibility, yet still held an appreciation, a secret waggishness for the thought of it. "My turn for questions. You know it's coming," Jacob continued to look at Ruby. "How in the hell...?" He pulled Richie Ashburn's baseball from his P-coat pocket, concealed from the conversation until the prompt and the prop were relevant. Jacob handed the baseball to Ruby. "Here you go, Skipper."

"Twins," Ruby explained. "It was twins, as in twin mothers and twin children." Once you met the first, the others were less than a block away, also heading in your direction."

"For what reason?" Jacob had his brow beating forehead and face of *what's your thought* process here? clearly visible and on display for Ruby to explain to.

"Two things. First the technology of links. From that Podcast, fed into an Ellipsis server, we knew when your feed began, was paused, resumed, and concluded. Based upon interruptions, portable security cameras that anyone can stick almost any place, and the predictability of your behaviors – we knew how to interact with you. The twins? The women you met. Hired actors."

"But..." Jacob stopped himself. He did find Ruby's deployments and exercises entertaining. "Why do you put me through all of these capacities – to show off – to showcase our resources – to exhibit a little one-upmanship?" His teasing was met with a more serious answer than he intended.

Ruby answered, "You're a situationally educated man now. You are an experiential learner."

"What's that mean...to you?" Jacob asked.

"Think of it like this. If I were to say, 'Whatever you do, don't go for the hottest brunette you ever met...yeah, the hot stripper who made you the king of her castle. Stay away from that one. It'll be the best sex you've ever had. She'll make heads turn and not only look at her – they'll look at you too. You'll go from being a boring money manager to a Wall Street magnet. Oh, and your net worth will increase one hundred-fold. But whatever you do – stay away from that one. There is a one hundred percent chance that after she helps take you to the top of your game – the top of the world, she will ultimately be the one who brings you down and crushes everything you alone built. Oh, and one more thing...she only wants you for your money. Would you have listened?"

"Yeah, probably not," Jacob answered.

"Of course not. Most meatheads wouldn't. You needed to experience it, because you, my dear friend, are an experiential learner."

"You played me again, old man," Jacob slowly turned his head to see if there was any expression on Ruby's face. There was a grin.

"Groundswell. I have got to admit, this can be the amusing and fun part of our organization's training. You know, the onboarding of knowledge," he looked at Jacob, then the phone in his pocket buzzed. Ruby reached for it, looked at its face, and slid it back in his jacket.

"Okay – more resources I'm learning about," Jacob said looking at Ruby patting himself. "What are you missing?"

"I... um, where did that go?" The black man's hands double checked his pockets. "Need to get going Jacob. I have somewhere I need to be and seem to have lost track of time. Don't want to keep the lady waiting." Ruby kept checking the pockets of his trousers, and jacket – inside and outside pockets. "Oh, I remember." He stood and reached for the back pocket of his pants. "Alright Captain Paisley – we'll see each other soon." Ruby reached for the back pocket where a wallet might normally be stashed, grabbed something and handed it to Jacob. The child's navy-blue mitten.

Standing also, Jacob shook his head, reached for it, and nodded with a small smile, "Another toy for Kolohe, perhaps." Ruby had turned and was quickly walking away toward his next thing. He watched him walk away, briskly toward whatever his agenda called for.

When Jacob was out of sight, Ruby turned several times to ensure he wasn't being followed.

There she was. Sitting on a bench, Adele was waiting for Ruby and just sent him a text message five minutes earlier, informing him that she had arrived in the spot he asked her to meet him at.

After they greeted each other, Ruby informed her he had met with Jacob ten minutes ago, and he asked, "Are you two taking good care of each other?"

Adele looked at him oddly, answering, "We always have. Why do you ask?"

"Perhaps I haven't been a good friend. I've been thinking about his health and made some assumptions that everything was great – when maybe it wasn't."

"It is actually, I've got him on a strict...we're both on a Mediterranean diet, eating healthier options." Adele's brunette hair blew softly in the breeze toward her face. She pulled a few strands back from her mouth as she continued to explain its value.

Ruby motioned to an available bench where they both sat down.

"Other than red wine, we're off the sauce. Well, most of the time. Special occasions only. A cocktail or two or a few isn't a nightly thing anymore. But with the wine – red – maybe that's a new vice. That's...well, Jacob has a friend who owns a winery in Chelan Valley, Washington - and then he's always had a thing for Danica Patrick. Another spicy brunette, go figure."

"Who?" Ruby asked.

"She owns a vineyard and wine label too. Something Latin. Jacob knows it a little too well. Danica Patrick."

"Who's that?"

"Danica Patrick?" She checked to see if he was kidding. He wasn't, so she continued to jostle his memory, "You know, the race car driver? NASCAR – Indianapolis 500? Tiny little thing. Long dark hair. Beautiful woman. On the corporate speaker's circuit. I think she has her own clothing line. Uh... Good wine. Jacob buys it by the case. Pricey. She used to do Super Bowl commercials."

"The...that Go Daddy model?"

"Well, of course you'd go there. You guys..." Adele huffed playfully, "You're all alike." She gave him a soft punch in the shoulder.

"I can assure you, we're not all alike. But if you led with 'Go Daddy girl'...well, I'm just saying that's the way to start."

"She's very...intelligent" Adele looked forward. "Good wine too," she attempted justification. "PPCM held an event in Phoenix. She gave some of his top traders a few spins around the track. Then it was his turn. Jacob said they were only going a hundred forty miles an hour on the turns, but the back wheels left the ground, floating as they turned left."

Ruby chuckled, mostly to himself, "Well, how about that... Next, you'll tell me he's got a thing for Elizabeth Hurley..."

Adele gave him another teasing punch in the shoulder for that one.

"Listen, why we're really here," Ruby began, "I know you share almost everything with him. But... But not this. Not just yet. Soon. Not now. We've got to have an agreement on this... You can tell him you're helping your son, or that you have a distant friend from college going through a divorce, or that..."

"I got you. As we agreed. I'll drop into San Diego. Do the thing. Then, jump on a Hawaiian Air flight into HNL the next morning. There's nothing questionable about that. Silence. You have my word." Adele was wearing a new pair of Maui Jim sunglasses as they sat on the park bench. Large bronze lenses wrapped in dark chocolate frames hid her eyes from his. Her dark hair was pulled back into a low ponytail, draped on the back of her overcoat. She was mature, cosmopolitan, and graceful. Adele was pretty. It was the kind of beauty which grew with time. As it ticked forward, with a minute, month, year or decade – she became more attractive. In her appearance, yes – but in the important matters: those of the heart. It was how she carried herself within the meaningful moments, the gentle words which she spoke to a person needing to hear her kindness, and the wisdom in how the world worked which found a way to lift a heavy situation. Her beauty transitioned inside out, from what she was thinking to her results. In a conversation with Jacob, they discussed hierarchy. Beliefs, perceptions, feelings, thoughts, actions, results. If it was pretty on the inside, it may be somewhat pretty on the outside.

They were both dressed in earthy colors. Browns, greys, blacks. An amalgamation of autumn dress in New York City. His, dated and slightly frumpy. Hers, current, chic, appearing likely from a posh shop on 5th Avenue in Midtown.

He squinted into the morning sun at trees stripped of their leaves months ago. White twinkling lights would light several of the trees aligning streets by night. By day, the small bulbs reflected the sunlight.

She was about to embark on her first assignment with the Ellipsis.

"We'll meet again in a few days to work out some of the details. Who you'll work alongside, what to expect, what to avoid, where to go, and so on. Alright?"

"Roger that," Adele knew it sounded corny as soon as it spilled across her lips. It wasn't something she'd have normally said. She chuckled slightly, more to herself than anything else.

Ruby smirked, and rose from the bench, "Miss Adele..." he paused, nodded his head and softly spoke only one other word in her direction, as he departed, "Aloha."

She replied with a softly spoken, "Aloha", more to herself as he left. It seemed out of place from the eternal grey of the city. She too, like Jacob, missed the bright blue and green of Oahu in the middle of the Pacific.

Adele watched him walk slowly across the park and then after he crossed the crosswalk, disappear into a small gathering at the corner on the other side of the taxi-filled streets. The yellow cars brake lights red glow filled the gray city with a cheery brightness. Small puffs of white smoke extended from their tailpipes evaporating into the air as they drove away.

She reached into her overcoat pocket for her phone after feeling it buzz. She smiled, swiping the face of the device. "Hey. What's up?" After a minute of silence, she frowned and replied, "Okay, I'll be right there. Where are they taking him?"

*****

Jacob was walking up Park Avenue. At the corner of 63rd Street, he could see The Lowell, where he and Victoria would visit and stay in the three-thousand dollar per night penthouse suite – just because they wanted to spend lavish amounts of money on something completely unnecessary. It was a finely appointed property. Two terraces, two seating areas, a fireplace, marble bathroom with Jacuzzi, and a stocked kitchen. He remembered Victoria, tipsy from several glasses of champagne, giggling as the bubbles in the tub reached the bottom of her chin. After her bath, she reached for an over-sized Egyptian cotton white towel to cover her breasts. As she turned toward the mirrors to dry, the soft nap brushed midway to her toned thighs. He was lost in thought thinking of how she dropped the towel as she made her way through the suite to their bed for the night.

"Who the hell were you?" He said this to himself as he winced in disgust. The former Jacob Paisley was dead. Winter winds whipped through the towers above. *"Really... Who?"* he added as he pushed the thought of their sexual playfulness into another spot in thought. Not able to control his desire, he looked around at the crowded street of people dressed in dark colored jackets, bundled snugly against the December cold front approaching. Looking at every thirty-something-aged female with brunette hair. This was her neighborhood, Lenox Hill. His former penthouse was a little further, the upper east side.

"Stop it. She isn't here." This time he said it aloud, and an elderly woman walking toward him wearing a scarf ducked away from him, speaking to himself.

Jacob pictured her mugshot, holding a white placard with black letters for her name and case number upon it. In his thoughts he saw her orange jumpsuit. Without makeup, without the spunk and spirit she usually led with, without the hustle of her next new thing...she looked at the camera taking her photo...completely without hope. Sorrow for her filled him for a moment.

Then, he considered the trade-off: what he wanted then – for what he wanted most. Lust for love. There was no bedding Adele in The Lowell. The several times which they had been together romantically were meaningful and filled with a wholesomeness. The countless times he had sex with Victoria were transactional and now hollow.

Gone were the days of having a company-paid driver in a town car. Gone, too, were the fine suits from Michael Andrews Bespoke. The private dinners at Eleven Madison Park were in his yesterdays. The white linen tablecloths, sconces adorning the walls, twenty-thousand-dollar dinners filled with kiss-ass service were no longer in the upcoming calendar. The excursions to Boca Raton to board PPCM's private yacht, The First Trade, were now his once-upon-a-time elsewhere. His cameos on CNBC, the occasional call from a congressperson seeking investment advice, and the traders sucking up to his tower of power were in his rearview mirror.

He had to get her out of his head. There wasn't real estate for her anymore. The poison she had introduced him to, known and unknown, wasn't the way forward. It was slightly embarrassing that Adele endured some of it – on occasion, covering for him with the Board of Directors. She had to know that his squalid behavior involved filthy and unquenched desires.

He reminded himself of something. With Adele – there was no longer an unquenchable longing for more. She was enough. He just needed to groom the risk and reward behavior. The quest for the lascivious prize. It needed to end. Jacob realized he was getting older. The differences between him being older and the allure of the younger women...*well, borderline creepy,* he thought.

The two-bedroom apartment they shared in Midtown not far from the East River but not facing it...it was enough. At least until the Residences at the Waldorf Astoria was complete.

And then there was Kolohe, his well-behaved rescue from Kapolei. The adorable yellow lab with big brown eyes, he too, was enough. Their Central Park strolls on Saturday mornings, they were gratifyingly filled with something that once was missing. Unconditional love. It was then that he realized that between Adele and filling a whole in his heart with an unconditional love – that he was continuing to heal from the death of who he once was.

The shiny silver phone in his coat pocket buzzed. He reached for it to answer, looking briefly at the face of the device. "So soon? What is it, you miss me already?"

The voice on the other end of the call was Ruby's, "Hey old man, change of plans. Can you fly out to Seattle on Tuesday? An opportunity other than building a mountain of money has presented itself."

Jacob looked into the crowded streets filled with people other than Victoria's of the world. He knew his call was to generate twenty percent returns with the funds that Ellipsis had deposited for him. This is why he was involved, to create funds for magical things to happen. Listening, he replied, "Tuesday...like next Tuesday?"

"That one."

"Be careful what you wish for, right? I can do that." Jacob considered the last time he was in Seattle, with PPCM – hosting a Supersonics suite for bougie new high net worth clients. This new assignment, whatever it might be, would be nothing like buying his investors Macanudo's, the iconic cigars known for embarking upon journeys. This new opportunity wouldn't likely include a toast over a premium glass of thirty-year double cask Macallan. It probably wouldn't be about getting together with the players after the game in The Gold

Dust Room at The Butcher's Table. No Mishima Reserve Wagyu steaks this time. He had traded lavish opulence for he-did-not-know-what in this new realm. The sights and sounds and the scents of the rich life were still weighty to him.

Ruby didn't say much else, "Check your email for a reservation and some instruction about what's next."

"But you...you said..."

"It'll be alright. Nothing binding." The call ended.

Nothing binding. What the...? Jacob slipped the device back into his pants as he thought about the secrecy that enveloped this new dynamic he had opted in to.

His phone rang again. The number was unknown, but an 808-exchange lit up the face of the phone. 808. That meant Hawaii. He wasn't expecting anything. Nothing lingered from the Aicon, the luxury craft which two idiots sank. He stopped himself. *No. They didn't sink it. Maybe, just maybe, it could have been repaired if it was gently brought in.* The fantasy of what-ifs caused him a noticeable loss of good headspace. Wasted thoughts, Jacob concluded. *Don't go there.*

The number stopped ringing. He waited for a voicemail notification to light up the face of his device. It didn't.

On the other end of the call Tamsen Makua, six time zones away, spoke only to herself, "Answer your phone New York money man, I need to pretend today."

She looked out at the waves curling fiercely on Oahu's North Shore. She ran her fingers across seven surf boards in her back yard board cradle. Speaking to herself more as she looked out at the surf, "Double overheads. Looks like a nice day for Daisy." Tamsen selected a short swirly yellow and white board she had custom shaped several years ago. "Today we're going to go hard, Miss Daisy. For the love of what we can control – and that which we cannot." She lifted the bright surfboard, hoisting it under her arm and carried it through the wooden gate, latching it behind her. Her home near Oahu's coast, up on the ridge, faced the rumbling surf waves pounding their crashing weight like thunder onto the blueness of the Pacific's depths. "Better than fireworks", she said to herself as she saw the white foam in the distance explode from the crashing waves. "Let's go." Tamsen hoisted the board to her SUV, knowing that in ten minutes she'd be running toward the raw energy of the liquid eruptions sending a foamy white mist towering into the morning air. The salty smelling air would fill her lungs with life and soul with meaning.

4

The Offer

The meeting was ending. Unless Vendemer prolonged the agony, there would be less than five minutes to the torture. He was exhaustive in some topics. This time it was an eternal elaboration about T&E reporting. Travel and Entertainment was a line item under close scrutiny and one that Vendemer watched over like a hungry hawk eyeing dinner down below. He had an incremental options bonus which would be granted due to his control over earnings from operations, which was abbreviated to the term: EFO. This was what all the Directors referred to near the end of a fiscal quarter. EFO this, EFO that, EFO something, EFO something else. The interpretation meant Vendemer's big ticket bonus for squeezing expenses and maximizing margins which were often gossamer thin.

He stopped speaking mid-sentence. "That's it. Enough. You get it. Get out of here and go sell something!" The dozen staff looked at each other and simultaneously gathered their things: cell phones, laptops, padfolios, pens, cups of Starbucks in varieties of sizes and flavors. They quickly moved toward the threshold where a form of freedom from meeting madness welcomed them with fresh air opposed to the stale air from the stodgy meeting room.

"Sinclair," he barked her name as she was merely two feet from freedom, "...a moment, please. Couple things..." Vendemer motioned her to the end of the room she had just migrated from. "Let's have a seat. Sit. Let's talk." He slunk down in one of the chairs surrounding the long meeting table, which was to resemble wood, but was nothing more than vinyl with a faux grain on the surface.

"Sure, what is it? If it's about that bottle of wine at Bobby Van's I can explain, because they took advantage of..." Allegra dropped into a chair near him, keeping a professional amount of distance.

"No... Uh, what?"

"Never-mind," Allegra stopped herself from divulging any more detail.

He ignored further inquisition, "There's something else we need to discuss. Not expenses." His thinning long blond hair was extra tousled today and as if he were reading her mind, he ran his hand across his head somewhat grooming it. She looked into his piercing blue eyes and attempted to read into the invitation for a chair and conversation. He reached into a short stack of papers he had at his end of the maple boardroom table. Two crisp documents were drawn from the pile. She could see her company logo at the top of one of the documents. It was ominous.

She looked at Vendemer who looked like a college professor more than an intense revenue generating leader in her company. *Am I getting RIF'd?* she wondered. RIF was an acronym used to represent Reduction in Force. But her numbers were within range of hitting topline targets, and she had a get-well plan for her gap, and there were many other teammates she assumed were at risk...

"You've been vocal..." he trailed.

I'm getting canned for some trumped up charge? She thought to herself. *Shit, everyone bitches more than me...*

"...about requesting more opportunity. So, I have an offer for you."

Even worse. I'm getting more responsibility without a promotion.

"It's an offer, which I hope...you cannot refuse." It was slightly creepy the way he said it. He slid the first paper across the table, facing her. His blink less eyes watched her review the words. The company logo gleamed a bright and irresistible blue. She looked at the title and the dollar amount in the middle of the page before looking at her manager. "It's no secret that we've had our eye on you as a bench player for leadership. This is your shot to take. We believe you have tremendous potential with our company and would like to build around your talents and skillset."

She blushed at the material difference in base pay. It was nearly a fifty-thousand-dollar increase. "Holy shit," she didn't know what to say, but that's what slipped through her lips, and she was embarrassed at her uncontrolled reply. "Not - what - I -meant - to say, but it fits the moment." Allegra looked at the offer letter again. An empty line was at the bottom of the letter awaiting her signature. "What I really mean is, thank you."

Vendemer slid a second multi-page stapled document across the table, "It gets a little better. In this role, we view you as eligible for stock options. The ISO's you're eligible for come with an additional do-not-compete clause. So…" he offered a pregnant pause, "should you choose to accept the offer, you'll also be bound to our company for a minimum of twelve months." She glanced at the strike price and the quantity of the grant. "And you'll work closely with me to cross-board into the senior leadership role."

"I don't know what to say. It's like Christmas morning." The unexpected recognition warmed her to the point she fanned herself a few times with the offer letter, "I'm excited."

"Good to hear that." He looked at her. He looked at her too much. She knew there was more to the story. "Unrelated…"

"Unrelated?"

"Yes, unrelated to any of this," he looked into her eyes, "what would you think about drinks tomorrow after hours."

There it was. That was the point that he fucked it up. She looked at her hands in her lap. They were wringing themselves nervously, "You know that I'm seeing someone, right?" She wasn't seeing anyone. Allegra was far from it, swearing off men for the next quarter...maybe month...or at least until the weekend.

"No... No, I didn't know that." He drifted, "...but would that matter? It's just drinks."

"I...I don't know if that's a good idea," she fidgeted and was lost in thought about what 'just drinks' meant to Vendemer. It was a trade-off, or it was nothing. But she was suddenly certain she wouldn't let *just drinks* get in her way. "Forgive me, I don't know what I'm thinking." Signing the offer letter first, then the options grant - she slowly slid the half dozen pages without reading the terms across the table. She was stoic and wavering at the same time, queasy on the inside, a steely exterior, "Sure, drinks will work," she said unconvincingly, almost monotone.

"Good...was hoping you'd come around. I already put the requisition through the portal knowing you couldn't deny me. It's official as of yesterday. Drinks Friday, and we'll see where it goes from there."

She stopped talking. *Wrong*, she thought. *This is not how I played this in my head. Not the way I thought I'd be promoted. Is this some quid-pro-quo thing?*

"We'll have a lot to discuss. There will be some compression next week. We'll consolidate some positions, necessary to do, and you'll be along for the ride for a couple and manage to a couple on your own."

Allegra knew this was a pathway to disappointment. She couldn't contain her curiosity, "Maggie?"

Vendemer looked at her, tipping his head slightly and wincing, "First to go. But we'll consider saving her for you. You come up with a bullet proof reason why. I mean Kevlar or steel belted radial or something. We're cost conscious now. Your first real test." He stood quickly gathering the remaining pile of papers, tossing them into binder. "Call me with questions. And..." he held out his hand, "Congratulations." He smiled. She hadn't noticed how yellow his teeth were before.

They shook hands. His was unusually limp. Hers was unusually firm. His was dry, warm, confident. Hers was as sweaty and cool as she thought it might be.

*Great...*she thought of the promotion to that of a senior manager. *This sucks as much as it is awesome. Damn, that's a lot of money.* Allegra stared outside at the cloudy sky. It was sunny when the meeting began an hour ago. She watched white clouds of smoke billowing from lower building rooftops HVAC units evaporating slowly into the December afternoon. The campaign *Save Maggie* was underway. She wouldn't fail. She would do all that she could to save her teammate and friend.

The door opened. He was back. She spun from the lost-in-thoughts look out the window when she heard the door jamb bump from the swing of the door.

"Sorry to startle you."

"No, it's quite alright. Just taking it in. Again...thank you."

"I almost forgot. We cross-build on our leadership team. There's a mentor..." He paused, "Not exactly a mentor...a sponsor. Someone with some knowledge about leadership, and building things, and navigating business that we'll want you to connect with."

"Great, when do I meet Ed Mylett?"

"Not Mylett." When Vendemer smiled, his yellow teeth were too big for his face.

"Tony Robbins?"

"Sorry, it's a no there too. No Tony. With what we're about to pay you we cannot afford them." The door slowly sunk shut, silencing the hallway noise from the rest of the office outside. "He's a local guy. That's the good news. You two can meet face to face for chitchat or whatever. We have him or will have him on a non-disclosure agreement I should say, so it's okay to share anything with him. A former fat cat money manager down on Wall Street. Used to appear on Bloomberg with the talking heads once in a while. Look at your time with him as a consultant. A coach or counselor. He's...well, sort of retired now. Semi-retired, maybe?"

Allegra looked blankly at Vendemer, trying not to stare at his shiny head or his coffee-chugging teeth. She said nothing other than, "So he used to be awesome. Sounds great."

"I like the intensity. You bring an unusual amount of moxie to the show, no matter what the show is." Vendemer pointed his index finger at her in a go-get-them manner. He reached for the door, swinging it open. "You'll hear from him soon, I think."

Before he turned to leave, she asked, "Does Mr. Semi-Retired have a name?"

"Uh...yeah..." Vendermer reached for his phone in his suit coat pocket, entered a pass-code, and fumbled for a contact. "Of course, you were going to ask me his name and I have it...right..." He continued to slide the surface of the phone's face from the bottom to the top, digging deep into text messages or email. "Here. Here...it...is...some-where..."

Allegra looked at Vendemer who was usually crisp, decisive, quick with resolution, and sometimes abrupt. Now he was clumsy, struggling to come up with direction, and sheepish. She assumed at this level she might be exposed to things not being quite as tidy as they appeared as a line-level junior manager. There were questions beginning to form in her head about the additional opportunities she'd be responsible for. She hoped that's what tomorrow's 'just drinks' meeting would cover, nothing else.

"Jacob Paisley." Finally, he finished fumbling and found the name. "You'll be meeting with Jacob Paisley."

Allegra felt a small crease forming in her brow. "Paisley. Sounds familiar."

"See where that goes, might be a mighty good thing there."

Immediately she felt better, knowing he had said the same thing about their 'just drinks' meeting for tomorrow minutes ago. Perhaps Vendemer used that kind of language with other senior leaders of their tech organization. Perhaps this was just shop-talk. She had learned recently that channel competitors were not really competitors as much as they were drinking buddies while on the manufacturer circuit.

"Hey," he added, "Go sell something, your quota isn't going away just yet."

"On it. Quit talking to me, you're holding me back," she teased.

He gave her a quick thumbs up and smiled slightly with his lips, sparing her another glance at his flax smile.

"Who is Jacob Paisley?" she asked into her phone after he left a second time. She looked at the device and began to scroll through page after page of biographies. "Easy on the eyes...hello handsome, nice to meet you," she said to herself as she skipped over news articles from several years ago. Pausing on one, "Uh-oh. Hmm... Bit of trouble there." Allegra continued to read from the text of the article, looking into his piercing blue eyes, salt and pepper hair, and clean-shaven chiseled jawline, while speaking to herself, "This dude's got some edge."

*****

She pushed a red button on the face of the phone ending their call. She had the green light to go. It was a first assignment and trust would be the byproduct from the trip. Ruby gave her instructions to tell Jacob that she needed to help a friend from college in San Francisco. Nothing more.

"Hey, I have something I need to talk with you about. Call me back." Trust was what she built. It was her primary product. But this was different. Both she and Jacob had been included in the objective of Ellipsis. It was greater than the Administrative Admin trust she had devoted to Jacob over the years. It felt foreign. Yet, they had the conversation that there might be a time to deviate from the trust of each other for the well-intentioned outcome of the organization. She went old school on him and left a voice message.

Adele didn't expect him to respond so quickly. Tucking a tendril of her brunette hair behind one ear, she answered. "What a day..."

"I've got something I need to talk about too. I was just going to call you when you got to me first."

"Well, you go. This might take a little time."

"It's nothing really. I have some unfinished business with PPCM which I need to attend to. It's in Seattle. I need to make a trip to Sea-Tac. Might be a day or two, not sure."

"Somewhat...surprised...you're willing...to help. I thought you'd give them the finger." Adele tucked another dangling tendril behind her other ear, switching hands. Squeamish about blatantly lying to Jacob, she played along with the news of his trip and thought it might diminish her fib somewhat. The need to sell the fabrication of truth would be more subtle with Jacob preoccupied with whatever business with his old firm he needed to tidy up.

He explained that there was a financial component which would benefit him. *Them.* He said *'them'* right after he said, 'him'.

Whatever guilt she had just shed, she loaded back up on. "Well, first, my grandson...*our grandson*...was taken to one of those doc-in-a-box urgent care places for four stitches from the playground. He fell from the monkey bars."

"Bars can be tough. On adults and kids. How is he now? Where did he get the..." Jacob was keeping it light, taking the time to inquire.

"Oh, he's just fine. The other thing is that I have an old college friend in California that needs me. She's going through a hard divorce and called me for some mental health. I agreed to go visit her." It was killing Adele, the slight lie. She was indeed traveling. It just wasn't to San Francisco. At least it was California, and the city was a San-something. *White lie, right?* She thought as she spun the untruth.

Jacob thought Adele was speaking quickly, zooming right past the concern for her grandson...*their* grandson. That was a new thing. Adele merely tapping the breaks in a speedy conversation about family was also a new thing. She didn't answer his question...where did he require stitches? *It was their grandson.* His elbow, his knee, his forehead?

"Hey...do what you got to do." Keep the pace of the conversation the same. Parity. He was considering how he wouldn't need to sell the lie through his lips if asked about additional detail for the Seattle trip if Adele was preoccupied with her old college friend in San Francisco endeavor. He'd never heard about this person, but this wasn't the moment to inquire – it was a moment to embellish the fact that he was indeed going to Seattle.

"I fly out Tuesday. We can talk more about it later...if you want to."

"Me too," he thought that lying to Adele was for amateurs. Over the years in working with her as his personal executive administrator at PPCM, she was the consummate professional in sorting through bullshit.

"Kolohe." Adele was the most conscientious person Jacob knew. Of course, she'd think of the dog with a heart of the same color he was, gold. "He's never been away from both of us, since we brought him through the flight nanny."

"He's a Paisley, he's tougher than most. It'll be fine. I think." Jacob shrugged his shoulders, knowing only he could see them roll with his artificial assurance.

"Oh, he's a Paisley, is he?" She was attempting to believe that the playful conversation helped the bluff glide through to a believable task which she just had to go manage to. Maybe.

"I need to meet with a young woman at a technology company tomorrow. Mentoring calls. Or sponsorship, or whatever they want to call it now. Tomorrow, I think. No one talks on the phone anymore. It's all text." Jacob felt the need to move from the nebulousness of his Seattle trip to a true task which Ruby had assigned to him. He had just entered her phone number and name in his phone for what could be a meeting of an unknown purpose. This was his new lot in life. From the objective to the subjective. From physical to mystic. From founding a company of his own name created to build something from nothing:

wealth...to a role of delivering dollars in offshore and clandestine accounting principles while asking for additional responsibilities.

"You're so good with people. You know that, right?"

"I haven't heard that in a while. Thanks."

"Hey, my son is calling in, probably with an update. Meet you at home." Still guilt-ridden for her fudging of the upcoming trip, it wasn't really the truth about her son on another call. She wanted to get off the call to dilute the deception. This was tough stuff on Adele. Keeping track of lies was busy work. It was easier to tell the truth.

Jacob looked at his phone. Her social media profile pulled up as he summoned her name, Facebook, LinkedIn, Instagram, Threads, and others which he paid little attention to. She was pretty. Her eyes were blue, and her smile was bright white. Her long blonde hair, slightly curled, with curtain bangs surrounded her pretty face and fell below her shoulders in her profile photo. *Thirty-something, he assumed, maybe mid-thirties?* Jacob thought, *the resemblance is there, to Kate Hudson.* He had met her at a PPCM fundraiser in the city years ago. But this wasn't a call to Penny Lane, or to Andie Anderson, or to Tess – seeking gold with Finn Finnegan in the crystal turquoise waters of the Caribbean. He slid his thumb onto a green button to launch a call to an alluring Allegra Sinclair.

*****

She counted the hours separating them. Six. Tamsen called the New York number Ruby shared with her. It fell to voicemail immediately.

"Hello Jacob Paisley, it's Tamsen Makua. I don't know you and you don't know me. Ruby's connecting us. So, let's get to know each other. I heard you're a bit old school, which is why I'm leaving you a voice message opposed to a text like the rest of modern civilization. Give me a call at 808. 213...and there you are..."

"Hey, Tamsen - Yes, Jacob Paisley here. I was hanging up with another call as yours came in." Kolohe, the yellow lab stretched out on the couch, granting Adele a small area to sit and scroll through her phone. She scratched his ears occasionally causing the dog's tail to wag randomly. Wearing a robe for warmth, she and Jacob were dressed for bed. This was a subtle game they played nightly. Seeing which one of them would call it out first, as if surrendering to the day: "I'm done, how about you?"

The dog would rise, eager to join the loser heading to the bedroom. Kolohe's bed was at the foot of theirs. Its fluffy padding was the warmth he needed for a long winter's night. It wouldn't be until five or six in the morning that he'd nudge with his big black cold wet nose that it was time to go out.

"Working late?" She was sifting the warm North Shore sand through her toes and listening to the waves break while she pictured him looking out of a window into the Manhattan city lights of nearby towers. Perhaps at a desk, maybe with a scotch glass in his hand, possibly even in pajamas.

Jacob hadn't thought of work in a long time. "If what we do is work, working late. If what we do is a little something more...purpose-driven outcomes, perhaps...then, just getting started." He didn't know much more than that a Hawaii call would from a Tamsen on Oahu's North Shore would take place soon. Ruby's team was scaling, or had already grown, and seemed to be beyond Jacob's original thoughts of a tidy little unit acting upon good intentions.

"Nice. We're speaking the same language already. Ruby tells me you liked your time here. With that, it's *Aloha* with you."

"Well, he had most of that right. I adored my time there. Absolutely loved Oahu. If you can find a way to get me back out there, count me in." Jacob used his free hand to draw the gold curtains aside, peering out into the sodium lights of New York. The darkness swallowed the city hours ago. A low rumble of street noise could be heard, but only if it tried to be. The television was on and turned to CNBC, but the noise was muted.

"Hawaii is like that for some visitors. I didn't have much of a choice. Grew up here. "

"Ruby says you're quite the surfer."

Tamsen wondered what else their mutual friend and partner had shared. "Again – didn't have much of a choice. My uncles and cousins had me swimming as surfing before anything. Choppy conditions – we go out. Ankle slappers – we go out. Bombs – they go out, and I watch. And now I'm addicted to dawn patrol, trying to catch the next perfect hollow barrel. I can hang but don't like getting worked as much as I used to."

"I could sit there for hours. Between mile markers seven and eight..." Jacob searched for the words, squinting at his reflection in the glass window. "Pupukea? Is that it? Near the lifeguard tower."

She giggled. "Tower number twenty-five. I'm looking at it right now. Banzai Pipeline."

"You kidding?"

"Nah. I live nearby."

"Lucky."

She found excitement in talking with him. Prior to the call, Tamsen thought it might be a drab call about how he was going to position her grants to help them grow beyond fluffy returns. "We had some heavy chunder earlier this week."

"Chunder?"

"Sorry, surf slang. It was a washing machine out there. Foam soup."

"Oh, wow. Did they have the jet skis out there towing anyone in? Or out?"

Jacob did know the scene.

"Nothing was peeling. Offshore winds made it impossible to stand. A couple headers, no lulls, plenty of grubbing."

"I need a cheat sheet to keep up with what you're saying."

Tamsen had questions. Time to ask. Not a time for surf-speak. "Always fun to watch. As long as no groms are out there giving Tower Two Five extra work. Like Mother Nature's fireworks - watching the mavericks crash and explode their foam against the deep blue."

"I can see it." Jacob had sat down at his desk and faced a large monitor. The National Oceanic and Atmospheric Administration website known as NOAA was pulled up. His time with the Aicon, The Final Trade, on the other side of the island had caused him to pay close attention to small craft advisories and become quite weather ready. He toggled through the surf history which featured swells, surf conditions, warnings, and 4K satellite imagery. He scrolled over the KoOlina Marina quickly, which was saved in his browser history – recalling his time on the leeward side.

"Ruby told me a little bit about your time here. About your yacht."

"He did, did he?" Jacob scrolled back to the North Shore. "Ah, there you are?"

"Dude, are you on satellite? Stalker..."

"I can see you waving. Looks like a nice afternoon." He wasn't really using the eyes in the skies to view Tamsen.

"You mistook me flipping you off for a wave."

"Oh, is that what that was?" he asked.

"Creeper," she teased in return.

Jacob smiled as he spoke, switching from his handset to an earpiece speaker. The was some rustling in the kitchen. Adele was stewing two cups of tea. Black for herself, green for Jacob. She tried not to eavesdrop on the call as she approached him and dropped off the steaming cup on the glass surface. "About Oahu. Adele and I wouldn't say 'no', but we have some family in the northeast, so there's that."

"Ohana," she mentioned the Hawaiian word for family, "bring 'em with."

"Maybe...someday." Jacob scrolled through the crystal-clear imagery of the homes doting the island's lush side, often referred to as *the country*.

As if she were peering over his shoulder, Tamsen shared where she was, "If you have the North Shore pulled up, locate Pupukea Road, follow it up the hill, once you're past the trees you might find Mankana Road. I'm there somewhere."

"I'll have to check it out," he pretended that he would, however he was already there. Homes from two to seven million dollars on large parcels of greenery aligned the hilltop neighborhood.

In the distance, Adele stubbed her toe on the baseboard spilling her cup of hot tea on herself. She let out a small painful whimper and turned quickly to whisper an apology. Jacob quickly converted his frown to a smile as he saw her bounce around in her slippers. He mouthed the words, *'you, okay?'*.

She waved him off and disappeared into their bedroom.

Unknowing of the mild toe-bending injury in the Manhattan night, Tamsen presumed Jacob was scrolling. "Can you see the Foodland on the Kam? Near the Pupukea Beach Park and the Hakuola Gulch?"

"Best poke in Hawaii..."

"So ono," she interrupted, indicating the word for 'delicious' in the Hawaiian language.

"Spicy Ahi?" Jacob asked.

"Hawaiian style, mac salad, and Kim Chee on the side. Chee-hoo. Ah – every Friday. I'm throwing you a shaka right now, money man."

"I can see it."

"Naw, that's me flipping you off again."

"Hey, switching gears on you – why does Ruby want us to connect?" Jacob was seeking a task, opposed to another island acquaintance.

"He's building his team. He's got something up his sleeve involving Oahu. He knows something you and I might not yet know." Tamsen knew her friend and mentor could only share so much, that his intentions were aligned with his, that his objectives were pure. It didn't take any convincing.

"*Yet.* There's that word that describes Ruby. He's knowing, *yet* only shares so much of the story. The minstrel which, at times, shares parcels of information."

"That's him. One hell of a poet, right?" She thought of him as a masterful architect or as a grand, yet uncredited, composer of a Billboard Chart hit ballad. From the sorrow of something broken rises triumph. A piano and a violin were surely involved in his compositions. Tamsen had more history with Ruby than Jacob did.

"A troubadour, a tease of sorts. I don't know if I ever get the full story from him all of the time. Perhaps just enough to keep me safe, wanting more, seeking the next turn in the road to somewhere – knowing the purpose solves a few things that can't be solved with the construct we've got."

"Yep, that's our guy," she said.

"Well, let's see where this goes." Jacob yawned.

"I'll let you go. Sorry to call so late. Good to put a voice with a name. We'll be in touch, I'm sure. For some reason."

"No, you're not. You did the math. Six hours. And you know New Yorkers stay up late."

"You're not as innocent as Ruby makes you out to be. More than a pretty face. Fair enough. Talk soon?"

"Talk soon, Tamsen Makua. Thanks for calling. Or...Mahalo."

"Mahalo, Jacob Paisley."

As they both hung up – they knew that they had done their research on each other before the call took place. The assessments checked out. They were two people who knew the mark. Money would meet meaning.

Born of their intended accomplishments, *yet* deprive of any firm definition, Tamsen knew that Jacob held an ambition to breed divergences. He wore a wholesome exterior, *yet* he had some history otherwise.

Jacob had a strong sense that Tamsen was determined to propagate a virtuousness – perhaps from the pang of a relationship or as a resolute atonement. She was strong, *yet* there was more to her story. *Yet* – a word to describe Ruby as well as anyone.

✳ ✳ ✳ ✳ ✳

Steve Booth was managing some conflict. It was written on his face. His forehead mostly. The lessons learned from his Momma were to respect young women. What he saw on the internet didn't appear respectful – but alluring – and Momma wouldn't approve. His desires of today clashed with his lessons from yesterday. What was happening now was at a discord with what he was taught back then.

"*Sometimes things change, son... Occasionally, what mattered then just don't matter no more... That's called evolution.*" Either he remembered her voice, or he remembered the memory of the way her voice sounded. A slow and soft southern draw, clear enunciation so that Steve could better understand, and often a gentle hand to stroke her son's head – running her fingers through his hair when he was a child and even as an adult. When he'd look into her eyes, those with wisdom of things beyond his comprehension, he would see the wrinkles around them crinkle as she smiled at him. He felt that her cautious reassurance and tender direction kept him safe.

Maybe this was the change she spoke of.

He reattached the fallen camouflage to the side of the metal container. It was warm and humid but not unbearable. If Momma were here, she'd tell him to have a lemonade and she was not, so he didn't. The steel wire from the spool was nearly gone. He used what remained to reinforce the repair cutting and twisting with a slow and methodical precision. His breathing was becoming raspy. Pausing to take a puff from his inhaler, he wiped the small beads of sweat from his brow. It was musty out here. it was time to return to the work yard.

The black bulky bubble earphones covering his ears made him look like a bug. They played the same soundtrack over and over and over again. It was on his boom box in the work yard too. His musical choices were limited to hard rock, acid rock, classic rock and a mix of rocks. Not understanding the depth of the lyrics, the melodies served as reminders of what he had done, connected him to his memories, and what Momma liked. Although his Momma would listen to the music, Steve blasted it loudly and aggressively turning the volume to a level that caused the bass to rattle. It also prevented him from hearing the noises. Love-song free, Steve preferred the shrieking, screaming, beating, banging, and pounding songs. Love, he thought, was for those girls on the internet – the ones his Momma might not approve of. *Maybe, this was the evolution that Momma talked about.*

He adjusted the clunky black bubbles onto each ear. Steve was sensitive to some sounds yet felt comfortable with the annoying volume of the tracks that repeated. His musical tastes, perhaps, were his evolution, he thought. His shrug was his way of considering the possibility and agreeing with himself. Another shrug took place because he liked the way it felt. He continued to shrug until he forgot why he was doing it while he finished his work.

Taking a deep breath, Steve decided that his breathing was better. The wheezing was gone and the tightness he'd felt and the irritation was already improving. As far as keeping track of prescriptions went – Steve was misunderstanding what to do. Once the prescriptions ran out, he migrated to the over-the-counter inhalers for relief, opposed to the preventative inhalers. Sometimes when he had too many puffs, his heartbeat in his chest, loudly and fast, sometimes out of control and skipping beats. He was figuring it out as he went, relying on the Pharmacist at the Piggly Wiggly to help him make choices. Momma would have done that for him. Now he relied on others. He spoke to her, "Lookth like you were right again, Momma. Evolution." He paused, placing the backs of his wrists on his hips for a few seconds, "I mith you, Momma." Returning to work, he twisted and re-twisted the remaining wires.

Steve heard a pounding noise, like a steady beat against a metal drum. The volume dial on his earphones wasn't all the way up. His greasy fingers, black oil which was under his nails and surrounding cuticles, reached for the control and cranked the volume louder. Iron Maiden's, *Run To The Hills*, screeched loudly in Steve's bug-looking earphones, drowning out any outside noise. Rocking his head, out of step, with the drumbeats, he finished twisting the wire to secure the camouflage to the container.

In the distance, to the east, nimbostratus clouds were forming and heading in his direction. To Steve they were scary clouds, dark and threatening and could soon be filled with strands of lightning and thunder and unpredictable downpours. Thinking of watching the unpredictable spark of electricity reach across the Floridian sky made him cower. The unsettling shock from an engine's starter which wasn't grounded was frightening enough. He knew the danger, its hazard, and the torment of the jolting tingle from electricity. For that, he was cautious. Momma made Steve wear rubber boots when outside while there was lightning in the sky.

It was time to prepare for it. Gathering his pliers and the remaining spool, he held what he could with his nine fingers. Turning the volume down enough to hear the gravel crunch below his boots, he returned to the encampment where countless projects, work assignments, unfinished business and his exposed tools were. Momma wanted him to clean as he went. But this too, was Steve's evolution. The way things were wasn't the way they needed to be. His evolution of conflict was evolving too.

5

Expectations

Aiden Ashford's struggle and pain was real. Days and months and periods of time were at work on his emotions. Today was an anniversary marking the day they first met. She saw him, he saw her, and everyone else was diminished to background noise. The immediate vivacity between them was giddiness. An effervescence which some might refer to as love at first sight – others might call destiny. Still, others described their meeting as mathematically timely, reciting Falkland's Law – the pragmatic and stress-free assumption that some things merely happen because we did not make an unnecessary decision in a prior instance.

"You're not doing enough." It had become his battle cry. He said this to his handsome reflection in the mirror. The same mirror by the front door of their condo which Ashley used to look into on her way out the door. The thought of her glancing into it made him feel that her presence was not lost.

It had been three years. Ashford's faith was that he'd hear keys jingle, the handle to the front door wiggle and she'd burst in, running for his arms. He fantasized that there would be frantic and relentless knocking – shouting his name for him to open the door and scoop her up. His daydreams of her were delusions. Things which might never happen – but could. The hope kept her here with him. The expectations of her sudden presence had given way to a false sense of hope, and that too had migrated to a 'someday' appearance. Ashford didn't want it to evolve into a 'never going to happen' thought. That would be too much to handle.

Three years since they last made love. A morning of sunlight flittering through the blinds, waking them for an intimacy only two could share. She straddled him. He felt her softness and desire simultaneously. Her fingertips stroked his chest while his hands held on to her hips. Long hair, golden and chestnut, swayed in the air as she rocked upon him.

As if to cry, Ashford held his fists over his eyes, grinding the knuckles into the tear ducts. One bead of salty sadness drizzled down his cheek for his chest. He sniffed away the sorrow and wiped his eyes from a buildup of emotion.

Focus. He needed to focus on the baiting. He logged back on to the dark web portal. His years as a software engineer were paying off. Meandering around the civility and proprieties of a normal browser user, he had stumbled across a backdoor in security. This led him to a glitch in communications. It was a conversation. He was not supposed to see the dispatch, but he did. Once inside, with access to the exchanges, he was able to isolate partitions of access to the messaging.

He had become someone he wasn't.

How did a Monday afternoon in a Tampa schoolyard come to this? Ashford played it in his head, just as he had done thousands of times before...

"Hey baby, let's get gelato when you pick me up today. I want the pistachio again. So, call me to confirm when you get this. Okay? Okay...bye. Love you..." the voice message was her last. He shared it with the police, and the Marshall's office, and the first investigator he hired, and the second, and the third. He listened to it until he fell asleep at night. The sound of her voice – before their situation had changed.

Following Ashley's last call to him, Ashford hung up from the programmers call he was on to call her back and say that he was running a little late but would be there in time for the parent pickups. He pulled the Ford Explorer into the parking lot where the teachers parked. From this spot, Ashford could glimpse her occasionally, between the bushes, as Ashley walked the small children out to their parents from the exterior classroom door. Since he rolled into the lot as she was chauffeuring the kids to their mothers and fathers and family members from their day at school, he didn't know how many there were left. The hallway door to where her students gathered while waiting wasn't visible from the position he was in. Gelato could wait. He scrolled through his phone, reading the meeting notes from a conference call earlier that day. That's when he heard the shouting. He didn't know what she was saying, but it was highly unlike her. Another teacher came to her aid.

Ashford climbed from the car to see what this disturbance was all about. A minivan was poised at the curb. A woman and a man were outside the entrance shouting at Ashley. "But we are family!" was yelled at as the other teacher huddled two remaining children in the hallway, away from the scene. The small girl behind Ashley watched the couple approaching Ashley. Out of surprise, Ashley said something, and they struck at her. It looked like an open fist. The other teacher reported to the detectives that it was a gun. Ashley's last known words, as reported by the other teacher were, "Over my dead body." That's when the child ran, and they abducted Ashley. She kicked her legs as they carried her quickly to the van, its door ready to capture her. They jumped in behind her as they threw her petite frame inside. The tires screeched and Ashford jumped in front of the grey vehicle. Tires screeching and swerving onto the curb, the only piece of the van he could grab was the driver's side mirror. It accelerated too quickly for him to grip, and he ran after it. After a block, the van turned right, into a neighborhood. It was out of sight. Ashley had been taken.

His expectations were that ransom would be requested. He was wrong. His expectations were that she would find a way to flee, returning to him. He was wrong. His expectations were that her captors would tire of her – unknowing what torment or hell she was enduring, so much was only so much, and they'd release her. He was wrong. His expectations were that somehow, someway, someday – they would find their way back to each other. To date, he was still wrong, but hope consumed him.

Then the darkness of thought crept in. He pictured far worse things than an imagination should have to take on. From her fears to her tears, to her struggle, to dire and darksome things which her captors might do to her – he struggled to conceal the nightmares and vile distortions.

Ashford channeled the thoughts of her Ashley's pain and suffering into vindication. Retribution for her desperation would be his focus. Revenge would be painful. Her sorrow would become their new normal. Her grief, their misery. Her hurt, theirs multiplied.

He checked again for a clue, a message, something, anything. There was nothing. It would require him acting scrupulously. With rigid and strict caution as not to spook them. He had learned about chasing away leads with an eagerness that was cause for pause. Acting to swiftly to jump in was a fool's method of infiltrating this cesspool of miscreants. The monsters. They had a network. He would be required to act as one of them to receive any intel from the rogues. This wasn't a bad boys club. It was a criminal syndicate, enlisting modern slavery. Human trafficking. Painfully, he had to act with diligence, which required patience. It was hard playing a game of cat and mouse with the wretches.

*****

The next morning was clear. A lapis blue sky with small cotton ball clouds dotted the Manhattan sky evenly.

"You're a little bit...well a lot of bit...sometimes, not always...impatient," Maggie said tenderly to Allegra.

"I'm intense!" Allegra shot back, pounding her knuckles on the shiny surface of her desk. The office had clean lines featuring whites, grey-tones, and black accessories. A few books were on a small bookshelf opposing the desk situated in the middle of the office facing the door. A matching white credenza sat behind Allegra with a water pitcher and crystal glasses – which secretly on occasion not only held water.

Silence consumed the space between them, there in her office. She looked out the floor to ceiling glass at the cloudy city outside. Low, foggy pewter colored clouds were off in the distance. "Sorry Mag – I just...I don't know...thought it would be somewhat different than it was. I said 'yes', but there's a cause for pause." She bit her lip, still staring out the window into the deepening hues of grey. The plum tab front business dress she was wearing made her golden locks extra bright and shiny against the dark purple color of the knit. She added, "I said 'yes'. It will lock me in for three years. I didn't sign the offer letter, but I said 'yes'."

"So, you said 'yes'," Maggie repeated. "Sounds like there's something else."

"Maybe, maybe not." Allegra was thinking about her *just drinks* agreement with Vendemer, yellow teeth and all.

"Restless spirit. That's what my mom calls it, what you are. A restless spirit."

"Is that a bad thing?" Allegra finally turned to see her friend and co-worker which was her Admin-to-save. She looked at the woman in front of her, coaching her to leap and reach for the promotion, not knowing that her own neck was on the chopping block. Maggie's hair was pulled back into a ponytail. The navy Miller Jacket which she wore had big bold gold buttons. It was versatile, but Allegra didn't tell her that she thought she wore it a little too often.

"It means you have a good thing in front of you, an incredible offer from a company that has legs in the channel, and the biggest thing of all is that you've carved out a cult following on social. You're an AI god for so many other women in our industry."

"That's going to change quickly over the next several years...couple years...hell, several quarters."

"Yeah, and you'll lead the charge like you always do."

"I don't know, Mag..."

"You got what you want, and now it's on to something else. Go figure out that 'else' thing and I'll hitch this caboose onto your train. That is if you'll have me?"

"Of course," Allegra lied. "We're a team." She thought about Vendemer's request to build a business case for saving Maggie.

"Your schedule is blocked from eleven to one today..."

"I just need to shake off this funk." Allegra flung her fingers back and forth in the air several times.

"Yeah, that'll do it. Find your inner Taylor Swift and shake it off."

"Hmm, we need a drinks night soon. What's this weekend look like for you?" She continued to shake, but not as spastically as she didn't really care for Maggie's over-bearing obsession with the most prominent celebrity songwriter of the 21st century. *No disrespect intended, Taylor Alison Swift,* she thought.

There wasn't a time where Maggie said no to Allegra. Then came the new boyfriend. "I'll have to check."

It stopped Allegra from the exercise as she looked at Maggie and smiled.

"There it is. There's the eternal spark. That hot blazing smile that everyone wants to see."

"A pilot light, maybe," Allegra added as the smile became a frown for what followed, "Eleven to one, I'm meeting up with a mentor."

"Since when do you cancel one-on-ones with your staff for a lunch date?" It was intended to be a tease but was met with a quick correction.

"Not – a lunch date. An older gentleman. And as of yesterday. When Vendemer told me to meet him. A money man from Wall Street a couple years ago that fell from good graces. I don't really know why, but I'm open to finding out. He is..." She held back from saying more.

"He is?" Maggie was taking a note on an Apple tablet she always had with her, looking up from the shiny device for words from her boss to fill the void as if the words were floating in the air somewhere.

Allegra hesitated in saying that he was attractive in his headshots and online press and that their brief conversation the following evening left her wanting to meet him. "He is meeting me close by – so I don't know if I'll need the full two-hour block," she added, keeping her meeting with Jacob Paisley to herself.

"How about Saturday afternoon?" Maggie wore the question on her forehead. Allegra thought she was being a diligent Admin, managing to Allegra's schedule – only to realize she had been texting Chris, *Mr. Remarkable,* who beat her to an "I Love You" while they were entwined.

"Multi-tasker." Allegra added, "Fitting me in for an afternoon. I'll take it. But where?"

"Yes, where shall we go, her majesty asks – you of thee luxurious Four Twenty Kent in Williamsburg. One who travels East from the city after work. And then there's me of Jersey City, the one who travels west."

Eagerly, Allegra interrupted, "Hey, at night, we're looking at the same Manhattan skyline."

"A slight exaggeration, as I am also facing west and directly into the next buildings windows peering into mine."

"Jeez, Mag – I know what you get paid, it isn't nearly as bad as when we were starting out ten years ago. You've come a long way."

"God...it's always enlightening thinking of the run. It's been a decade, hasn't it? The days of bagels *without* cream cheese for breakfast, leftovers for lunch, and top ramen for dinner are behind us. We've moved from the bottom shelf wine to the shelf above that for happy hour too." Maggie tossed her tablet PC onto a chair which she usually sat on as they talked shop to tighten her hairband.

"And you met the man of your dreams there."

"Who'd have thunk I'd fall for a Jersey man?"

"Thunk?"

"Thought," Maggie corrected herself.

"Well, he sounds incredible." Allegra nodded to affirm what she meant, and trying to be genuine that her friend was in this good place – wherever that might be, Jersey City and all. "God, if my mom knew I was forking out six thousand a month for rent. Rent!"

"Please. Everything sounds expensive to your mother. She lives in Phoenix."

Allegra thought about the distance between them. "Yeah, still getting her cowgirl on or something."

"Arizona's the one next to California, right? I always get New Mexico and Arizona mixed up."

"Maybe, don't tell anyone else that. Showcases your Ohio education so well..."

"Only you. Geology wasn't my thing."

She paused, turning toward Maggie. Allegra couldn't contain her giggle. "Geography. Girl...you're losing it."

"Okay then. Glad we had this talk. Saturday afternoon in the city somewhere. Let me know how it goes with your lunch date and if there are any deliverables afterward. Unless its geography or geology – then you might be on your own." Maggie spun around on her heels for the door while Allegra was still smirking at her friends' gaffes. There were several of them – always harmless and usually brightening any given moment. She always appreciated the reprieve from the constant grind of productivity.

Allegra checked her watch. The silvery shiny timepiece caused a deep breath and a slow exhalation. It was time for the day to accelerate into action and she had a head full of motion already running. She glanced at the laptop on her glossy white desk and picked up the matte black phone on her desk pushing a couple buttons to summon and then deliver the never-ending deluge for data. Wrapped with purposeful outcomes, the information technology industry as she navigated it didn't exist thirty years ago. Allegra knew that the total addressable market for IT spending exceeded five trillion dollars last year. Next to labor costs and real estate, technology was a necessity. And the necessity was ever-changing, making it evasive to cut. There it was. There was her business case for Maggie's retention. She'd need to carefully craft value statements surrounding the message and sell it. That she could do.

*****

Hawaiian-born Brian Kekahanamanui sat on their couch, stroking his wife's long dark chestnut hair with his fingers. He was listening intently. They were enjoying morning coffee in the quiet of their small home in Oceanside. California mornings in December were cool and sometimes damp. The heat kicked on warming their living room where they were.

Laki continued talking about the fundraiser. "Twenty thousand dollars is what they're trying to raise. It's just going to get her, and the kids stood up for a few months if they're tight like us."

"Like us?"

"You know – they don't blow it on ridiculous things. Food, utilities, the essentials. She's going to have to learn to be average. Probably tough to do when you had money."

"From the sounds of it, they had nothing but debt and other people's money for a long time."

"That's why the SEC took him away in jewelry."

"Handcuffs are for criminals. Jewelry is for..."

She interrupted, "Imagine. Just last year at this time, we were driving to their McMansion in Rancho Sante Fe. And now...there's nothing. No cars, no furniture, no savings, no toys for the kids, no food in the fridge. They took it all."

"It wasn't theirs, and I hear you, but the fake lifestyle was his investor's money – being lavishly spent so that other people would admire his mocked success and want to invest in his phony funds."

She sat up to sip from the still-steaming cup of coffee sitting on an end table offering up plumes of gentle billows into the still morning air. "So, you're telling me…"

"I'm not telling you anything. It was all unreal. It was a counterfeit lifestyle that yes, he hid from her which was wrong – but the investors have their wants and needs too. They're out what they gave him and are protected by regulations. When the SEC comes knocking, you'd better have your story buttoned up for battle, no shams."

Laki rubbed sleep from her eyes and reluctantly replied to her husband, "Yeah…I suppose you're right."

"What?"

"Punk," she gave him a soft slug with her small fist on his broad shoulder next to her. It caused him to dribble coffee from his cup onto the lap of his pajama bottoms.

"Ouch…" He winced slightly.

Knowing the spill of hot coffee found its way to the place no man wanted hot coffee to seep, she giggled. "Oh, I didn't hit you that hard."

"I'm scorched," he teased back, pointing to his groin. "You did that."

"I'll inspect it later – to see if you need nursing."

Over it but raising an eyebrow in her direction. He returned to the go-fund-me event they were to attend to raise money for her friend of a friend, "Do they expect people to show up with hundreds of dollars?"

"No silly, it's a holiday drinking event. They know I married a poor shoe salesman from San Diego. If we give them a hundred bucks, that's too generous. Rich people have rich friends. It just takes one or two of their wealthy friends to front most of what they're trying to stand her up with."

"I gotta' get me one of them…"

"She hasn't been to yoga since the raid, and this will be the first time I've seen her since…"

"Was it the FBI?"

"Pretty sure. Maybe the Marshall too."

"Money laundering, probably."

"Well, there's not going to be any laundering, because they took their washer and dryer too."

"Disputing that stuff, the civil or criminal forfeitures, is going to drag on for a while." Brian took a deeper sip of the hot brew to lower the liquid from the mouth of the mug.

"We've been watching too much Law & Order, haven't we?"

"Let's get back to talking about your yoga moves."

She looked at his longing glance at her. "I'll show you some of my yoga moves…later…tonight maybe."

Brian smiled and changed the subject again. "What would you do with twenty thousand dollars?"

"That's a hell of a bribe for showing you my yoga moves. I'll do that for free."

"No seriously, for the fundraiser. If someone dropped twenty grand in your lap, would you save it, spend it, I don't know…" He shrugged his shoulders.

Laki thought about it for a moment. "Ten thousand per kid – in their college funds."

Brian thought of their two little monsters that would start stirring any moment now. They were growing up so fast. "The two 529's that have a hundred dollars each?"

"Yeah, those college funds."

He stood up revealing that the spill was a little more than a little in his lap.

She stood up too and tip-toed to kiss him good morning again, wrapping her arm around his neck for balance.

"No more coffee for you." She reached down to feel the wet spot.

'I saved the sofa."

"Oh, is that it? Thank you."

"Welcome," she muttered as she groped him again.

"Why's it on a Monday?"

"Holiday break. You know, this thing called Christmas." Laki lowered her voice to a whisper, "Where Santa Claus, God bless him, gives presents to good little boys and girls. But you're bad. You're getting coal in your stocking. Naughty." She smiled broadly.

Brian sat the remainder of the cup down and stretched. "Okay here we go. Happy Aloha Sunday. Time to rise and shine." The battle cry wasn't as effective as he had hoped. They both shuffled toward the kitchen for a bowl of Cheerios in the morning's remaining stillness.

"Who do the Rainbow Warriors play today/"

He paused before answering, "Oh...honey...college football was over several weeks ago. And...and they play on Saturdays usually. Thanks for trying. But you smell good. You're kind of cute too. Make a helluva huli-huli chicken." He gave her a pat on her butt before they meandered to opposing sides of the Santa Cecilia granite island.

"Well, there's that. I make good kids too, right?"

"Those little monsters?" Brian motioned with his thumb. "We'll keep 'em."

"What, you don't want to give them back?" she asked.

Brian shook his head slowly, teasing, "That just sounds like too much work."

Laki came around to his side of the island. "So...you said I smell good?" She blinked her eyes prominently, snuggling up closer to her husband.

Deeply attracted to each other, Brian hunched down next to Laki and whispered, "I'm really surprised."

"Surprised at what?" she asked quietly and seductively.

"That we haven't had like…about…ten more kids," he continued whispering. "Ten more little monsters."

"Then we'd have a dozen demons," she added.

"Twelve terrors," Brian countered as their exchanges continued.

"A bunch of banshees."

"A grip of goblins."

"A slew of specters."

"A dense deal of devils."

Laki looked up and paused. "I got nothing more…" she concluded. Then added, "But I smell good. You said so. It's Flowers. It's what I wear when I want to get frisky with you." She tiptoed, still whispering. "You can kiss me now."

* * * * *

Adele hung up the phone. Her call with Ruby was not as enlightening or exciting as she had hoped. She thought this inclusion was for goodness. That it may be free from illicitness, that only well intended acts of kindness and generosity would take place, and that charitable and philanthropic activities were excluded from the purpose of this Ellipsis organization was the simulation she played in her head. This was not what she thought she would be getting herself into. Not this.

Replaying the call in her head, Ruby had made the arrangements for her to pick up a manila envelope with cash in it after she arrived at San Diego. A locker box at an offsite storage facility would also contain a handgun. He mentioned that she'd likely encounter some shady characters and that the gun was for her protection. "Do you know how to use a gun?" he had asked her.

She did. The only time its trigger was pulled was at the range where her salesperson sold her the small shiny silver piece. She had one. Jacob did too. They were stored in the safe in their apartment, tucked in the back of the locked box hidden in the closet. It wasn't a comfortable call, just as the thought of holding a foreign gun potentially in the direction of someone, reprehensible or not.

Tuesday had become Monday, so there was another white lie to be told. He must have sensed her unease. "You got this," he coaxed. His voice was filled with confidence while hers must have sounded hollow, like it had none.

"Is...?" Adele was fidgeting with a pen in her hand, taking notes as she was accustomed to doing when detail was involved.

"Yes?"

"Is a weapon really required here?"

"You want to live?" Ruby had no hesitation in asking her the pointed survival question. "I don't want to see bad things happen to good people. So, we take precautions to prevent...unfortunate situations from presenting themselves."

Adele's silence and note-taking caused additional gaps in her responsiveness. "And you said there will be two of them. On the side of the road. Off of the Ronald Packard Parkway. Around two o'clock. Keep circling between El Camino Real and College Boulevard until I see them? How is all of this so certain?"

"Adele?"

"Yes?"

"Peace. You're going to need to find that inner peace. Take a deep breath. Make sure you take the safety off of the gun only after you pull over. It will be loaded. You got this."

Slowly, she assured herself that goodness, unknowingly would come from this. Her role as a secret agent in its doing was as foreign as she came to the controlled chaos she ran for Jacob while at PPCM as his executive admin. It found its way to her throat, into her mouth and through her lips, "I got this." As she lifted her chin and stroked her smooth neck all the way down to her chest, she thought of the limited amount of jewelry she wore. Adele was resolute that kismet prevented her from the man of her dreams for the years she was without him. The bling which sometimes followed a relationship was absent from her fingers, neck, and earlobes. '*One less thing*', she allowed herself to assume, not thinking of its missing presence often.

"One more thing," Ruby added. "Commit this to memory. Destroy those notes you've been taking. Jacob cannot know about this mission you're on."

She looked around behind her, and within the apartment for a camera blinking somewhere. This new environment seemed to be invasive to her privacy, but she was still willing to team together with Jacob and Ruby on the good intentions of the Ellipsis endeavor. "And what about the trip to Honolulu?"

"It's off. Sorry, I forgot to mention. When he returns from Seattle, you two will have a little something else to attend to. And he's helping me with an assessment right now."

"Yes, the lunch meeting." She was faking it – as if she were in the know.

"Something...like that," Ruby.

"Must admit, a little disappointed about *not* seeing the little one on Oahu."

"There will be another time for that. Trust me. You know which number to call if you have questions or run into...something, right?"

"Correct. I do, I do have this." she assured him, finding assurance in the sound of her voice. Assurance was a cousin to conviction. There it was: convictions. Hers were, at this time, borrowed – relenting to the Ellipsis to call the shots.

"Remember Adele, we hold accountability when it cannot be held. We put the bad guys away. And not in a Dexter way. Although I like his rationale. We lift the downtrodden up to higher ground providing hope where there is none. Ellipsis has reconnected families, solved mysteries, unraveled the most knotted situations, and delivered a difference where one was needed. We are the middlemen or middle women, the game changers, the advocates of pushing things along when the administrations we have created cannot solve our problems. We put the score on the scoreboard when a zero was showing."

It was the affirmation she needed to hear.

As Adele listened to the silence on the other end of the call for several seconds after Ruby hung up, she looked at her notes again. She would spend several minutes memorizing the location, and destroy the notes – safeguarding Jacob from having awareness of the potential danger which she was placing herself in.

Placing the cell phone on the counter-top in the kitchen, she reached for the stainless and fingerprint free door of the refrigerator to plan dinner. For a brief period, maybe it was a two-day thing, Adele pictured them raising the child from the Pacific together in their condo in Kapolei. Her knack for finding the goodness, or for trying to, in almost everyone she met was in no short supply. She had been with this man for more than a decade. Seeing him at his mischievous worst and at his generous best - putting her son through college and funding a 'girlfriend experience' on his company's balance sheet – she stuck with him. Her thoughts dashed to Victoria. Beautiful, irresistible, sinful, elusive, mysterious, and distrusting Victoria. *What did Jacob see in her? Everything he shouldn't have.* A frown found its way to Adele's face.

She looked toward the bedroom where the two of them slept together now. The past decade taught her, if anything, that there was a deep-rooted goodness within each of us. It sometimes needed nurtured, and unearthed, and chiseled like any masterpiece. Jacob had it in him and she saw it – when and where others might not. He was a standout. A real human potential example. And now they were together. A smile erased the frown as she thought of him holding her in their bed at night.

God, what is it about him? she thought the familiar thought. Warmth found its way to her heart.

She didn't know what Jacob might have at his lunch meeting, but chicken breasts were thawing. Heart-healthy something was in order. "Woman, what have you gotten yourself into?" It was said aloud. Pausing as she said it, because she didn't know who was listening –

probably not, but maybe so – Adele wondered if this was the way it would always be as she selflessly served the unknowing recipients of their sacrifices. Would her privacy always be compromised? "Lemons," she added quickly while stooping over peering into the appliance. "You've got yourself into heart-healthy chicken and lemon something...of course."

Adele looked toward the bedroom again. Perhaps tonight would need to be something somewhat special. She didn't know what tomorrow held. A flight to San Diego, *not San Francisco*, a locker box trip, pick up an envelope and the weapon, get the car, drive east toward Vista, do the drop with the gun in tow and just in case, you know, for reassurances... Who knew how the 'job' would go? She knew she was more risk adverse than others, exercising her sensibility. *Would this be their last night together?* She put the thought on hold as Jacob's ring came through her phone.

"Hey."

"Hi. I was just going to call you, how coincidental."

"My Tuesday trip morphed to Monday. I just got off the phone with the lawyers and I'll need to..."

"No problem. I'll see if I can fly out too. For San Francisco." She felt she was overselling it.

He paid no attention to her little while lie as he was occupied with telling one himself. "Great he added. On the way to meet up with an Allegra Sinclair. See you after lunch."

"Have a nice lunch. Chicken-something for dinner. Just so you know."

"Salmon-something or salad-something it is. Thanks for the heads up. Jumping in a cab now. See you soon."

"See you soon," she echoed before the call ended.

Long gone were the days of calling a car for the CEO and co-founder of PPCM. Gone were the first class and business class flights to anywhere in the world, an opportunity took Jacob Paisley. Gone were the not-so-secret weekends he travelled with Victoria on his arm.

The gorgeous ghost was gone. The stunning seductress was no longer in his orbit.

Tonight, might need some magic, Adele thought. She reached for the candlesticks above the microwave and retrieved a bottle of red, the Lafite Rothschild, from the cradle holding other varietal thrills from around the world. The bucket list vintage just might set a tone.

*****

Allegra was laughing. She didn't think this would be a laughing lunch. It would be an obliging, stoic, align with yesteryear's leader, do as Vendemer requests, lunch meeting. It was much different than when she played it in her head.

'Only in high finance, she chimed in. We could never get away with something like that in tech."

"But why not?" Jacob challenged.

"You Yahoos have gross margins at what thirty, forty percent?"

"Something like that," Jacob nodded his head while smiling, and knowing that it depended upon the service classification.

"See, that's what I'm saying. The OEMs have something like that, but it's netted out with their investments in the partner community. The value-added resellers are left with five percent, if we're lucky and wrapping everything with a cosmetic."

"I don't really understand everything you just said there, but I believe you."

"AI, artificial intelligence...to answer your earlier question...that's my superpower at the moment. It was security, then it was cloud, then it was edge, then it was augmented reality and digital twins. It's always tomorrow's hype. But AI – it's the real deal, like what the internet was to 1995."

Jacob looked off into the distance for a moment and excused himself, "Pardon me, Allegra." He waved in the direction of the receptionist waiting area, "Charlie?"

The young black man resembling Ruby reluctantly walked to their table, "Mr. Paisley?"

"Hello. What are you..." Jacob stopped himself, knowing that the unknown was revealing itself slowly in this new juncture. "It's good to see you again."

"Oh, hey, yeah. Running some errands for my dad. It's good seeing you again Mr. Paisley." He looked at Jacob's lunch date.

"This is Allegra. Allegra Sinclair, meet Charlie." She extended her hand grabbing his as it made its way toward her.

"Pleasure to meet you, Charlie."

He smiled slightly. Looking at Jacob, he was hesitant to say more. Then after a slight pause did so, "Pleased to meet you."

Allegra tilted her head. They had previously met. She was attempting to place the whereabouts of their encounter, and even though it was just two days ago – and he handed her a shoe left behind – she sought the assurance that this was him. Saying nothing she continued to smile at him, wondering if he would mention anything.

"What brings you to this area of the city, Charlie?" Jacob asked while sorting through his salad with a fork.

"Yes sir...Columbia. I have a good friend attending. I was up here visiting with him this morning." The young man shook his head slightly while he talked.

She threw it out there. "I like your shoes." He was wearing a pair of retro Air Jordan's. The white and red sneakers appeared new as everyone looked at Charlie's feet. "You have both of them."

Jacob looked up to his lunch date, seeking more from her probe. She looked at Jacob warmly and then at Charlie wryly.

Charlie smiled and said briefly, "Yes ma'am, always better with both." Her baited comment caught nothing.

"Well Charlie, I'm sure we'll be seeing each other again. By the way – friends at Columbia are a good thing. Most of them, anyway. Maybe there are a few bad apples." Jacob didn't understand the connection between the two, if there was one, but didn't want to share too much information with Allegra. Just yet anyway. As things had a way of turning out with Ruby – perhaps something was in play already.

"Yes sir. Good to see you again Mr. Paisley. See you soon." He waved to her nervously and quickly indicating his departure. In a quick and nervous turn, he abruptly left their table, heading for the exit.

They both watched Charlie depart through the lunchtime crowd within the restaurant.

"Do you know anyone who went to Colum...?"

Before he could finish, Allegra interrupted the diversion question. "Two questions for you. Who is the stalker? And what is it with you? That's the third person that you noticed, or they've recognized you - all in the past ninety minutes."

Jacob needed to share a little detail to prevent a prickled response. "Like I may have mentioned, the son of a fairly new business acquaintance. I met him a couple days ago. And I was going to ask you the same question about the kid. How did you two know each other – if you did. Most people wear two shoes."

"You caught that, did you?" She looked off into the clattering silverware noise of the plates and dishes being cleared from the oak tables throughout the restaurant. "Maybe, Jacob Paisley, he's a stalker...I don't know." She was playful and didn't really mean what she said. A small wrinkle landed between her eyebrows, "I think I met him two days ago as well." She looked back at Jacob's face filled with curiosity as well. "Let's stitch some things together here. How exactly do you know Vendemer?"

"Who?" Jacob asked blankly.

Allegra smirked, shaking her head. Looking up at Jacob, she said, "Kind of interesting, isn't it? A mentoring conversation and you don't know my source – and I don't know yours."

It was then that they both realized that they were there, to meet – and it was under false pretenses. A minute of silence stood still between them as they tried to piece together the randomness or the ulterior motive behind their connection.

It was Jacob breaking the silence, "Trust me. I've had some crazy situations thrown at me in the past couple years. This doesn't make the cut in terms of the bizarre or some whacked out coincidental happenstance. I'm in a mentoring and sponsor network for women. I'm an ally – what can I say?"

"Okay – I guess. Makes sense, somehow..." She believed him. He wasn't selling. He was concealing. He wasn't hiding an agenda. He was as interested in 'why' as she was. Her watch showed her that two hours had slipped away. "I didn't think I'd be here long. Then you sat down, and we hit it off. Your charming stories and worldly wisdom about business and finance and leadership and all. I've enjoyed meeting you, Jacob. Thanks for your time and interest in helping me. I really look forward to our next conversation or seeing where this goes. As surreal as it's been so far, I may be in for an interesting ride, right?"

Jacob looked into her eyes. He saw Victoria looking back at him and wondered if when she kissed, electricity was generated from her lips too. He looked away – toward the kitchen to answer her, "Some people believe that there's a master plan for everything. Others believe that it's cold hard math. Things happen because of things happening. Data..."

"That's what I believe in. Facts. What got you here, won't get you there because there's no road map."

"Yeah – that's what I bought into long ago too. But then there's the combo. That our lives are ruled by randomness. And..." He paused, looking into the eyes that were no longer those of Victoria. It was Allegra, he assured himself.

"And?"

"And with randomness comes an odd combination of intention and chance and suggestion and a host of other things which deliver," he paused, "different outcomes."

Her eyes squinted and she stared at him. "You have some secrets."

"We all do," he jumped in right away. "You do too."

She considered the few secrets she held, the ones she didn't want anyone to know really. Then she answered, "I'll bet you have better secrets than I do."

He smiled at the challenge, replying, "We'll see. Maybe the next time we meet and each time after that, we can share a secret or two along the way."

"Is it a secret, or a lie?"

"What's that?" he inquired.

Allegra twirled her hair, contemplating one of her secrets. "College game – drinking game - tell a secret or a lie and your friends have to guess. Guess wrong, you're doin' a shot."

Jacob said nothing, curling up one side of his mouth. She had no idea how hard the traders at PPCM partied. The strip clubs. That one strip club where he met her. *Sowing The Seeds of Love*, playing loudly – so very loudly that one could feel the ground shake. The stage dance featured Rorschach wearing his necktie as a headband. He pictured her as he first saw her, Victoria. He felt himself drifting off in thought. The present was here, now...sitting across the table from him. Now.

Allegra - she didn't need to know about the solicitousness which dictated his demise. Then again, perhaps she already did. More than a pretty face, Allegra could read a situation.

"Wasted. So drunk." Allegra subtly chuckled.

"How about no drinks...?"

"Well...not as fun, but okay." She stopped twirling her hair, realizing that she, intentionally or not, was flirting with him. "In the spirit of mentoring, because you're experienced in business, I'd really like to know what regrets or unfinished business you have." She expected more of a response than she received.

He was stuck on the word, regrets. Shifting from a reply to misdirection, he said, "Listen, I have a little project. Will take a couple days. Early freaking flight tomorrow for Seattle" his eyes widened when he thought of 4:30am at JFK. "We will connect when I return, alright?"

"Alright. Alright, Jacob Paisley." She reached out to shake his hand confirming the deal. As their hands clasped, they were mutually warm to the touch. "Looking forward to learning from you. Look forward to hearing what you might have to say, listening to some more of your stories, and..." She looked for the words to say on the ceiling but found none. Finally letting go of his hand and stumbling for what to convey, which was unusual for her, she finally added, "and...unraveling why we're even here. I must go. Don't really want to but must."

He nodded his head slowly and slightly as she stood to depart their small table. He began to stand too.

"Don't get up," she added.

Jacob did anyway.

She looked at him and smiled, rolling her eyes, "I'm off."

Jacob sat back down at their table. Her business overcoat swaddled her as she bundled up for the departure into December's brisk breeze outside.

She said her piece but placed her hand on his shoulder as she left. For the second time within a week, she thought to herself, *something had just happened there.* As Allegra walked a block away from the restaurant to hail a cab she stood there with two fingers in the air. A cab driving the other direction honked it horn to attract her attention. Another yellow and black car parallel parked, facing her, darted out to meet her request. The two cabbies exchanged words that we undetectable and aggressive. Allegra paid no attention to the heated exchange. She was calming the heat in her chest. Ever so quietly to herself, to hear it spill through her lips, she said it: *'Girl, you gotta' get a grip on your daddy issues.'* The tires screeched to a stop, and she hopped in.

Jacob was now sitting alone at their table and said softly to himself, "Regrets?" He sat idle, no one to hear the evaluation playing in his head. "Regrets. No more Victoria's."

*****

It was later the same day. Kolohe was tugging on the leash. Too many new smells. There was the stink of the taxi exhaust, overcooked and stale hot dogs warming on vendor carts, wafts from the sewers through sidewalk grids and steel manhole covers, and New York's signature scent: garbage. Garbage from the alleys, trash cans lined up outside of delis, and nearly every street corner.

To Kolohe, there was street meat, pee from a friend, a potential snack, and the smell of success. Dogs smelled it. People could only occasionally picture it. But to a dog, each day was one more than they expected the day before. Each day was one of success. The moments were more filled with 'What's Next?' than the "Been There, Done That's'. He tugged, causing a grunt from Jacob once in a while.

"Easy, boy. Lots of city left." Jacob's phone rang and he noticed the Hawaiian number from Tamsen again. He needed to list it in his contacts.

"Tamsen?"

"Hi, hope you don't see this as too soon," she had a concern he thought as he heard her.

"Not at all," Jacob tugged at Kolohe's leash as a piece of pizza crust or bagel just out of reach presented a nice treat before dinner.

"What are you doing? Are you working out?"

"Uh…just a minute…down, sit, no." Kolohe restrained and did as he was told now that the carbs were out of reach and off the table. Jacob rewarded him with a healthy treat from his coat pocket. "Walking the dog."

"What's his name and what kind of dog?"

Jacob was certain that this wasn't why she called and made it short. He needed to walk Kolohe, eat dinner with Adele, make the fib about Seattle more convincing, finish packing and find the sheets for an early departure to the west coast. "Kolohe, a yellow lab, 'a good boy'" he said speaking to the dog and answering Tamsen's question.

"I had you as a dog guy before we spoke. Not why I'm calling..." she hesitated, then finished, "I'll make this quick. You said you thought that Ruby had ulterior motives. And I just wanted to weigh in on..."

Jacob interrupted, "I said that he had his ways and means of doing things. I respect it. It's his process.," He tried to clarify, "If I did misspeak, it wasn't intended that way. I believe that there's a sophisticated velocity of idealization in what we're doing. Not understanding the evolution of Ellipsis, I lack..." Jacob listened to himself talking. A memory of running PPCM jostled. He remembered ridiculing a trader on the street corner adjacent to the one he was now standing on. The world he left behind was present and past at the same time. What had changed was himself. Jacob Paisley the Wall Street titan of finance was talking with a woman six times zones away about doing good in the world. There was nothing to do with stock trades, options, or triple witching Fridays at the calendar quarter's end. No longer were the Dow, Nasdaq, S&P 500, the foreign exchanges, nor the cryptocurrency markets topics to torture his poor-performing traders with. They were now instruments he leveraged to make trades for Ellipsis himself – responsible for his own success, not that of hundreds of others.

"Are you still there? Hello."

Jacob was distracted, and pretended that it was the reception, "Tamsen, can you hear me now?"

"Yeah, you drifted off." She had him on the speakerphone while she finished drying dishes in her kitchen. "Maybe it's my device. I just switched to Verizon. Thought it was better..."

"Sorry, standing next to The Plaza at Central Park." That part was true. Jacob looked at Kolohe, wagging his tail, watching children playing soccer on a cold grassy lawn, absorbing the last light of day.

"Nice. About Ruby, you were saying?"

"I dismissed the thought leadership required to recruit, assemble, and lead a diverse team of secret keepers. Collectively, competencies including vision, strategizing, communication, and delegation – they make up the building of a well-functioning team. It's not for the meek.

The results of the right people in the right roles at the right time – they need to be free of dysfunction. Ruby's a master at building a crew. I need to observe and support where I can, boldly supporting him and forging forward in trust."

"Poetry," she said.

"What's that you say?"

"I just heard angels sing. You said it the way it needed to be said. There was a small concern after we spoke which spooked me, but you just killed it. I see why you were a successful CEO when you..."

"Those days are behind me, behind all of us. We've all been through things that other people can't understand. Sometimes...the more we talk about them, the less we smile."

"Hmm...I never thought of it like that. Our baggage does tend to get in the way of what we leap and reach for, doesn't it? Weighs us down..."

"Something like that. Are you sitting on the beach kicking sand off your toes again?" Jacob pictured the North Shore. A long stretch of a sandy beach engulfed by a blue sky peppered with white puffy clouds and met with a deep blue sea. The lush greenery of the rising Ko'olau mountain range was in the distance.

She ended his illusion of Oahu, "Naw – it's raining here today. Flooding actually. The river's making Waimea Bay's sparkly blue water brown. A good day for Netflix or drinking a Longboard on the patio with a good book and my dog. Tamsen looked around for him. He was sleeping on the sofa, like usual.

"Well Friday's coming." Jacob was a listener.

"Friday? What's happening this Friday?" Tamsen tossed the towel from dishes on the granite counter.

"Poke. Foodland. Traditional Hawaiian.

"Ahh, yes. Happy Aloha Friday. You were listening.

"Ever been to New York? Manhattan?" Jacob watched the city begin to light up. Tower after tower, more twinkling lights illuminated the dusk.

"Many times. We did a Bravado photo shoot there a couple months ago. Next time I'll give you a heads up and we'll all get together. But something tells me you'll be back in Hawaii before I make it to the city." Tamsen didn't know anything but teased that she did.

"What do you know that I don't...?"

"Nothing, gotta go Jacob Paisley. Thanks for saying what you said and how you said it. It was eloquent."

"Wait! What...?" Jacob heard nothing as the call ended. "She doesn't know anything..." he said out loud and to himself. *Or does she,* he thought.

6

SAN

He was looking at a text message on the screen of his shiny phone, "You have got to be - fucking - kidding - me!?" Jacob said it out loud. A young man wearing a Seahawks sweatshirt and jeans walking alongside him heard the comment and tried to look away while giving Jacob a side-eye.

Jacob lowered the device to his side and looked up at the screens offering the departure and arrival information in the terminal's corridor. He'd just arrived at SeaTac and was being summoned to grab a flight that left in 23 minutes to SanDiego. The salty words for Ruby were marinading in his mouth. He was standing at gate 3, needing to get to gate 27 – pronto. Boarding had begun. *What's this shit?* Jacob asked himself: *seat 33B, a middle seat?* Perhaps he would need to remind Ruby who was financing Ellipsis now. Much of it, anyway. Okay – some of it.

Don't we have people in SanDiego? He considered. Ruby makes Ellipsis out to be a vast network of do-gooders with extensive reach and capabilities beyond the well-groomed, experienced, hierarchical organizations of governments and social structures of the current day. *Don't our Philanthropists know I got my ass out of bed at 2:30 to catch a 4:30am east coast time zone flight?*

His phone spoke in a gentle woman's voice: "Flight departing soon. Make your way to the gate.?"

"Fuck you," he muttered under his breath. "Don't tell me what to do. I need a fucking cup of coffee. Just Joe." He wasn't going to get it, knowing there was a purpose, a call, which needed answering. He would have to set aside his need for the moment to appease the need for him to rally around catching the next flight. He could get a cup on coffee or two on his way to San Diego. *Worst damn coffee ever, airplane coffee, yuck,* he thought. It was a necessity.

When they had a conversation a few months back, Ruby asked Jacob, "What's off the table? What aren't you willing to sacrifice?"

Jacob thought about it for a few minutes and came up with a short list. "Red wine. Good for the heart – or so some articles on the internet state." He paused. "Coffee – give me coffee in the morning, no one gets hurt." He paused. "Adele. I don't want anything harmful to happen to her because of my sacrifice."

"She's along for the ride, though," Ruby added.

"Yes, but... No harm. She's had my back. She's, my partner. No detrimental inferences or situations which cause her distress."

"I...we...will do our best." Ruby shrugged his shoulders.

He played the conversation in his head – thinking of coffee as he walked past a small Starbucks with a line of customers nearly two dozen long. The ticker for the company, SBUX, danced in his thoughts. Some habits are hard to break, the former trader himself thought. With a strong debt to equity ratio, earnings per share encroaching $4, and a lift in the dividend he simply thought, '*What's not to like?*'

Jacob made his way to the queue for the flight to San Diego, uncaffeinated and not a contributor, this morning anyway, to Starbucks profitability.

*****

Adele's early morning had a copious amount of activity. She dropped Jacob off at JFK, made her own way down to LaGuardia – which was on the other side of Long Island – parked their shiny black X5 at an offsite facility, then she shuttled, flew, light-rail trained it, and bussed her way to the locker. Her she was, punching in a code to gather the materials Ruby instructed her to pick up at the offsite storage facility. The private room was hers. She entered the numbers, realizing just then that it was Jacob's birthday: 0629. June twenty-ninth. Click. The tumblers were electric. A door gently opened revealing two manila envelopes. Surprisingly, they were about the same weight. One containing money, the other containing a handgun. Immediately upon touching them, she knew which was which.

Then, she noticed a third envelope. Lying flat on the bottom of the locker with red lettering reading: DO NOT OPEN. She tucked it into an inside pocket of her gray light jacket. "Probably not a Christmas card from Ruby", Adele muttered.

She checked the rental confirmation. It read pickup time for another hour away. She had some time to catch a cup of coffee and think about the action plan which Ruby had laid out for her.

But her thoughts were compromised. It was her evening with Jacob that she kept returning to. Their lovemaking was what she had hoped for, what she dreamed of, and was quite exceptional. It couldn't be his experience with other women, namely Victoria. It could not be the various known and unknown lovers and acquaintances she was aware of, and he was not aware that she knew of. And it could not be what she did not know about him that managed the memorable evening which they had just shared. It would need to be an appreciation, a mutual appreciation, for each other that she cherished. She did. He was not only the most important person to her. She felt as if she were becoming the most important person to him.

A protein bar with her third cup of coffee, an Uber back to the rental facility, a trip to the ladies' room, an escalator to the second level, a text message to her son, and a deep breath – she wondered what people found so alluring in business travel. She was missing the meaningful connection, the pain of presentations, the positive conflict, productive debates, and say/do ratio of getting the job done. She was also missing out on the fine dining, booze, unforgettable moments that cemented business and nurtured lifelong relationships.

National. The rental car company which allowed you, depending upon your status, to choose the car of your choice. It was simple, she found an X5 in the Executive Isle. It was even black, just like back at home in New York.

Adele tossed her small carry on in the back seat. It slid across the black leather to the passenger's side. She climbed in, behind the wheel, and took a deep breath. "'Woman, you can quit if you want to." Then she thought of the purpose, or the challenge, or the opportunity that Ruby had described to her: *Helping toward a greater cause than your very own awareness could comprehend.*

Perhaps, she thought. Calibrating differently, she asked herself, sitting there behind the black leather steering wheel, 'What if it's all just bullshit?" Adele smiled, "Well don't you sound a little bit like Jacob Paisley now?" Her thoughts ventured back to the Turkish sheets they laid together in the night before. *Would she even be doing any of this without him? Probably not.* "And here we are, the throes of the moment," she added, tapping the brake and striking the push-button key to fire up the engine. Slipping the gear from park to drive, she nudged forward toward the task.

She glanced at the rental agreement that was emailed to her on her phone and slid the RA into a folder: TRAVEL. The push button starter fired up the engine of a familiar sound.

*****

It had been a minute - since he had felt perspiration in an airport. Flight to flight, rental car shuttle, a barrage of text messaging from Ruby with a specific time: "Don't be late", and a precision of coordination as if he were being watched, tracked, monitored, controlled. But here he was – as instructed at the National Rental Counter for the Executive Isle. He looked over at the Premier VIP Isle which he normally would have chosen as the CEO of PPCM. *Better*, he thought to himself.

Jacob slipped the phone to the booth attendant assigning cars. She punched a few buttons on the screen, several more, then several more.

"Did your wife already pick up your car?"

"What?" It was what one would normally say when in shock, or to process information, or to genuinely ask someone to repeat themselves.

"Says here that your car was picked up two minutes ago, by Adele Paisley."

Adele noticed him ten seconds before he noticed her. She pulled up to the booth next to the check-out gate and rolled down the window facing Jacob. He looked befuddled as she slowed the roll and approached him in the X5.

"Hi honey!" She tilted her head in his direction while raising her eyebrows, which was their longstanding soft code for "what the hell just happened here?"

"Hello darling!" he chimed back artificially, reaching for the passenger door handle. "Shot gun!" he declared as he fell into the seat without a seat-belt on. Recognizing the familiarity immediately, he added teasingly, "What the...did you drive here?" Adele tipped her head toward him. Her brunette hair tossed slightly his way, and she rolled away toward the exit of the rental car facility. The BMW still had a new car smell, just like at home in New York.

Within minutes they were on an on-ramp onto the Golden State Freeway, heading north. The questions were plentiful: How was Seattle? How was San Francisco? Where did you really fly out of? What time did you land in San Diego? How often have you heard from Ruby today? How much time was there between flights while connecting at

SeaTac? Do you think there's an agenda we're not aware of? Are you hungry too? Why are we fucking doing this?

The answers to all the questions were either trite, thoughtful, or hypothetical in their nature, or added some degree of comic relief to the moment of 'the test'.

The eventual question that was asked last was the question that changed the moment. Jacob asked it at the end of the barrage of the logistics questions: "Wasn't last night incredible?"

"I love you." She said it first. The X5 shifted lanes slightly as she looked across the console at him.

"I love you too, Adele. I really do." He quickly followed. Looking over at Adele behind the wheel, gripping it firmly, he saw her eyes well up with tears. Her chin moved up and down, toward and away from her chest as she took a deep breath. The affirmation was not new. He had lived within and shared her radiance for years. "I really do," he added as the first stream of tears fell down her cheek facing him. She looked at him, nodding. The alarm beeped, indicative of an unauthorized lane change. Jacob smiled at the beauty of the moment and chimed in, "Don't kill us."

She tipped her head toward him, acknowledging, "I do have a gun in the back seat."

Jacob looked forward to the cement, the guardrails, listening to the click-click, click-click, click-click, click-click sounds of the wheels meeting the highway…wondering what she was talking about.

"For what?!" he finally blurted out.

"Ten grand, a handgun for protection against the nefarious characters, and an envelope that says DO NOT OPEN."

"Well, that's what we're opening first. Where is it?"

"In my bag, back seat. Be careful, I didn't even check. I assumed the safety is on."

Jacob wrestled her bag from the back seat retrieving the contents from her carry-on. The manila envelope was flimsy, containing a single piece of paper or two. He ripped the sealed package and pried the letter from within. He read it to her aloud so that they were understanding and comprehending it together:

'Hello Jacob!' it read, 'Just knew it'd be you, 'Good news – bad news...knowing you, you'll want the bad news first.'

"That's so...so Ruby," he added, not referring to the letter he was reading to Adele. He looked at her, blotting the remaining wetness from her cheeks. He reached for her forearm now resting on the console. Holding onto her he continued reading.

'Bad news – after this, there's a little something else. Good news – here are your first-class tickets back to New York. Safe travels.'

"What a huckleberry."

Adele was doing all that she could to keep the vehicle between the dashed white lines, continuing to think about the, 'I really do', he had said moments ago. The click-click, click-click, click-click, click-click of the tires eased as the cement gave way to quieter pavement. Their exit was approaching. He pulled the handgun from another manila envelope and sat it carefully under his feet on the passenger's side.

"I'm so glad you're here," Adele said watching him check the safety and set it down on the floorboard.

The third envelope contained the same thing which Jacob came with; what Ruby handed him before he left. Ten-thousand-dollars, cash. The currency had a delicious smell. New green bills flipped through the fingers of the former CEO. He had held ten thousand grand in his hands a thousand times before. It never failed to excite him. It never got old.

In the distance an older minivan was pulled over to the side of the road. It was a dark colored vehicle pulled off safely into the berm of the freeway. Several cars sped by it, between where Jacob and Adele were and their target: the minivan.

As they approached the vehicle which may be in distress, it appeared to be engine trouble. Adele spoke, "Could this be our gig, or is it just random?"

It appeared to be attended to by a man closing his passenger's side door, moving toward the hood of the car. Another passenger was likely behind the wheel.

"There's that word again," Jacob added to hear himself speak, "Randomness. A kissing cousin to Team Hope and Team Logic."

Adele shrugged her shoulders as she gripped the wheel tighter, "True." She tapped the brakes, pulling up slowly behind the vehicle that they could now see was weathered and grey like the gloom of the clouds above. "You ready for this?"

"I really do," he repeated the comment he made earlier which made her heart flutter with excitement. "Leave it running," he nodded toward the instrument panel. "I'll see what we're getting ourselves into." He looked into her eyes, filled with admiration for him and a sense of concern. Reaching for the door handle, Adele grabbed his forearm and leaned over the console. He fell back into the car, giving her a look, "It is what it is...until it isn't. Then...then it's something else. Let's see what *something else* is arcing this horizon, shall we?"

It sank in, she grabbed the lapel of his light jacket and gripped him tightly. In another circumstance she would have leaned over the console to kiss him. But in this situation, she released her grip. The words diminished her concerns. They were there to change the game. They were in this place at this time to meet these sketchy characters and make some unknown and intentional or random thing happen to make some uncertain persons or function better.

Adele watched him approach the man under the now raised vehicle hood. There was a complete minute where her mind raced in curiosity. A stirring in the vehicle from the driver made her look for the handgun on the floorboard of where Jacob was sitting. It glistened in the dim light reaching the X5's carpet. The driver of the minivan appeared to be reaching into the back seating area. Was it a woman? She appeared to be dark and with long hair. There seemed to be an item, perhaps two in the bench seat behind the driver's side. Was this the questionable character reaching for something? Maybe a gun as well? Jacob was still talking with the man in front of the minivan.

She reached for the handle of her door, clutching the silver handle, then let go, hearing the spring snap back. They gun and the money spoke - she would need to stay with the handgun and the dough. Her ten thousand dollars and the small stack of bills with a bank wrapper which Jacob brought too. Surprisingly, $10,000 was only one-half of an inch thick. Sticking her nose in the unsealed envelope she smelled the luscious smell of money intended for the potential hoodlums in the vehicle she was positioned behind. Checking her rearview mirror, then the driver's side mirror, Adele saw the wide variety of vehicles slightly slowing down but not stopping and changing lanes to avoid the lane closest to theirs speeding by.

Together, they walked back to Adele's SUV. She wasn't paying attention. It startled her. Jacob was smiling. Unusually. Perhaps he even chuckled while saying something to the man next to him. He was handsome, dark complected, and with a slightly larger frame than Jacob's. Maybe he was a Pacific Islander. Their gate was comfortable, and the man followed Jacob to the passenger's side door – away from the traffic. Adele rolled down the window next to them remaining in the X5. *The gun! Should she have grabbed it? Good things can go bad quickly.*

"Hi honey! This is Brian. Brian, I cannot pretend to pronounce his last name. And his wife is Lucky. Lucky?"

The Hawaiian-born man smiled a full mouth of pearly white teeth and answered, "Laki, like lock key. Ma'am, how do you do?"

Adele smiled and could only find a "Hey..." as she sized up the situation.

"Anyway – triple A is on their way to help them along. Their kids are in the backseat of their minivan, and we can just wait here with them to ensure..." Jacob's phone rang interrupting him.

"You are with the mark. It is confirmed." Ruby spoke plainly.

It wasn't common for Jacob Paisley to misjudge or mis-characterize someone. How could this guy, his petite wife behind the wheel, and two kids in car seats be the target? With the phone still next to his ear, and the call still live, he looked at the young man who looked nothing like a hooligan. Several scattered thoughts simultaneously dashed through his mind. He was no threat. There wasn't going to be any tomfoolery with this couple at this moment, was there? Why the gun, Ruby? Something was up. Something Jacob knew that he didn't yet understand but would eventually. Perhaps another one of the small tests. A pop quiz from Professor Ruby. Like Baskin Robbins' old slogan of 31 Flavors – Jacob concluded that deception existed. Some flavors were easy on the eyes, disappointing to the pallet. Wolves in sheep's clothing. This man next to him was an inviting flavor that for an unknown reason required a handgun. *'Welcome to fucking southern California'*, Jacob muttered to himself.

"It is confirmed." Ruby said it again, without any additional color or emotion.

"Got it." Jacob used his thumb on the red button at the bottom of his phone's screen, ending the quick call. He opened the passenger door, grabbing the manila envelope he came with, and the identical one Adele picked up when she arrived. Now $20,000 was in his hands. He handed both envelopes to Brian what's-his-name.

"What's this for?" Brian Kekahanamanui held them in his hand, slowly peering into one of them, which caused his eyes to dart back to Jacob.

"That's between you and them." Jacob shrugged not knowing what else to say.

Just then, Laki opened her driver's side door. She shouted against the sounds of the highway traffic, "Brian! It started."

Adele watched it play out. Of course, the car started after they received the drop. She glanced at the handgun, out of sight of Jacob and so-called Brian, but within her grasp if need be.

"Go now? I don't know what to tell you. Less might be best here."

Brian looked at the envelope again, and back to Jacob with an unspoken question on his forehead. He bent over to look at Adele.

She sat at the ready, to grab the gun and battle here off the freeway north of San Diego. Her hand was two feet away from the piece. If she needed to, she could grab the gun, flip the safety and fire when ready. None of that happened.

Brian took slow steps away from them, back to Laki and the kids in the weathered minivan. Unsure of what to do, he looked back at Jacob reaching for the door of the shiny X5. He reached for the handle that jiggled and listened to it creak as he pried the handle open.

"It just fired up. I tried it a couple more times like you suggested and 'ta-dah', it turned over." She looked at Brian holding two manila envelopes with a look of disbelief on his face, "What's that?"

"Money," Brian said, then he whispered while looking into one of the envelopes, "A lot of it."

"Huh?"

He handed one of the two to her.

She sat there in her sundress with sunglasses on even though there was no sun. Removing them, she glanced into the back seat at their children occupied by the screens they were holding. Cartoons consumed them. Peering into the unsealed envelope, she cried out, "Those are hundreds!" Laki began scrolling through the clean unused bundle.

Brian said, "This one's the same...I think." He pulled out the tidy collection of Benjamin's and began counting. When he was halfway through, at fifty bills he knew it was ten grand and stopped counting.

"Ten for you," she said.

"Ten for me," he added. "But it isn't ours."

"Drug money? They mixed us up with someone else?"

"Silly Haole's." Brian muttered and Laki giggled, smelling the heap.

They looked at each other. She spoke first, "We're on our way to a fundraiser, where the goal is to raise twenty thousand dollars."

"Remember the other morning," Brian asked, "when I asked what you'd do with twenty grand, and you said $10,000 for each kid in a 529 account?"

"I did, didn't I?"

Speechless, they sat there as the AAA van pulled up behind them. The driver quickly approached them, as Laki rolled down her window and shouted into the freeway noise, "It started, we're good!"

The driver informed her that they'd still be responsible for a surcharge of some sort, and they haggled some. Brian wasn't really paying much attention, just as the kids with their noses in the tablets weren't motivated to divide their attention.

As Laki's window squeaked shut, drowning out the truck and car noise, Brian looked at her and with some difficulty spoke, "We...we do what's right, don't we?"

Laki gripped the wheel tightly with both hands. Facing forward she jerked herself back into the cushions of the bucket seat and looked into the rearview mirror. "Oh shit, Brian, they're still there! What are they waiting for?"

"Probably to make sure we can move forward," he smiled. "Why not...drive?" he giggled.

She smiled, placing her hand on the gear shift on the console to the steering wheel, slipping the van into drive. The radio crackled to life. David Bowie's song, *Changes*, just began playing as they drove toward their destination with few other words spoken.

✳✳✳✳✳

"There they go..." Adele watched the van that had seen its share of the Golden State Freeway, a copious number of June-gloom days, and for that manner of counting - the better part of two decades roll away.

"For a couple of pseudo-dubious characters, it was an interesting exchange. It's just twenty K. Why did we have to cross the country for that? I don't get it."

"See... that's why you're good at this and I might not be. You look through the situation to the logic of it all and..."

"...And?" Jacob prompted her to finish, as she slipped their SUV into drive. It nudged forward as he fiddled with the radio. David

Bowie's song, *Changes,* surrounded them, playing halfway through its duration and crisply on the eight high-fidelity speakers within the cabin.

"And I almost peed my pants out of fear," she finished.

"Well, that's over now. Ruby mentioned that there would be one more thing. Let's see what that's all about." Jacob reached for the gun under his feet. He began wiping its shiny surface down with the sweater under his jacket.

"What are we going to do with that?"

"It isn't going back to the Upper East Side with us, that's for sure. Is anyone behind you?"

"Way back there, there are a couple cars."

"I thought all of California had traffic..."

Before he could finish, and because she was well aware of the school schedule, she added, "Holiday break started. Christmas is coming. You'll get coal in your stocking, I'm sure. All the schools are out. And because of schools, we make most of our traffic happen."

Adele felt the breeze as he pushed a toggle lowering his window. As it was all the way down, the warm air was quickly replaced with a moist Pacific and cooler rush of wind. She shouted into the wind as he swung his arm back towards her to throw it, "Maybe we should..." It was too late.

Jacob tossed it like a Frisbee into a wooded area at 60 miles per hour, looking to the side of their speeding vehicle and back, watching it bounce down a tall grassy knoll into a ditch filled with cattails. They blew slightly with the wind, their brown spongy flower heads looked like dozens of hot dogs on light green sticks.

"That's that." Jacob said, satisfied with himself. His salt and pepper hair, tussled from the wind, resembled a morning's bedhead. Her tendrils too, were lofting in the rush of breeze. The window lifted, calming the swoosh of wind.

Adele grinned at his fluffed hair which resembled a rooster's crown, as he ran his fingers through it. "Cock-a-doodle-do," she tittered playfully at his attempt to coif his normal boardroom look without a comb. "I like it," she added with a half of a grin.

Unknowingly to the two of them at that moment, a car that wasn't as far back as Adele thought sped up behind them and lit up its flashers. The red and blue lights strobing from inside the black sedan didn't capture Adele's attention, until it did and nearly a quarter mile later.

When she finally noticed their penetrating bursts, the blood in her arms and legs iced. Adele felt panic rush into her chest, and she pumped the brake slightly, hoping that the garishness of the light was not intended for her. But it was. The car approached them quickly. It tailed them aggressively with its invasive pageantry of red and blue blinks.

"What are you doing?" Jacob asked, uncertain of the vehicle behind them.

A squelch and a siren which sounded like a phaser sounded at the end of the early seventies' song about change. Like the rocker's eyes, one blue and one with a pupil so large that it appeared hazelnut brown, they too were different than they were a mere minute ago. Once again, randomness, that playful presence which mysteriously leant itself to pattern-less influences and probabilities had arrived.

He used the side mirror to affirm what he assumed.

Tapping the brakes, holding them firmer as they coasted to a crawl and eventually a stuttered stop, Adele, slipping the SUV into park and pushing a button on the dash to turn off the radio as a saxophone softly bellowed its final deep notes, turned her head slowly toward Jacob looking for a form of reassurance. Any.

"Well, this might be delightfully entertaining." He faked the confidence with a look of concern. As he raised his eyebrows, small folds stacked on his forehead. Focusing on her eyes, which were seeking but not finding what it was that she wanted. There was a salient absence of certainty. The illusion of control, just a minute ago, mirrored by a sense of relief and David Bowie - had yielded to randomness accompanied by silence.

*****

Maggie wore a little more makeup than usual. She had a little more pep in her step. Her wardrobe had taken on several new items. It was more than several. From shoes to low-cut blouses to sexy dresses to accessories for each outfit, and to the silky bra and panties in a rainbow of colors, which only her and her knew beau new of – she was remaking herself. There were some hand-me-over items from her bestie, Allegra, too.

If she knew that Allegra was in blitz-mode, building a business case to substantiate saving her job, she'd have spent less on the makeover. But she was clueless to that task which her boss's fingers were blistering over. She left Allegra's office, returning to her cubicle with a small stack of papers in her hand. Once she logged on, she opened Outlook. Her unread email was building faster than usual. Opening what was intended for her, she deleted, filed, flagged, and forwarded tasks.

Then, the mistake was made. A workflow document was opened. Workflow documents tracked who opened, read, forwarded, edited, or deleted a file or folder or body of work. It was Allegra's offer. As she read it, she was shocked at the dollar amount. Double – maybe. She always assumed that Allegra earned twice as much as she. Not quadruple.

Staring at the number, not understanding the options element, squinting at the bonus structure of a plan and something called a 'leadership MBO guarantee' – she looked in the direction of Allegra's office. She'd have to come clean that it arrived in her inbox, and she clicked the enter key accidentally. Truth. And truth soon. It was the best way to handle this situation.

Not understanding her diversion of why she had picked it up, the phone in her hands had numerous distractions. The offer was still open but minimized on her monitor. Setting the shiny silver device down, she fidgeted. Then, she stretched it back open to read the document once more adding, "Girlfriend, good for you." Only she heard this. Maggie stood up, rolled her chair under the desk, took a deep breath and marched back toward Allegra's office where the frosted heavy glass door was closed but not completely.

With a small double knock, she swung the door halfway, allowing herself in.

Allegra was two cups of coffee short of being in the zone. She didn't show it though. Dressed especially professionally with her hair pulled back into a bun with several tendrils hanging near her pink cheeks, she looked pitch ready. Her Monaco silk blouse from Ravella was sage green and fit perfectly. It was one of her favorites and a closet classic. An over-sized strand of pearls hung loosely around her neck. The alabaster-cream dress slacks were her favorites. They felt like pajamas. "Mag – I'm buried, can we..."

"I saw your offer letter. I'm sorry, God am I sorry Allie - I opened it up by accident, I swear. I never meant to. I thought it was another services delivery doc and didn't read the full body of the title. It didn't really have an 'Offer Letter' type of declaration popping out at me." She didn't hear Allegra tell her that it was alright. The ramble resumed. "I know what is for your eyes only is for 'your eyes only'" She pointed toward Allegra emphasizing the earnest mistake she felt she made and continued apologizing until she saw Allegra saying nothing and smiling broadly, showing perfect teeth within her pink lipstick. "And you're smiling. Of course you are."

She closed the platinum-colored laptop on her desk with the task she had been laboring over, still smiling.

Maggie whispered: "If it were me, I'd be smiling too!"

"So...what'd you think?"

"It might be more money than I'll earn the rest of this decade."

"There's another one. A little bigger."

"What?"

"People – they always do that when they need more time to process. They add the *what* in there."

"Only you, girl. Who's the other with?"

"Doesn't matter. It isn't that impactful people leadership direction I want to go. It's specialist stuff, a Digital Transformation Officer for a small shop in Philly. I don't have anything against the City of Brotherly Love – but it isn't that *better elsewhere that* I want to go."

"Allegra Sinclair, you are one restless spirit. Is their logo blue too?"

"What's that?"

"Blue. Blue's all you do. Your brand is blue."

She frowned thinking of her track record of companies across the years.

"You do know that right?"

Allegra took a deep breath, reminiscing at the lineup in her roster of blue brands: Epson, Dell, HP, Intel, IBM, Vimeo, and now her transition to the channel as a reseller. It was a lot of work in a short amount of time. *Where did those twelve years go?* Their blueness was nothing more than coincidental.

She learned tech at Epson, hitting the phones as an inside-selling rep. Then, the quick succession from one brand to the next is where she learned quality skills as a Partner Business Manager. What she remembered most were how to golf, drink a lot, bullshit like a champ, and host an especially memorable event also known as a party. In those roles, people wouldn't necessarily remember what you said, the data, or even the call to action. But they would remember how you made them feel and perhaps how you said it. she said it, whatever the *'it'* was, with a smile on her face and a transition of emotional conviction. Her prowess in being a natural geek helped greatly in engineer to technologist to solutions architect scrutiny's. She could pull it off – the brains and the brawn. More than just a pretty face, Allegra was becoming a Titan in the channel, recognized as one of the city's 40 under 40 for a second consecutive year.

She snapped back to the moment. "Yeah, I've heard you say that before. The *brand of blue thing* – those are coincidences. We've had a good run, haven't we?"

"Uh-oh..." Maggie read something else in Allegra's.

"No - no 'uh-oh' just yet." With translucent oyster-white colored nails, her fingers made air quotes. "There's something, and I can't talk about it just yet because it's not even in the incubator, it's a...it's just concept – something really different. Really. Different. But maybe some transferable skills would help me...I don't know...get to that better elsewhere? I haven't been offered anything. Just the idea of something has been, I don't know...teased, maybe. Does that make sense?"

"No, not really. What I'm hearing is you're entertaining offers instead of having to interview. Must be nice."

"I don't know if I'd call it nice. It's a bit confusing. I really need to talk to Vendemer some more."

"About that – Mr BenVen won't be in today. His kidney stones are back."

"Ugh. Got all gussied up for nothing." Allegra's eyes returned to the unfinished Word document that her nails had been clicking on. She was 95% there. But there was some unfinished business to discuss with the one and only, Mister Benjamin Vendermer. She looked up at Maggie, shaking her head.

"Girl, I've seen you crawl out of bed with a raging hangover. You look like that," she motioned the total head-to-toe gorgeousness, "no matter what. God, I hate you."

Allegra ignored the compliment. "Any idea of when he might be in. We were supposed to have *drinks* at some point."

"He cannot catch a break, can he? Vendemer's fate. Like the song..."

"What song?" Allegra's face was blank. The question hung in the air while Maggie found the answer on the ceiling.

"You know the old rockers...years ago..." Maggie's hand circled in the air like a wheel turning, "It's on the tip of my tongue. Rush!" she exclaimed proudly, that she cited her source.

"Vendemer?"

You know... Maggie continued to attempt to explain and began humming the tune from Freewill. Her head bounced slightly, tussling her hair against her shoulders. "Na, na, na, na...na, na, na, na...Vende-mer's fate!"

Allegra squinted at the show and finally giggled.

"Hey, I'm trying here." Maggie joined her friend and boss's giggle with a small smile.

More giggles fell from Allegra's chest, and she blurted it out, "Venomous... it's venomous."

She switched from a smile to a frown quickly, "Oh. All this time." She shrugged her shoulder's and added, "We good?"

"We good." Allegra nodded firmly, letting out an occasional chuckle as Maggie spun on her heel, pivoting to leave the office.

Before Maggie completely left, she turned with a query, "The mentor dude? Is that part of your secret mix?"

There it was. Allegra nodded her head ever so slightly up and down. Then, she gently bit her lip.

"Don't you bite your bottom lip!" Maggie shook her finger at her friend. "I know that when you..."

"He's so handsome...and charming...and experienced..." she rolled her eyes.

"Girl..."

"And taken. Of course. And taken." Allegra looked out at the city outside. Neighboring towers of glass reflected other towers surrounding theirs. "He's with his Admin Assistant from his old firm. They're a thing, I guess."

"The fact that you're checking..."

"He was a bad boy." Allegra said it as if there was potential of some kind in the conversation they shared.

"Is this something firm, or..."

"They vet people for years. It isn't an interview process per say, there isn't a panel...it's like a vetting process that you may or may not know of. And they've had their eyes on me for a while. I'm told. But this was not an offer. It was a discussion. It was just a discussion with a very distinguished – "

"And older..." Maggie chimed in.

"And older, gentleman."

"Vendemer's fate!" Maggie shook her index finger once in the direction of her attractive friend as if it were Hermione's wand and spell, vexing off whatever lively fantasies may be flying around within Allegra's racy imagination. "God, I can't believe you and Chris haven't met yet. Oh, for six in trying to get you two together. I won't stop trying."

"You never do," Allegra repeated.

"I never do indeed. You and my dude – a meet up. Soon." Satisfied with herself, she smirked and turned to leave.

Allegra pulled up the Canadian rock band's song, *Freewill*, from her phone's playlist. Geddy Lee's vocals, Neil Peart's percussion, and the guitar from Alex Lifesong extended by Bluetooth from her iPhone to a small speaker on her credenza. With the volume much too quiet for such a classic, she boosted the volume on the shiny white speaker to a point where a teammate walking by looking in her office through the glass, gave her a quick hand horns, the rock 'n' roll salute.

*****

Steve made frequent trips to the container housing the product. When the organization came to swap the product, he intentionally stayed away from the metal housing unit. His position as the caretaker was to supply meals, security of the compound and the product, and occasionally to administer sleep aids in the food supply. If there were to be a power outage, and south Florida had its fair share of them, Steve would need to fire up the gas generator to provide backup power to the compound. This temporary electricity would ensure that the security cameras, the motion detection, and the server providing the ciphered contact and potential instruction with the outside world. If the juice went out, he was instructed to power the generator and sit in front of email – awaiting orders. No porn-surfing allowed.

Instruction came through an encrypted email account. He read the directions from the organization, then typed any reply with his remaining fingers. Occasionally, at his personal mailbox at the Postal Express, he'd receive a threatening article about what happened to a random and unknown person. Most were articles from the internet or a newspaper. They were all about a gruesome death or dismemberment of the victim. Steve knew these were from the cutter. The cutter was perhaps the kingpin or the honcho of the organization, he thought. Steve's thoughts were simple and far from what was transgressing. The true violations of the unalienable rights of life, liberty, and the pursuit of happiness were loathsome and atrocious.

Once, when retrieving mail, he received a small poly-bubble envelope bag. Once outside, and while sitting in the cap of his old pickup, he opened the white plastic baggie which contained something. Inside it was Steve's pinky. Shriveled, dried skin held the bone and ligaments and few muscles together. He couldn't help himself; he smelled it. Surprisingly it had no smell. The last place he saw it was tucked in the pocket of the cutter. A handwritten note:

Look Steve – your finger!

If there's a next time – it just might be your thumb!

Then, you'll resemble a chicken.

Happy Birthday, Thdeve Booth!

It was the only birthday greeting he received. He reexamined the digit, tucking it back inside the bag. Then, looking at the back of his left hand without the pinky, he tucked his thumb under and into the palm showing just the three remaining fingers. Resembling the claws of chicken feet, he brought the thumb back into view. He couldn't work without a thumb. Getting by with the missing pinky was difficult enough.

Once back to his rundown shanty on his property which he called home, as his truck drove behind the gate and unobtrusive cameras, away from the product in the corrugated steel container, Steve removed his detached pinky from the poly bag and gently laid it on his workbench. He used one of his drills with a quarter-inch bit to grind a small hole through the bone at the base of the finger where it would have connected to his remaining knuckle. Carefully sliding a black plastic cable zip tie through the finger, he attached it to his truck's key chain. Then, he changed his mind and used wire cutters to slice the plastic of the cable tie, freeing the finger with the hole through the bone.

Steve admired his dismembered former piece of his body which helped him daily, before it was segregated from him in that vicious act. He pictured cranking a wrench, gripping the steering wheel of his truck, surfing pornography on the internet. *"F, f, f, fucker. You'll get yourth. Don't know when, but thome day."*

He logged on to check the encrypted mail server. There was no new message. It wasn't time to feed the product. Steve could surf porn from a while. He knew porn like someone knew their own name. It was a form of identity for him and what led to the situation he was now in. Addicted, he also knew in the world of smut there were Tube sites, Cam sites, Premium sites, Fetishes, Virtual Reality, MILF, Voyeur and Cosplay choices. Opening a browser, careful to use the guest account behind a firewall securing his true identity and location he was quickly sorting through categories of lesbian, gay, racial, interracial, older person, younger person and celebrity options. He finally landed on a "For Her Pleasure" category of videos. He clicked with, in Steve speak, *'hith fingerth he thdill had on hith handth'*, clicking clumsily from one video to the next, saying to himself, "theen it...theen it...theen it," as he looked with beady eyes at the screen. Finally, landing on fresh material for Steve, he said with mild enthusiasm, "Oh, thath nithe."

As one hour slipped into the next followed by another at the keyboard, he realized that it was feeding time. It was also the unfortunate time of the week for him to slide the metal excrement box from the end of the container. He would need to shovel shit. From the box, into a wheelbarrow, sometimes two, he'd begrudgingly galumph through the task he disliked most. It wasn't because the reason for the excrement was heinous. Nor was it because of the putrid smell. The scraping of the shovel onto the metal bin was what Steve despised. A scratching sound reverberated against the corduroy bottom of the bin grinding the steel head and blade of the shovel against the ribbed reinforcement in the compartment's foundation. The shoveling noise lasted no more than ten minutes but haunted him for what felt like hours. Like some people reacted to a dentist's drill in their mouths, or others loathed the sound of fingernails scratching a chalkboard, and others reached frantically to calm a blaring alarm clock – Steve would shovel, pitch, and stop, seeking the moments between the dredging sounds.

*****

As they sat there on the berm of highway, the dark sedan was idle behind them. Its flaring cherry and imperial blue lights were invading this point which they would be debriefing from the cash drop. The stage was set for things to go one way or another. Jacob and Adele watched as the driver's door opened. A trooper slowly climbed out of the car. Jacob squinted to make out a Dodge Charger, dark grey or black. It appeared to be a man. He had a gun and a radio on each hip. His campaign hat, the most common hat resembling what Smokey Bear would wear was tan. Drill sergeants in the Army derived superpowers from the Stratton felt headpieces. He slowly walked to their vehicle, pausing to call in their license plate number into his radio. As he held it close to his mouth, he had his other hand poised to draw.

Adele had reached her left hand to her armrest to fully lower the driver's side window while keeping her right hand on the steering wheel.

The trooper, noticing that the window was down and not all hands were on the dash or the wheel, knocked twice on the side of the car with his knuckles and called out, "All hands on the dash, please."

They looked at each other and complied by placing their hands in front of them, leaning forward slightly.

He leaned over. "Hi folks. I'm Officer Sanchez. Ma'am, driver's license and registration, please." The Hispanic man was pleasant in his demeanor. His badge was a shiny gold seven-pointed star.

Adele reached for her driver's license from her bag at her feet, "Slowly," he added, reaching for his sidearm.

"It's a rental." She was showing concern. Her normal coolness was missing meeting Officer Sanchez. "The rental agreement is on my phone. It's in the duffel in the back seat." She handed him her driver's license.

He took it and inspected it. "New York, huh? You are a long way from home, aren't you?"

Adele froze. She hadn't planned a story. What if she was called out. Was this vacation? Perhaps it was business, and they were on a sales call? Was it to visit a nephew? Maybe he was moving or broke his leg or had invited them for Christmas. That was it.

Jacob spoke first, "We're here to visit a friend of hers, going through a divorce. She needs some help with the kids while she's ramping up life without the asshole..."

"You lose something in those bushes back there?"

The worst possible words they could have heard were just spoken in a question, requiring another quick falsehood. Who was the better liar now? The trooper saw the gun tossing incident. Perhaps. Maybe he saw something but wasn't sure what he saw. Maybe the gun found water in the marshy area with the cattails. It was quite possible that it did not, as well, and was conceivably laying in the deep grass awaiting discovery.

"Worst taco ever." Jacob continued the storytelling, intentionally coloring the fiction with additional detail. "I thought I was going to be sick. It was supposed to be chicken. Tasted like a dog or cat. The salsa was like ketchup. I'm sorry..."

"I like tacos," the Officer interrupted Jacob's mendacity.

Who doesn't? Jacob muttered to himself quietly. His head swung from studying the officer's dark brown eyes to looking down the road in front of them. He was contemplating options. How simple it was making money, something from nothing, on Wall Street. The options traded there, puts and calls and covered calls, were nothing like the options of lying in the face of a man with a gun. These options were real. *I think I can outrun him, but then there's Adele. Need to protect my Adele at all costs.*

The jacket and pants matched the stiff brimmed hat. He held Adele's license, flipping it over. "Organ donor..." he made slight a 'Humph' sound as he flipped it back over. Then added, "well...that's good to know," as he stood back up straight. His right hand remained near the gun on his hip the entire time. "Look, I'm going to give this to my partner and have him call it in – maybe see if you have a littering charge or two in New York. We try to keep our roadways free of tacos here in Southern California. Meanwhile, since I like tacos so much, I'm going to have a little look back there where your bag most likely landed. If I find what I'm looking for, and you don't want this to happen, my partner will be making a little trip up to speak with you. We clear?"

Adele nodded her head nervously, and softly spoke, "Yeah...yes...yes...clear..."

"You two sit here, just – like – you – are – right – now."

Officer Sanchez left their SUV, slowly strolling back to the passenger's side of the dark sedan with the red-light, blue-light, red-light, blue-light blinkers behind them. Watching him intently in the side-view mirrors, they watched him hand Adele's license to a dark character they hadn't observed earlier. A silhouette reaching for the license was all that could be made out in the shadows. Then, Officer Sanchez went on that small walk he said he was going to make.

"Whatcha' thinkin' Captain Paisley?" She found it, her coolness.

He found a reason to smile. It was her. "Wasn't last night incredible?"

They giggled. It was the levity they needed. To think clearly, to strategize, to contemplate alternatives, sometimes it just took one lofty comment to be able to sort through the clutter in one's mind. Adele took her right hand from the wheel, finding his bicep, and squeezing it slightly. "What's the worst thing that could happen?'

Jacob shrugged his shoulders slightly, lowering his hands from the leather dash, disregarding the instructions. "Well, I was thinking I could outrun both of you."

"Oh...yep...yeah, my white knight in shining armor, thank you,"

"But I don't know about the other yahoo..."

More time had slipped by in the unpredictability of Officer Sanchez's trek into the grassy area than they had realized. What wasn't supposed to happen, might be. The passenger door opened. One leg, then the other. Another Officer of the Law stood wearing an identical uniform. It appeared to be another man with the brim of his hat riding low, hiding his face. Walking slowly, he approached their car. Then he stopped.

"What's he doing?" Adele barely moved her pink lips as she asked. The rearview mirror was easier to see than the side-view mirror since the officer was approaching Jacob's side of the X5.

"Nothing." Jacob answered dryly. "Standing there looking at us." He saw a small dip in the knees of the official. Then, the feet took small steps toward and away from them. Back and forth. The officer's arms were now into it...making small circles like the cranking wheels of a steam locomotive. "He's..." Jacob tilted his head, squinting to make out what he was seeing. The officer continued to dance, moving toward them. Finally, taking off his hat so that they could make the likeness, Jacob started shaking his head, drawing his hands to rub his face, wiping away the lapse in memory that he too could still be surprised by his friend.

"He's, well, he's...dancing. And by he, I mean Ruby. I think."

Adele had been holding her breath. She exhaled dramatically, exuding the pent-up stress within her. A chuckle spilled from her chest.

Tap, tap, tap. The sound of the black man's knuckles struck the back window. Leaning over to see them both, resting his forearm on the car in front of Jacob, he finally spoke, "I like tacos too!" Ruby laughed at their expense. Processing the sarcasm quickly, they all did, Ruby more so. "Welcome to SoCal!"

Before they stopped sweating, prior to any interrogation, and ahead of a simple, '*What the hell are you doing here?*', Ruby opened the back door and jumped in. "Let's go!"

"What about Officer Sanchez back there?"

"Oh, that's Tony. He's awesome. He works with us. Seriously, hit it. We've got an event that is going to make this all feel so much better...I think." Ruby paused on the last part of what he said.

'He's legit? CHIPS?"

"What's that?" Jacob remembered Ruby's poor hearing in one of his ears. He asked the question because he didn't hear, not because he did not know.

"California Highway Patrol?"

"That's the one." Ruby kept touching one ear, slightly above it. Then, slightly below it. Jacob knew he had an earpiece in one ear, working some kind of job. His friend was a master of acting casual and comfortable, while truly being quite busy.

As they flaunted the countless questions Ruby's way, they were met with a triangular reality. Jacob trusted Adele. Adele trusted Jacob. They both trusted Ellipsis *just enough* to protect each other from their cheeky fibs – whopper number one and whopper number two - about traveling to Seattle and San Francisco.

"There was a degree of uncertainty and danger and risk in this little field trip. Along comes the element of surprise and a gun, getting you out of your environment, in the field. Guys, sorry for the test. You wanted to protect each other at the risk of doing good. That's what sacrifice looks like. Living up to what you agreed to, the welfare of unknown others. That's the warrior's creed we need." He double touched under his ear again.

'Where's the couple with the twenty-grand off to?" Adele asked as she merged into the oncoming traffic.

"That will end up going to a good cause, and... "

"And you're an eternal recruiter." Jacob knew he was working the bench, seeking good talent for another day. Starters, utility players, cleanup hitters, bullpen relief pitchers – like a ballclub, Ruby was always building a team.

"And I'm scouting for new recruits, yes. Constantly testing character. The good and the questionable. Look at you, Paisley. Who'd a thunk a CEO fat cat from Manhattan would end up in the field and funding project to project?"

Jacob thought about funding. "The Bloomberg terminal pays for itself yet again."

It was a bone of contention between them. Now that Ruby had to manage costs of running a small team in the field in addition to his talent acquisition role, he actually paid attention to the costs of each job, the price for performance.

"The thirty thousand, that's a subscription? Per year?"

"Worth every penny. I made seventy-five overnight last week. That's while I was sleeping off of the OTC derivatives."

"OTC?" Ruby's skepticism was mild. Adele knew what Jacob spoke about. Her understanding of financial gibberish had broadened from her years as his Admin while they were at PPCM.

"Over the counter. Trades that take place off an exchange, outside of a third party. The Bloomberg terminal operates from real-time market data. It's a proprietary trading platform. And because I'm a little bit selfish. It's what I want and it's what I know.

"Fair enough. Keep printing the dollars." Ruby changed topics on them. "Here, stick these in your ears. Just one each." Ruby handed them what appeared to be a small piece of tan fabric, the size of two grains of rice. Tuck it in, deep."

They did it, first Jacob, then Adele as she toggled hands on the wheel. They heard what he was likely listening to. Chatter over a radio signal. Rustling.

"What is it?" Jacob said. "All I can hear is commotion of some sort."

"Shhh..." Ruby held up his hand.

A man's voice spoke clearly. "Target is identified. Confirming, target has been identified."

A woman's voice followed, "Takeout approved. Proceed with caution. Be careful out there, Tango team."

"Affirmative. Target is currently pulled over. Looks like a lunch break perhaps. Heading south on Campo Road. Over."

Adele, Jacob and Ruby listened attentively as their X5's tires slapped the cement freeway heading south passing through Miramar to the I-8, heading east passed San Diego State University toward La Mesa. No one spoke, they listened to the engine noise on the earpiece.

Finally, Jacob broke the silence, asking Ruby a question. "What should I make of Tamsen?"

Ruby paused, thinking of how to respond with Adele in the car. "She's a piece of..." holding back from the word 'work', he replied in kind, "of our extended team. I wanted you two to meet. Maybe there's something there, maybe not."

"Should I be jealous?" Adele asked in a joking tone. "You're quite the matchmaker, Ruby...the women...Allegra...and now Tamsen? If you mention *Victoria*, I'll wreck the car. Just sayin'." She gripped the wheel firmly. The smile slipped away from her lips. Nonchalant about the first two, deadly serious about the third. Jacob's Kryptonite, his ex, his former lover – she was perhaps what might wreck the goodness they had going. Victoria was perhaps the one and only risk for the growing relationship between Adele and Jacob.

"Allegra is an up-n-comer, an eager beaver, one to watch. Tamsen is emotive," Ruby quelled Adele's drollery about the other women, leaving the topic of Victoria stand alone. "Tamsen is someone I'd like you, Jacob, to have an opinion about. Call it an assessment of personnel. You have an eye for talent. She's – Adele, I'm counting upon you for some confidentiality here...she's just a tiny little bit of an alarmist.

Not everything can be a crisis. Tamsen wants to act expeditiously for her causes. Ellipsis as an organization, well, we vet the considerations without lone wolf agendas. Vigilantes? Sure, you could say that we are, for lack of a better description, but consensus is king. We don't care about every single ailment along the way because we have our eyes on the issues, we believe we can adjust. Those with broad and meaningful outcomes. Tamsen can allow herself to get distracted."

"I'll treat it like that – a conversation with a teammate." Jacob felt that Ruby was seeding yet another beanstalk of some kind.

"Believe it or not, they're the same age. Allegra is mature beyond her years; Tamsen wants to save every stray she meets."

"As long as they're not pretty," Adele added, looking up into the rearview mirror, seeking Ruby's reaction.

Jacob turned to see Ruby's face. Wrinkles formed on the old man's forehead, unable to conceal the fact that he thought they were both beautiful. Giggles broke out between them.

Ruby shook his head, "I hate to talk shit about one of our own, but if someone became a rogue agent, spinning off to take on saving rainbows – it might be Tamsen."

"Well, she's from the right state for that," Jacob added, speaking mostly to himself.

"She's from Hawaii?" Adele asked.

"A North Shore surfer," Ruby added.

"Well, this just keeps getting better," Adele was teasing again. "I might just need to go find me a new dude." She looked over at Jacob, looking back at her.

Tamsen - she's a good looker too. Mm, mm. Brown skinned local girl. Long dark silky hair. And competitive. A real brand ambassador now. An icon over there on Oahu. People adore her charm." Ruby was egging her on. "Allegra's prettier, my opinion."

"Do you think Jacob can handle three women, Ruby?"

"I don't know," he smiled shaking his head slowly, adding to the provocation, "Maybe I didn't think that through."

Jacob sat in the shotgun seat, feeling the barrel of the talking guns upon him. He shook his head at the targeted banter.

Rolling green hills flanked them as they approached Highway 94. Traffic and the commercial city-busy way was quickly traded for an almost rural drive with lush low trees with hunter green foliage, grasses, and brush with tiny yellow flowers. Large boulders protruded through the rising hills snuggled up against the roadway. Tiny white flowers against the crocodile green colored vines wrapped the telephone poles and tree trunks. To the New Yorkers, it was a trade-off, the concrete jungle of Manhattan for this warm scenic drive into the mouth of dangerous activities.

"Could you live here?" Adele glanced quickly at Jacob, then back toward the lines on the road ahead. "I think I could live here." As the city gave way to occasional single level ranch homes, cars and pickups parked in their driveways, some with Christmas lights on small trees, a simple middle American lifestyle had its allure and welcoming call on Adele. "The high desert, if that's what this is has a beauty of its own."

There was an extended pause where he shrugged his shoulders. Cracking the window for a burst of cooler outside air, then cranking it back up, "I...don't know that this is our kind of place. Hawaii...Oahu...Honolulu..." Looking into the back seat at Ruby who was paying no attention to him, "We could have a little New York in the middle of the Pacific, couldn't we?"

Ruby was listening all along. "To which I'd say enjoy your twilight years of retirement, President Paisley. There's work there, sure. But for you to trade, leveraging the U.S. exchanges, you're getting up at what, two in the morning? Every weekday morning that the S&P and the NASDAQ and the Dow open? That's good for a short stretch, maybe. Now that things are escalating for the two of you, generating funding from your disbursements – New York is what we had in mind."

"You can make money from anywhere..."

"You can. Yes. But you yourself, you asked for something more. You asked for something more too," he pointed at Adele. "The two of you…we see an up-town cosmopolitan couple in Manhattan. Maybe swinging by the United Nations building quite often. Cocktails at Tryst. Dining at Le Bernardin. Black tie affairs at The Met. Broadway shows. Bottle service the Marquee. Perhaps a sleepover at the Mandarin Oriental? You know, Billionaires Row kind of people. That's a good fit for you. Sophisticated, but not notorious. Makes your intentions believable. Got to learn to lie through your teeth a little better though. We can teach that."

"The U.N.?" Adele whispered to herself, questioning the relevance, listening to the extravagance while her eyes focused on the roadway ahead.

"There are bad actors at the bottom. The salt of the earth has its nefarious villains. The middlemen – those heinous ding-a-lings have next level needs and wants. Unreasonable plans and unlikely goals which they can be compromised over. But the undoubtedly results-based criminals, the top of the ladder wrecking balls – well, they have handlers and fixers and screens and all sorts of methods of filtering who might get to their desires for power, greed, lust, gluttony."

"And these things take money." Jacob assumed.

Ruby pointed his finger at Jacob without saying a word.

"The arousal of curiosity. Intrigue. Mining for truth, for intent, for confirmation. That's a part we may play…"

"One hundred percent." Ruby reached into his pocket for a different cell phone. It was shorter than the iPhone he had been toggling and was black, not platinum. He handed it to Jacob. This is to connect you with Sydney.

"Who's Sydney?"

"She's an IT specialist. Cannot have enough good people in the emerging technologies these days."

Jacob peered into the back seat toward Ruby. Their eyes met. They were both thinking of Allegra Sinclair.

"Do I need to call her for something?'

"Nope. She'll find you. That earpiece you're wearing has a filament thin RFID tracker in it. She knows where you are - at all times. Oh, and I forgot to tell you, it's touch sensitive. Three taps on top of your ear lift the volume. Three gentle taps below your ear, lowers the volume."

Both Jacob and Adele demonstrated volume control, amazed at the technology from the minuscule earpiece. Miles of roadway slipped away under the tires of their vehicle as they continued their trek south, toward the California – Mexico border.

"Um, where are we going?" Adele asked.

At his direction, they had turned onto a smaller freeway, heading toward the unknown event ahead. The cement still slapped as the SUV powered into a less populated area. Tonal clatter waned to a gentle hum as the uneven cuts in the road's mortar were replaced by asphalt.

'What's going to happen here, Ruby?" Adele gripped the wheel while trying to meet his expression. He was checking his phone while listening. They knew that there was a sting operation of some sort happening or about to take place. They also didn't think they would face danger other than the kerfuffle they had already experienced in their mad dash of cash.

Ruby continued to be preoccupied with his iPhone but was able to answer her question two full minutes after she asked it. Still observing his cell, "Our mercenaries are badasses. Some really bad dudes are going to go down, and we're going to free their hostages – also known as *The Product.*"

"The Product?" Adele repeated. "People? Are the product?" She lowered her chin to her chest and frowned at the windshield and the changing landscape ahead. Rolling green hills flanked them as they approached Highway 94. Traffic and the commercial city-busy way was quickly traded for an almost rural drive with lush low trees with hunter green foliage, grasses, and brush with tiny yellow flowers. Large boulders protruded through the rising hills snuggled up against the roadway. Tiny white flowers against the crocodile green colored vines wrapped the telephone poles and tree trunks.

"To these assholes they are. We've been tracking this ring for a while now. Unfortunately, our intel has revealed that it's a little larger than we originally thought. They're several cells that, over a period of time, we'll...we will extinguish."

Adele affirmed out loud her assumption, "So...human trafficking."

"Human trafficking. Mostly small, young girls. Young women. But human trafficking can be anyone. Not just the vulnerable or the compromised or the naïve. Anyone." A moment of silence to recognize its significance dominated the space between each of them. "Damn right shameful. We're going to end it impacting nine young lives today. Eight confirmed, maybe nine. This is Ellipsis. This is going to, hopefully, be another favorable outcome from what we do. What we quietly do."

"Where? Ruby, where are they heading?"

Ruby looked at Jacob, then Adele, "Tecate."

"Mexico? But how could they possibly cross the border?" Adele remained under a broadly false assumption that human trafficking was an elsewhere thing. Not here. Not in the beautiful countryside of San Diego.

"A blind eye will be turned, several guards will be threatened, a payoff or bribe or some other form of exchange will be accepted, and a small white truck will slip through from the U.S. into Mexico. Adele – it's hard to listen to this number, but it involves tens of thousands each year."

"Ladies and gentlemen, our target is moving." The radio crackled. There was some static, then silence.

"We're almost there. I think." He touched his ear and asked, "Sydney – how much further." He listened to his earpiece and shared a response with Adele and Jacob. "About five more..."

Pop, pop, pop, pop, pop! They all heard the gunfire at the same time. *Bang! Bang! Pop, pop, pop! Bang! Pop, pop! Bang! Pop, pop, pop.* Thudding sounds which resembled shots hitting metal and glass shattering and a ringing sound of steel were loud through their earpieces. *Dot, dot, dot! Bang! Pop! Pop, pop, pop!*

"Target taken out. Tango one, check in: Check! Tango two? Check! All accounted for." Several voices weighed in over the same frequency. "Going offline. Sending in the custodian."

It began in a flash and within a minute, it was over – the gunfire.

"The custodian? The clean-up?" Jacob asked Ruby, without finishing his question.

"Crime scene cleaner. Might as well call it what it is." He was so matter of fact about it. Adele looked slowly in his direction, then quickly back to the veering roadway.

Speechless, Adele drove toward a scene that she knew would forever change her perspective toward the general goodness of mankind. It would aggravate her heartening wish that people in whole were well-intentioned. Her outlook may very well be tarnished. Human trafficking. She was too far down this road to turn back and return to a Pollyannaish conviction that out of sight meant that *maybe it didn't really happen.*

Jacob knew what she was thinking. Ruby knew what she was thinking. They said nothing.

Ruby continued listening to something only he heard. Jacob assumed that it was Sydney calling out their GPS and proximity to the situation.

"Turn here Adele."

The turn signal blinked a quiet, clicking sound. She veered off to the left, under the telephone lines which had been running congruent with their journey. A small home with a dog sitting looking in the direction of where they were now heading was on the corner. The sound of gravel scrunching underneath the tires was the only noise made other than the soft drive produced by the vehicle's engine.

It was a half of a mile down the gravel path. Serene. A gentle rolling grass field with small, rounded brown and golden colored granite boulders occasionally breaking the surface. In the distance, a couple miles away were foothills to a range. The distance between was dotted with some desert brush and fifteen-foot trees of olive and moss green foliage.

"Giddy up." Jacob broke the quiet of the car. He knew that what they might find would be memorable.

"*Give me your tired, your poor, your huddled masses yearning to breathe free. The wretched refuse of your teaming shore. Send these, the homeless, tempest-tossed to me. I lift my lamp beside the golden door.*" Ruby quoted the poem at the base of the Statue of Liberty. Emma Lazarus's, *The New Colossus*, was committed to his memory, parts of it, for moments like this.

"Where do you come up with this material?" Adele found a small smile, happy that she was no longer alone in her thoughts.

Jacob used his thumb to point toward Ruby in the back seat, "He's a preacher's kid, or so he says..."

"Adele – I think this is going to end well for you." He smiled with his eyes crinkling as his thick lips created an upturned crescent. "Uh, you can turn it off. We'll be here for a while. And...if what happens which I think might happen, there isn't any place you'd rather be."

Together they noticed the dust from a van trailing off into the distance away from them as they approached a white utility truck. A faded and peeling painted logo about MexiCali Fruits and Vegetables was the only distinguishing feature on the once-produce carrying cargo area. One mercenary, carrying an assault rifle walked to the back of the delivery truck, and was standing in a guard position at the roll-up door. He wore sunglasses, was dressed in umber camouflage cargo pants, a tawny field jacket with no insignia identifying himself, and Timberland boots. A sidearm and a hunting knife were tight against his hips. He made no motion as they slowed down, sending more dust into the air as they came to a stop.

"Stay here for a minute." Ruby jumped out first, leaving his door open. He approached the armed soldier and the two had several words. The soldier disappeared around the truck and returned with a bolt-cutter which resembled pruning shears. He snipped the lock in one quick jerk, causing the remaining piece of a copper lock to fall to the dirt.

Ruby looked toward Adele and Jacob and motioned them to join him.

In the Arcadian stillness, Adele glanced over at Jacob, stalling but then eventually breaking the silence with her words, reciting Ruby, "...yearning to breathe free."

They climbed out of the now dusty rental, leaving the car doors open like Ruby did, as not to create more noise. The chiming from the keys still in the ignition rang several times before Adele removed them, tucking them into her jacket pocket. Slowly they walked to the back of the delivery truck where Ruby and the mercenary were standing.

"Hi. I'm Jacob." Paisley held out his hand. Ruby looked at the warrior and the two exchanged shakes of their head. Nothing else was said and the clean-cut fighter disappeared once again.

Ruby turned to Adele to focus on his instruction, solely with her. "I'm going to open the door. It's a rolling door, so it'll make a sound rolling up into the roof. The people, the children inside, they'll be frightened. They won't know what to expect. Jacob..." he looked at Jacob, "...and I – we'll step to the side. It's you they might want to see. We'll boost you up and you just stand here. You just stand right at the back of the truck bed. And it should all be good."

"Shouldn't we tell them we..." Jacob attempted to offer a suggestion but was interrupted by Ruby with a quick but gentle hand in his direction.

"No. No, this is Adele's minute. Just...just let it happen. The last thing they'll want to see is intimidating warriors with guns. They'll scatter. That's happened before. Likely more of them than of us. No cat herding out here. They've been through enough already. Adele will be that maternal consolation they may be drawn to." He looked into her eyes for her composure. She shook her head, 'yes'. They took a breath of the desert air, which had its own unique smell: of creosote bush and dried grass. It was what they smelled before they opened the latch.

"He was on his radio," Adele whispered.

It wasn't as simple as the serviceman made it seem. With a third crimp and a small grunt, Ruby managed to cut the bolt. He pointed to Adele. She reached for the handle, nervously, and turned it. With the boxes of soundproofing out of the way there was no more than ten feet in the truck's bed which would have left another ten for a small room. She turned the handle and pulled open the unfinished door her way. A small rustle was heard.

No one moved. Intentionally, they waited patiently. It was a full minute of nothingness.

Ruby reached down to the handle, gripping it slightly at first, un-latching the steel clasp. He lifted it slightly, then proceeded to lift it the rest of the way. It made the noise, he explained. They all stared into the darkness of the body of the truck, with blank expressions, not seeing what they expected. Brown, corrugated boxes two feet tall were stacked to the ceiling. Ruby reached first, Jacob next, for a sample box. They were filled with filament. Soundproofing. Upon removing the first layer, a second layer was found. Once they removed the second layer, they could see that the walls of the truck were also soundproofed with insulation. Digging further into the truck, a wooden door was seen latched. It too, had a padlock. Ruby turned to jump off of the truck bed. Before he could, Adele had the silver cutting device in her hand. Now she was in on it, climbing onto the wooden bed. Closer to the door, the scent of the desert was exchanged for the smell of the formaldehyde glues from the plywood and the stench of sewage.

Out of the darkness, a small blond-haired girl, thin and frail, with tear-stained cheeks wearing a yellow sun dress appeared. She looked up to Adele. Her big green eyes were wide despite the light filtering into the stale and gloomy place she had emerged from. Slowly and hesitantly, she took small steps toward Adele who remained still. The small girl looked to Ruby and Jacob and stopped.

Adele slowly reached out her hand. The child reached up and took it. Taking another step closer, and another, and another. She had a zip tie on her left hand with numbers on it. She had the same zip tie on her right ankle, again bound tightly with an air tag tracking device attached to it. They held each other's hand as additional sounds came from within the cargo area. Another small child, another girl, perhaps Hispanic approached Adele in the same manner. She was younger. They may have been seven and nine. Adele looked down at her and they also held hands. Then, the two girls joined hands and the three of them were connected in a hands-to-hands-to-hands circle. This meaningful connection brought large tears of joy to Adele's blue eyes.

Ruby looked over to Jacob. Jacob looked over to Ruby. Nothing was said in this quiet moment of re-establishing a morsel of trust with these children. Slowly, two more small girls came out of the darkness of the room. Then, four more did. Eight in all. Several of them were as young as the first two, several of them were slightly older. Just as Ruby said, maybe eight, maybe nine. Each of them had the same plastic tie, firmly wrapped around their left wrist and their right ankles. A radio frequency identification tag was affixed to the ankle bands. Attached to them so tightly, there didn't appear to be room for even a finger. Each of the numbers was slightly different.

Adele, tears now streaming down both of her cheeks onto her blouse, nodded toward the exit of the truck where Ruby and Jacob were. One of the first two girls pointed her finger back to the room where they came from.

"One more?" Adele asked softly, trying to be strong for them.

The child shook her head slightly and slowly in the direction of 'yes'.

One last child appeared. All small girls. Nine. Nine souls on board after all. Nine reasons to drive toward Tecate today. Nine lives which might change the world for the better, or for worse. Nine reasons to celebrate the potential which each one of us has within us.

Together, there, they embraced – Adele, the center of the flower, surrounded by the petals - reentering the daylight from the darkness, joining the living world instead of the modern slavery they were bound to, encouraged by an oncoming better elsewhere.

Ruby and Jacob watched.

"Trauma-bonding. They way they emerged from the container," Ruby said gently to Jacob, informing him of the children's behaviors coming from the metal box in the desert.

"Trauma-bonding?" Jacob, seeking understanding asked.

"The way they comforted each other...the band of human concern they had toward each other...how they held hands and looked out for one another. Children seeking solace. We have a lot to learn as adults, don't we..." Ruby watched the alleviation Adele provided in the huddle of calming cluster.

* * * * *

"Dude, what are you doing?" Ashford looked at himself in the mirror, noticing the changes. But for what? Where was this going? His square and chiseled jawline was now covered with scruff. He needed to shave and reached for his Norelco shaver. As he trimmed the stubble, he spoke to himself.

"What's the next step?" The neck work was first. "Hell, what's the plan?" He stroked the grain up, then down. "Yeah, I hear you – Get Her Back." The sideburns needed to be raised and evened. "But, like, really – what are the specifics?" Longer strokes from the ears to the chin began to reveal the man that Ashley would remember.

"Sure, get fit, prepare, be strong – mentally and psychologically – but what is the actual tactical objective here?" The chin was a little more delicate. The trimmer had done its work. Ashley's lover's, Aiden Ashford, face was back. She wouldn't have cared for the beard too much. "There he is." It was a slight smile, but nonetheless counted. "When was the last time that was there?" he asked himself. The man in the mirror didn't have any answers but did have the identical questions that were asked, and statements made.

Aiden Ashford, the adopted son of a pair of hardware engineers looked like he used to. He had taken himself out of the dating market the day he met her. Looking at himself, he repeated his new tagline, "Not bad for a broken-hearted software developer from Tampa..." Immediately, he choked up, thinking of Ashley, somewhere, alone and afraid or worse – compromised.

He struck his image in the mirror with his hand, where the palm meets the wrist, cracking it. His reflection was askew. The awry face looking back had lost its smile. Ashford, without the facial hair, looked back with a scowl at what he'd done. When Ashley returned, he'd have to explain it – or fix it before then, whenever then might be.

Counseling didn't solve his problems. The loss of a loved one, a spouse or a child was the pain that words didn't fix. Time was as much of an enemy as a requirement. He fought the tears, but they won. He wiped the wet salty stream from one cheek and watched several drops of tears fall to the vanity from the other.

Leaving the bathroom with the now broken mirror, he walked into the kitchen and dragged his chair, not Ashley's, away from the table to sit down. On the glass top was an article he printed from the internet. He had previously read it twice and wanted to read it repeatedly. A man, unrelenting in his search for his girlfriend of several years, yet taken two years ago, dedicates his life to the underworld work of becoming and being a vigilante.

The vigilante becomes a zealot in his search and pursuit for his girl. He dedicates his life to finding her – referring to her as *the underrepresented*. Eventually everyone else gives up, the article stated, and the only people seeking her were her parents and him, the vigilante.

This was Ashford's world.

Detectives take on the cold cases with passion, then with persistence, then out of object, and finally out of project. The intensity waned with time. It was typical. But the activists crusade was undone. Therefore, the mission to represent was only as strong as the will to carry on. The author, an idealist and promoter of taking control into your own hands found his girl.

He thought about what he often thought about. The difference between accidental loss and deliberate loss. Accident versus deliberate. If it were luck, bad luck, that she was struck and killed in an auto accident a year after he rescued her. Somehow, some way, her loss at an intersection was alright. Her disappearance, her missing – perhaps assigned a place in the dark world of modern slavery where technically she was living, was not an acceptable form of loss. Her freedom, stripped away - a hopeless existence filled with doubt and fear was a hell when compared to an accidental death.

Balances, whether by legal jurisdiction, faith, or natural occurrences were unequal – sometimes unfair – but occasionally just. The vigilante's work was of balance. Acting as an equalizer in unequal and often lawless situations, the author proclaimed that enough from law enforcement was indeed not enough to solve the crime of abduction. Shackled with budget constraints, the good work of the men and women in blue was often limited in financial support and sometimes scope. This man's cry for more.

Rising from the reading to nuke a burrito in the microwave, he again saw his reflection of a clean-shaven face. Agreeing not to strike the appliance, he wondered what more he could do to act as an equalizer, seeking Ashley's freedom and his vindication for her abduction. What would a vigilante do?

He picked up the paper again, seeking the name of the author and chastiser. Again, he read it: *anonymous*. What would make someone advocate for the righteousness of a nemesis, and fall short of full castigation?

"More questions than answers," he said to himself again. He wanted answers, some answers, even if they weren't the right ones to listen to.

The burrito's cheese and salsa smells made him hungrier than he was. Ashford opened the cupboard for tortilla chips, finding none. He substituted pita bites for the crisps. Without the garnish of jalapeno peppers, a pickle was substituted. Diet Coke? No, other than tap water, lemonade was all that was available. Seeking an avocado buried in the refrigerator's fruit and vegetable drawer was hit or miss. As he looked, he was missing Ashley's shopping rigor and diligence – not the green fruit with the oversized nut. The mishmash of food mirrored his bachelor's days. He missed her – every little thing about her.

* * * * *

"Where's Kate? I can hear her, but I don't see her on the call yet."

"Kate? You logging on?"

"Just a sec," she shouted from the den.

Tamsen acknowledged the rest of the girls for being on time and said something nice about each of them while Kate logged in to the Zoom call. Ashley got accepted into USC; Zoey was going to Portugal with her family before taking a role in her family's real estate business; Terri was the best surfer on the team and had a competition in Tahiti next week; and then there was Kate – the project. Kate was cute, the cover model of this new group of Bravado Surf squad. She was a little ditzy at times, saying off-color but unintended things which caused pause, and then a giggle, and maybe even sympathy for her approach. The thing about Kate was that she wasn't unlike-able. Everyone seemed to cheer her on for some reason or another.

Kate's camera finally lit up. She was making a face, crossing her eyes, sticking her tongue out the side of her mouth, and lifting her nostrils with a pinky.

"Loser," Ashley teased as Kate came on camera.

Terri tossed popcorn at the camera, as if flicking it at Kate, picking up a few kernels to munch on them. She said nothing.

"You owe us Kate," said Ashley.

"Yeah, but I won the trip to Hawaii and y'all didn't. Ha! Bitches. What is that kettle or cheddar?"

"Neither" Terri replied, "It's Skinny Pop...uh...original."

"That stuff is tasteless, isn't it?" Kate added. "I just l-o-v-e the smell of buttered popcorn. The kind you get at the movies."

"When was the last time any of us went to a theater?" Ashley asked.

Their playfulness told a story. The get-together in San Diego was a success. They bonded. Hopefully not like an epoxy, Tamsen hoped. She needed a task today and wanted to divide and conquer, not cure a bond that separated them from her mission.

"Okay," Tamsen began, "dearly beloved, we're gathered here today... Why are we gathered? Why do you think this is necessary? You're all surfers, you're pretty, you are the next face of our brand, but why do you think we're onboarding you the way we so meticulously are into Bravado?"

The usual silence followed.

"I got all day..." Tamsen allowed the quiet period to become uncomfortable, until Zoey spoke up.

"Because you care and you're trying to make fine representatives of the brand out of us?"

"I think that was a statement but came across as a question. Yes, thanks for speaking up, Zoey. This isn't a charm school. It's an insurance policy for our Talent Acquisition team. We've done some background checks, we've kept our eyes on your surfing talents, we've even dug into the volunteer work you've done with local agencies and some of the national charities you've worked with. Now you're on a larger stage and there's eyes on you. Eyes you don't know about."

"Like the guys in SoCal, Kate," Ashley taunted something that happened involving an incident. There was a secret among them.

"Let's start there, please." *Here we go, feels like a sorority. How did I ever become the Matriarch of this rabble?* Tamsen thought to herself. "Those are just some of the eyes on you. Guys, lots of guys, girls too, lots of girls - if that's your thing." Tamsen looked at Terri longer than she intended, thinking that Terri would react at the comment. Poker-faced Terri had no reaction. "We'd like to think that they all admire your cute face or body, but sometimes the intentions aren't pure. Sometimes they're downright evil. Sometimes..." she paused on purpose, "they are as evil as they can be. So, this is me telling you that the spotlight that will shine upon you isn't always warm and bright. There will be times when it illuminates things about you that you don't want it to."

"You sound like my mom," Ashley said.

"You sound like my dad," Zoey said.

"Good, and good," Tamsen replied.

"You sound like my bestie," Terri said.

"Great. That's the best bestie to have – the ones that try to keep you safe." Tamsen was merely touching on the admirer topic. It would become part of their onboarding cadence. Each call would need to address the fandom that would accompany being the face of the brand. She had a responsibility that she knew too well – to protect these young recruits, some innocent and some maybe not so much.

"Tamsen, I'll tell you about what Kate did in San Diego if you promise to ground her," Ashley was past the last lesson and back to the teasing.

Quickly, Kate replied to the bantering, "Works for me, can't think of a better place to be grounded." She picked up some binoculars from the desk and pretended that she was looking out the window. "Look at those Volcom boys out there shredding. Oh my, there's more on the beach. Yum. Yum."

"Alright, alright..." Tamsen needed to reign them in. "Cathouse talk one-oh-one, We talk trash, and it can be as gossipy and gritty or dirty as you want. But. But - it doesn't leave this circle. Deal?"

Heads nodded and four deals were committed.

Zoey added, "Tamsen, I didn't take you for a dirty talker. You like that kind of thing?"

"Oh, I can talk dirty. I've been a woman for a while now. Stories to tell." It was worthy of several giggles and Terri tossing more popcorn at the screen's camera.

"Okay – let's get down to the homework assignment. Who's got their charity of choice, their noble cause prepped and ready to pitch?"

Surprisingly, and welcomed, there wasn't silence like there was earlier. Each of them volunteered to go first and alphabetically they pitched why their cause might be the one which the other's would potentially rally around.

Best for last, it was Zoey with her charitable cause, *BOTA Benefits*. BOTA was an acronym for Be Open To Anything. The organization focused upon the potential for young abandoned pregnant women with newborns. Supporting them in their search for significance beyond motherhood, helping them with careers, clothing, baby items, simple necessities, and the important things such as purpose and self-esteem – Zoey provided the most compelling presentation, backing it up with data.

After her new teammates commended her, it was Tamsen's turn to turn on the compliments, "Well, it won't take much to convince HR to throw some cash toward BOTA. Very nicely done, Zoey."

Perfect teeth. Dark auburn hair. A surf hoody, navy with a white rope drawstring gathered at her small neck. The girl smiled, "Thanks." It was a heartfelt glow which was short-lived.

Tamsen sensed a little more there and asked, hoping it was a coaching moment. "Zoey, only if you're willing to share, why BOTA Benefits?"

Zoey paused, swallowing, "Well, I had a friend, years ago. And... And her younger sister disappeared. She went missing. And... And if that wasn't tough enough, it absolutely destroyed her family. Her dad left after a year. Her mom had her younger brother to care for, and that didn't go so well. And. She..."

"You don't have to finish if you don't..."

"I have to. I must. I must tell her story. Not my friend, Sara, but her mother, Sally. With Sally's daughter, Sara's younger sister, missing - and we don't know where...it was her mom, Sally. She committed suicide two years later. She took her own life, because all of her hope was lost." The girl had told the story before, fighting back tears and doing a good job at it. The noble cause of BOTA had ingrained itself in her.

Tamsen hearing it, and feeling the bravery within Zoey, cut into the stillness of the call, "I'm sorry ladies, I'll be right back." Her image-sharing dropped and the likeness of her filled her square on the Zoom call. The mute function lit up. Reaching for a tissue, Tamsen wiped the water gathering in her eyes away quickly. She reached for another to blow her nose, but there were none remaining. Her tee shirt served a necessary purpose. *Gross*, she thought.

The girls, Ashley, Terri, and Zoey briefly talked about the charity, Zoey's friend, and the tragedy of what happened to the mother, Sally. Kate was quiet, listening more to the sniffles in the next room than what was said on the call.

She took deep breaths to still the emotion. Four seconds in - slowly, four seconds out – slowly. Then, a dozen quick breaths to increase her heart rate.

Kate could see her prepping for a return to the call in the reflection of a mirror by the front door.

Tamsen's serenity was impressive. The tranquility was rehearsed and intentional. "Sorry. Had to let my dog out. He was scratching at the door. When you gotta go, you gotta go, ya know? Okay, back to it...*Zoey*, my goodness, Zoey - it's a 'yes' from me. I'll help champion your cause. We'll get a little help lodging the presentation to your liking onto a PowerPoint deck and you can tell your story. Going to cut the call short this time, because you made it all so easy today. Thank you, each of you for coming prepared. Aloha for now..."

Kate knew that there was no dog emergency. It was a fib. But, for what reason? Tamsen didn't even stand up. She watched her composure and surrogate strength command her true compassion for the abducted girl and the eventual misfortune that followed a mother's loss. Kate didn't understand a world of pain like that. It was material for a series on a streaming service or perhaps a fit for someone else's story – but didn't anchor itself within Kate. She realized she had much to learn from Tamsen, like how to fib for the right reasons and how to reason within the right fibs.

7

Secrets

A week later, and back in Manhattan at another coffee shop, a different location in the city, they met for the second time. There was more laughter, Allegra giggling at Jacob's colorful stories of his time leading Paisley Pierce Capital Management. The Day of Decadence made her ask questions about how quickly the prudence of reporting sexual harassment had changed over the past two decades.

"The compliance training we must do is ridiculous. Can't get those hours back. Same thing, over and over. Especially as line level managers and junior, seniors." As she spoke, Allegra fiddled with a sugar packet between them She told herself, '*No flirting this time. Keep it professional.*'

"Gilbert's Law," Jacob professed.

"Say what?"

He swirled the paper cup on the maple tabletop, stirring the milk he'd just charged his cup with. "The biggest problem with anything is that no one tells you what and how to do it. Want to fix the issue? Do this, not that. Want sexual harassment to go away? Report it. Hashtag me too. Said another way, you're a bit responsible for initiating things toward resolve."

"Who's Gilbert?"

'Long ago...an American politician, a newspaper man and business-man."

"Newspapers. Rest in peace."

"Not just yet. They're in a state of transition, like much else. History teaches us that the successors are the ones who meet the needs of the future. Which side would you rather be on? Perception or perspective?"

She clutched her notepad in front of her and leaned forward into the table separating them, "Jacob Paisley, you going deep on me?" She looked into his piercing blue eyes. *Easy,* she said to herself, *there's a sexual undertone there somewhere.*

"I wouldn't do that," he said. As he glanced into her sapphire blue eyes, he had Victoria's fire ignite within him. Her eyes were like the Ko Olina lagoons: deep, cool, and inviting. He swam to safety, finding Adele at the shore. "Naughty or nice? Did Santa Clause visit you?"

"Naughty, I guess. No Saint Nick this year." She tucked the sugar packet back in the bamboo cradle it came from. "Oh well, I'll try harder next year."

"And how about the offer letter. Is it signed?"

"Signed."

"Well, you gifted yourself a nice pay increase then, right?"

Allegra paused, flipping open her notebook to jot something down, holding it close to her check so that he did not see her script. "Right..." she said ever so slowly. Her sweater was a deep mulberry color and cashmere. A size smaller than she might normally have chosen, because she wanted it to fit tightly showcasing her breasts. Black tights hugged her hips. Mule kitten pumps with a small strap wrapped around her size seven feet. She crossed her legs, dangling one leg into the space between them knowingly feeling for his pantleg. The material from his trousers barely touched the toe of her shoe as she gently rocked the leopard skin print on the vamp of the soft leather pump between them. *Are you trying to play footsy with him? Pathetic.* "Right!" Allegra finally repeated, scribbling another note. She snuck a peek at him from the notepad jotting. He was taking the white plastic top from his coffee watching the steam rise slowly from the mouth of the brown paper cup. "What about you?"

"Me? Oh... Well, I'm the Kriss Kringle."

"Well," Allegra leaned forward again and said softly, "you missed me Kriss - this year. My stocking didn't get stuffed," God, *can you be any more obvious?* She blinked her eyes several times. Looking down at what she had written on the notepad, her faux lashes batted against her pink cheeks as she attempted to tone down the inklings and unintended cues.

"Maybe next year."

There it was. A spark of hope for something more, which she wondered if the randomness of the universe would help conspire to happen, was twinkling in the air between them. She gave him a slight smile and took another stroke at what she was scribbling.

"Old school. I didn't picture you as one to resort to paper and wet notetaking. Thought you'd be double thumbing it if at all."

Allegra was about to say, 'wet is good', but refrained, instead quoting herself, "You remember one hundred percent of what you write down."

"I used to think that too, until I lost a notebook much like yours with things I couldn't afford to lose. Then, simpleton me, lost a thumb drive which I couldn't lose, and things really got cagey. Just saying, be careful out there."

Allegra saw the open door and jumped in on the topic. "Cagey? As in how things transpired at your company, like..." she read his body language for permission to proceed. "Like with that woman, near the end of your run?"

"Victoria." He was comfortable enough to mention her name but said it without warmth. "My character. My ability to judge. My rationalization of right and wrong. All compromised. But if I didn't make those poor choices, I might not be in the position to make these substantial choices I'm making today. In other words, and not knowing it then, I needed to fail for something to transition."

"There's the Mentor." Allegra was beginning to see the man of influence Vendemer wanted her to meet up with. "And it didn't end well, I'm assuming with her?"

"She's... Well, she's..." Jacob, in his imagination, pictured her wearing orange with an eight-digit number on her clothing, sleeping on the top bunk, working in the laundry, reading every Dean Koontz book ever written, and nibbling at the highly processed foods in the cafeteria. He pictured beautiful Victoria being the apple of every inmate's eye, and not fitting in at the same time. "She's a part of my story. Whether I like it or not, I wouldn't be here if it didn't work out the way it did."

"I like that. Even though we fuck up, pardon the French, the mistakes can make us great too." She wanted to explore the edginess in this talk further.

"Fuck isn't French at all."

"Oo," she teased, "Do tell me more."

"I had a trader who wanted to build a fund, a public fund for exchange trade. Of course, 'F U C K' for a ticker. Salty and scandalous companies were the makeup of the constituents. Sin stocks. Microcaps on the pink sheets, mostly. The SEC would never go for it, but he researched the history of the expletive, and it turns out everyone wants some credit for it. The Scottish, the Scandinavians, the ancient Greeks, bastardized Latin and Middle English. It isn't an acronym like originally thought for people who wanted to get down and needing to have permission from the king, Fornication Under Consent of King or the one I like, hookers in old England tried for Forbidden Use of Carnal Knowledge. To the Norwegians, 'fukka' means to copulate and to the Swedish, 'focka' means to strike or push. So, no mention of French."

"So, what you're saying is we're fucking fucked in trying to find out where the fuck, fuck comes from?"

"I'd say, no one gives a flying fuck. You might have fit in nicely at PPCM." Jacob took his first sip. It had gone from steaming hot to lukewarm.

"Then I might not have become the tech tigress which I am today." She lifted her chin playfully into the air, bouncing her golden curls with one of her hands."

Before it landed, Jacob added, "you just would have become something else. Perhaps," He reached for his phone to check an incoming text message, "something more?" Looking up to her from the device, he took the pulse of the table.

"Perhaps. I'd say it worked out alright."

"I used to say that too. When I was at my best, giving cameos on CNBC, regional speaker engagements, meeting down at city hall with the pension planners, leading five hundred traders who made from four hundred net to ten million gross, annually. Seeing your name on the door and having a tribe of zealots hang on your words...it's a drug. It's a narcotic in a sense. Having people bring you things just because you're a CEO or the cream of your crop...is...well, it's wonderful. In a luminous event well after I expected what had happened to happen, floating in a leaking life raft in the deep blue Pacific, with my dog, Kolohe, and an infant in my arms..."

"You found God?!"

Jacob paused, surprised by the interruption, "Uh, no. but we're friends now, instead of enemies or strangers."

"I'm sorry, I'm cutting in. What did you find out?"

"That your success is an inhibitor to your potential. Don't get complacent. Don't settle. Don't let that vanity or arrogance get in the way of who you could become. Listen, there was a time that I thought I had it all. But 'all' wasn't ever enough. I continued to seek something, anything, everything – which I did not have. There was a desire...this want inside of me...that could never be fulfilled. When I was in a position where I had to manage that, I was capable of change. Change for the good. Otherwise, one hundred million would need to be two, then five, and so on."

"Wow, there's my Mentor again. You mean like become what you were meant to be."

"Well," Jacob squinted at the wooden grain on the table, "her name is Adele. This is who I'm with now."

"Adele?"

He nodded. "I hired her twenty years ago. She was married, had a small child, experienced a divorce, put her son through school then college, now has a grandson, and stuck with me for some reason through all of my mischief. We built a company together. She was my spine, my backbone. We were friends. Good friends. There might have been a point at the end where she was my only friend. And all along..." Jacob looked back to his coffee date, his mentee, this beautiful woman – breathing shallow breaths and hanging onto every word. "And all along I felt, there's something there. There's something more. The crime made was that I never explored that. I never told her. I never listened to love."

"Oh..." her shoulders slumped. "You two are deep. You go way back." Her shoulders slumped.

He became wistful in how he said it, "Way back. The days are long, the years are short."

"Like a child," Allegra paused, "and your company was your baby. You two raised it together."

Jacob made a clicking sound from the side of his mouth, and twisted his head, steering his eyes away from her, "She's all grown up now."

Music which was playing so low and quiet in the coffee shop that it couldn't be understood was turned up in volume. 10cc's, *I'm Not in Love*, played. Jacob smiled at the nostalgic and hauntingly beautiful sound from his early childhood, the pre-digital and mid-seventies. Allegra frowned, struggling to identify it somewhere in the past, but before her time. The coffee grinder made a deafening noise, difficult to speak above when it did its job of crushing the beans. Occasionally the fresh smell of a mocha latte or a hazelnut Frappuccino would envelope them.

His phone beeped again; a voice message appeared as a banner on the screen. Jacob looked into Allegra's eyes, "Would you like to meet her? She's close."

"Well, I..." Allegra was shaking her head 'no'.

"You'll like her. She'll love you."

"Sure." She couldn't say 'no' to him, could she?

Jacob and Allegra spent the next fifteen minutes discussing her skip-stepping through the brands of blue in the technology channel of original equipment manufacturers and value-added resellers. She was able to avoid telling him, this man she was encouraged to confide in, about any of her secrets. He was able to avoid a trip further down into the pit of his regrets.

Allegra explained her thought process at the volume of content that had been created in just the last ten years. How it acted as a distraction toward innovation and its abuse could plunge us into a period of cultural period which was opposite that of the Age of Enlightenment. Her opinion was that we were becoming narrower, instead of broader. He tallied with the ever-thirst for curiosity and development.

"You'd fit in nicely at my organization. Looking for a mid-level management position? We might have an open requisition."

Jacob chuckled, "I've got a good gig."

"Hey, you're supposed to watch the caffeine, doctor's orders." Adele appeared with Ruby. It wasn't what Jacob had pictured.

Having had Jacob to herself, in her imagination and at the table in the coffee shop, listening to the oldies, Allegra was flummoxed. *Who's the tag-a-long with the woman?* she wondered, looking to Jacob for an introduction. They stood, the four of them, shaking hands, introducing themselves. She looked up to the elderly black man, his hair was more white than grey. "I like your freckles on your cheeks," she said, pointing to her own cheeks.

Sheepishly, and in character, Ruby said, "Why thank you. You're Jacob's daughter?"

"Oh, no! God no! I'm too old for that." As she shook her head strongly, her blond curls jiggled. Allegra thought about what she had written in her notepad a half hour ago, which no one could ever see.

Adele, also in character, introduced Ruby as a good friend of theirs and from the neighborhood.

Allegra looked at Adele, admiringly. She was pretty. There was a sophistication to her. Together, standing next to Jacob, Allegra thought that they looked like a strong couple. As they collectively spoke further, Adele and Jacob finished each other's sentences and came to aid one another in what might be missing in a description. Allegra pictured them in a tower on billionaire's row, walking their dog in Central Park, having a picnic with their neighbor, Ruby. She also observed the way Adele looked up to Jacob. The wanting. It was there too. As much as she might feel a tinge of disappointment, she felt that she was in a class of distinction with these people. *Something's happening here*, her intuition told her.

The music played another tune which Allegra couldn't easily identify until the chorus called it out. Sly & The Family Stone's hit song, *Everyday People*, played on the speakers. The horns blasted the song of unity, taking some of its inspiration from Mother Goose through its lyrics. *Maybe I was just born in the wrong decade*, Allegra thought to herself. Watching Adele touch Jacob's forearm, giggle at the words coming from his mouth, drawing Ruby into the conversation, complimenting her on what she was wearing...Allegra couldn't disrespect the boundaries here.

After they agreed to connect in a couple days, perhaps over a glass or two of wine at The Plaza, Adele asked Allegra where she lived. When she explained her riverside apartment in Brooklyn, Adele pivoted, "Oh right across the East River. We can get together in East Village or the Lower East Side if that's more convenient for you..."

That was what people of true influence did, Allegra acknowledged. They enabled your success, comfort, and ease of adaptation. Their compliments hit the bullseyes. She touched her jacket, commending it softness. She endorsed her bag, caressing the soft leather and acknowledging the color choice. It was camel colored and matched little in Allegra's wardrobe. She congratulated her on her promotion – stating that the Women in Technology Network was a rising force which they donated to. As welcoming as Adele was, she felt a bit outclassed by her. She also knew what she had to do the moment they left each other's company.

They said their goodbyes with Allegra remaining behind to make a fake call. At the bottom of the page which she was pretending that notes were being taken on, she wrote *I want to screw him – so hard - right now!* She ripped the page from the spiral ring binder and ripped it into twenty pieces before tossing it in a trashcan where final sips of coffee and their dark grounds would surely drown the salty wish which diminished when she met Adele.

*****

As he was driving there, he thought about target practice. His marksmanship had improved considerably. Aiden Ashford's aim, stability of hold, breath control, trigger control, and follow through were each enhanced through target practice, the simulations, and range drills he had been taking. Even in the paintball and laser tag arena, he partook for the agility training of leaping and firing. He'd attained top score, taking out a team of seventeen-year-olds. With the handguns, the rifles, and the shotguns, he was beginning to master his shooting skills. The automatic rifles, his qualified instructors told him, take longer. He was nearly 20,000 rounds in. A year's practice – and he was just obtaining a marksmanship score of 75. No one achieved a score greater than 90 while in combat mode. This is what he was preparing for: combat mode.

He turned off the engine, sitting in her driveway. *"Where are you?"* he whispered to himself before he opened the door.

She took his money, eagerly. The room was dark. Three small dim mood lights - a midnight purple, an azure blue, and a seaweed green – were lit behind the ruby sheer curtains which they sat face to face within. Her request was that he remove his ball cap, shoes and any jewelry. He kicked off the dress sneakers and had no jewelry to take off.

"Aiden?" the medium asked. "What kind of a name is that?" She spoke slowly and tranquil as she asked a few questions. Her balmy demeanor was serene and tranquil. The robe she wore was silky and indigo as it shimmered in the Stygian lighting. She was much older than he pictured her being. Almost frail, she moved slowly.

"The kind my biological mother gave me. The one who didn't want me or couldn't keep me...or...whatever." He had his doubts about what was about to happen but was desperate. The research online suggested just that – that this sixth sense was a claimed ability to acquire information beyond normal sensory contact.

"And Ashford? What kind of name is that? Is that, Irish?"

"It's the kind that my adopted parents gave me. Lovely people." He shrugged his shoulders at what he said next, "I don't really know what I am. No 23andMe for me."

"Shh. Allow me..." She held her hand between them in the air. Her fingernails were long, painted gloss black and tickled the air as she pulled her hand back to herself, then toward gentle plumes of incense off to the side of them, smoking in the still air. The movement of her fingers was slow and the coordinated finger grabbing of the nothingness in the air caused the incense smoke to waft toward them. The smoke smelled like sandalwood and jasmine.

Ashford took a deep breath, liking the sweetness. He did feel calm and serene.

The she...? It was Lady Barbara. Her mascara was thick. Much thicker than his Ashley, who also liked the smoky look, wore. Eyeliner, painted on her upper and lower eyelids, added to the ghoulish vibe she was showcasing. Lady Barbara played her part. Mysterious and haunting, yet soothing and peaceful.

Ashford was listening to flutes and soft instrument sounds playing quietly from speakers that surrounded. He felt that she was approachable and was fluid in managing the excitability which he had coming into her home, to a state of sereneness.

"Tell me a little about yourself" Lady Barabara directed him, again speaking slowly and gently. Her voice was deep and raspy.

"I grew up in New Mexico and we moved to Florida when I was young. My parents worked for a fab plant north of Albuquerque."

Lady Barbara cautiously held one finger with an exceptionally long and curling nail in the air between them. "Mm. Fab plant...what is this fab plant?"

"Intel. A fabrication plant where they make chips. Processors for computers. Rio Rancho, New Mexico. Intel had...or still has...a large factory there."

"Shh. Say no more about this. For this is not why you are here."

"Tell me about yourself and the woman you seek. Tell me about the two of you together." There were slow and deliberate pauses between her requests. "About how she made you feel. About your desire for her. You're longing for her back into your life... No?"

"Yes." Ashford was never so certain about anything. This was a clarity session if anything.

A black cat with green eyes, watching their every move, licked its lips out of boredom. It wagged its tail through the air gracefully, just as she did with her long fingernails, and disappeared into a darker corner of the room.

Divination, the practice of determining hidden significance's of events, foretelling the future, and attempting to gain insights into questions or situations, includes scrying. Scrying is the seeing or sensing the guidance, the revelation, and the inspiration from spirits. Some forms of scrying include rituals or altered states of awareness or even consciousness. Reducing mental clutter and enabling an emergence of visual images or auditory sensations was what practitioners commonly induced. The dark colors, soft lighting, gentle and quiet sounds in the background aided Lady Barbara in purposefully alleviating any anxiety walking in the door with Ashford.

Lady Barbara had done her research. She knew, and shared in a small way, the loss he was coping with. Her craft was accustomed to helping with closure, be it ongoing or well in the past.

Scryers attempted to induce the feedback loop through various tools, such as water, crystals, stones, smoke, or mirrors. Crystal balls, trances, and an item of importance from a victim or lost one were mechanisms to assist in revealing the past, present, or future state. Lady Barbara resorted to all these resources for her clients. The two hundred dollars, in twenties, sat folded in an olive bowl near where he took off his shoes.

He spoke slowly at first about Ashley. As if in a trance, describing when they met. The joy he saw in her eyes, deep into the soul, the person she was. Ashford told the woman about how she made him feel, what holding her hand meant to him, the smell of her skin, the warmth of her smile. It was only once that his eyes welled with tears – when he shared that he thought she was a courageous spirit.

Describing Ashley's final known cry to her captors as they attempted to abduct the child in the schoolyard, "Over my dead body..." was the heroism which led to that heinous moment.

"Hold my hand, Ashford." Lady Barbara's skin was paper-thin. "You are strong. You are preparing for a battle." Then, she whispered. "You are wise in this conquest. You will face evil spirits. You must be stronger than they, but..." She paused. "But not for your woman..." Her eyes remained closed. "For you..."

"What do you see?" Ashford felt a spookiness in the whispers from the clairvoyant. The hair on the back of his neck rose and a tingle was felt down his back. He shivered.

"I do not see..." Lady Barbara squeezed her closed eyes tighter, "I hear. I am listening to a woman. It is not your woman, but another." Lady Barbara's breathing was faster, "She is showing me the way. A long and flowing gown she is wearing. It is golden."

Ashford watched her describing what she saw with her eyes closed. She was quiet, saying nothing, but gently rocking her head in several directions in small turns of her neck.

"Ashley. Ashley, where are you?" The medium's voice grew louder... "Ashley, show yourself." Lady Barbara attempted a gentler approach, "Ashley – my darling, please. Please Ashley, I am here with Ashford. He is trying to reach you. He is searching for you... Do not be afraid."

Ashford felt perspiration forming on his forehead and under his arms as he held Lady Barbara's hand. The still air grew stale. The smoke from the incense billowed up into the canopy of the curtains surrounding them. Sweat formed on his back and the midriff of his torso. It was creepy.

"Vindica te tibi," she spoke as if in a trance, speaking in tongues. She said it again, louder, "Vindica te tibi..." Lady Barbara's hand gripped Ashford's as she pressed on with the chant, "Vindica... te...tibi..." Ashford watched as her face contorted in what appeared to be from a painful and oblique vision: "Vindica te tibi!" she shouted.

Then she stopped. Quickly she released his hand, and pulled away from Ashford, clutching a crystal necklace dangling from within her robe. She opened her eyes wide and looked at the crystal. Large, gaudy, reflecting the dim jewel-toned lighting, glimmers sparkled against the sheers. She looked into Ashford's eyes, seeing what he did not, and whispered the Latin, "Vindica te tibi..."

Ashford paused, allowing it to sink in. "What does it mean?" he asked slowly and carefully.

Lady Barbara's words were hallowed, sanctifying the meaning, "Claim your freedom. Get your power back, Ashford."

"What about Ashley?" he said glumly, "Where is she? What did you see?"

"I saw nothing, I heard a voice from a place where the woman took me. It is not here. It was not a light place, nor a dark place but a cry from a neutral plane saying '*Vindica te tibi*' which means emancipate yourself. Lay claim to yourself. It means stop time from being stolen from you. Do not let it slip away. She, Ashley...she is not here. If it was her voice, speaking, she is away from here – I do not know where."

"What did it sound like? The voice?"

"It sounded like a gentle warning. A murmur perhaps. *Ne obliviscaris vivere.* This means, 'remember to live.'

"Like Carpe Diem?" Ashford asked.

"Yes." Lady Barbara reached for a plum-colored candle which was tucked between pillows. Out of thin air she lit a match. The flicker illuminated the dark space they were in. The sweat which had been forming on him, in his pits, up and down his back, on his forehead – now cooled him. The enclave which they were in changed from warm and humid to cooler, adding a peculiarity to the moment. The match lit the candle and immediately he smelled a rich and creamy depth.

A velvety embrace surrounded him. A subtle hint of sweetness enveloped the small space. He felt comforted. "I... I didn't expect this sensation." Ashford's voice was free from judgement.

"Remember you must die, therefore do not forget to live." Lady Barbara said as if someone else were within the sheer curtains with them. There was no one. She turned to Ashford again with the warning, "Vindica te tibi – this was as far as the spoken words would travel."

Ashford knew recurring revenue better than anyone else. Software engineers knew that software makes the world go round. Create new software and it drives the demand for new hardware. He felt it coming.

"Should we see each other again – to see where the voice leads next?"

Ashford paused, calibrating what had just happened and what might happen next. He needed to process. "Yes, perhaps," he said. 'No, *maybe not'*, he thought. There it was: recurring revenue. But maybe, just maybe – another two hundred dollars would find its way into an olive wooden bowl. This, after all, was as close as Ashford had felt to Ashley beyond his memories of her, the pictures of her, the moment-after-moment reminders of his purpose – to reunite with her wherever she might be.

After they said their goodbyes without an affirmative action for their next meeting, Ashford walked to his truck which was parked in her driveway. He stopped and turned back toward the small porch. He knocked on the thick wooden door with no window and she opened it slowly.

"I'm sorry. But maybe you can help me. You said something about preparing for battle…?"

She did not invite him back into her home. The black cat made a nosey appearance by her side. Seeing that it was him, it again curled its tail and dismissed him as unintriguing. "Be strong. Be strong for you. Your heart is tender, but your strength is increasing. This body you are making…it is your armor from evil. Live. Do it for you."

"Can you tell me…"

She slowly closed the door on him.

"Well, that's a bit of a cliffhanger." Ashford said it to the closed door between them. He thought that the workout ahead of him today might be special. Do it for yourself…*and do it for Ashley…*he thought. Prepare for battle. You'll face evil spirits. *Solid advice? Or poppycock?* Ashford returned to the Ford and once inside looked at her picture on the face of his phone. He remembered Lady Barbara, attempting to summon her: *…Ashley, my darling…*

✳ ✳ ✳ ✳ ✳

The pickups rolled onto Steve Booth's property with a speedy force. Two had Florida plates, the other was from the Peach State. Although some referred to it as the peanut state. Peaches aren't in the top ten agricultural products of the state. Peanuts, on the other hand, account for half of the nation's yield. When the Franciscan monks first introduce peaches to the islands along Georgia's coast in 1571, they had no idea that they were introducing controversy.

Spanish moss stretched from tree to tree. It's grey-green reach smothered some branches of the cypress trees and adorned others. The tiny leaves on the brush and low-growing trees surrounding the property were thick and dense. It was difficult to see into the marshes, water lands and swampy areas close by, the places where the rice rats, snakes, and alligators called home.

"Thdevie Booth!" the pinky cutter exclaimed as he crawled out of the first pickup. That was all that was said. Steve placed his hand missing a finger in his pocket. "God, it stinks here. Smells like something died."

The Dodge was in much need of a rinse as mud splatters covered it from grill to bumper. Only the windshield was clean and only in the areas of the wiper blades. Since Steve was short, and the cutter was slightly above average in height, Steve was a head shorter than his tormentor. As the others climbed from their pickups, five men and a woman, they stretched – indicating they had a drive behind them and were tired. Only the cutter was addressing Steve. The others gathered at a picnic table and dug into the white paper fast food bags. Since they had not yet reached Everglades City where a couple additional choices were offered, the bags from Subway contained build to order sandwiches, chips and fountain drinks. They argued over the wrapped contents and jibbed each other, excluding Steve from the conversation. Ignored and left alone, he had no portion offered to him out of inclusion or acknowledging his presence.

"I alwayth liked Mommath thubs," Steve whispered to himself as he turned to the outdoor refrigerator for a cold Coca-Cola. He thought of his Momma's subs, the leftover spaghetti on the toasted Wonder Bread bun. A slice of Kraft singles was melted on top as it cooled. He pried the tab of the can with his right hand, the one with all the fingers. It sprung into life, the sugary fizzy carbonation hissing with a whisper that a refreshing beverage and the accompanying "ah" sound was soon to follow.

Steve watched as the six of them teased each other, joked, laughed, and whispered secret things so that he couldn't hear their discussion. He felt left out, alone again in the company of others. "Thath okay," Steve said to himself. Looking down to where the pinky might have been, he knew now not to think for himself – especially when it concerned the product.

This was unusual. Three pickups. The exchange of the product usually involved one pickup and one white panel van. They normally traveled in from Miami and southeast Florida coastal cities, across the everglades to Steve's hidden location. It was far away from a missing person's search and ripe with a large population. Florida ranked third in the United States in the number of mission persons, behind California and Texas.

They let Steve know of quantities but didn't allow him to watch the exchange due to his previous interest and engagement. He no longer knew where the emergency key to the padlocks was located. Merely, 'three out, two in', or 'four out, one in, or 'one out, three in' to balance the inventory of the product to a net number between nine and twelve. He had become a slave to the maintenance of the product, never again seeing the faces which came and left under his care.

He had learned to adapt to this. Occasionally, as an exchange would take place, Steve would be asked to face away from the back of the unit – to face his shanty. A small mirror in the outside area where his refrigerator was located would let him glimpse them. Black, red-headed, Hispanic, boy, girl, blond, Caucasian, young, too young, older, surprisingly older. This small peak at them was his only connection. That, and the cries from the first nights. As faint as it was, suppressed by the layers of insulation inside and outside of the compartment, the crying was something which he closely listened to while not wanting to hear at the same time. He no longer responded. Instead, he looked at his left hand, missing the pinky.

The product. It was how the organization...the side hustle or in Steve-speak, his 'thide-huthle'...referred to the victims. From missing to forever gone, the location of Everglade City which was hidden away from it all and easy to forget about, would cleverly conceal the victims. They would be out of visibility for a lengthy period following their disappearance. As the urgency surrounding their disappearance would die down, they'd be exchanged for a new product. The Ten Thousand Islands National Park off the coastline of southeastern Florida was the cell which Steve worked for. He was bonded to this syndicate until he was no longer required, which meant to the cabal that Steve would no longer exist.

Serving to live had become Steve's lot. The coven of criminals discarded him seriously. He couldn't speak clearly. His intellect was short of their standards. As a generalization, society had found him somewhat odd. Only online relationships with others somewhat like him were his connection in a form of a community. Left to think for himself, Steve's intentions meandered but were genuinely not pure. He knew all of this, able to evaluate where he stood. Momma's boy, Thdeve, missing most of his four front teeth was always on the outside, looking in.

"Hey Steve," they finally called out to him, "come here, brother." He'd never been called a brother before.

He set down the red can which was nearly finished and burped as he stood up. As he walked to their table, he let out another belch. "Ethcuse me," he said.

A man in their klatch which Steve hadn't seen before was speaking to him. "No problem, Steve. Listen, one of our cells in Southern California was ambushed by some do-gooder militant types. We're beefing up security in Cali, Texas, and your fortress here in the Everglades."

He didn't know they referred to the trailer and his property straddled by brush, non-navigable swamp, and countless acres of marshy alligator infested sprawl as a fortress.

"We're putting in more cameras, alarms, smoke bombs, and some air detection devices. You know, a no drone zone. There will be several areas you can no longer walk in. We'll point those out to keep you safe. Sound good, buddy?"

He was nice. The finger cutter watched and sneered and turned his back to Steve while finishing the rest of his sandwich. The nice one repeated himself. You hear me? Sound good there, Steve? Keep you safe."

"Thoundth good. Thank you." Steve shook his head, glancing at the trailer where the product was located.

"No prisoner exchange today, just some tech work. That's why all these people are here."

A kerfuffle of some sort had broken out at the small table where the six of them sat. There was the nice one, the cutter, and the other four who were laughing at each other. They were all wearing jeans or cargo pants, light green or camouflage tee shirts, boots, and had handguns strapped to their hips. The sidearms appeared to be Army issued SIG Sauer M17s. The 9mm pistols were coyote brown and black. The safari-colored holsters held them tightly to each hip of the sandwich eaters.

Steve listened to their banter. Two men were talking to the woman. They were the kind of young men which would pick on him, make fun of him, perform some sort of mean-spirited prank on him if they were in high school together. He could tell. Their bravado was loud. *Too loud,* Steve thought. The woman was standing up for herself, she seemed to have the better of them in their discussion.

"You want to know what a real man has to offer, look no further..."

"That little pickle isn't getting anywhere near me," she interrupted him.

The others laughed, which only made their banter louder. He was sitting next to her and stroked the side of her shoulder, touching the back of her arm. Tattoos on his forearms were in cursive. The immortal script of a word Steve didn't understand was flanked by an eagle and a wolf. The verbal volleyball escalated in its bragging volume as the others chimed in too. The six of them were exchanging words and it appeared that there were two sides. One of the men stood, clutching his crotch offering a service of some sort. They were loud again. *Too loud*, Steve whispered to himself. She stood her ground, "I don't care for baby dills and sometimes cucumbers are best peeled and sliced!" A ten-inch Bowie Knife was pulled from its sheath on her other hip and with incredible force, stabbed the table in front of them in one fell swoop. She looked at the fondeler, and added, "Keep your hands to yourself!"

The table erupted, "Oh Billy just lost his dangling ding-a-ling..." This was the most noise made in this area perhaps ever, Steve thought. The ribbing continued with the woman wiggling the point of the knife from the table, waving it toward another of the men, slipping it back in its sheath at her waist.

The laughter and finger pointing diminished as soon as the nice one who was the leader commanded their direction. "Okay you bone-heads, we've got work to do. Grab the gear."

The cutter walked to the truck which meant he walked by Steve. "What do you think about that, *Thdeve*? A little amputation humor."

Steve thought about it all the time. Whenever he turned a wrench on a diesel engine. He wished as he installed a fifteen-pound starter in a tight space, that the extra finger would help lift the part. His hand dexterity and strength had left him periled in some mechanical work. What took him an hour before the missing digit, now took two. Occasionally, he would need to jimmy alternate ways of doing what he once did in new and more dangerous ways.

"Where's your sandwich, Steve? Awe...we didn't get you one. Well, maybe next time," the cutter said as he returned with a heavy box on his shoulder, passing Steve heading toward the metal container housing the product. Short in breath from carrying the load, "Maybe chicken fingers are your thing, *Thdeve*." He chuckled, then grunted, as he dropped the box. It made a clanging sound which caused Steve to jump. No one saw it. "Next time. A binding contract, just between us buddies. Pinky promise." The cutter held out his hand with his dirty pinky extended in the air toward Steve. He chuckled to himself, let the hand fall to his side after it wasn't met with Steve's missing finger, and returned to the dirty pickup for the next box of materials.

The phantom sensations from the missing finger were still present. He read on the internet that it often takes two to three years to subside. It may never vanish completely. Steve looked at the missing area, scared and blunt at the knuckle. He too had work of his own to do. The small block heat exchanger on his workbench wasn't going to clean itself. Grabbing the acid and end gaskets, Steve went on about his normal routine while stopping occasionally to see all the technological enhancements the team was making to his southern Floridian fortress.

*****

A $20,000 anonymous donation was made.

Brian and Laki Kekahanamanui were the "anonymous" donors. They felt genuine joy this great several times before their random benevolence. When they met and fell in love, when they got married, when their daughter was born, when their son was born. The $20,000 may not have gone to the neediest cause. Their friend and her two small children – their financial hardship and emerging predicaments weren't as dire as they might have become. Perhaps things would have worked out.

"Resolution enhancers were at work within the universe." Laki believed in fate. Supernatural powers beyond a person's control, an unexplained and unknowing occurrence toward a plan, the mysterious causes drawing an event to happen – these were the unseen things which lived above the clouds and within us.

"That was plain bizarre." Brian believed in those things as well, when it was pillow talk. His foundation was grounded in the grind of the football field. Falling off a surfboard because you lost your balance, then paddling back out to catch the next wave off at Makaha beach. Standing up for yourself, because no one else would. The cause and effect of things happening because of reasons was the moxie he brought to the show. His loadstone was grounded in points on a scoreboard from something you and your team did. But he couldn't put his finger on the event. Why? Why did two strangers roll up behind them and hand them two installments, seconds apart, for exactly $10,000 each which coincidentally equaled the grand total amount they were heading to a fundraiser for? He lost sleep over attempting to solve the 'why?' in thought.

"Should we ever, like ever, mention to anyone, that we were the benefactors?"

"Never," Brian shook his head slowly. He used the remote to turn the TV off.

"Never?" Laki asked, turning to see him for doubt. There was none to be found.

"Some secrets are yours to keep." He shrugged as he looked around the room at the lines where the blue room met the Arizona white ceilings. Almost perfect. *DIY good enough*, he called it. "Their faces. Like, they thought we were drug dealers or something. Like...they were as baffled as we were. Like...like they didn't know what they were doing there."

"Like maybe they thought we were gangsters?"

"It was strange. But at the same time, he was nice. And she was prim and proper and pretty and...I don't know. Whack-a-doodle bizarre."

"Sound like you're Auntie and your Uncle there, Bri. Thought I heard some Pidgin there too." Laki smiled at the eternal Hawaiian in him.

"Can't take the rock outta' da boy, cuz." He teased.

She thought about what he said of secrets. "You have secrets you keep from me?" Laki was brushing her long chestnut hair. She was ready for bed, sitting in front of the mirror in their newly painted true-blue bedroom. "What don't I know about you?"

"Ugh…" Brian was tired and didn't want to get into it but would if required to.

"I'm serious. Tell me a secret."

"Alright. You want to know about me making it to third base with Malia Iolana my senior year?"

"Oo, gross. Keep that secret to yourself. I met her at your high school class reunion. She's still into you. She's a little skanky if you ask me."

"I didn't." Brian was happy with himself for fending off a deep conversation as he began to drift off.

"Well, I don't have any secrets like that because you know all the boys I've been with and what we did together. Open book, complete honesty. No Malia-like secrets from me." She looked in the mirror to see his eyes growing heavy. "I think we should tell someone."

"Why?"

He wasn't as asleep as she thought. "Put it out there and see if karma finds its way back to you, maybe?"

Brian propped himself up on one elbow on the pillows. Their print matched the color of the room. "Do you think we should crack the window?"

Laki took a deep breath. "Smells good to me. Clean. Fresh."

"Karma… It means," Brian sat up. "Karma is about action. Knowing that you took an action, good actions and bad actions, is part of a journey. It isn't about being perfect, but rather about becoming more of what you really are and undoing what you aren't. There are twelve laws of karma which serve as a guide for how to live."

"Alright Mr. Philosophy, so you do have an affirmative opinion here."

Brian scoffed at the borrowed conviction, "Professor Hatfield did. Intro to Philosophy, Freshman Year. Go Aztecs." He slipped off his tee shirts and dropped his jeans to the floor, kicking them with his foot up into the air, catching them midway through the arc in the air. Tossing them in the white wicker laundry basket in the corner of the room he collapsed back on the mattress into the fluffy goose down-filled duvet. His broad shoulders and brown skin were a contrast to the stark white comforter on the queen-sized bed.

"On...?" she looked at her husband lying on the bed, staring at the ceiling "or...off?"

"What's that?" He looked at her.

"My PJ's?" she pulled the top draw string revealing an abundance of brown skinned Polynesian cleavage. "On because it's chilly outside and you're too frugal to turn the heat on in winter."

"It's San Diego," he whispered playfully. He smiled at where he thought this might be going.

"Or off, because you'll...well," she looked down at his boxers, "you know, warm me up."

"Off. Definitely...off." Laki flipped the switch on the lamp and took off her pajamas. Climbing into the sheets naked, she said. "It'll be our secret, the money. No one will ever need to know."

"There's something special - about doing something amazing - for someone - and they don't know much about it. You can revel in the mystery of it with them, knowing all along what happened. But you...I guess...maybe you, foster a deeper faith and understanding in the power of human kindness." He closed his eyes again. "Something like that," he added, yawning.

Together they lay there, in the fleeting heartbeats of another day turned night, feeling the warmth of each other.

"I love you, so much." Laki snuggled up to Brian. "You are a good man. You know that, right?" She looked at him in the dark of the room filled only with shadows from the low lights outside, she could see him slowly closing his big brown eyes a final time.

"Mmm…" He held her in his left arm, and she laid her head on his chest. He gently stroked her long brunette hair a half dozen times before drifting off into a deep slumber.

Secrets were sometimes crafted in tender moments like these. Others were long drawn-out strategies with sophisticated plot lines and layers of benchmarks ensuring their undoing. Others were made from simple pinky promises.

*****

Maggie was surprised at the cancellations in Vendemer's calendar. *Push, recall, cancel, postpone, modify, withdraw,* and *virtual-only* were the various descriptions which populated Allegra's now less-busy Outlook assignments in the coming weeks. This was her integration into senior leadership should be taking place with strategy sessions, speaking engagements, cross-boarding, and taking the quiet chair at the executive table should be taking place. None of that was populating her month ahead. Perhaps it would follow. She became distracted when her boyfriend texted her sexual suggestions. A smile, a shake of the head, and a look up from her phone to ensure no one was watching her guilty pleasure at work occupied her more than the unusualness of Allegra's lack of productivity ahead.

Working in a private equity value-added reseller company wasn't much different than their tenure in working with the public companies. There were still end of month and end of quarter timelines. The quotas never went away and were always higher than the sales reps found attainable. By the miracle of God and the power of man, those same quotas would be crushed, and Administrative Admin, Maggie, would scramble with the same divine dominion to source a venue for an epic celebration for record-setting performances. The Chairman's celebration would feature the most progressive performers for even-loftier recognition. She participated in none of it. But it sounded awesome. Maggie was on Allegra's coattails, to a degree. It was satisfying, playing with the house's money. Prying the corporate credit card from her wallet in her hand-me-over designer bag to pay for thirty grand of tickets at a Yankees game, or C-row seating on Broadway, or restaurant buy-outs with or without the Prix-Fixe menus was a rush. Maggie felt like it was a big deal when she was booking an arrangement with the partner's money. It was good enough.

Allegra's number lit up her cell. "What are you doing?"

"What's that?"

"Like, you still work here, don't you?"

"I'm working from home today. Yesterday I had a mentor-thing that Vendemer set up..."

"With the hot older gentleman?" Maggie said it, rolling her eyes, "You watch yourself there, girl."

"Yes, with George Clooney – or maybe Patrick Dempsey – I don't know."

"He's off the table, that ship has sailed, the bus left the station, and all of that." Allegra, on the other end of the call, stuck out her bottom lip, pouting. She wouldn't share the thought alive and well within her that she still wanted Jacob Paisley. This consumption didn't happen often. But when it did, it absorbed all the imagination between her ears.

"Good to hear it." Maggie nodded, having to play the parent to Allegra didn't happen often enough. "Stay strong woman..." she said holding a fist in front of herself, "Stay strong there."

"Met his lady friend and she's awesome too. She's pretty. A sophisticated kind of beauty, like when you get better looking with age. She even smells good." Allegra scrunched up her nose at the thought of Adele. Refined, polished, well-mannered, anyone-might-like-almost-anything-she-does Adele. She was what a handsome and smart and sugar daddy like Jacob might deserve. Although his naughty side needed a little more exploring. *There was a flicker of intimacy in how he looked at her*, she thought. Silence filled the minute.

"Graceful, good looks – I think that's called," Maggie suggested. Maggie held the phone away from her face to see if the call had been dropped. It didn't. There was just an unusual and elongated pause. "Earth to Allegra, are you hearing us Allegra Sinclair...?"

"What's with all the calendar jockeying going on?" Allegra finally asked.

"That's what I want to know. I thought you would be taking on more in the new role and all I see is less. You're like a free agent." Maggie was curious.

"I'm sure it's the calm before the storm." Allegra played her part, knowing what she knew.

"Enjoy it, I guess. The next quarter will be here before you know it."

Allegra toggled through her email and said, "Oh...that's interesting."

"What is?"

"Speak of the devil. Vendemer wants me to meet him tomorrow at the United Nations building."

"I didn't know we had a proposal out with them. You and what sales rep? Who owns the UN?"

"We don't. It wouldn't be in my jurisdiction anyway. The UN would align to a Fed rep in public sector."

"Hmm..." Maggie spun her chair to her desktop and clicked on the company's application, the Account Lookup Information System they called ALIS, because everything in information technology seemed to need an acronym including the name of the industry, IT. "ALIS doesn't have it assigned to anyone."

"You got to break it down. It would be parceled out by the departments and agencies. There's like the general assembly, and the economic and social council, and the security council and like blah, blah, blah...I don't know what else. Civics class wasn't my thing."

"The teacher probably wasn't old enough or hot enough."

"Ah. Take that back." Allegra was smiling as she said it, and Maggie knew it. "I was what fourteen or fifteen back then."

"And when did you know you had a thing for older, confident, wealthy..."

"I have a relationship with my father, I'll remind you..."

"No, you do not. Girl, get a grip with your reality. You have a thing." Maggie caught on to Allegra's thing soon after they met. In the world of men at her feet, the twenty and thirty-something-year-olds which threw themselves at Allegra and her wit and her beauty and her *Joie de vivre*, which meant zest for life – were emaciated gestures. She liked what she liked, and it wasn't what was easy. It was what she didn't and couldn't have. Maggie also wondered how the trade-off of getting someday what she wanted would alter her friend. Allegra was riding the restless spirit thoroughbred from one race into the next, jockeying win after win. This wouldn't always be the case, and Maggie knew she'd have to fend for herself at some point.

"It's a shit-ton of people that call on the UN. I found...oh, it keeps going..." Allegra's voice trailed as she investigated the same tool that Maggie was wincing at. "I'm not coordinating anything on such a short order, I'm just going to show up and talk shop. Say what I've got to say about generative AI, and digital transformation, and data-sharing, and..."

"And you're going to do your thing where you look beautiful, dress awesome, talk smart, and people love you and give you a PO."

"I walk in with a look of humble determination. I never walk in expecting a purchase order, but I walk out with a PO sometimes – and maybe a smile on my face."

"Yeah...whatever. It's still an industry dominated by dudes..."

"Less every day. Got to sharpen your saw."

"Okay – so you and Vendemer are on at the UN for looks like ninety minutes and you have just three other appointments for tomorrow?" Maggie asked, clicking into the day after tomorrow.

"Yeah, I'll get some time with BenVen to go over the buildout from here."

"Hey. Allegra. I've got to cut – the other lines are on fire, and they sent me an instant message to help run point on routing."

"You go do that. Ciao for now."

After the call was dropped, Allegra went to Jacob's page on LinkedIn again as a ghost. Incognito mode, to the best of her knowledge, allowed her to browse without storing search history. The discreet queries led by non-tracking search engines was a big of a guise. Even Allegra should have known that behind every click on the internet, there was a commercial curiosity behind the consumer's curiosity.

✷✷✷✷✷

Ashford's simple God Questions were legitimate, "Why did this happen? Why do bad things happen to good people? Why was Ashley taken?" They were, now, asked but unanswered. He had too much time on his hands. All idle time was filled with meditation – revenge therapy – strategy sessions – delving into the darkness online, seeking clues – and God Questions.

The Gun Show was this weekend. He had leveraged his savings, cashed out on the I-series bonds which they'd saved, sold his prized baseball card collection, and redeemed a cash-value life insurance policy his parents gifted him – all to buy more ammo and anything of projectile interest while at the Expo Hall. His arsenal was growing. From the knives to the Ak-15s to the handguns to rifles and shotguns, he had more artillery and firepower than he thought could be shot his way. It had become an obsession. Automatic and semi-automatics with bump stocks, he traded and brokered deals into cash into the hoard of weaponry. He often wondered whether the same captors were walking alongside him at one of the events.

The captors. There wasn't a clear description which Ashford could provide the police with when Ashley was abducted. Most of the time, they had their back to him, facing her. Their clothing was of no use, although it stated what they were last wearing. The suspect description was three years old.

He needed a new name for these contemptible assailants. Their sordid ways were atrocious. Ashford took to the internet to study evil. According to an article he favored on the nature of evil, there were two descriptions. Moral Evil, which covered the willful acts of human beings against each other. This included rape and murder. Then there was Natural Evil, which included natural disasters. Famines, floods, hurricanes, tornadoes and other Acts of God or misdoings from Mother Nature fell into this category. The malfeasances were clearly Moral Evils. His study then led to the reasons behind the vile deeds which were the face of the Moral Evils. The behaviors behind what made a person evil included neglect, hatred, psychological traumas, selfishness, expediency, ignorance, and destructive values.

Ashford played up and downplayed the motives for evil, depending upon the euphemisms of what he was reading. The volume of content about the topic of evil was overwhelming. One thought fed another. Roads twisted quickly as one web page provided a course of corruption and another a course for recovery. In all his research, he was sure that this was where the dark passengers climbed aboard their bus to hell's depth.

Left alone in his thoughts, he was able to return to how he got here. Recanting his bachelorhood in his twenties and half of the thirties – he knew how acting as a lone wolf wasn't as joyous and the wonderland which the two shared. Yet here he was alone, required to play the part of the carnivorous beast which could feed on a deer, a moose, an elk, or a beaver. But wolves would not eat other wolves. Only if it was a dire condition, and another wolf had died would a wolf cannibalize from its own kind. These wanton wolves needed to be hunted, skinned alive, and burned – feeling pain upon pain.

Was it just her? Or was there more to the story? The unanswered questions were haunting him. It was worse than Ashley's parents blaming him. "If you two weren't together, none of this would have happened." There was no unifying of force. After the first year, their blame casting was strong. Their thoughts...Ashford had a part in her disappearance because in some odd way – she would have returned home or moved elsewhere, or some other fate of favor would have found her. Not this disappearance.

The wanton wolves. This is what their pack was. Savage. Merciless. Oppressively preying upon women and children. Ashford's desire for vindication grew.

But first, Ashley. She would be saved.

He returned to the website, using Ophcrack, a password cracking tool he was most comfortable with, he returned to the dark web – attempting entry. The first two digits were a number: 61. The next eight characters were either letters or special characters, and they could be in an arrangement of upper-case and lower-case use defaults. The tumbler deciphered an upper-case, "T". It had been running in the background on a high-compute tower server under his desk for hours.

Fifteen minutes later a lower-case "r" was made available. After one available IP address was locked out, the software tool would locate another available IP address and revolve around the algorithm until it too was locked out. After ten attempts an alternate address would be leveraged, cycling through the available addresses he had purchased online. Many, hacked and useless, simply wouldn't be able to log into the website titled in some uncommon gibberish.

It froze. "Shit. That's not good." Ashford looked at the locked screen of the site. "Someone's on to me. Time to go quiet. Quite quiet." He was talking to himself since there was no one to listen to him.

He reached behind the server and unplugged the cat-5 cable from the box. His laptop had the email link open. It was a lead, and the leads were good, but he'd need to protect himself, his snooping, from suspecting cyber-pointers. The clues and cues found online fed the vengeance beast growing within him.

8

Understandings

They weren't that nice to him when they first met. A lot of people weren't that nice to him. He was used to it. But as the day progressed, they talked to him more and even offered him a sandwich of his own as the day became evening. There wasn't a seat at the table where the six of them scarfed down their foot-longs. Steve pulled up an orange Home Depot bucket. Flipping it over to serve as a seat next to the picnic table, he was shorter than anyone else but was part of the meal.

Long after they were gone, Steve looked at the shell on the table. The brass casing for the .308 Winchester was shiny. It was a bullet made for hunting big game like bears and deer. A Remington 700 rifle would host the round. He heard what they had to say to him as they gave him the "buckets of thunder" as they called it. The heavy containers were hauled to a locker cabinet, and Steve was given the key. They trusted him enough to be a custodian of some of their weaponry. Where to walk, where not to walk, which alarm to turn on and off, and the stainless key to the weapons locker.

He remembered their commands. Over and over and over, they instructed him of the intruder protocol. Repeating it to himself after they left, "Steve, don't you use these bullets on them gators out there now. These are for people. Ya hear? Bad people. Bad people trying to take from us. Poking their noses into some place they don't below. You're our first line of defense, Steve. You understand, don't you? Steve?"

Steve kept saying it, but not exactly as eloquently. In Steve speak: *"Thdeve, don't you uthe thethe bulleth on them gatorth out there now. Thethe are for people. Ya hear? Bad people. Bad people twying to take from uth. Poking their notheth into platheth they don't belong. You are the firth line of defenth Thdeve."*

His recollection of what the cutter of the pinky said to him was clear too. "Look Steve, this bullet – it's about the same size as your pinky finger. There you go, Steve. My calling card. You serve and protect this place, and I got you. You can have this one. Steve? Hello Steve..."

He was gazing at the ammo just erected on the table. Listless, he was hearing the words. He just wasn't responding as quickly as he could have. Passive listening was in play. "Hello..." he finally uttered.

"I got you, dog."

Steve had never been called a dog before. Maybe it was a good thing. But dogs didn't last long if they poked their noses too close to the water's edge. He wouldn't do that – if he were a dog.

The big bullet shell was the size of his finger. Duller and copper colored on the point, shinier and brassier on the shell – the ammunition stood at attention on the table where they dined, and he didn't. The calling card pointed toward the sky. Steve smelled it. It smelled like nothing, but he did catch a whiff of the metal-smelling grease cleaner remaining on his fingers. The goop was still under his fingernails, cohabitating with the eternal black crud that lived there.

The instruction about helicopters was clear as well. If a helicopter hovered above any part of the immediate area where the product was, take them out. At all costs, use the rifle in the cabinet to eliminate the bad people. They weren't patriots like Steve was. They were interventionists. Steve didn't know exactly what that meant, but it didn't sound good. "Dum-dumth."

"That's right Steve, they're dum-dums. You see a helicopter close by, you don't even give them a warning shot. You take them out. Now drones are a little trickier. So, we've installed devices that will kill the signals to the drones. So not to worry the technology we installed today will wipe that out. These people – the interventionists – took some of our products in California. But they're not going to get through Steve's fortress here in Florida. They don't mess with Florida boys, do they, Steve?"

He shook his head 'no' while sitting alone at the table.

In the stillness he heard snaps, hisses, roars and snorts from the alligators. The babies made small chirps. The most dangerous sound they made was no sound at all.

Silence was dangerous in this area. The alligators were plentiful and definitely would hunt if food were scarce, but not as aggressive as crocodiles. Both lizard's scaly backs were nubbed with bumps and spikes, called scutes, and protected the creature from predators. Their bellies were soft to the touch like a snakeskin, and much lighter in coloring, taking on a tan or lime white hues. Alligators could hide their teeth when their mouths closed. The crocodiles had a toothy grin. Together, their eyes were brighter green than their bodies, with pupils, vertical like a cat, eerily glowing when a bright light would shine on them at night.

Steve was wearing his alligator boots today. No one noticed. They were $39 on Amazon. He had to go pick them up at the Postal Express in Naples. The russet and sepia-tan tinge was scuffed and dulled from so much wear. He pulled them off his feet. Still had all his toes. All ten. Not today, cutter. The dry heat of the day had succumbed to the cooler humidity of the evening. A trade off from what hunted by day gave way to what hunted by night.

The ecosystem and food chain within the wetlands was complex. The foliage of plants and algae fed the insects. The herbivores fed the fish and turtles - which fed the rats. Predators such as wading birds and alligators were next. And then there was the human factor

– which in ways known and unknown was killing them all. From shallow beach waters to the labyrinthine system of waterways through the lower third of the state, it was a place for creature, not man.

The soggiest and most desolate areas began here, where Steve and his vinyl alligator boots protected the product in Everglades City. Here, not even man was safe from man.

They lived eighty miles away, in Miami, across the Everglades. When Steve's side hustle companions weren't around, when the organization which he worked with, the one that wasn't his day job as a south Florida boat mechanic, wasn't present, he knew very well what the product was...what it represented...who it was. Once, so desperate to fit in with anything, and now obligated - he had separated the knowing from the unknowing, which was bolstering immorality and wickedness.

The young women and sometimes men, mostly girls and occasionally boys in the container were on their way somewhere else. This was a weigh-station to parcel them out for a price. Steve did not understand and would not know that the waterways and marshy islands south of Chokoloskee Bay made tracking and discovery of the human trafficking taking place difficult. He wouldn't understand the unwillingness of the young people or how they would be deceived or threatened to go along with their captors, risk harming their parents or families if they didn't participate. Steve's ability to reason wouldn't fathom what would happen to them after the small boats carrying them through the Ten-Thousand Islands area would find bigger boats. Those larger boats and vessels would find open international waters bound for Cuba and the Yucatan peninsula. Gone. At that point, the product, the too young people, girls and boys – they would be gone.

The counties of Palm Beach, Broward, and Miami-Dade accounted for most of Florida's GDP. Money. 27% of all of Florida's population also came from these three southern counties, stacked upon one another. In fact, Miami-Dade serves as the seventh-most populated county in the country. Based upon the available livable area, it equals

1,408 people per square mile. 46% are native-born, and 54% are foreign-born which adds to a large variety of socially acceptable optics, languages, cultures, and norms. It was a people on top of people on top of people situation where confusion sometimes dominated situations. If you see something, say something basis was not always dominating situations. A perfect storm for abductions and human trafficking, the side-hustle Steve thought he was involved in created a conundrum for him. His Momma taught him better. His Momma taught him to respect young ladies and young gentlemen. His Momma would not approve of Steve's conduct.

Steve would not understand the complex nature of the children stolen out of parking lots in broad daylight, the missed signals at day-care pickups, the middle of the night apprehensions, or the young women taken for modern slavery. He kept his thoughts to himself, to his missing finger, to his alligator boots, to the pornography which he occasionally watched, to the boat motors and parts and diesel grease. His intentional ignorance made the simpleton complicit. He heard an occasional moan or a cry and knew it did not come from the swamp.

The guilt within Steve was a skirmish. Building uneasiness was sparing inside of him. Grappling within him, it fought for relevance. He was wrestling with an internal conflict, subtle at first, but growing. It was dangerous, as was the Everglades. Like someone's pet, wandering too close to the hissing noises in the wetlands, the wrestling would not end well for the pet. His Momma taught him better. Steve understood that something was not quite right. It wasn't as it should have been.

It was time to go inside to make *thupper*. He tucked the bullet in his grimy jeans pocket.

* * * * *

Tamsen's call with Jacob was pointed. "I get it," she said, with less Aloha in her tone than normal, "my grant isn't as large as some, but I want what I want."

"I understand. My gig is to grow it, to dole it out when the receipts are presented, not to assign it." Jacob's defensiveness was not intended to dodge her scrutiny, nor was it to caste blame elsewhere. He thought she may seek a kindred spirit to lay eyes on Ruby's distributions. "Ruby has visibility we don't have. You know that better than I do."

"When I have a point, who's doing the listening?"

Jacob wasn't about to be defensive. This wasn't his battle. "I don't know. Sort of surprised you don't."

"What's that supposed to mean?"

"I don't know, Tamsen. Not trying to ruffle feathers here. Learning as I go, but I'm not the all-be-it influencer you might think I am."

"Do I need to threaten to pull funding? This slow-moving action is pissing me off. Do I need to yank what I've contributed?"

"Maybe," he replied calmly.

"Maybe? Maybe?" She realized it wasn't Jacob's function and finally listened to him instead of attacking the idea that he was the decision maker.

"Yes. Perhaps." Jacob played it cool, knowing the way to diffuse a lit wick was often a collected soothing response.

"I sound like a bitch. A spoiled little rich kid, which I'm not – married into my money. Sorry I sound so bitter. I'm trying to be intense. Passionate. Not opinionated." Her voice softened as she redirected the fervor. "Sometimes I do that. I get wound around my own axel."

Jacob let the silence do the talking.

"I shouldn't vent to you. It's a discussion with the gatekeeper, I know. And he has a lot going on. It's not just about me."

Jacob repeated something she said, seeking harmony within the moment, "He's got his hands under a few spinning plates."

She asked, "Old money or new money for you? You can still smell the ink on mine."

"Stolen."

"What's that?"

"Mine was stolen. I took it."

Tamsen let out a giggle.

"No, I'm joking, I know. But it feels that way sometimes. Right place, right time, right convictions." Jacob was remembering building Paisley, Pierce Capital Management with his old partner nearly twenty years ago. Full of piss and vinegar, the young Jacob Paisley dedicated each waking hour toward learning, adopting money making mechanics, applying the charm upon the suits up and down Wall Street, convincing those with the deepest pockets to test his potential. Luck. Luck had a way of finding him in those days. It turned out that making the most of one's potential wasn't all that personal. It was collaborative, where one was born, what drove your ambitions, how you were influenced, why you made the particular choices you made. The big things. The little things. The things in between.

"Anyone who has new money can say they were involved in the game of timing."

"One hundred percent." Jacob knew the randomness well. He didn't tell her about the timing of hiring Adele, making his first one-hundred-thousand-dollar trade, the first million-dollar commission check, the strip club visit following the quarterly Day of Decadence - and where he met Victoria. He didn't mention the fall from grace. She wouldn't hear of his yacht on the other side of her island and his discernment into Ellipsis due to Ruby's vetting. Tamsen wasn't there – at that level of trust.

She was on the beach again, sifting sand through her toes again while on the phone with him. The large sun hat covering her face was drawn low on her forehead. A cover up protected her shoulders from the rays but her legs were exposed and soaking up the North Shore's radiance. The swells had diminished. Her eyes were squinting at the horizon, seeking whales breaking the surface. Earlier, she watched the spouting and blowing from a mother and her calf, followed by the fluking which was the tail breaking the Pacific's surface before a deep dive. Tamsen was hoping for the whale sighting trifecta of catching a breach.

"So may I ask, if you've got all your money, stolen or earned, whatever...why are you interested so much in being involved in the field operations?"

Her question was in itself a conversation. But Jacob provided the bare essentials, "I wanted more. It was an illumination of purpose, and I wanted a greater role than I had in making money from money. Hey, I'm still JV, still trying out for the varsity team. Don't jinx me."

"He's been poking his nose around Oahu a lot, you know that right?" Tamsen was illuminating something of her own. "Ruby – he really likes it here. Or found himself something to latch onto. Or something."

"What keeps you there?"

"The Aloha Spirit. It's home. But just 45 minutes away I've got a mini–New York in the middle of the Pacific. Honolulu."

"I sure liked the Ko Olina. That's my speed. Living in Kapolei was a nice break, the reset that I needed." Jacob's dog, Kolohe, was tugging at his leash trying to reach for a piece of a pretzel with yellow mustard on it lodged in the curb's corner and surrounded by dirty water. "No! Kolohe, no!"

"What are you doing? Out for a slice of New York pizza?"

"God no. Some of that is like drywall covered in ketchup. Some of it is good, but the diet I'm on..."

"So, you're walking your dog again? You're a good dog dad."

"Yeah?" Jacob asked, "Well, for what it's worth, it's a bit more challenging in the city than I thought. Sometimes I feel guilty he only gets two or three walks a day. And when we have to travel – it's pure torture having to board him and say goodbye. We rescued him from a shelter in Waianae.

"Oh yeah? That's my hood. Makakilo, Nanakuli, Waianae."

"West side, best side."

Tamsen smiled, "Exactly. It's where I can go and appreciate everything I've experienced. It's my respite – where I find the most tranquility."

"North Shore livin' is tough stuff, I bet," Jacob teased. "Tranquility – that's important. Well, I don't have your roots, but I can imagine it is. From what I picked up living there the short time that we did – and beyond the perfect climate and beautiful scenery – that especially strong sense of community and connection to each other, the *ohana* and the *kuleana* living – that's what I like."

"There you go, city boy. Each Hawaiian has the responsibility and the privilege to care for their community and the land. You were just born on the wrong side of the country. A Hawaiian at heart. Has New York always been home?'

"Ohio, actually. I was born in Ohio." Jacob didn't need to explain the middle name of Columbus and the clunky manner in which it came to be.

"Ewe. Ohio. You're not one of those O – H guys, are you? From Thee Ohio State University?"

"I – O. Go Buckeyes."

"Gross. I knew there was something about you I found revolting." Tamsen's ex was from Michigan. It dawned on her just then that cheering on the other side of the field might be a good thing, but she refrained from admitting it.

"Want to know a dirty little secret?"

"Maybe." Tamsen saw a whale watching boat slow its float, which was indicative of the passenger's seeing activity at the surface. She stood and could see dolphins splashing about. Their white-water churn was short lived.

"You just missed a pod of dolphins Mr. Manhattan."

Jacob curled the left side of his mouth, "I look at the surf report every day. The wind speeds, tides, forecast, winter storm warnings."

"What? Winter?"

"Teasing there, of course. My short-lived stay, but admiration – maybe even an allegiance is...I don't know." Jacob tugged at Kolohe's leash slightly, indicating the turnaround point on the walk.

"Island fever. Works both ways. Some haoles want off the rock, some want on it. It isn't for everyone, but it's for me. Sounds like it's for you too."

Jacob realized he'd softened her tone from the money conversation earlier. He found common ground – the fascination of and their mutual respect of the culture. *Mission accomplished*, he thought. Building a bridge with Tamsen, even across the mighty Pacific, wouldn't be as difficult as he thought minutes ago.

"Hey, I've got another call coming in. It's a Bravado-type call which I must take. Can we connect in the next day or so?"

"Take it," Jacob said, being pulled by the yellow lab against his will back to Adele and home and kibble. "Aloha."

"Aloha, money man."

No longer was she the Hawaiian rooster like at the beginning of the call, crowing randomly and apparently at nothing at all. Tamsen Makua was excitable, readily aroused from her own ardent desires as well as irritated from the lack of progress. The monomanias she held boosted her accelerations and acted as her own deterrents.

Jacob, having navigated the treacherous terrain that the legal and illegal tender of Manhattan could sling his way, thought that he knew how to meet the needs and govern the obsessions of someone like Tamsen.

As he walked further with Kolohe pulling again as if it were an Iditarod tryout, Jacob restrained him and commanded the lab to "Sit!" Kolohe pranced in place and did as he was told, looking up to Jacob for a treat. He reached into his coat pocket retrieving a stale morsel. The dog munched it quickly from Jacob's palm. "We're not going any further unless you can act like an uptown boy and walk instead of pull." Seeming to understand, Kolohe licked his lips and continued to sit, occasionally looking back up as if he were apologizing.

In the distance was Romero's, an Italian eatery which Victoria loved. It was a regular hot spot for them to dine. The vodka marinara sauces stewed all day, filling the air wafting outside of the restaurant with scents of basil, oregano, and garlic. The brand of heavy cream, secret spices, and source of the tomatoes used were the Italian owner, Vincento Romero's, secrets. Even Victoria, dressed in sexy short skirts and unbuttoned low cut little-left-to-the-imagination tops, doing her best to be convincing couldn't talk him out of divulging. The epicurean had his boundaries: primarily, Mariella, his wife who was disapproving of Vincento's wandering eyes. Guarding Adele from an uncomfortable conversation, Jacob made sure he didn't return – and missed the couple's love of operating their family's fine-dining establishment.

There she is again, Jacob thought. *In my head. This must change...eventually. Why – why are you still here?* She haunted his thoughts at random, but especially with the physical proximity of the city. A random certain time of day, article of clothing, street smell, or gesture triggered a memory of her. He had established guardrails when running into an old acquaintance or friend to distance himself from who he was then. Ten years of a girlfriend experience were tough to dismiss.

"Know of a good priest? I might need an exorcism." Jacob spoke to Kolohe, not knowing that the yellow lab was the only one listening. The dog looked at Jacob, cocked his head, then looked at an elderly woman standing behind Jacob. Kolohe lowered his ears.

"Go see Father Patrick at Saint Paul's. Always seems to work for me," she said matter-of-factly as she passed, only stopping to look into his eyes to see if he was all there. Once he appeared normal, she smiled without showing her teeth. Wrinkled crinkled at her old and tired eyes. She held her hand out for a brief moment for Kolohe to sniff. He lowered his ears further and bowed down on the pavement. She continued walking slowly, more of a wobble in the direction she was heading.

Jacob looked around. No one was close enough to hear what he said next, "No more sidewalk talk. After that. That was it. Last one." Knowing that next to Adele, Kolohe was the best listener, Jacob knew there would be countless more conversations with his tail-wagging companion. He took one last look at Romero's red sign above the front door. Romero's : Traditional Ristorante : Delicious.

Victoria. Perhaps they were serving spaghetti and meatballs at Rikers Island tonight. *Only the best for perhaps the East River's most attractive inmate.* Jacob imagined her spinning the pasta around her fork, thinking back at the experience with Jacob. It was a peculiar revelation for Jacob: *Perhaps her memory of me is as unsettling as my recollection of her.* Something inscrutable was still present as much as something discrediting was missing.

*****

"Fernby, Sydney," she said, responding to the security guard.

"Will need to see a passport or driver's license, please."

"Yes, right. Right here. There you go."

"All items on the belt please. Through the detector."

"Yes, yes of course – keep us safe. Just this and this for me." Sydney laid a shiny laptop without a bag and a tiny black purse on the conveyor belt devouring items from the people in front of her. Her two items joined the lineup for the large black box resembling a refrigerator laying on its side, swallowing items for investigation, spitting them out on the other side of the metal detectors.

She was slightly taller than the average height of a man. Black leather skintight to the ankle pants and two-inch heels made her tower above most men in the lineup. Sydney's mocha-brown skin glowed like a moon shadow. Her angel-bright film-star smile was almost as luminary as her almond-brown eyes which lit the moment with their blaze of wonder. Her hair was tight against her head. Short graduated black coils required little attention. She was a get up and go woman.

Sydney Fernsby was British. She lived in London some of the year, dicing the calendar with trips across the pond to The Hamptons, jaunts down the coastline to her family's beachfront estate in Hilton Head and a masterpiece of a property in Miami. Here, the zip-code of 33133 was no stranger to the twenty-to-fifty-million-dollar properties lining the edge water inlets where the luxury yachts tethered to private docks were deemed almost essential. The wealthy looked east across the bay to Key Biscayne, where the other wealthy held their winter getaway homes.

When in England, her time was quite busy – residing in Covent Garden which was at the heart of London and in the middle of many of the attractions the capital city offered. Her flat consumed an entire third floor of a charming red brick building located near The Savoy. The theater district was close by. In the other direction was Trafalgar Square. Buckingham Palace, Westminster Abbey, and Big Ben were a short Saturday morning walk for a frothy latte and crumpets.

Sydney has frequented the United Nations complex. She knew her way around. After the security check, she was required to receive a sticker for her lapel which was indicative that she was a visitor. Either a lanyard, always to be displayed publicly, or a sticker was required for identification purposes. This was a place of no secrets and the greatest of secrets.

The high ceilings and materials used in the lobby were of metals, concretes, and checkered dove and cloud-grey tiling on the floors. The cold industrial look and feel was softened with drywall partitions featuring the good intentions and deeds, conquests, and relief provided by the agencies of the UN. Some were black and white, which were indicative of despair and need. Others following the first two dozen were sepia tone, warming to the thought of actions required and of hope. At the end of the walkway, color photos told a cheery and propitious story of what things could be like. It was a follow the favor story of the human conditions. A glimpse of mercy and grace were dispatched in the images.

She walked past all these which gathered small groups gawking at the visions while reading the captions below them. The elevator bank was segmented. Ground to fourteen, fifteen to twenty-seven, twenty-eight to thirty-eight. There were three basement levels and a secretive fourth that the public did not have access to and didn't have general awareness of. This was not the United States. The land occupied by the UN was technically extraterritorial which was an agreement with the U.S. government. To receive local police, fire, and emergency services, the UN had to abide by the local, state, and federal legislation. Few of the specialized agencies were actually housed in the headquarters building.

The 193 sovereign states, nations which comprised the UN , had equal representation within the plaza and complex. However, the more you give, the more you get was an unsaid universal practice. The assessed member contributions, a complex formula factoring in GDP and population, was a strongly recommended guide, not club dues. Nations could then fund certain economic and social council, general assembly, or secretariat funds which collectively rolled up to the United Nations.

Sydney was aware of her need for discretion. Operatives had a story, an alibi, a plan for their intentions which was buttoned up with loopholes for pivots. There was no chit chat in the elevator. Waiting until the man in the black suit and silvery tie made his selection, in her British eloquence, she prompted the floor button to be summoned, "Twenty-two, please."

What appeared to be a Japanese businessman accommodated her request. The frames for his glasses were thick, but not as thick as the lenses. He gripped a small attaché case is his left hand. They were the only two on this vertical journey. Once he departed, she pressed an additional floor, twenty-seven. After the quick stop at twenty-two, she departed at twenty-seven and then made her way to the staircase for a trip down two floors. She opened the heavy metal door on the twenty-fifth floor and found her meeting room.

There he was. Benjamin Vendemer.

"BenVen!" Sydney spoke softly as she broached the crack in the door.

It startled him. Engrossed in a message on his phone, he jumped in his seat, jolting his elbow onto the corner of the desk. Wincing, he retracted the elbow.

"Funny bone?"

"Nothing funny about it." Rubbing the bumped bone, he found a smile and rose from his seat out of respect for the lady.
"Old school. You're a sweet bloke. Sit." After placing her stainless laptop without a case on the pewter colored laminate table, she plopped down on an office chair next to him. "It's been a minute, hasn't it?"

"What's it been, nine, ten months?"

"A proper good time was had by all. Perhaps we needed a cooler?" Sydney pried open the laptop which was already powered on. The calendar jumped across the screen to her attention. "Oo. Six of us today. Big mission?" Her eyes dotted over the briefing document with a seal stamped on its digital cover sheet. Toggling down the instrument she observed the need-to-know audience.

"An important one."

"No more faffing around. Time to go be..." She stopped speaking and looked at Vendemer, "Sinclair. Is this the woman?"

"We're doing a soft roll on this one, but she's got the AI-savvy, and solutions smarts that will be meaningful for our outcome. Yes, the one I told you about. I've had the pleasure to see her in action – at her best and at her other best – for years. She gets beaten down; she stands back up. I wouldn't bet against..."

"And what makes you believe she might be an asset in the field?"

"Like I just said or was attempting to – you don't bet against her. No Field for her just yet. IT Ops. She's got the Cloud, Data, Edge,

Cyber smarts. She serves us best as an additional powerhouse on all things IT."

"The other two: Adele and Jacob – also new?" Sydney saw the lineup of rookies and was quickly uneasy.

"To make you less comfortable, I haven't met them. They came to us from Ruby."

A smile made its way to her face. "Oh, you should have led with that. If their vetted by Ruby, they're fine by me." Sydney opened a web page, clicked into a phantom-browser, and studied the neophytes. "She was his number two?"

"An executive administrator. His handler. The adult in the room sometimes, fun committee chair at other times, a trusted confidant of sorts – or so I'm told."

"And now they're a thing?"

"Are they?" Vendemer shrugged his shoulders not knowing what they were.

"Oh...my...he's a bit naughty. A scandal of sorts." Sydney scrolled through links leading to tainted and valid stories about Jacob and his tryst with dishonor.

"In the long term, he's a big bet. In the near term, we're grooming him." Vendemer looked to Ruby for more, but the old man added none.

Sydney continued, "I don't even need to say it out loud, but just adore my English words so I'll hear myself speak. Our boundaries are beginning to be defined. We must...be careful there..." Her statement lingered. The pregnant pause in what she said was filled with what they both knew. Including Ruby's sentiment, what the three of them knew. A suspicion was growing that Ellipsis was not as contained as they had wished. "A kerfuffle in jurisdiction is something to avoid, wouldn't you say?"

"I'd say." Vendemer looked at his watch. Five minutes or thereabouts. He ran his fingers across his scalp. His jacket bunched up around his shoulders as he hunched over the phone to swipe left through email, archiving them. Then, feverishly typing, he said, "They're here. Downstairs. I'll pick them up on twenty-three and walk them up."

"Thank you, Benjamin," she spoke into her small laptop, glancing up at his as he passed by her, leaving the small meeting space which was only identified with a room number on the door. Digging in on Jacob Paisley, Adele Kirby, and Allegra Sinclair – she settled in on quick assessments. He was a handsome man, perhaps spicy and perhaps a maverick. She was proper, a bit sophisticated, probably stable and predictable. The youngster was an enigmatic force. Sydney dug in here. "Who are you *really* Allegra Sinclair?" After her fingertips vigorously clicked keys between military and police-force background checks, and drawing blanks, she moved to social media sites. Little was offered between the prominent applications. She went into Allegra's search history and was redirected to alternative Sinclair's. "What are you hiding?"

Adele, Jacob, and Ruby arrived at the door to the small office with Vendemer. It was time for the sapiential circle to meet, sharing their collective get together of intentions, resources, and knowledge.

It was Adele who spoke first. "I could never pull off that look."

Sydney's smile was slight, hiding her megawatt smile. Her hourglass figure was met with a small needless black belt as she stood to shake their hands. Moments before they walked in, she was deducing their characters from what the internet would share and was comparing her blind judgment to feeling their hands clasping hers.

She piled on, "Love those pants. Wish I had some of that confidence." Adele's compliment was all about what Sydney wore underneath the black leather – it was for her self-esteem and certainty. Anyone who met Sydney would notice her pert nose, silk-brush eyelashes, and kiss-inspiring lips. They might even go there – only to be minimized as Sydney's intelligence would hush the aesthetics they may have led with.

"You must be Adele?"

"That's me."

"And Jacob?"

"That's correct."

"Ruby." Sydney tipped her head, acknowledging the architect of the meeting. "One mo...?"

"Later." Ruby was quick to head off the question, so as not to alarm Jacob.

It was time to stitch it all together.

Sydney, Ruby and BenVen had worked together for a decade as Ellipsis scaled and accelerated. Ruby scouted and had on-boarded Adele and Jacob for his special ops pod team. The only person who knew of Allegra Sinclair's history in the technology sector was Vendemer – who had locked her in on a pseudo contract within his leadership team. Knowing Allegra was seeking a blockbuster leap and reach role within tech, she was ripe for a project like this.

Jacob had met Allegra to discuss managing a bourgeoning career and because the old man asked him to offer an opinion. Ruby and Adele had managed a 'fly by' to meet a technology prodigy which Ruby was scouting.

No one, just yet spoke the name, nor mentioned Allegra Sinclair as they pieced together their relationships,

"How about that commute?" Ruby asked Jacob.

Jacob looked at Adele. She wasn't dressed as racy as Sydney, but her smart choice in what she wore made her dynamic appearance lustier and more vivacious than how she dressed at PPCM for years. Adele was always masterful at playing her part. He pressed his lips together and thought that some leather skinny jeans might need to make their way onto Adele's wish list. Breaking free from his daydream detour he replied to Ruby, "I could get used to these walk-to-work days."

Vendemer asked, "Close by?"

Without sharing specifics, Adele added, "MidTown East."

"Oh nice, Kips Bay area for me, not far from Bellevue, just down the FDR."

They refrained from mentioning Park Avenue would be home base as they compressed living spaces. The Waldorf Astoria Residences, among a few other properties they owned artificially made them feel affluent. They didn't know that Benjamin Vendemer was a donor-philanthropist incognito. They had no idea at the time of Sydney Fernby's massive net-worth was of old-money wealth. None of them knew about Ruby's rise to financial abundance. His superfluities remained interred and concealed as he guided others to see his servile and unpretentious lifestyle.

Following the introductions and pleasantries, they overviewed the situation, the opportunity at hand, and a call-to-action outline.

The mission. It was as fuzzy as it was clear. A greyness between the black and white filled the gap in the plan. What they thought would be a two-dimensional rescue effort for victims of human trafficking in south Florida quickly became a three-dimensional blueprint. When the complexities of the security investments made in their modern-slavery compound were shared, they realized a zero-kill plan may require a tesseract – or a dimension within the dimensions. The unknown variables would need to be calibrated, and a foolproof strategy would need to be developed.

Unknown to Adele and Jacob, they were all waiting on the woman. They were waiting for the *A Little Bit of Heaven* lookalike, Marley Corbett, but without the health-related prognosis - to join them for a broader planning assessment.

Vendemer looked at the ping on his phone. "She's here. I'll get her." He stood, tucked the device in his jacket pocket and said nothing more as he left to retrieve her in a similar manner.

*****

"Aiden? Aiden Ashford?" The nurse called his name in the lobby. He followed her down a corridor lined with maple doors to patient rooms. She followed him in the small room and asked him to disrobe down to his skivvies. He complied, leaving his socks on too. Asking him to stand on a scale, she read the weight back to him, "Two twenty-five? That sound about, right?"

"Something like that." Ashford knew he was two-something but didn't think he was 225 pounds. It must have been exercise. His muscle mass was continuing to multiply.

"Let's check your BP." Her hands were cool. He hadn't been with another woman behind closed doors since Ashley went missing in the schoolyard. She pumped the air into Velcro compress. It scrunched and made the ripping sound as it tightened around his bicep. "You're almost too big for the standard model." Her notepad was a thin computer. She jotted down a number and said, "Let's do that again. How about the other arm." Again, she pumped the air into the restrictive compress and after she received a second reading, must have adjusted her findings. "Okay, the doctor will be in to see you shortly."

Ashford listened to the white sterile paper covering the bench under his butt crinkled with every move. He listened to second hand from the clock on the wall tick seconds away. Tick, tock, tick, tock, tick, tock.

It was short. His doctor was an older gentleman. "Aiden?"

"Yes." He'd accept using his first name in this situation.

He didn't say anything else as he looked at the data. "Question for you..." he paused. "What are we going to do about that high blood pressure of yours?"

Ashford didn't know that he had any high blood pressure. His thoughts about diet darted to the extreme meat consumption, some of it from the butcher in the grocery, others from the processed meats he devoured to maintain muscle mass. They began their conversation about the increase in size and strength. They talked about the lifestyle choices and Ashford assured the doctor that substance abuse and recreational drug use might have been a possibility, like five years ago, but that he was more of a candidate for a straight edge lifestyle than a user.

They discussed the supplements he had been taking to support the strength and mass increase. The doctor latched onto the culprit. "The problem there is that one, your blood pressure is going to do other damage – it's fifty points higher than it should be - and two, once you go off of those protein enhancers, you're going to lose what you've built. Do it naturally. They're going to impact more than you know. We're going to check your blood work. I'm guessing your cholesterol will be sky high too."

"So, it says here that you're not in for a free sermon or a general checkup, but rather that you're seeking steroids?"

"Yeah. That's right. I want to know what..."

"Can I stop you right there? The juice is likely to raise your BP higher. We'd be going the wrong way. And look at you – you don't need that crap. What are you trying to do to your body and why?"

Ashford left out the response, *I want to stop a truck,* and simply answered – "I'm just trying to be the best me possible."

"What doctor doesn't want to hear that? Do it naturally. Lay off the sodium and watch the processed foods. Whey and pea protein drinks are good. Meats and eggs for days upon days or weeks upon weeks, probably not as good."

They wrapped up their little talk with the doctor leaving the small office, returning with some printed handouts about controlling one's health when alerted about high blood pressure.

He left the office blanked. A choice could be made. Do your own thing or go about it another way. Ashford would consider the options while he logged on to research other supplements which might not impact his heart health. After his password was entered, a ping appeared in his notifications.

RE: help wanted – special projects

It was a reply from the dark portal, the potential human-trafficking lead. The message read, *"Yes, looking for a strongarm. Must be knowledgeable in technology. You seem to have a fit here. Weapons know-how is pretty good. The special project is all the way down in the Everglades. Busi-*

ness is expanding. No per-diem. 50% cash up front, 50% at project close. No show for project – well, you won't want to know what happens if you no-show."

He had the IP address. Ashford had the missing link – what he needed to track down the wanton wolves – perhaps even his wanton wolf pack.

He could now track not only the sender of the message – but the tentacles of communication, including wherever in the Everglades. After frantic clicking he found the backdoor but needed a ripper to unclutter the cypher. The encryption was sitting on top of a coder application. He knew how to get under it. It would take some work. Ashford might not sleep tonight, but he'd finally be one small step closer to the nefarious villains within this ring.

Ashford thought of Ashley. His hunching over a laptop, spending his days and nights lost in thought of finding her, longing for her without a material lead – the lost hope, it would have killed her. She'd have encouraged him to move on. "But – I – won't do that girl. I'm here, you're there. We just need to close that gap. I – will – find you." He spoke to her picture, assuming in some ethereal sense, she could hear him.

Returning to the dumbbells, he picked them up and counted reps, talking to himself. "Got to get prepped for a showdown. Gotta be stronger than strong, tougher than tougher, faster than fast, smarter than smart..." Veins in his biceps began to bulge as her continued to curl the weights from him hips to his chin. "Twenty-eight, twenty-nine, thirty." He puffed and switched arms, curling the forty-pound hunk of steel in his other hand.

He finished the sets, followed by planks and hundreds of push ups as sweat began running down his forehead. "Think," he said to himself. "Think. How is this going to happen?" Code cracking wasn't his specialty, but a discipline he thought his skills could transfer into. "if this, then that," he said to himself, wiping the perspiration with a white hand towel. "If this, then that." The digital logic of computation, like the combination of a lock, was spinning through his thoughts – seeking the tumblers to click into place. He had so little to operate from that something, anything, was everything to feed his obsession toward finding her.

9

Fact of Impact

Unknowing what she was truly in for, Allegra assumed this Vendemer-prompted meeting was an Artificial Intelligence tech talk with the IT Department at the United Nations. The only thing that she was leery of was a presentation without a Microsoft PowerPoint deck to reference. She followed his instructions – to arrive at the plaza in front of the complex and call him on his cell phone.

Adele and Jacob didn't realize that Allegra was being drawn in so quickly. The mention of her appearance was a surprise to them.

"Why the kid?" Jacob asked.

Ruby lowered his chin to his chest and in a scowl added, "Not a kid."

"You're all novices as far as I'm concerned." Sydney became known as the outspoken one of their small crew.

"No, seriously – why the intrigue in her?"

"Because we like her more than you." Ruby's feathers were ruffled. He needed to stand up for the diverse team he was assembling, and his leadership would require a typical triangular dimension with Jacob. He continued, "We want a healthy mix of young relevant experience. Her perspectives and intel are not like yours. She's nimble, coachable, agile. Want a Hawaiian word for it, Captain Paisley? She's akamai. Allegra is Eleu."

"I still don't see... Did she get three votes of confidence too?" Jacob's challenge was persistent.

"You had to get out of your head! Out of your own way! With her, we don't have that hurdle. She can be trusted! We know we can count on her." He was agitated. "We've been vetting her. Not like with you. In different ways. She just doesn't come to us with as much baggage. Yes, yes, she got votes of confidence!"

Nothing more was said for nearly a minute. Silence filled the air where words were shouted, filling the void. Jacob looked at Ruby, then to Sydney, met eyes with Adele, and returned to the architect of the project.

Finally, Jacob broke the verbal stalemate, "Red teaming the decision, Ruby. Scrutiny is the Breakfast of Champions."

"Fair enough," Ruby replied calmly. He quickly composed himself. His red suspenders, checkered shirt, and weathered brown trousers were replaced by something UN worthy today. A navy suit and periwinkle dress shirt pressed, and crisp in the collar was worn. He even wore black shiny dress shoes.

"You're stressed," Adele finally said something. "Why? Why Ruby?"

Ruby contemplated saying something and paused. He looked at Sydney. She stopped clicking keys on her laptop to look back at him. The old black man opened his mouth again, then pressed his thick lips together, still seeking just how much content needed to be shared with the newbies. "We need to keep our secrets secret. What should remain hidden, clandestine."

"Paramount privacy," Sydney added in her British accent, the soft "i" as in 'igloo', in for the hard "i" as in 'iceberg', like an American might pronounce it.

"We need to be extremely mindful of the calls, the texts, social media, web traffic, browser history, anything tech. We're suspect to our boundaries – beginning to be defined." Ruby spilled the beans because he trusted the room and everyone in it.

"A breach of some sort?" Adele had a concerned look on her forehead as she asked Ruby for specifics.

"No, nothing like that. Thank God. Just some chatter over intel about rouge vigilantes – out to make good on what the government couldn't accomplish. We need allies, not regulation or worse, a shakedown since we don't have the governance from the FED and State or local agencies."

Sydney seemed to know a little bit about everything. "Curtain twitchers," she said under her breath. "Meddlesome duck of some sort, I suppose."

Adele smiled. Then, Jacob smiled. Finally, Ruby smiled. "You make everything sound just a little better." They collectively chuckled and didn't notice the entrance of Allegra and Vendemer.

"I must be in the right place, everyone's happy here." Allegra sized up the room with a long look at Jacob, a quick glance at Adele, a pause at Ruby who she met briefly at the coffee shop, a new person, and Vendemer.

"We've met – several times," she said as she addressed Jacob. "Met you, met you," referring to Adele and Ruby, and pausing at Sydney. "I'm Allegra." She held out her hand for a firm shake. "You're pretty."

"Like you," Sydney added.

"Mm, prettier," Allegra countered. "And BenVen."

"How was the detour?" Adele inquired, assuming that she had received the same elevator field trip which they had.

"Which one? Climbing the exit stairway or in what Vendemer briefed me on in our ascent?"

"Either." Jacob was curious about the briefing from her career boss.

"The first diversion, I got in a few steps. The other – I may have some steps to take."

"Well said," Vendemer acknowledged.

It was a time for some interaction, but after the assessment. Ruby, who was leading the charge, sized them up. He did it verbally for all of them to rally around what he saw.

"Jacob Paisley. Influential. A masterful manipulator – in a good way," he smiled and added lightly. "Has some stories to tell, the sweet and the salty. A good soul I've had the pleasure to get to know over the past several years. And a trusted ally - who now foots most of our expenses. Our Captain of Capitalism."

"Adele Kirby. Thinks things through. Completes Jacob's snap judgments," he smiled again, pointing at Jacob. "I said that lovingly." He returned his attention to Adele. "Offers the human element that's sometimes missing. She knows what good looks like. Compassionate, thoughtful, knowing, perceptive. The Ambassador of Goodwill."

He moved to Sydney. "Sydney Fernsby. One of our architects. Wicked smart, courageous, abrasive, worldly, ingenious beyond comprehension. Sydney knows more people that get shit done than all of us do, including you, Captain. Sydney is our most capable and creative counselor."

"Benjamin Vendemer. A steel-belted radial retread that just won't wear out. My resourceful fixer. In fact, causes the ails to go away with good medicine he prescribes, Doctor Vendemer. Benjamin is a good friend. A cohort I've worked with in people-development over the years. Brings us the newest member of our team." Ruby slowly rolled his eyes over to Allegra.

"You. Allegra Sinclair. Dynamic, creative, tech-savvy, vibrant, flexible yet reliable. More than a pretty face. Our soon-to-be Distinguished Technologist."

Allegra's eyes wandered over the cast of characters. She sized them up in her modern and abbreviated way. Jacob – sugar daddy material. Adele – sugar daddy prevention. Sydney – British sophistication. Ben-Ven – one smooth operator, playing the part he played for so long and being involved in something so secretive. Ruby – the hub of the wheel, drawing the spokes together.

"Shall we get started?" Sydney asked, "Draw together the odds and sods perhaps?"

They sat where they had been before Allegra walked in with Vendemer. Allegra joined them in the last chair at the table.

"Allegra, pull your seat over here by me. You won't want to be there. This is why we're here."

Allegra rolled her light chair easily across the office carpeting. As she did this, a screen, once hidden rolled down from the ceiling completely filling the wall - exposing a whiteboard of details, photos, schematics, and elements of description.

"Wow. We gotta' get us one of these, Ben." Allegra watched Sydney approach the front of the meeting room and begin a deeper discussion about why they were there.

Sydney began. "High level, as in a satellite view. Here, at this back brush dodgy location in Everglades City, Florida is a shipping container holding about nine people, young people mostly, women and girls, little girls sometimes, captive. Modern slavery. Human trafficking."

Allegra swallowed as she listened to Sydney's buildup.

"What we wish to accomplish is to not only free them, returning them safely to their families, but to send a message to the blokes running this operation. We'd like to let these plonkers know just how rank they really are."

"American's present here, Syd." Ruby reminded her.

"Yes, of course." She looked directly at Allegra, then at Jacob, and at Adele. "If necessary, we want to take them out. Okay no roundabouts here. We will eliminate them and their vile organization. Or at least our mercenaries will."

"Mercenaries?" Allegra asked, looking at Vendemer first, Ruby second, Sydney next for an explanation.

"Impressive. Just had a glimpse at what they can do in San Diego," Jacob tucked it in before Ruby held up his hand, preventing any more about that from being said.

Allegra whispered to BenVen, repeating the question, "We have mercenaries?"

"We'll get to that, later." Ruby added.

Page after page after page of information was shared in what Ellipsis knew about the human trafficking clan. She shared on the wall, flipping with the wave of her hand, one category of information after another, what they believed to be intelligence followed by what they assumed could be intel. The coven of criminals killed and captured – how they could be strewn together was shared as they studied the expansive network of evilness. Possible victim after victim after victim which might be held was studied. The flurry of questions, seeking to better understand, the wickedness and immoral capabilities of the cursed organization was met with fact of impact.

Fact of impact.

The phrase affected them all. When they observed the victims, and their families, their friends and coworkers, the roadside memorials where they were taken from, the stories of anguish from the person's left behind to wonder, the hopelessness that swallowed their faith in goodness and decency – when they saw the photos shared from social media and police files about the abductions, known and unknown – they paused.

The fact of impact was a real and devastating condition. The crime deserved one's condemnation and potential elimination.

"There isn't a fiery furnace of hell, hot enough or deep enough for them." It was Adele who said it.

"Yes, we should all agree to that." Sydney stated and followed it with a lane-changing comment, "I'd love to get my mitts on a warm scone and a cup of tea. Anyone else need to use the loo?"

Allegra assumed she meant the ladies room, and chimed in, "I do."

A short break in their afternoon session took place. When they returned, Allegra had a moment with Vendemer. "How does all of this get coordinated with our day jobs? It's a grand gesture, sure, doing the right thing in a social sense. But our work, what we were doing, or what I was doing – that doesn't go away, Ben."

Sydney was listening to the quiet conversation. She saw the questions building within Allegra. "In need of a little cocktail napkin calculation, are we? How about a dollar for dollar plus one contract?"

Allegra was pleasant in asking the question, leading with a smile, "What does that even mean?"

Vendemer jumped in, "Your role, hidden within our private, not public company becomes a project-based position. You do your thing, talk about anything cloud or AI or sustainability or whatever emerging topic we slip you into. That...that's a part time thing. This...this is a project-based opportunity too. You'll load balance. I've watched you do it quarter after quarter after quarter. I've been doing it for years."

When she shook her head in amazement, her curled blond hair tasseled gently in her face. Allegra tucked a strand behind her ear and added, "I've known you all this time and just thought you were a little... I don't know... Weird?" She looked at his expression, "Sorry?"

"I am weird. Intense. Creepy. Rich. Poor. Aloof. Brilliant. And a hundred other things. I play the part I need to play. Like you will."

"So, payroll is a..."

"Nonissue. If I gave you more time to think about it, how much time would you need to take?"

Sydney looked up to the two talking about money. "Money isn't important here, bonnie. Purpose is. If it's the dollar holding you back, bugger off. Maybe there's another noble cause for you. Beach clean-up, slinging bags of rice, pitching quality education in the backwoods of Kentucky or wherever... "

"No, that isn't it. It's, it's just the shock of all of it. At once."

"Spose...that happens." Sydney spun in her chair back to the laptop screen.

"You've been at this a while, right?"

"Since we began things, a dozen years ago. An angel investor I ran with scooped me up." Sydney identified Allegra as a technical peer, "Smart with technology like you, he was. Handsome bloke. Loved him, really." Lost in recall, she finished, "And then he died." Her fingers were idle from typing as she remembered him.

Allegra was speechless. A small moment of silence joined them.

Sydney pressed her full lips and continued, "You give up a piece of yourself, of who you were. And then you take on another piece of identity, filling in the loss. What you bring aboard is a better side of yourself. A human will to leave the world in a better condition than it is now...is that transition."

Adele, Jacob and Ruby returned to their meeting room. They brought a cup of tea to Sydney and promised a scone or crumpet or biscuit after they finished for the day.

"Alright, now the fun part. The part I favor anyway," Sydney smiled. "Let's talk about blowing some shit up!"

*****

Maggie received the news late in the afternoon. She was being re-assigned as a Sr. Pool Admin, which meant she would help additional Directors and Senior Managers at their tech firm. It wasn't a glamorous title. At least she had "Sr." affixed to hers, whereas the three others did not. Her long run of working directly with Allegra was at its end. For the time being, she told herself, maintaining the optimism that they'd find their war to be reunited. *Their force was undeniable*, she continued the delusion. It was unusual that she didn't hear this from Allegra, though. Her two texts and the call of affirmation dropped to voice messaging. Unusual. Why did the client meeting with the UN run so long? She re-read her first two texts and decided against sending a third.

First text: *Hey! Remember me? WTF just happened w/ the shuffle? Thought we were BFF. Haha! Call me, geek!*

Second text: *Don't call me 'geek'! It's you. You're the geek, Geek! Seriously though. We got some drankin' to do! Cheers!*

In her message, WTF didn't represent 'Water The Flowers' and BFF didn't represent 'Best Friends Forever' as it did with everyone else. Bonded For Fucksake! was their fortitude. Even though it may not be grammatically correct, the work stuff you concoct while hammered following a company paid Happy Hour found its way into the following work week and thereafter maybe.

Now it was Maggie's turn to play it cool. She'd let her boyfriend preoccupy her time and attention until Allegra freed up.

Ping! Allegra's personal account within the company's order workflow popped up with a 'Request to Process' prompt. She ordered three tower servers, five high- compute desktops with bundled 4K 30" monitors, four pimped-out workstations, twelve security software licenses, and a services quote for something which Maggie couldn't see. The Scope of Work was a unique document that would only arrive in Allegra's personal inbox. "That's weird," Maggie uttered to herself.

It would take Vendermer's approval of the order before anything would happen to process it. Just then, another workflow prompt appeared: 'Your Request to Process has been APPROVED! Thank you for your order!'

"That's weird too." Maggie assumed they were at the UN still, perhaps showing off the portal outside of the demo tool. She presumed a cancellation request would pop up causing the electronic data interchange to prevent the actual order from sourcing to a distributor like a TechData or Ingram Micro. Nothing.

Maggie looked at the screen and shrugged, "Eh...not my circus, not my monkeys. She knows what she's doing." Realizing she was talking to herself, she continued in thought, *'Accept with the dudes.'*

Ping! One more message popped up. 'Request to Process with Alternate Ship To Address'. Maggie looked at the order, same as the first with an additional location. She compared the two, the first with a United Nations Plaza address, and the second with a JW Marriott, Marco Island, FL address.

Fraud? Maggie never noticed order requests like these on the portal. The first and the second identical in revenue size: $28,700 in hardware. What was more unusual was that the order with services intended for Marco Island came with a $15,777 services request quote.

She picked up her phone to text and call Allegra again, noticing the potential scam. It was the right thing to do. *Sorry to bug u – FRAUD ALERT on your personal / corp account. PLZ call me asap*

'Request to Process with Alternate Ship To Address'.

Ping! 'Your Request to Process with Alternate Ship To Address has been APPROVED! Thank you for your order!'

Vendemer approved that too? She didn't care what it sounded like in her head: fraud, demo, whatever. Maggie was doing the right thing. The next course of action was to reach out to their Compliance Officer and report the...

Her phone rang. It was Allegra. Of course, it was. "Hi Mags – thanks for the texts and the calls. It's okay. How's it going?"

"Uh two things." Maggie was going to address the order of IT equipment first, and then get to the org structure shake up.

"Yeah...I can't wait."

"A little sarcastic are we in the new role?" Maggie asked.

"No... no, like I meant I can't wait. Talk fast. I'm in between meetings and I'm going to piss my pants." Allegra's acting wasn't her best performance, but she thought she pulled it off.

"Gotcha. The orders – are they legit?" Maggie asked quizzically and slowly, seeking assurance.

"Yeah, it's good. Let them process. Vendemer is here with me. I'll explain it later." Allegra acted as if it were nothingness which needed a mechanical push of the approval button.

"Alright, fine. Strange, but fine. The second, since you have to pee can wait..."

"I know, I know – we'll find an excuse to get the band back together. Drinks this weekend?"

"Uh..hello. Born to drink and live vicariously through your let's-rip-the-night-apart partying. Say 'when' and I'll hop off of my boyfriend for a few minutes for you."

"You are a little skank. Where did that little skank come from?" Allegra said and asked but was happy with the distractions which Maggie's boyfriend were presenting. It diminished the grilling of questions and focused interest which Maggie constantly had upon her. Before him, she'd have her friend all to herself to entertain.

"I'm good at it. Or so I'm told."

"Naughty." As soon as Allegra said it, slowly and precisely and with Sydney's proper British accent, she recoiled. She knew she'd have to work on the transfer skills in the novel and discretionary capacity.

"Going Queen's English on me, are you?"

Damn Bridgerton or Downton Abbey or whatever English bullshit she's streaming on Netflix... Allegra optioned for, "Mags – the piss is about to stream down my leg, it'll be an embarrassing pool of yellow under me and I'll blame it all on you. Gotta' go."

"We don't buy drinks, we rent them. Go pee." Maggie's words and the voice put a smile on Allegra's face. She tipped her chin to her chest knowing that she'd miss her dear friend as this new and meaningful sequence of agendas consumed her.

"Lying to friends and coworkers already? You just visited the loo. The fibbing usually starts the second day, not the first. Overachiever!" Sydney walked past her on her way out of the room they were in.

Only Allegra and Vendemer remained in the room together as the others had stepped out for connection calls into their 'other lives', trips down the hall to restrooms, or to look out the window at the fading daylight.

"The mentoring with Jacob. That was a smooth move, BenVen. Now I see why you did it." Allegra thought that Paisley was more of a Team Sinclair supporter than he really was.

Vendemer just smiled and added, "Yeah, he's a bit of a good judge in character."

"In women, really? Which one, the mistress or Adele?"

He knew most of the story about Jacob and Victoria, not all of it, and didn't care to. "Adele, of course."

"Hmm..." The small and subtle sound of judgement fell from her chest. Then, in her inside voice, Allegra said to herself – *Well, I only thought about boning him a dozen times today. Work to do, girl.* And in her British accent she added, '*You manky tart, you*'.

On the other side of the call between the two of them, Maggie fidgeted with Allegra's shared email inbox. A short meeting invite had been requested from their internal auditor. You don't turn those down. She went into Allegra's calendar to see that three days had been blocked off for "Travel – West Coast". Things weren't as they were already. This new course of conduct was uncanny. They had gone from sharing too much to ambiguous agendas. Maggie raised an eyebrow of suspicion and scrunched one side of her mouth.

Something was up.

* * * * *

"Listen to this next part," Brian was sitting on their sofa, stroking Laki's hair with his nails slowly massaging her scalp. Like a Golden Retriever getting its ears rubbed, the dopamine was strong. She loved it. The Hawaiian continued reading the inscription, describing the inscription at the Statue of Liberty, a poem titled *The New Colossus*, from Emma Lazarus, affixed to the base of Lady Liberty in 1883... "From her beacon-hand glows world-wide welcome; her mild eyes command the air-bridged harbor that twin cities frame. 'Keep, ancient lands, your storied pomp!' cries she with silent lips. "Give me your tired, your poor, your huddled masses yearning to breathe free, the wretched refuse of your teeming shore. Send these, the homeless, tempest-tost to me, I lift my lamp beside the golden door!"

"Beautiful." Laki reached her small hand to stroke his, touching her. "We don't speak like that anymore, do we?"

"Like?" Brian looked down at her deep brown eyes seeking his.

"Like with kindness, and compassion, and acceptance for differences."

"Hey, we're Californian's here, staunch Democrats, c'mon…" He tipped his head into her direction.

"No, not a political statement. Just an observation. It isn't about us versus them. It's become competitiveness versus a collaboration. Politics aside. We're fencing off. Walls being built are supposedly easier than conflict resolution. 'Let's fight!' is sometimes easier than, 'Let's fix.' Do you know what I mean?"

"Right, left, middle, I don't care." Brian took the last sip of the room temperature ale on the table next to him, adding, "We're seeking politicians, council-members, people leaders, community members that seek a unity in what we want to accomplish. Together, we have the potential to achieve. Divided, we have the opportunity to destroy our potential. It really shouldn't be so difficult."

"Where did you get that? The poem?" Laki pointed to his phone indicating what he read to her.

"Someone sent it to me by accident. Someone from New York, I think.

"Hmm. "You should run for Governor."

"Or as da bruddahs in Havaii call it, Govna'", he chuckled as he reached for his phone.

Laki giggled. "Govna' Brian, conjugal visit permission tonight, please. Please…sir. May I aboard her majesty, your Grace?" Her British accent was sub-par.

Brian Kekahanamanui chuckled as he drew a Jack Johnson song to his iPhone. Through the boon of Bluetooth, *My Mind Is For Sale*, played on the speakers surrounding them.

Together, they listened to the lyrics of the song.

As the song finished, Laki jolted her head toward Brian, "What are we watching? It's your night to pick. Choose wisely, my friend, hot sex is in the balance." She looked at the slate-colored screen of the TV on the other side of the room. "Comedy, rom-com. Comedy, rom-com," she whispered.

"Well…" Brian pulled up Amazon's Prime on the channel options. The screen illuminated with options. Immediately, he clicked down to the action-adventure genre.

"Why you little motherfucker…" she spoke as she yawned.

"Would you have it any other way – than me being a mother fucker? At least twice." He chuckled some as they playfully jabbed at each other.

She was speaking softly and laggardly, nestling against him. "Twice? Twice? Why? Because we have two kids to prove two times?" Laki sluggishly questioned him. "We've had sex…what, over two thousand times? What can I say? You can't resist me." She held the back of her hand to her forehead finding a pearl of potency at the day's end. "I'm irresistible to you."

Brian watched her dramatic presentation, "Yeah. Pretty much." He scrolled through the options. "How about?" He toggled further and deeper, "How…about…? How about National Treasure?"

"First or second? Like, first, best." It was a murmur as she spoke. Laki's eyes were heavy as she lay there with her head in his lap.

"Good choice," she muttered as she reached up to touch his chin with a stroke of her fingers. Her hand fell to her side silently. Eyes closed; she fell short of what she may have wanted to say.

He hadn't made a choice. She was drifting off. Brian looked down at her beautiful, brown-skinned face. He stroked her soft and flowing hair more, and then returned to the channel-surfing options.

His phone pinged. It was the same 212 exchange number with the same text message he'd been receiving the past two days. It read: *Choose Thrill over Chill. Why have a lame job or a vanilla career when you can deliver a real difference. Are you wasting your time running the circular race? Want more than the bore? Interested? Type Y for 'yes'. Or go back to what you were doing and type O for 'opt out'.* He ignored it again.

"If that's my pimp, tell him I'm off the clock," she mumbled the masqueraded role, carrying on their *'What would you rather do if you had to do something different?'* discussion from earlier in the day.

"Ha-ha. Okay, I'll do that. I thought you were asleep."

"Mmm…" was all that she was able to get out, nodding her head slightly just twice.

Oddly, the text messages from the New York number fit in with their discussion. Brian remembered their clowning discourse from earlier in the day…

Brian: "I think I'd like to be a carpenter. Love working with wood. Creating and building things – that's what I like to do."

Laki: "Two answers. First, the serious one, a bakery chef. Working in the kitchen. Dreaming up sugary delights. Everyone's excited at what you've cooked up for them. You're giving them something they want."

Brian: "And the second?"

Laki: "A high-end call girl, for sure. Same answer. You're providing a service they want!"

Brian: "Well, I see you've given this some thought. What am I going to do with you?"

Laki: " Oh, I can think of something!"

He laid down next to his wife, leaning close to her silky long brunette hair. It smelled like pikake flowers and honeysuckle. The teasing from the text message cycled through his thoughts as he considered himself running the circular race. He thought to himself: *Was he actually running the circular race, or just jogging through it? What was the risk in seeking to understand? It would just be asking questions. Right?*

⁂⁂⁂⁂⁂

They were at dinner following their strategy session, sharing stories, observations and hacks - just like any of the other co-workers breaking bread together in the expansive restaurant. Dish noises, laughter, conversations, and background music which no one could really make out added to them speaking loudly across the table to each other. The restaurant, Lupa, was true Italian, specializing in Roma trattoria fare of the highest quality. The Thompson Street treasure's otherworldly pasta and sauce smells were rich. As they watched dishes prepared for other tables arrive, they grew hungrier.

"The hard part for me..."

"Say it again, please," Allegra giggled: "the haaad paaat faah..."

Sydney was amused with her new teammate. "Ah yes, the British lack of ahhhs. As if I was from Boston... No seriously, the hard part for me is fencing off the social interests from the work at hand."

Vendemer swirled his fingers in the air next to his ears, out of synchronization, "This is too much. Let's go somewhere else where we can hear each other."

"We just sat down," Sydney rebutted.

"No, seriously, cannot hear a damned thing."

Jacob made eye contact with the waiter, and as they came to his edge of the table, he whispered something. A quick exchange took place with the waiter holding up one finger in Jacob's direction, smiling at everyone, and walking away.

Adele had an idea of what was happening.

"Is he being Jacob Paisley, like I think he is?" Ruby asked Adele. Before she could answer, the manager approached them and said, will you all please gather your personal things and follow me.

The private room, the Writer's Room, was typically reserved for corporate events and could hold thirty. To keep with the private dining namesake, excerpts from great books were found on the walls, playing homage to great literature from the past and present. It was just the six of them. The warm earth tones met with golden accents, bronze lighting fixtures, glowing wall sconces, and ornate gold frames provided a cozy setting. The noises from the main dining room were muted. Here, they could speak and be heard.

"There, there – we have the whole place to ourselves." Jacob pulled out a chair to seat Adele.

And he's a gentleman... Allegra only played it in her head. She was sitting between Ruby and Vendemer facing the rest of them.

"Nice job, Paisley. Thank you for this." Vendermer grabbed a water glass not yet filled with anything and raised it in Jacob's direction. "A proper toast is owed, with wine, of course."

Adele leaned over and whispered in his ear, "You'll make a helluva Exec Admin someday." She had reserved countless private dining experiences for Jacob and his trader team back at PPCM hosting CEOs, Board Members, sophisticated investors and the likes of it but never at Lupa. The smells of roasted chicken and simmering tomato sauces, rich in garlic, oregano and basil, permeated the establishment.

"As I was saying," Sydney began. "The separation between church and state is essential in what we do."

Ruby bobbed his head up and down.

"It can be quite difficult. We all have something which can compromise us, and that is what we must protect. We protect it by taking it, putting it in a little compartment within us, and bring it back out when it's convenient."

Allegra watched her speak, enunciating words eloquently, apart from the R's. She thought her secrets would remain just that, her secrets. The sound system in this private dining room was much better than outside. She observed Jacob, watching his casual conversation and confidence in slow motion. It was like poetry from a lover in a garden of falling cherry blossoms, slowly trickling down to land gently on his shoulders.

Get a grip, girl. Not here, not now. The self-scolding stopped nothing. He was in his element: navigating, being chivalrous, commanding opportunities within his city.

Soft club music filled the warm room and her warmer and dreamy thoughts. No Doubt, played, *It's My Life*, when they walked in. The Dave Matthew's Band played *Where Are You Going* and Colbie Caillat now sang *Brighter Than The Sun.*

She watched him speak without hearing words. He was talking with his hands in motion in front of him. Casually, he'd smile and look across the table. He looked at her. He was looking at...

"Don't you think? Allegra... Allegra...? Allegra!"

"Oh sorry, lost in thought," she replied.

Sydney continued her conversation. "Easy to do. I was saying...there's this bright light beacon of goodness within each of us – delivering a difference for the world – the work we do. But there's also the secrets we all keep."

Oh fudge, Allegra thought. *It's as if she's reading my damn mind.*

"No need to let the rooster out of the cock shed," Sydney looked at Ruby and then paused at Allegra, adding, "Just yet anyway."

A waiter arrived with menus and bottles of flat and sparkling water. Shortly after, a wine steward approached them, but only had eyes for Jacob.

"May I?'

As if anyone would deny Jacob from the magic show he was putting on, as all of their heads nodded, he ordered for them, "We like the Elena Walch, the *Beyond the Clouds*, and the Benanti, the *Pietramarina*, the 2018 please. One more, a Lombardia – how about the... The Balgerra, the *Sassella*."

"Deliciosity. You have exquisite tastes, good sir."

"Thank you." Jacob watched him leave, pleased at the selections.

"What did you just order? I'm not challenging, just curious." Allegra tucked a tassel of her blond hair which had lost its curl through the day behind one ear.

"Hell if I know. Two reds and a white."

Ruby chuckled. Vendemer felt his pockets searching for a roll of antacids. Sydney wished Jacob had ordered the San Leonardo. Allegra giggled at Jacob's charming performance of bullshit. Adele tipped her head away from him, admiring the changes she saw him make through the years – three steps forward, one step back, three steps forward, one step back – transitioning from the man he was to the man he is to the man she felt he would become. She thought she had the best seat in the house and sat back up straight, smiling at these new friends, these change makers.

"A bit more about biz. Miss Allegra, in a few days when we all meet next, we'll need to have you sync with the Tango Team about your proposal. Perhaps brilliant. Give it all the more some thought. It will need to be buttoned up tight as a penis fly trap." Her British explanation of what tight meant caused a chuckle-storm at the linen table. "What? You'd rather I say Kitty? Foof?" Sydney had a serious face in her options presentation while the rest of them laughed. She continued, "Box? Puff Muff? Beef Curtains?"

"We got it, we got it, we got it," Allegra said, smiling and pumping her hand in the air toward the table. "I think I want to talk like you when I grow up."

10

Sixty-One

Two days later, late in the morning and back in the same secretive room within the United Nations building. The Microsoft Teams meeting opened. Allegra, sitting with Sydney, Ruby, Jacob and Adele, was expecting to see troopers decked out in camo, uniforms of gruff resistance, impenetrable by the mere look of their toughness. Instead, they were smiling at her. Wearing various colors of pastel polo shirts and backgrounds with books on shelves or a ceiling fan swirling in what appeared to be a dining room. One of the warriors set down a kitten as the call began. These were regular guys. Four of them. Granted they did seem physically fit with their thick necks and square jaws, but none of them resembled tough guy commandos like Arnold Schwarzenegger, Chris Hemsworth, or John Cena might appear. The warriors, rangers, and in her mind, guerillas appeared to be dudes you might find at a clubhouse drinking beers following a round of golf.

Allegra's hair was pulled back. She wore a black knit top and dress jeans. It was an unusual look for her. She decided that she was after a tactical look today. Don't try to be cute. *Don't go for the allure of a decision maker at a client, buying hundreds of laptops for a tech refresh. Don't dress to impress Paisley. This was serious stuff. Lives were at risk.* It was a discussion about freeing victims of human trafficking while ensuring that the Ellipsis rangers remained safe.

A moment she had been prepping for, here they were. On the call was Bing, Chuck, Jude, and Marco. Their names appeared under their images on the call. She was assured these were not their names. Their coded monikers were all that she needed to know – all that anyone might need to know. Each of them had short hair. Only Marco had facial hair. His neatly trimmed beard was golden blond.

Her first impression quickly changed as they made their introductions, and she heard about tours of duty, honorary decorations, paramilitary operations, and number of kills. There wasn't any selling. There wasn't any buying.

It was her turn to introduce herself. "That's impressive fellas. I'm Allegra. Allegra Sinclair. With me today are Sydney and Ruby who you know well, and two others on our strategy team, Adele and Jacob." They waved their hands as they were introduced since the room was displayed. "Guys, quick question here: what should I have as my code name?"

Their immediate responses were as if they were rehearsed and given a heads up – "*Foxy, Sweet Cheeks, Hottie, Bunny, Sunshine, Candy, Pudding, Baby Cakes, Dreamy,* and *Cookie,*" were offered in rapid fire from each of them as options. It was Jude who offered one final name, "*Jude's Girlfriend...*", in which they teased him.

"Fair enough," she said with a small smile on her face, "I admit, I had that coming, guys. I'll give it some thought. Thanks for the suggestions. Even you, Jude."

Jude added, "We're missing Tucker and Rave today. They're on another assignment. "Rave is the crazy one."

"Why's he crazy?" Allegra asked.

"She..."

"Oh, right. Sorry," she tipped her chin to her chest, then rolled her eyes briefly and turned her head to Sydney sitting next to her.

Sydney led the conversation following their 'hello's', laying out the most recent intel they had captured. "Even though this is a backwoods operation, they are not backwoods in their sophistication and use of technology. We foil the bloody bastards plans and their back at it. Relentless little pricks, really. The souls we saved in Texas from the containers was a good thing. But unfortunately, those containers are filled with victims again. It's a sad state of affairs, seeing demand – and supply. If we cannot break the chain, we'll bonk their operation by eliminating their headcount – yes, their people handling 'the product', the women and children. Listen, we're all brassed off about what's happening. We take the wankers out - like what happened in San Diego - and we've delivered a true difference. Cut off their willy's and knobs and send them to their mums."

She continued with the briefing, "You well know what usually happens, local authorities defer to State and Federal which potentially, may or may not, lead to convictions and legal ease. Meanwhile, nothing changes. The deterrent controls and interference methods of the scoundrels do not contain their repellent and horrible actions. This is one of the reasons we're including Allegra in a tech strategy. She has a few ideas to help jam communications and accentuate your presence. So...I'll turn things over to her and she'll share a witty thing or two. Tata for now, boys. Allegra...?"

Allegra was pitching a solution again. Just like she had a thousand times before. "Hi guys, me again." She was stone cold serious. It wasn't a time for cuteness or verbal volleyball. It was time to pitch. "Like you, or much like yourselves, I believe a change is required. We don't have to do this; we get to do this. What's the cost of indecision? The despicable continuance of what these bitches and bastards have been doing. So, let's start with 'why'. 'Why' are they doing this we ask our..."

Ruby cut in. "Allegra. Sorry... Perhaps I should have framed this up better. We've been to the beginning of this so many times, we've worn it out."

Jacob and Adele looked at each other. Within a glance, they knew that he was controlling the controllables, cutting to the quick. Allegra was comfortable in presenting a solution, but she was needed for a potential solution, not for laying groundwork. It was odd that Vendemer and Ruby had bestowed so much trust in her. After all, Jacob was vetted for what seemed to be years. *How long had they truly had their eyes on this mid-thirty-year-old? Why the sudden volume of trust in her contributions?*

Adele asked the group, matter-of-factually, "Is this one of the largest organizations of human-trafficking which we've had...?"

Jacob abruptly joined her, "Yeah, is South Florida an unusually large part of their...syndicate? Why...there...and why now?"

Ruby's interruption continued, "Why? Well, a one hundred fifty-billion-dollar global industry is the answer. That's why. Their slice of that pie, that's what they have to gain. Because there's demand, which is sick, they have a corrupt business model. I hate to even think of it as an industry. Money over morals. The human trafficking industry is like a real estate investment trust. Rent them out, the people – mostly helpless women and children, for whatever purpose. And when they're done with them for that purpose, for who knows what, sell them for another purpose. In the meantime, they get them addicted to substances, demoralize them, abuse them any way they might, threaten to harm their families, and strip them of any shred of remaining self-esteem. Hope..." He had a hard time finishing his words. Ruby took a deep breath, pausing from the thought of the pain the victims endured. "Hope," he tried again, taking a deeper breath, "Hope is sucked out of their world. It's *fucking* insane that more isn't being done about this. Are we upsetting their supply chain with this type or a commotion?" He shrugged his shoulders instead of speaking. "Can't really say that we are. But you fight this form of evil with a wicked form of strength, not fairness. First, we disrupt the supply chain. Then, our hackers go after their capital, all forms of it."

Adele leaned over toward Jacob, "We have hackers?"

He winced and returned to looking at Ruby to see if there was more of a rant.

Ruby's hand wrung over his face. "The traffickers even leverage the trafficked individual to open bank accounts and set up credit cards using money remittance services to funnel and launder money, large amounts of cash, structuring deposit which might fall just under the triggers for inspection. Cleverly deplorable, creatively hateful, cunningly vile. I apologize for my segue," he looked at her and pointed to her, "back at it, Miss Allegra."

Allegra acknowledged the coaching and his affirmation, with a nod of her head. She continued by pivoting to explain the intelligence she'd been unearthing over the past two days. "Unfortunately, in looking at their build out of security, encumbrances, and interference – they know what they're doing. We don't want to admire what they've done as impressive, but reactive to what happened in Texas and then San Diego. They're playing defense in a big way. It's going to take more than a takeout, take down, shoot 'em' up session. The intel we've gathered shows that a firepower fortress has been set up. Here's what we know. Here is some of the structure and detail we've been able to gather."

Allegra was sharing her groundwork with the legionnaires. She wasn't getting to the point - how to infiltrate the Everglades City compound.

Sydney interfered, looking at Allegra, "They're quite speedy learners. Expeditious in comprehension. Let's get down to it."

"Alright," Allegra began pulling up a satellite view of the area on the screen to share with everyone on the call. "This is the EC compound. Sits on the outskirts of town, away from the community, the good people and families of the Stone Crab Capital of the World. Population five, six hundred or so, depending upon which source you use. Gateway to the Everglades – and also..." she paused as she pulled up the mouth of the channel near the air park. "Ten Thousand Islands. Acts as a cover for smuggling people in and out. Off to Cuba and the Yucatan Peninsula. Once they're gone – they could be gone forever."

They all paused observing the beauty of the multiple shades of blue from Marco Island to Key Largo.

"Sometimes..." Bing spoke, "Sometimes it's almost hard to believe something so terrible could be happening, from a view like this, where everything looks so peaceful." They looked at the hues of blues and greens and turquoises on the satellite imagery. Allegra was reminded of Maggie. *Blue – it's all you do.*

"I hear you." She spoke softly, mesmerized by the pallet of tranquil colors displayed for all of them to observe. "What's your preferred brand of blue?"

The question was unanswered. No one spoke, knowing of the ground level corruption hidden within the stilly and serene image on the screen. The soldiers looked at the coastline as if they were staring into a lover's eyes, lost in the moment.

"So, what are you thinking, Allegra?" It was Marco.

"Drones. Lots of drones. Three thousand drones. Black Falcons loaded with frequency jammers confusing the GCS, ground control station, which is scrambled. How do they get in? Glad you asked. The first UAVs, sorry, unmanned aerial vehicles, these big boys here, the GRIFF Aviation drones have a payload of up to 500 pounds and will drop the Brince LEMURs. Tactical drones to take out the four detectors. Here, here, here, and there." It was quiet and Allegra presented the concept without interruption. "You've heard of IT, Information Technology. We're employing OT, Operational Technology; DT – Defensive Technology; and AT – Aggressive Technology."

She continued, "The turrets we're taking out are in these locations. This is a danger zone, within the red dotted lines. Launch from this point here, fly to the location here, and jam their comms. When the communications are down, the motion detection won't pick up on movement. Option one – attack from the land and roadway. Option two – go in by water. Once the comms are down, we go in guns blazing. This is where you guys have it on the ground. I would imagine there would be manual firefight opposed to tripping the intercept."

"One if by land, two if by sea," Chuck added, "Revere's ride."

"Unfortunately, there's more. If we take out all power, we're at the liberty of a custodian on the ground at the facility, triggering another source of communication. Something unexpected perhaps or harming the very people we're attempting to save."

"Do we have info on the ground character?"

"A Steve Booth. A boat mechanic. Not a tremendous amount to operate off of. Watches a lot of Netflix, mother died a few years ago, uses their encryption email to communicate with the organization. We'll get into that in a minute. We can't crack that, just yet."

"Let's learn a little more about this Steve Booth character," Marco recommended.

"I thought so too. White male, thirty-two, like I said, mommy who owns the property still, died a few years ago, a loner, surfs a lot of porn."

"What kind of porn?" two of them asked at the same time.

"I don't know. We don't have a screed of baseline, so not sure of any subcultures or categories. All we know is where he goes for it – the usual Pornhub, Xvideos, and the like. We don't know what the perve is into, if that's what you're implying."
"Back to the org for a minute, please. Where's the money for their guns and technology coming from?"

Sydney spoke, "A Cayman Islands holding company, an umbrella company that works with cryptocurrencies..."

"Of course. It all leads back to not tracking the money." Bing was quiet until now. "Dark money."

Jacob, who had been listening, spoke up. "Lots of reasons. Tax efficiencies, international recognition, a sophisticated banking system which leads to yes, money laundering, but transparency – or should we say the lack of it, the privacy and nominee services are elected to maintain anonymity."

After a pause, Allegra said, "Thank you, Sydney. Thanks Jacob." She smiled at him and jumped in on the rest of the plan which she and Sydney had concocted. "Following the elimination of the...I should say the containment...following the containment of the scumbags on the ground, we rescue – we liberate – we emancipate... whatever you want to call it..."

"We like to say we extricate, but the way you said it sounds even better. We save them from the hell they're enduring as captives."

Ruby had been responding to text messages on his phone. "Once the danger dies, once the bullets lose their fly, after the body bags are out of site, when the noise quiets, Adele will work with our abductees. She will begin the follow up outreach program. She and Jacob will help with the ingress hand-off, getting them home safely. They're non-weapons-authorized at this early point in their work with us, working on the social and care projects. Adele and Jacob, they'll need a chopper with twelve to fourteen passenger capacity."

"Done," Jude said. "I'll outsource it through the DoD."

"Thanks Jude." Sydney was taking notes. "What about the bag count?"

No one said anything. Jacob, Adele, and Allegra looked at each other. *Body bags?* Jacob didn't consider that planning a coup would include the aftermath of planning the actual number of bodies to haul away. Human remains.

"Allegra?" Sydney drew her into the planning of it.

"Uh...that's where it's either seven or eight."

"What does that mean?" asked Chuck. "What are we working with here?"

"There are six..." she was at a loss for her bad guy descriptions, because the evil they did didn't have a strong enough depiction, "thugs, and I hate to even call them that because they're worse than that. It's a compliment to them, almost. Six vile and immoral and ugly and just horrid...." Allegra's eyes filled with water but didn't fall to her cheeks. She took a few deep breaths. "Six on the ground and the caretaker or whatever we want to call Steve Booth." She took a couple more deep breaths. There's been a lot of chatter with an IP address in the Tampa area. There's potentially a seventh, bringing it to eight. Eight bags are what I'd plan on." She used the back of her index finger to wipe away the tears forming. It smudged her mascara. Adele reached for a tissue from her bag and handed it to her.

Bing ignored the emotion, "What more intel do we have on these hooligans?"

"Not a tremendous amount. Four of them appear to be in an extremist org."

"Which ones?" Bing continued asking the questions.

"Which four or which organization? Sydney, your territory." Allegra looked at her feverishly clicking keys, "Sydney?"

"Be a dear and share the screen, would you love?"

Allegra prompted screen sharing. There on the wall was a simple logo, two fists, facing forward. On the middle finger to the left was a tattooed six: 6. On the middle finger of the right fist, was the one: 1. The tattoo's font was Rebel Bones Bold.

"Sixty-One Tributes." Sydney pressed her lips tightly together, "A validation of when slavery was still legal, yet losing its acceptance. The year 1861, before the Emancipation Proclamation. Sixty-One Tributes. 1861: the year that eleven states seceded from the United States to form the Confederate States of America. Homage to slavery in the United States at the time when the Civil War defined the divides between the Confederacy and the Union. When the struggle to preserve the Union and end slavery set a decisive course for how this nation would be reshaped. They, the Sixty-One Tributes, are just that. Sixty-One of them. And their affiliates. Only sixty-one members and as many affiliates as they choose to align with."

"Sixty-one," Ruby said. "Sixty-one and then some idiots that believe we're getting softer, weaker, misaligned with the time when America was tough. They revel in the thought of going backwards."

Adele asked Ruby, and then the group, "On one hand, they, and I dislike common ground here, but they think like Ellipsis thinks – institutions can't be relied on alone to advance us. We also believe that societies and consortia can only do so much. Our coalitions are responsible for moving us forward, not backward. We're fragmented. Completely over here, on the other, they want to manage by strength and hatred and fear. We want to advance and maintain where we think we've diminished or lost a step."

Sydney spoke again about the Sixty-One Tributes, making eye contact with each of them, "We had limited access to this site," she referenced the fists on the big screen. Something changed recently. None of our pass-code breaking tools help us crack our way in. Not Hashcat, not John the Ripper, not Brutus."

Vendemer, who had been quiet, asked, "Have we tried THC Hydra or Medusa?"

"Tried them too." Sydney replied.

"RainbowCrack?" Allegra asked.

Sydney glanced at her new tech-savvy teammate and shook her head for affirmation on that tool also. "Looking for some new tools, we are. May lead to something. May lead us to nothing."

Bing spoke again, "Well, let's just go kick some asses in the meantime. When does the fun begin? What do you propose?"

Sydney spoke again, "Well that's up to you guys, but every day is a form of hell. We do know that the second Saturday of each month they convene, swapping out 'the product', in other words the victims, checking the parameter, sometimes just fucking around for hours watching sports or playing cards or whatever. Like a clock, second Saturdays and they are there for about six hours. They arrive at nine o'clock. Can't explain it other than it's likely the contract driving the discipline."

"So, three days from now?" Marco asked.

"Correct." Sydney replied.

"If we don't go in now, when we think we know they'll assemble – we might spook them off. And another thirty days isn't a favorable option."

"It isn't," Sydney prompted, "But can you guys pull it off with such short notice?"

A moment later, it was Chuck that responded, "Hey Syd, give us a minute or two. We'll get back to you later today."

"Thanks Chuck. Thank you everyone. We cannot do this without your courage and bravado."

"We're going to hang on this call and talk among ourselves if you all wish to drop."

Allegra addressed them, "Bing, Chuck, Jude, Marco...it's been a pleasure, but wish we were meeting under different circumstances."

Their goodbyes came in rapid succession. *"Later, Bunny- Bye-bye, Sweet Cheeks - Farewell, Foxy- See ya- Sunshine."*

"Out." Sydney hung up the meeting room's end of the call. A battleship grey blank screen remained on the wall where the four freedom fighters were seconds ago.

"Well, you sure were a hit. Brightened their day," Ruby babbled without emotion.

Allegra asked, "Does this plan meet the need?" No one answered.

Everyone was thinking about the danger ahead. Asking the brave soldiers to consider a firefight. The cause was worth it, but the imperilment was a cause for pause.

Their reserve consumed a minute.

Sydney spoke first. It was a question she asked while looking at her screen, "Are we letting ourselves dream too big? Too big for our britches, are we?" The question hung in the air between them, unanswered.

Allegra had another question for no one in particular, "Do we really have enough data to make a decision here?"

"What opportunity does the three days present? What additional risks?" Vendemer quietly spoke, as if asking himself, calling into question the timeline.

"What if the drones don't do what they're supposed to do?" Ruby queried no one while looking at the logo of the two angry white fists facing them on the screen.

"Is it seven, or eight, or more we might anticipate? Are they scaling in headcount?" Jacob referred to the evildoers anticipated to be on the ground, casting additional doubts.

The silence was deafening. Only the ballasts in the lights above made the slightest buzzing sound.

Adele finally contributed to the interrogatives, "What do you think...those people... in those metal boxes...are thinking about right now? How much...hope...do they have left?" Her soulful conundrums caused them to see into each other, finding obstacles which they knew would be overpowered by their collective sinew and capabilities to deliver virtue. By their good grace, they knew that they would find a way.

*****

Steve Booth had been surfing porn for two hours. It was time to do something about it. He unbuttoned and unzipped his jeans when his cell phone rang.

"Hello..."

"Sthdeve Booth! Guess who?"

"Oh...hey there."

"Hey buddy! You'll never guess why I'm calling..."

Steve didn't know how to reply,

"What kind of sandwich do you want? We'll see you Saturday as usual, at nine o'clock."

"Oh, nithe! Thcore." He pumped his fist in the air, finally feeling apart of the team. "How about...hmm, let me thee...how about...hmm, let me thee. Well, I don't know. What are you...?"

"Steve, dude. I don't have all fuckin' day here."

"Hmm...meatball thub, pleathe. And chipth if thath pothible."

"Man of distinction. You got it buddy. See you at nine o'clock, Steve. You got that, buddy?"

"Okay, thoundth good, thee you then." The call dropped before Steve could finish saying what intended to say to the pinky cutter. Inclusion. Something to look forward to.

Nine o'clock. Said twice, 'nine o'clock'. It was a decoy.

The croaking from the swamp had begun again. Uncertain of its origin, bullfrogs or cicadas or small gators, he held his hands over his ears until it subsided some. This panging irritation would come and go. The scraping of branches against the container steel container with The Product inside it bothered him also. Nothing was worse than shoveling the metal container. He'd shovel the corrugated bottom, scraping it - then need to take a break from the noise, repeating the sequence: shovel, take a break, shovel, take a break. The noise sensitivity which Steve experienced was getting worse as time passed. It began shortly after his Momma passed away.

Steve's desk was cluttered with machine parts. Wrenches, vice grips, pliers, screwdrivers, and tubes of engine grease with oily exteriors which were once white covered the surface. More tools were out of the toolboxes, than were in their intended compartments.

Momma, she was always so organized. She'd say that there was a place for everything, and everything had its place. To Steve, if it's out and you can see it...there it is! If you have to look for it...well, that just takes more work. "Thorry, Momma. You dithlike metheth, I know...I know." Gone she was, not there to hear the apology he was giving her.

The grime had made its way to the keyboard of the computer. Once a shiny silvery platinum color, the keys were barely detectable, and the touchscreen sensor was losing its ability to detect his fingers. He plugged in a mouse to do the job.

He checked email as he was instructed to do daily. There was an additional reminder about the routine nine o'clock meet up. Steve's thought was that nine was a bit early for lunch, so he'd have breakfast after noon and the sub for breakfast. "Problem tholver," he said to himself.

Large towering thunderheads were building in the sky. A wind had picked up causing the scratching sounds on the container. He scrunched up his nose and held the palms of his hands over his ears again.

He forgot why his pants were unbuckled and unzipped and re-assembled himself. It was time to feed and shovel the shit. Food first. That horrible scraping sound from the steel box second. He shuddered at the thought of the scraping.

His thumb drive was sticking out the side of the laptop. It had images he'd download from the websites. It also had a worksheet with all of his passwords, account numbers, his bank routing number, bitcoin accounts, and reminders of when his bills were due. Steve was careful with the drive. He unplugged it and placed it in the backpack where he stored his laptop.

Before the scraping of the container's bin housing the Product, he'd grind a few more stakes. The stakes would be driven into the ground to help secure more of the camouflage netting. Five down, four to go. He turned on the bench grinder which was harnessed to a heavy worktable. Steve placed his headphones back on to limit the noise and eyewear on to prevent sparks from shooting into his beady eyes and leather work gloves. The diamond tipped blade caused a humming sound as it was turned on. As Steve inched the metal stake closer to the blade, the vibration shook him. He was careful not to grind into the blade, but rather away from it. The sparks flew away from him toward the work yard. The sound was like that of a plane's jet engine, of which Steve had never flown on before. The heat from each bar of metal grew warmer the longer it was held to the machine sharpening it. An iron-ore smell filled the air along with the flying sparks.

In between the stakes, Steve turned on the music by cranking the small black dial. *Round and Round,* a song by RATT coincidentally played as the grinder's blade spun round and round and round, causing the sparks from the steel to arc wildly in the air.

Steve Booth was busy. From one project to the next, the side hustle consumed his time. He never stopped to consider what else he might accomplish. To him – any direction was what he deemed his purpose. His considerations were limited. His curiosity was squelched when his Momma passed away. His intentions toward any form of a better elsewhere were hijacked. Like the sparks flying aimlessly from the grinder's wheel, Steve haphazardly contributed to the malfeasances of his ignoble and lumpen coven. Unknowingly aligned to Sixty-One Tributes, he went about each day filled with slapdash tasks, like the sparks, moving their sinful agendas forward.

* * * * *

'61Tr' was as far as Ashford could get with the password-busting system. The website was unresponsive. *Perhaps they were on to something? '61Tr'.* That was one angle, something which led to something else - perhaps. *But to what?* He had a couple *fizzles* and three *maybes* in play. There were some pops and drops. Nothing solid. This occasional texting with a Miami number from his burner phone was another attempt with slight promise. The communication about a future meet up was the most intriguing so far. The last time, it led to a white supremacists' neo-Nazi skinhead drinking party. Or at least that's what it appeared to be. In other words, he concluded, that particular faction was more hype and talk than anything else.

His phone pinged again, *"Would you consider yourself a true patriot of the old world?"*

"We were better then than now, weren't we, my brother?" Ashford typed with his thumbs, just like Ashley did.

"Amen, brother."

He told himself to play it cool and to not appear too needy. *"Anyone who screws with the righteous parties I affiliate myself with…well, FAFO!"* Perhaps the acronym for Fuck Around, Find Out would offer a glimpse of his pretentious incivility. Ashford would need to temper his boorishness with respect for unruly authorities of shared doctrines. This was not his lone wolf moment. This was his pack-tending infiltration play.

A long pause between texts caused Ashford to think he blew it. Then, ten minutes later a reply. *"Like what I'm seeing from you. Maybe there's something we can do together. What are your thoughts on being a contributor for a cause of taking back strength?"*

Ashford forced himself to be patient. *"I could be down for that. Maybe a meet up at some point."*

"Tampa, right?"

"That's the one. Correct." Ashford was locking triangulation upon the location of the phone number but couldn't get more exact than the metro-Miami area code. It was probably a burner phone, but the texts pinged the area code within its jurisdiction. A call would help him get close to a cell tower. It would require taking a meeting to gather more information on this potential scumbag.

"There just happens to be a project we're at work on south of Naples. Could use a good man or two, know of anyone with a short leash interested in some side work?"

"Me, yes. I don't trust anyone else right now though. Looking for a unit to join up with."

Several minutes passed before the final text came through: *"Good answer. Nothing more for text messaging. We'll talk about the rest of it. Is this a good number for that conversation?"*

"Affirmative." Ashford typed.

"Southern boy, we like that too."

"Rebel Yell, hell yes." Ashford tried his best to appear like a redneck embracing the Confederate soldiers charging battle cry. It was the final text message he received.

Ashford's tuna sandwiches were crunchy. He had filled the mixing bowl with two small cans of StarKist brand, four stalks of celery which was a copious helping, small-cubed apple pieces, raisins, and pine nuts. The sourdough bread was the over-sized loaf type from the bakery at the grocery store and was sliced thick. Not sure of what truly went into tuna salad sandwiches, as he took a bit of the first, he decided that this wasn't the combination. But it smelled good and tasted…different. Perhaps his tuna took on a chicken salad flair. Again – he was reminded that Ashley had all of the kitchen skills, and he was lacking in that category.

One hour later, Ashford's phone rang from the same Miami-based phone number. He looked at it. The fish was on the hook. "Let's see if I can reel it in," he said to himself before answering.

*****

In the framework of transparency, they asked each other not to leave the room for personal calls, but rather to take them and share a silhouette of what was taking place. It was standard practice while in the war room discussions with Ellipsis.

"Hey! Remember me?"

"Hey Mags, yeah…uh, sorry. I'm slammed on this build out Vendemer assigned me."

"But he's there with you right?" Maggie said it before she thought it through. "Oh, and he's like *right there*, like *right now* and you can't get away from whatever. Just say 'yes'."

"Something like that. Yes." Allegra lied and winced away from the phone knowing that Maggie had a built-in lie detector.

"I totally get it," Maggie said, and did.

It worked. Still got it. Allegra thought. "Listen, we gotta' get together. Lots to talk about."

Ruby, Sydney, Jacob, Adele, and Vendemer all looked up from their laptops and at Allegra as she said it. To calm her new cohorts, she scanned the table and held out her hand as if stopping traffic, assuring them that she too was staging – simulating something that would not happen – divulging not even a trace of what was taking place.

"Oh yeah? Like the way you said that. Like, the mentor guy you're in to? What is he like fifty-five years..."

"Not the time or place, sister. Conversation for another time."

"Ewe," she said quickly, "Make good choices."

"Text me some places and times."

"You owe me detail. I'm picking pricey."

"Okay. Alright." Allegra was hoping she wouldn't ask any more probing questions about Jacob. Especially with Adele sitting across the table, within earshot, Maggie's volume might cause a suspicion of her impish imagination, which had been piloted to a placid place so far.

"You're talking fast again. I know what that's code for. Ciao Bella, girlfriend."

"Okay, Ciao," Allegra repeated bobbing her head from side to side wondering when Maggie, who clearly missed her friend, might stop blabbing and spilling an indiscretion.

"As in goodbye beautiful, not where I'm going to have you take me."

"Got it, Mags,"

"Bye. Loser."

"Was a Geek, now a Loser. Love you too." Allegra clicked the red button on the face of the phone, ending the call.

She still had Vendemer and Ruby looking at her. "Maggie – bestie – knows much, but not this – not any of this - clueless on the detail of things – loves the spicy stuff." It was the simplest need-to-know synopsis of her all-time best friend. She felt it wasn't the proper respect Maggie deserved but required of the listening ears audience.

Ruby gazed at Vendemer for verification. Following Vendemer's single nod, Ruby also returned to his laptop. They were partitioned in their potential assignments.

Allegra glanced in Adele's direction at no reaction. Apparently, her secret was still safe. She added to the strategy, "We'll want to install a few checkpoint cameras on the road, there's only one, in and out of

Everglade City. This is to monitor traffic, civilians in the area, or unknown backup, eyes in the skies can only do so much on a cloudy day. Before you ask, I'll pay close attention to the forecast."

"Use NOAA," Jacob added.

She looked at him, unknowing where he'd encountered the use of the National Weather Service tracking system – perhaps from his time on Oahu, and reaffirmed, "Of course, will do."

Then Sydney's phone rang. The call was less than thirty seconds. "The boys are a 'go'," she said. "We're on."

"Well, that was fast," Jacob said.

"Real fast," Adele added.

Breaking from her British demeanor and proper etiquette, "They don't fuck around much, do they?" Sydney gave her conviction of certainty, adding, "Alight then, time to crack on."

"What's next?" Allegra asked, directing the question to Ruby and Sydney.

"There are three tiers of field agents. Primary, locked and loaded, fire at will. Secondary – like Sydney here, firearm carrying, former special forces or defense operative, fire if instructed to do so. Tertiary, like Vendermer and me and now the three of you – no weapons – civil services duties. You're chipped and tracked and..."

"Microchipped?"

"It's a patch, like a thick Band-Aid, you wear it on one of your butt cheeks and there's a tag in your shoe. Maybe another in a bracelet or watch. You'll need a physical. Jacob had a heart attack. He's high risk. Why he's working closely with Adele, gentle eyes – easy to look at. No good in a street fight."

"Wait...back to Sydney...you were what MI-6?"

"Perhaps," she said, not looking up from the keys she was tormenting with her fingertips. Following her own advice, she was cracking.

"The drones, you assured us they could be programmed in an afternoon?" Ruby asked.

Allegra shook her head, "It's easy, but just takes repetition and a mask for the program, assigning each drone a unique configuration so that they don't mash up."

"So manual, not automatic. Meaning each device needs touched, but again – not too time consuming. We've done this." When Vendemer spoke, Ruby and Sydney appeared comforted. When Allegra, Jacob and even Adele spoke – an additional question or peek to Vendemer was required for assurance.

Jacob looked to Ruby. "What now, what's next?" he asked.

"Got a better place to be?"

"No, old man. I gotta' take a piss."

Ruby giggled. "We've been at it a while. Enough for now, people. Keep in touch on the burner phones. Anything, I repeat, if anything doesn't feel right about this – meaning if you have reservations, concerns, ideas, you get it – bring it up on a group chat on your burner phones. Keep it off the cloud."

Vendemer stood first, "I'm with Paisley. The men's room calls." He snapped his fingers and pointed in the direction he was expeditiously heading.

Collectively, the Ellipsis teammates reassured each other that should anything come up, they would work together to resolve it. Pre-supposed that they were doing all the right things, or the best-of-their-ability things, or necessary things to help – they falsely assumed that money was the overarching mechanism which drove the intent of Sixty-One Tributes forward. It was the well-known artist, Jimi Hendrix, which is attributed to the quote, "When the power of love overcomes the love of power, the world will know peace." The Ellipsis organization, formed and forming, had some storming, norming and performing yet to do to catch up to the love of power. Unknowingly, their power of love was growing in its seedling strength, but the love of power was deeply rooted within Sixty-One Tributes.

*****

"Why did you think that was a good idea?" Tamsen was angry – or acting as if she were. It was a staged phone call, intended for listening ears. Some of it on speakerphone, some of it off of the broadcast in her home on the ledge of the North Shore. "Why on God's earth would you ask me to send a text to a former boyfriend of mine – who's married I should add – taunting him to engage? Why?"

He needed to pretend here as well. For the other end of the call, and for his. "You did it from your 808-burner number, right?" Ruby wasn't at all rattled from her attack as he was playing along. He too had some mild entertaining to do. This was an intentional conversation – and for the ears of Kate, Tamsen's house guest and within earshot when they performed these rehearsed phone calls.

"That isn't the point, Ruby!" Tamsen's tone caused her dog to cower and migrate to its bed in the den. It was drizzling outside and strong enough to not see the shore any longer.

"That was totally the point. I've had my eye on him for a year now. There's something there." Ruby was impressed with his improv.

"There's nothing there."

Ruby paused, "I don't know why you're so upset. It was a text to someone who's got some potential. He doesn't know it was you. I could have...should have...used another resource, but there are few in Hawaii. You piled on to what I sent, compelling him to engage. He'll think it was someone from SD State, some former Aztec football player pranking him. This kind of volley is what we do to uncover character. I'm scouting. I'm doing my job, uncovering talent..." Ruby paused for a few seconds. "You still listening?"

"Well, yes Goddamn it!" Tamsen faked the anger into the call. "He'll figure out it came from me, then there will be needless drama..." Tamsen picked up a cup of coffee gone cold and tossed the liquid in the sink. The splatter soiled the hand towel draped over the ledge. Kate peeked into the kitchen and quickly retreated, seeing a ferocious

Tamsen having a heated conversation with a mysterious man named Ruby.

"The only drama is the one you're creating...T."

"I fucking hate it when you call me that! I can't believe this is happening. Do you know..." Tamsen pressed her lips together, fighting the fake fury. "I don't stand for those kinds of shenanigans. A married man, happily married with kids too, shouldn't have any engagement with an old flame from high school."

Ruby had been waiting for it. "Didn't he turn you down? Weren't you the one with the crush?"

"Oh...oh, them's fightin' words, my friend." Tamsen was shaking her head and began to pace. The beauty of the North Shore was special when it rained. The waterfalls filled in force. But for the sake of Kate, she couldn't act pleased or smile at the lush valley below them reaching out to the beaches and the sea. She needed to pretend to be intense and pissed-off.

Ruby's turn for some faux dialogue, "There isn't going to be any fight. I'll drop you from the pursuit. We'll recruit him and you won't know about it. You'll be in the dark and not have any contact with each other. If you don't want to know what's going on, you'll operate on other tasks and in the dark, autonomous of each other."

He's good at this role play, Tamsen thought, going with it. "Well, now I'm getting pissed off about that." Tamsen wanted something, anything to feed her fire she felt.

Ruby held an unlit cigar in his hands as he sat in the bar of The Bowery Lobby. He didn't smoke but thought about it because he did twenty years ago. Occasionally he ordered one, carried it around a week, and threw it away. He was enjoying the squirming Tamsen was enduring and hoped it was being heard by her temporary guest, Kate.

Sammy, the former trader from Jacob's former firm, PPCM, and Charlie, Ruby's son sat there listening to one side of the conversation. They were surfing the screens of their phones, perhaps playing an online game against each other. Charlie raised his eyebrows when he heard his father beginning to speak, presumably being cut off, then picking up calmly where he left off. Unrattled, Ruby smiled at Charlie and Sammy occasionally whether they were looking at him or not.

Ruby's glass was nearly empty. Little of the amber whiskey remained and not enough to float the single ice cube in the middle of the cut crystal goblet. Sammy, who occasionally worked at the Manhattan establishment made eye contact with Ruby, pointed at the drink and then at the bar, motioning another round. The old man waved him off and mouthed a 'thank you' followed with a small smile.

The Bowery Lobby bar in Manhattan's Bowery Hotel was adorned with warmth. Cushy velvet's in hunter green, golden wheat, and camel colors within the dimly lit and oozing atmosphere created the never-leave and have-just-one-more or let's-get-a-room utterances from couples congregating. Oriental rugs covered dark hardwood throughout the establishment. The expert bartenders in their red velvet vests serving creative cocktails caused lingering conversations and meaningful connections to happen.

She wasn't at all penetrating him in this moment of peacefulness. Her synthetic and manufactured need to get something off her chest was important to convincing Kate. Ruby continued to listen, adding less logs to her bonfire.

"Are you still there?" she asked.

"I'm here, Tamsen. You done?

"No, I'm not. That charity I wanted to support. Did you have a chance to look at their website? I sent links."

"Support them. Ask Paisley for a withdrawal and do what you got to do. I support it. You don't need me for that."

She was quiet. "Alright. I'll call Jacob and ask for a hundred thousand."

"Cool. I'm sure he'll arrange a wire transfer on the dark wallet accounts." Ruby held the cigar close to his nose sniffing it. Sammy and Charlie looked up from their phones and Ruby made a mouth mocking gesture indicating the woman on the phone he was talking with was rambling. They chuckled to themselves and returned to the devices.

"No. Bitcoin."

"Okay – Bitcoin it is."

"You're making this easy. That's concerning." Tamsen's tone softened from the attack and became suspicious, "Why?"

"Your sense of agency is distinct. You're a valued teammate and this is what's important to you. Not as important to me, no disrespect..."

"Supporting women in need isn't im..."

"Let me stop you right there, Tamsen. Supporting women in need is exceptionally important. But the checkbook only has so many zeroes. The pockets only contain so many dollars. And the BOTA Benefits program is honorable. But you can do that on your own and shield Ellipsis from awareness. We're not going to ACH a hundred thousand dollars or any amount into an existing org. Not ever going to happen. Thank you for your due diligence and in determining it is a legit cause. Go do it if that's what's important to you. I'm not holding you back. I'm encouraging you to drive it. Go fast."

"You're not seeing the big picture there. You know that, right?" Tamsen was speaking quickly and adding needless spices to a warming discussion which was one-sided and could have ended differently.

"I hear you. You're..." Ruby deliberately stopped speaking into the phone. Then picked up again, "...when we have the time..." He intentionally caused his own disruption, while acting like his few understood words were a retreat, "...and then we'll..." He smiled at his own acting – as if he were concerned, faking the concession. "Is that...with you? Tams...Tamsen? Oh damn..."

As he clicked the phone he smiled and raised his glass to Charlie and Sammy.

On the other end of the call, Tamsen swore to herself, "Fucking skyscrapers. Always cutting me off when I have a point to make."

She looked in the distance and saw Kate duck back into the bathroom.

"Kate?"

The blond girl edged her nose back out of the doorway. "Do you two want to kill each other or what?"

"Or what," Tamsen replied. "Sorry you had to hear that."

"Your ex?"

"What's that?"

"Was that you ex, you know on the call?"

"Oh, God no," Tamsen answered, "That was just business. An associate that I need to spar with once in a while."

"Fierce," Kate said. She thought of the text she had just sent her new Bravado surf girlfriends: *Testy Tamsen is torturing some dude on a call. Think it's her ex. Why can't Gen Geriatric just text?*

One quick reply was returned - from Terri: *IDK. Generation playing-for-keeps just needs to chill. Live in the moment. Too many good waves out there.*

Another replied, Zoey, ignoring the context: *Aloha Bitches. Kate, when are you back?*

Kate responded: *Tomorrow*

Ashley responded a minute later: *Looking forward to the Long Beach party. We drinkin'!*

Tamsen's mission was accomplished. She had shown a ferocious side to the new Bravado teammates, substantiating her corporate presence and verifying her involvement and branding stewardship.

Kate walked on eggshells to the kitchen, peaking around the corner, careful not to piss Tamsen off any more than what the call may have done.

"Hey Kate!" She spun around, startled, to see Tamsen in a bikini and nothing else.

"Oh! Shit! You scared me!" she breathed short, startled breaths, and held her hand to her chest.

Tamsen's abs were that of a bodybuilder, their definition showed the small tight muscles, a six pack complete with obliques, lack of much body fat – a surfer's perfect body. Her perfect breasts were barely covered by the tangerine and white neoprene. "Looks like it's clearing up. Wanna go see if we can catch some waves?" Her smile was bright. She nodded her head toward the ocean where it looked promising.

"Sure. I'm packed. Let me change." Kate hesitated and confirmed, "You're not still...pissed off, are you?"

"Oh, honey...I just got a little enthusiastic. You have got to stand up for what you believe in. Take it out on the waves, what do you say?" Tamsen thought...*and the Academy Award goes to: Tamsen Makua.* She nodded her head to the Pacific again, curtain bangs waving as she did it. "C'mon, let's go shred."

"Let's go cut it up," she giggled and had more pep in her step than when she, seeking a glass of water, slunk in.

"We'll see if you can keep up," Tamsen mentioned, looking at Kate, winking.

* * * * *

"Do you think he's running at full capacity?" Tamsen was at it again. Her rant was unusually long. Jacob had been tolerating her verbal countenance for fifteen minutes.

"I think..." he was cut off.

"Because I don't. I'm alarmed that I have to request a claw-back. Has that ever been done. Is the FBI going to investigate this? It's an unusual transfer of funds, don't you think? You're the money man."

"Well, I wouldn't worry..."

"And has he even talked with you about the BOTA Benefits..."

"Tamsen, I got to ask you. And I'm hesitant to, but here it goes – is this about you, the cause, or what you committed to do with your surf company or for one of your Bravado protégées?"

"I can't believe that that's what you think. Is it really? Or is that Ruby thinking for you? C'mon man," she paused, then added, "Birds of a feather..."

"That's all me. Like it or not, I want to know." Jacob stood his ground because he really did need to know. Ruby did ask for his assessment. Her insistence caused him to question her motives. Her usual stability gave way to recent inconsistent rants and emotive outbursts.

The was a soft knock on the door. Jacob looked from where he was sitting, in the living room, into the kitchen. Adele, brewing a cup of tea for herself held out her hand, indicating she had it. Jacob continued to listen, watching Adele approach their condominiums door, opening it slowly, and interceding with Ruby. The old man tiptoed while smiling as he approached the sofa Jacob was perched on.

"It's a conversation for another time." She was agitated. "I'm hot, you're hot. It's a conversation for another time."

I'm not hot, but you sure are, Jacob thought.

Jacob wasn't going to alleviate her frustration. Ruby's presence with Jacob would surely turn stone into magma. They exchanged smiles and silent giggles with each other, Ruby knowing whom Jacob was speaking with.

"I'll make the time for you, Tamsen."

"Is this going to be when you pretend to utter words, fake reception problems, and hang up on me?"

"Not going to do that."

She huffed. "Awe fudge. I'll give you back the rest of your evening. Sorry to be such a pest. Talk later, brah." Tamsen hung up.

He looked to ensure the call had ended. "Well, I got a 'brah' at the end of the call." Jacob looked at Ruby and assumed something. "You drunk?"

Ruby laughed. "No. I'm not drunk. I tossed a few Old Fashions back with Sammy and Charlie at The Bowery Lobby bar. But, no, not drunk. Tipsy maybe."

Adele chimed in from the kitchen while retrieving ginger snaps to go with her tea, "We love that place, Ruby. Thanks for introducing it to us. Jacob's taken me there several times since."

He was about to say that he didn't live far from it, then stopped himself. He had been to Jacob and Adele's condo several times but had not yet disclosed his place to call home. "Yeah, it's a go-to, for sure." He looked at the glass of red sitting on the table next to where Jacob was perched.

Jacob noticing, offered, "You want a night cap? Have a seat. Sit there. Best seat in the house."

Ruby sank into the chestnut brown buttery leather recliner. "Oh, nice. A place for naps." He wiggled in and leaned back, sinking in the comfort. "Listen, I'm sorry if I'm here too late. Would you like me to leave?" Ruby's jacket wasn't yet off.

He shrugged when Adele let him in. Jacob assumed she offered to take his coat, and that Ruby didn't accept. "No, you're not here too late. You're right on time, as usual. I have a few questions."

"Old man Paisley isn't going to fall asleep for another hour or so, Ruby." Adele offered him tea and a cookie, and he declined.

He did look at Jacob and accept the glass of wine. "What is it liquor before wine, feeling fine. Wine before liquor, never sicker?"

"What are you seventy?" Jacob asked.

"Five," Ruby quickly added.

"And you're still relying on nursery rhymes to get you through..."

"What is that, a Cab?" Jacob's old friend asked. "Success?"

"Succession. An old friend owns the winery in Washington." He flipped the label around so that Ruby could see it better.

"Suc-ces-sion. Hm. Well, that's coincidental," Ruby said.

"What is?" Jacob asked.

Ruby shook his head, "Nothin'. Just an old black man rambling."

Before either of them said more, Adele delivered a glass with flakes of gold speckled on the bottom of the goblet and stem.

"Fancy glasses," Ruby commented.

"From Italy. Don't ask. Real flecks of gold. The taxes to import the 'gift'..." he looked over at Adele, was more than I'd pay for a set of four fine wine glasses."

"And you're not poor," Ruby added.

"I still think you're drunk," Jacob tagged on as he poured the bottle. *Glunk, glunk, glunk, glunk, glunk* sounds filled Ruby's glass as the jammy-scented and Byzantium-purple colored liquid rose in the glass, its bright bubbles clutching the sides.

"A new bottle. Did you let it breath?" Ruby raised his eyebrows jokingly.

"So, what's up? Why are you here?" Jacob was still wearing his clothes from the day, jeans and a soft brilliant blue cashmere sweater. Secretly, the sweater was a gift from Victoria, given a year before the waywardness. He liked it so much that he felt a need to fib to Adele about it – when she asked about it.

"Based upon the call you just got off of, I think you might know why I'm here. Well, one of two reasons. But first, Tamsen. There's a recalcitrance in Tamsen. Miss Makua seems to have a mind of her own. I'm growing concerned." He sipped at the vintage. "Mm. Smooth. This is good. Soft and velvety."

"Yeah, they know what they're doing." Jacob wasn't about talking grape juice at this point, "She wanted to throw you under the bus. You know...'thunk-thunk'. But I held onto the wheel and avoided squashing you. What's going on?"

Ruby looked at Adele, pretending to be busy cleaning the counter top.

She paused and smiled, looking back to the old man. "Busted. Right? Time for some man-to-man talk. I'm used to it." She looked to Jacob, recalling the trader discussion at PPCM.

He didn't know how to respond and simply smiled at her.

"What's the second reason?" Jacob asked Ruby, acknowledging Adele leaning on the counter top with her elbows, now in full voyeur mode.

"I need a favor. How's your card game?"

"Card game. Poker?"

"I'm assuming you've played..."

"I'm a force to reckon with," Jacob answered.

On that note of surprise, Adele piped in from the kitchen, "Oh, really...?"

"But I don't think that's what you've got up your sleeve, is it?" Jacob asked, prompting Ruby to connect the ask. He also looked at Adele and added, "I can hold my own."

She replied teasingly, "I know how to read that face of yours, Paisley. Say when."

"Okay, here it is," Ruby began, "Bump stocks, as in firearms, are back in the legislative process. There have been Presidential Executive Orders, Supreme Court rulings, lobbying, blah, blah, blah...and now it's heading back to Congress for yet another congressional vote. This time...may be different. Two congressmen on opposite sides of the isle, a Republican and a Democrat are crucial in a bump-stock vote. A couple of good old boys from Georgia and Florida. They're friends. Good friends with history...a mischievous history we'll call it." Ruby paused, choosing his words carefully, "Perhaps they share some secrets together. They may be compromised by the NRA. We need you to help..." he paused, "sway their vote. Less guns and automatic rifles good – more ways to kill each other – usually bad – if you know what I mean. Doesn't take much to figure that one out."

"How in the hell am I going to do any of that over a card game?" Jacob asked.

"It's more than a card game. They are a bit gluttonous." Ruby held his hands outside of his own body's size, "not just in food and drink, but in other things. They live, how should I say...large. And naughtily. And waywardly. And a bit selfishly. And... I'll stop there."

"Work hard, play hard? A couple of rascals?" Jacob sought some confirmation, looking over at his yellow lab, Kolohe, looking back at him.

"I would say they work hard, but they definitely play hard. Enter gambling. They bet on anything and everything. There's a private club in the city here..."

"Private house underground poker." Adele called it.

"Correct," Ruby looked her way. "Adele's heard of it." He didn't say more, thinking that she'd be thoroughly offended to take part in the task. She was, a lady.

"I read about it in a novel." She glanced Jacob's way, "Like in Molly's Game – that movie we liked."

Jacob looked at Adele blankly, then toward Ruby. "What do you want me to do? Beat them at poker and tell them to..."

"Is it a black-tie type of event? Like a James Bond thing?" Adele added. "Can I pick out a glamorous flowing gown and ask to have my martini shaken, not..."

"You're going to want to sit this one out, Adele." Ruby shook his head as he looked at her. "This might not be a place for a classy babe, like yourself."

Jacob looked at Ruby. "Not only do we have a couple sleazy politicians, but we also have a disrespectful environment?"

"Underworldly seedy. Gunrunners, drug dealers, ex-cons, money launderers, terrorists, embezzlers, lobbyists, prostitutes, the most questionable characters..."

"I get it," Jacob interrupted.

"All mixed in with celebrities and sports stars," Ruby continued. "Basically, anyone that can be bought and sold or is famous and just loves to play in the underground gambler's space – mixing it up with a very risqué environment."

"What specifically do I need to do? Befriend these yahoos in some way?"

"Fly them to JFK," Ruby answered.

"Fly them to...?" Jacob attempted to ask.

"We'll arrange for you to have a private shared ownership jet in Savannah, where they'll jump aboard two open seats to New York. They have a meeting in NYC with a few other lawmakers – dudes from Vermont, New Hampshire and one of the Dakotas. Jimmy and Bobby will meet with the NRA a day later to firm up..."

"Jimmy and Bobby?" Jacob asked.

Ruby shook his head, acknowledging that he was getting ahead of himself, "Jimmy Gaines, Congressman from Georgia. Bobby Fonteneaux, Congressman from Florida. I'll let you figure out which side of the isle they sit on. Doesn't really matter. They know it's a doomed vote, split down the middle, fifty-fifty. Half of their constituents want no bump stocks, half of them do. They'll please half of their potential voters and piss of the other half."

"They're in it for themselves." Jacob surmised. "They just want to have fun along the way."

"Gambling. Girls. Booze. Often testing the guardrails of a lawmaker's boundaries – these big-time betters need a fun friend to fly with."

Adele had been quiet, listening. "Enter Jacob Paisley – the fallen falcon of finance."

"He's got an authentic story to tell – and will know just how to convince them." Ruby had details to share. But, stopped himself to guzzle deeply the red wine still filling half of the golden goblet. "Engage them in conversation. Offer to be their host for a dinner at Del Frisco's or The Old Homestead Steak House – we'll be listening in and managing all of the logistics. Bet on anything and everything that you can between Savannah and New York. Lose two of three bets. We'll help that happen along the way. Just do your best to get yourself invited to the poker game."

"What if I don't. I don't know – they're preoccupied. They don't cotton to us Yankees. Perhaps they won't..."

"Don't worry about that. You'll have a little help along the way." Ruby attempted to assure him.

"I don't need to know about all of that right now, do I?" Jacob asked.

"Not at all. When it comes down to it, you still a money man. They'll be interested in you. The genuine you, who knows how to get around things – to make money from money. If we get an opportunity to sway your wagering with them – either you'll know what gun company stocks to bet on or to short. Your interests will be pure and align with the knowledge you can pull or build with them in an afternoon and night.

"Night?" Jacob asked.

"The poker games don't begin until ten," Ruby matter-of-factly added.

"Old man Paisley is going to need a daytime nap." Adele giggled.

"When does this all take place?" Jacob asked.

"Tomorrow," Ruby answered quickly.

"Tomorrow? But we have Florida in prep and play..."

"Quick trip. Rest up on the way down to Savannah. You're going to go hard tomorrow night."

"Mm...this is going to hurt a little bit," Jacob squinched his eyes – thinking of how much more difficult it might be to entertain wildly now, and how easy it was with his PPCM traders just a short time ago.

"I'll go watch an episode of the Housewives of Silicon Valley in the other room," tossing a damp dishrag into the sink, Adele, in her blush-peach satin pajamas approached them, said her 'goodnights', and gave Jacob a soft kiss on the side of his forehead before she retreated to their bedroom, closing the door gently behind her.

"She's never watching crap like that," Jacob motioned with his thumb to the bedroom. "She's in their Googling and performing a data deep dive on Tamsen right about now or looking into how Jimmy and Bobby vote up and down their party's tickets."

"I love seeing how you always have her back."

"She has mine." Jacob's bottom lip protruded.

Ruby didn't know if he was thinking of Adele...or of the girlfriend experience with Victoria...or remembering a kiss from Mom.

Apparently, it was neither, as Jacob began, "I get that we're influencing the Congressmen. We're trying to turn a vote. Ellipsis business. But internally, risk awareness and management here," Jacob continued, "With your Tamsen. What kind of a pickle might we be in?"

"She isn't off the rails just yet, but the box cars are rattling." Ruby smelled the rim of the glass, "Cherry? Raspberry?" he paused slightly, "Maybe plum?"

Jacob realized that it might not be an early night and played alongside his friend, "I've got smoke, ball glove leather, and freshly cut grass. Oh! And pepper and chocolate. Maybe a hint of potting soil."

"Ha!" Ruby laughed, "I think I made a recruitment and hiring mistake. Notice how no one ever says that it tastes like grapes – the prime ingredient?"

"That would be boring, now, wouldn't it?" Jacob sat with the glass of wine in his hand, sniffing its rim, thinking. "What can I do?" Jacob took another whiff of the wine without drinking it, "to help you?"

"Not now, but maybe eventually, we make a tweak to our roster." Ruby leaned back on the armchair he was sitting on and looked up to the ceiling. He sighed deeply.

"I have questions," Jacob said. He poured himself another glass, meeting Ruby's level of a generous pour.

"Of course you do. That's why I'm here."

Jacob's reasoning skills in his investment firm were data based, fact based, based upon dollars and numbers – and occasionally the human intrinsic value of guesswork came into play. This wasn't as logical as it was emotional. "Is something, I don't know what, driving her manic panics? Is there an outside influence perhaps, which is compromising her?"

"Well..." he rubbed his hand over his chin feeling the stubble from a few days of not shaving. "Fuck if I know," Ruby said softly and mostly to himself.

"Maybe you do and don't want to say that you do. I've met most of your pod, your team, don't know the back end folks yet, but she seems to be someone you have trust in, but she an enigma – at least at this point." Jacob's assessment was more precise than what Ruby wanted to hear. He didn't want Jacob to be this in tune with his secret at this point.

The old man's response was a deep breath, apparently to Jacob, admitting there was an action which might need to take place.

"It's never comfortable," Jacob added, "'But what a leader sometimes must do."

Again, Ruby said nothing. He took another swallow of the red, from the golden flaked expensive Italian glass. "I suppose," he added, doing his best to convince Jacob that Tamsen was of growing risk. Then added, "Do you think the cost of the glass makes this wine taste better?"

"I do not. Looks like deflection there." Jacob continued, "Let me know when and how I might need to help...service...whatever your decision is with her."

Ruby shook his head slightly. He continued with his Tamsen masquerade. "We can't have people thinking for themselves. We can't have rogue operators or threads of secrecy broken. When we do, we shut things down. That can get uncomfortable." He didn't say more, allowing it to sink it. His conviction couldn't go overboard. Not just yet for full disclosure – even for Jacob, his rising protégé.

"Switching gears. I'd like to know about the money trail. Can we talk about it?" Jacob went for the source of funding benefactors as if it were a nine o'clock Monday morning meeting and not late in the evening.

"What do you want to know? Leaving my numbers out of it, of course."

"I don't want to know numbers. But really, just the rank of the philanthropic contributions." Jacob's curiosity caused Ruby to turn his head which was still looking at the ceiling toward Jacob.

"Ranking?"

"Who gives the most, driving the direction of Ellipsis?"

"Got it.' Ruby calibrated the roster of income and quickly came up with the answer, "At the bottom is Tamsen. Go figure. Least and loudest. Then, probably myself."

"You're out of it, but..."wow!'...I didn't know that about you."

"Inherited it. Another story. I'll tell you, soon," Ruby looked out into the Manhattan city lights configuring the contributions, "You'll know all of this eventually, anyway. Then Sydney. She is loaded. Old money. She's one hundred-x what I've contributed to the organization. Big gap there. And Vendemer. BenVen – way out in front. And these, these are just the people you know of. Private Equity, philanthropists, orgs that realize the social agencies our civilization has created isn't handily solving our modern problems... "

"Wait... Back up." Jacob held up a finger while he set his glass down. Vendemer?"

"By far. At the top of the stack. He's given the most to what we do and spend."

"Didn't see that coming. At all." Jacob frowned, disappointed that his gut assessment didn't factor into the actual fact that Vendemer was the highest distributor of funds for their clandestine organization. He would have pinned Sydney as the chief contributor to their cause, based upon a false assumption of her old-English and unknown wealth and stealth.

Ruby reached for his glass from the tabletop. "Benjamin Vendemer," he said. "Who in the world is BenVen, really?"

"What kind of name is that?" Jacob asked.

"What do you think it is? I know." Ruby teased.

"Um... Dutch? German?" Jacob answered, thinking of the spelling. He continued, "Maybe Norwegian?"

"Final answer?" Ruby asked.

"I'll go back to Dutch." Jacob reached for his phone.

"Don't do it. Spell Vendemer backwards." Ruby smiled from half of his face, like a Cheshire Cat with a canary hidden in its mouth, he had the self-satisfaction of the answer within his grin.

"R-E-M-E-D-N-E-V," Jacob, slowly, letter by letter spelled Vendemer backwards. "Remednev. Remednev," he repeated. "Sounds Russian."

Ruby pointed his finger in Jacob's direction and then snapped them for a 'yes'. "His great grandfather was an Oligarch. Veniamin Remednev. Veniamin is Russian for Benjamin. Benjamin Remednev – Benjamin Vendemer. BenVen - the largest benefactor of our group, our pod. Or as I like to call him, the Ben-efactor. Pretty cool, huh?"

"Not what I was expecting." Jacob annexed Ruby's appraisement with, "A diamond in disguise, for sure."

"Ha! Do I have an eye for talent or what?" Ruby's proclamation wasn't about talent at all, but rather about a source of fuel for their purpose.

Jacob left it alone, contemplating the money he was managing and growing for Ellipsis, and yet there was no accounting, no GAAP, no audits yet known for the growth or in bad market conditions, lack thereof. Finally, he broke his own silence. "There is no Board of Directors. There is no governance. No guardrails. No auditing. No hovering."

"You're getting there. When you find the right man, the proper people – un-leveraged – driven without regulators – toward the right causes... Well, then the correct things just might happen to right the wrongs."

"Does Allegra Sinclair know?"

"The girl? Hell no. She doesn't need to know, nor does anyone."

Jacob knew he meant Adele too. "Nothing will be shared."

"Oh, by the way. Can you cut her a check for a sign on bonus. One for you and Adele too?"

"Sign on bonus?" Jacob was curious.

"Yeah. One million dollars."

"What?" Jacob asked.

"Yeah, you heard me. One million. It'll be material to her."

"I... Sure. Didn't know that was part of the arrangement." Jacob acted surprised. "Tell you what, we'll defer ours. Payable next year."

"Whatever. It'll help lock her in. You two, not needed. Do what you wish there."

"When I ran my firm on Wall Street and had to cut a million-dollar bonus check from my ledger, Adele and I would go to Tommy Vans and drink."

"Or you'd go to the strip club and fifty grand on the lionesses." Ruby was matter of fact with his comment, which caused Jacob to consider just how much knowledge his friend had on him, for how long, and from what angle.

"Or that," Jacob admitted. "Lionesses, tigresses, leopardesses. Or that." His thoughts returned to Victoria. Her seductive and irresistible allure continued to play a place within his imagination. She was alive, but not well, within him.

"I think I know where you might have gone there. If so, get her out of your mind. If you can, that is."

Jacob said nothing to the comment. Instead, thinking, *get out of my head, Ruby.*

Ruby leaned back further in his comfy chair and downed the rest of the Cabernet that once filled the glass. He yawned. "Things happen, the known and the unknown, the remembered and the forgotten, well beyond what we can possibly perceive and outside of our limited understandings."

Jacob noticed that he was sleepy and beginning to close his eyes, but Ruby continued a rehearsed soliloquy, "The fingerprints we leave behind, they'll show our children and their grandchildren our awareness, our actions..."

He noticed Ruby's deep breathing as he continued speaking softly, "How we cared about our world... And theirs."

Ruby's eyes were heavy, yawning again, but managed to ask, "Say, remember when we first met? Well, when we first really met in the hospital following your heart attack?"

Not sure where the question might lead or for what reason, Jacob played along, "Yeah – I do. Why?"

Ruby yawned once more, "Oh...I heard you talk about stocks and options and trading on margin and what not." He was groggy. "But not so much lately. How are we doing?"

"We're currently seeing a twenty-two percent increase in capital appreciation. That's in unrealized gains but doesn't consider the cumulative return which captures some tax loss and cap gain harvesting. I've taken the proceeds and spread it across some cyclical closed-end funds that will guarantee double-digit yields should anything crazy happen. I spend two hours each morning as the market opens in front of the Bloomberg terminal..."

He looked over at Ruby, beginning to snore softly, and finished, "Yeah, that puts Adele to sleep too. I know why you asked me, old friend. You're a clever rascal, aren't you?"

Jacob reached for a throw that Adele normally snuggled up to while watching the non-sensationalized news at eleven - which was difficult to do in an election cycle. He held the soft grey cloak above the seventy-five-year-old prophet, he called his friend, careful not to awaken him. Turning out the lights one by one he opened and closed the bedroom door, knowing that there was so much more to know than he knew, and a responsibility was looming. Unable to identify it, he laid down next to Adele, but did not sleep – wandering and wondering in his thoughts.

He thought of two women – at odds. Adele was a restful sleeper. She awoke in the morning covered as she was when she fell asleep. Efficient. Victoria, when Jacob was with her, was restless. Tossing, turning, under the sheets, on top of the comforter, often waking Jacob in the middle of the night for a host of reasons. Sometimes to tell him she couldn't sleep. Sometimes making noises in the kitchen. Sometimes with an elbow flinging in his direction as she tossed a blanket or pillow. Sometimes, and sometimes more than sometimes, for sexual activities.

There was no disrespect intended for Adele and he wondered to himself quite often why he allowed Victoria to turn his head in the wrong direction. There was a regret which only time would heal, but the scar tissue would remain.

Peace. He preferred the placid partner at night he had in Adele. But was struggling to forget Victoria. Perhaps she'll always be along for the ride, he thought. An unwelcome and eternal passenger. He wondered if, in her jail cell, she was sleeping on the top bunk or the bottom bunk. When they were together, she preferred being on top.

Adele preferred to be by his side. She was loyal and true and above all else – his partner for all things, not just the finer things in life.

11

It Isn't Real

*A*llegra was daydreaming again. *In her imagination, she pictured herself and Jacob trading sexual innuendos. Jacob would look over her shoulder at the work she was doing on a spreadsheet and say, "We need to go deeper." Then, he'd lean over her, pointing at the cells in red and whisper close to her ear, "Here, and here, and there, and there..."*

Unable to restrain herself from her satisfaction of feeling the electricity between them, she would tuck her blond tendrils behind her ear and look up to him towering above her. She pictured herself questioning him, not to cross-check his intellect – but to taunt him. The intonation of her ask would open up her willingness, as she looks at him doe-eyed, "If I change this to that, would that be hard for you?"

He'd look at her, locking eyes for an extended period of time, "Hard is good – we've got to make it bigger than it is."

Allegra would look down to his crotch and say softly, "We can make it as hard or as easy as you want." She scrolled through the worksheet with him leaning over her closer to see the detail she shrunk.

"You're so fast with your fingers." Jacob would touch her back, slightly below her bra clasp as he watched her fingers click the keys. Her nails interrupting her work.

"I can be fast and effective, or I can be slow and deliberate – it's just what you want."

"I see..." His hand stroked her back intentionally, opposed to accidentally. She was sure that he wanted more.

"Let me show you more. If I come over here...and then I come over there..."

"Then you've come everywhere." Jacob acted amazed and uninterested in the work on her screen.

"Uh huh, good right?"

"Crazy good." Jacob replied, smiling softly.

"Do you want the work inside...or outside?" Allegra continues to tease him into a frenzy and highlighted the cells.

"Oh, definitely inside." As he said it his hands slid from her back down to the top of her skirt. She realized he was bending over further to smell her neck. His lips were and inch from her ear and she felt his breath. He was breathing harder and deeper.

"Yes. Yes, I agree, inside is best." In one fell swoop Allegra spun around in the office chair and grabbed him for a deep kiss, pulling him to her with his necktie. His hands were upon her breasts, feeling her when...

"Hello there, girl," Sydney had walked in on the fantasy. Her office sex imaginations were on hold. She'd have to migrate from hot to not and finish him off later.

"Hey," Allegra replied.

"Am I interrupting something?" Sydney was being British polite and not actually aware that she was interposing upon Allegra's growing desire for the attractive older man.

"Nope. Come on in and have a seat." Allegra couldn't mention that she was just about to reach for him as her breasts were being fondled. *This isn't real,* she said to herself. *Focus on the good work in front of you, not the selfish and naughty girl you want to be.*

Sydney asked, "Are the traffic cameras going to be live, for viewing a day before we execute?"

"There being installed today. And the altercation in the town is set up. Two cars will have an accident in front of the Collier County Bank. Down the street, a liquor store will be robbed. No harm to residents in either situation. Ellipsis actors, fake tourists in both cases.

The gun under the liquor store counter will be disarmed the night before. We pulled the city and county traffic camera footage. The white van which usually, like clockwork, rolls onto the premises at nine o'clock will be where we do our thing." Allegra looked at Sydney after reading her notes.

"Do our thing?" Sydney asked.

"You know...shoot 'em up, take 'em out...rock 'n roll... whatever they do."

Sydney just smiled at Allegra, and eventually nodded. Allegra felt judged, or new at this point, or perhaps missing something. She asked, "Am I missing something?"

"It's impressive how much you've added value and how quickly. So far, so good." Sydney crossed her legs and continued to look at Allegra.

Not sure what to say next, Allegra returned to the project management planner. "I don't know who to reach out to for the helicopters. Who to coordinate with, I mean. That's foreign to me. I assume you'll want to work with the mercenaries on all of that?"

"The important thing to remember always, especially when there's a firefight involved is that you leave in the same chopper you arrived in. Don't screw that up. Ever. Two helicopters of our own and a white van simulating theirs – for a good reason. The first helicopter is for speed and efficiency in an attack from the skies. The second is a larger bird, and for transporting our victims to safety." Sydney spoke with experience.

"I'll bet you've done something like this before, like with MI6?" Allegra's closest encounter with gunfire was at a country western concert she attended as a high school student, when three shots were fired a hundred yards away.

"They're never the same. Always best to be over-prepared. This is why you're of tremendous value. You help us think things through with new perspectives. Not all of it is new. But the thought process you bring for technology is enlightening. I think you'll be impressed with the trailer. It'll be set up in nearby Marco Island." Sydney was scrolling through Allegra's planner since it was on a shared drive.

"Yay. I've always wanted to go there. But...why? Why there?"

"Comms."

Allegra didn't comprehend, "Communications? But can't we hook up...?"

"Dedicated bandwidth. We own a dish there. The Siemens trailer requires a lot of juice – so the servers need 2,000 kWh per square meter. About twenty times the power consumption of a typical American home. We would have secure electricity from a reliable source, and our dedicated satellite wouldn't face the vulnerability of some unexpected altercation." Sydney had been here before. She knew what she was speaking about. Her knowledge of data consumption was from experience.

"We have our own satellite?" Allegra asked quietly, following Sydney's revelation.

"It's a small one. Shared. Not really dedicated. That was a bit of an embellishment. On the back of the UN's. But we paid for it. Shh... Don't tell anyone." Sydney removed he index finger from her lips. "Have you seen Jacob and Ruby or perhaps BenVen today?"

"No, why should I have? Did I miss a meeting invite? That's not..." Before she could finish, in walked Jacob, with Ruby and Vendemer. They were smiling.

He wasn't wearing a necktie, as he was in her fantasy. Rather casual in dress, he was wearing an open collar sky blue shirt, jeans, a navy jacket, and camel colored dress sneakers. The others were similar, but she focused on her man of fantasy, and he spoke first, "We have a sign-on bonus check for you."

"Uh..." she paused, "I didn't know that was a thing. Are you sure?" Allegra took several steps toward Jacob, and he took several toward her. Extending a traditional business type light green check, he said, "This is just for show, like one of those mambo sized checks you see people who won the lottery receive. It'll be a direct deposit."

She thought that he had made her panties damp five minutes ago and now he was giving her some money. "Thank you. All of you." She accepted it without checking out the sum.

"We're not here for any other reason than to see your expression. Look at it." Vendemer, he ultimate recruiter – her faux boss from the tech industry – the one who had his eyes on her for years cultivating her prowess and guiding her intentions knew the value of a dollar to someone in that industry, especially someone who had come from very little.

She dropped her chin to the top of her chest where her blouse opened up, and began chuckling a little, bobbing her head. Her golden hair rocked slightly as she came back up for, what she thought might be her face-to-face taunting from the group, "All right guys, thanks for the hazing. I get it. New kid on the block. Let's rib the gullible girl." Allegra looked up at them. They weren't smiling back.

"It's real, kid." Vendemer had his arms folded across his chest. Ruby had one hand in one pocket of his jeans. Sydney looked up from her laptop and back down at it, then back up, studying Allegra's assortment of expressions.

Jacob took a step back and added, "It's legit. You'll take your mind off of necessities for a while. Hell, if you're smart, you'll grow it ten times that amount over the next decade."

"It's a million dollars!" Allegra looked at the zeroes following the one again. "It's one million dollars. Oh my God, it's a million dollars." She looked back up at each of them to see if they broke out into laughter from some well-rehearsed joke, at her expense.

"It's a cool million," BenVen smiled. He still had the yellow teeth, but she suddenly didn't find them off-putting. "Comes without a quota, but does come with the strings of secrecy, responsibility, and significant intentions."

Allegra looked at each of them again. "Holy shit. I don't know what to say. Other than 'thank you'. Oh my god. Thank you."

Vendemer looked over at Ruby. Ruby looked over at Jacob. Jacob looked at Sydney, sitting quietly – breaking into a small smile. Sydney didn't take her eyes off Allegra.

"Are you sure? Am I dreaming? This isn't real, is it?"

"It's real. It's real," Vendemer repeated. He looked over to Ruby, "This was the best one yet." He moved in for a quick hug. "Welcome to our team."

Ruby was next with the hugging, and motioned for Vendemer to the door, talking about something completely different as they walked through the threshold.

Jacob was the last hugger. The best. He smelled good too. *Well...you made me wet and gave me a check for a million dollars today*, she thought as they embraced. It was a strong hug. She felt muscle under the jacket and a firm squeeze, but not where he squeezed her in her imagination earlier. He only said, "Work to do. Let's get after it."

"This isn't real," Allegra whispered to herself as she sat back down next to Sydney. She didn't know why she did it, but she lifted the silken pine green check to her nose to smell it.

Sydney looked up from her clicking, seeing her sniff the safety paper with the six zeroes following the one, and winked at Allegra. "You heard the man, work to do – let's get after it."

*****

"Thith ithn't real. Thith ithn't real. Thith ithn't real!" Steve Booth awoke in a cold sweat. He had a nightmare. In his dream, running from alligators and ten strangers who were chasing him with crimping sheers to cut off the rest of his fingers, he tripped, and they were closer. Then he ran into his workbench, and they were closer. Then, a white van pulled in front of him as he ran down the lane toward the highway into Everglade City, Florida – and again, they drew closer. He could hear the snapping of the Fiskars, the loppers, and the hedge shears as they approached. Some of them had a tight grip causing the sound of sharp blades to come together. Others we quick snaps that sounded like limb-limiting loud clicks. In his running away, he turned to see more alligators joining the chase. Their teeth snapped and their eyes blinked as they waddled quickly falling behind the men chasing Steve. "Thith ithn't real!" He would scream as he ran. Then his Momma appeared on the side of the road, calling out, "Run faster Stevie. Run faster baby! Momma loves you. Don't let them gators get ya, honey!" He ran past her trying not to look back. But now he could hear their footsteps on the crushed white shell of the roadway. Steve's legs were not long, and the cadence of his run was lopsided. *Snip, snip, snip.*

He sat up in his dirty sheets, dripping and breathing heavily. Looking around the bedroom for alligators or men with shears, he only saw a pile of soiled clothes and several tools laying on a small table with a lamp and a picture of Momma. They grey cast-aluminum streetlight that the men from his side hustle installed last week outside his window wouldn't turn off until daylight. Steve used a blanket to cover the window preventing the penetration of bright white LED from keeping him from a good night's sleep. The blanket wasn't doing its job well.

"Thith ithn't real," he said to himself one last time before he lay back down, lathered in perspiration.

Morning came quickly. Steve remembered the torment from last night's illusion. He shuddered. It was good to see Momma again. She was cheering him on as he ran past her, away from the alligators and the snapping blades of the hedge loppers coming after him. He didn't dream this way often, but when he did – it usually involved the uncertainty of the dark swamp, or the heavy weight of an engine part dropping onto his good hand causing him to bleed or being picked on by those mean school kids because he couldn't speak well. Those dreams didn't involve a manic panic where he woke up wet from fright and anxiety.

His cell phone rang. Eventually, he found it within the grubby sheets but missed the call. It was the cutter. It rang again, "Thdeve Booth thpeaking," he said.

"Stevie! Hey man, we'll see you in a couple days. Nine o'clock."

"Yeth thir, nine o'clock," Steve repeated.

"Remember that. Nine o'clock, just like always."

"Juth like alwayth," Steve recited his caller, holding his cell phone with the hand missing the pinky.

"Hey buddy. You haven't seen anyone poking their nose around the compound, have you? Anything seem suspicious? Anybody unusual anywhere around your place?"

Steve thought about the alligators in his dream chasing him and shuddered. Probably wasn't what the cutter wanted to know. Steve shook his head 'no'.

"Stevie, I can't see if you're shaking your head *yes* or *no*, so which is it, dude?"

"No. Ith a 'no'. Definitely a no''." Steve shook his head again, reaffirming that there wasn't anything unusual.

"Hm...Alright. It appears there might be a team of infiltrants, or maybe just a sole infiltrator out to shut us down, which would be bad for you, Steve. No sidehustle. You sure?"

"No action here. Thafe and thound."

"Well...alrighty then...keep your eyes peeled, Stevie. Might be a do-gooder or two out there. And that might be very, very, very bad. Doesn't help us much. We'll work on it on our end and see if we can't flush him out."

"Thoundth good." Steve was shaking his head 'yes', that he would keep an eye out for activity.

"Alright Steve. We'll see ya soon, little buddy." Click.

"Thee ya thoon," Steve said to no one. He clicked the red button at the bottom of his screen.

He waddled into the kitchen, opening the small black refrigerator to see if there was milk for his Froot Loops. Momma said it would be best to get a black fridge because sometimes her baby has dirty hands. Who knew that black could become grey? He looked at the uneven circle of grey grime surrounding the handle. Before he cracked the door, he wondered if he was still having a bad dream and an alligator would jump out at him, so he opened the door slowly. Only the milk jumped out at him in its odor. It smelled sour. He reached for the container, anyway, thinking that the Fruit Loops would hide the smell. Steve scrunched his nose, revealing his shortened front teeth. Their nubs which caused the speech impediment.

As Steve crunched at the candied cereal, he thought of the upcoming visit from his side-hustle companions. It was the only thing he was a part of. His only social interaction where he was a contributor in some sense was with the five men and one-woman group. Eventually they would tell him their names, instead of Steve having to listen to them talking with each other and overhearing their conversations. Momma said that wasn't a nice thing to do. And they were even kind enough to include him in a meal. Two days from now. On a Monday. He checked the calendar. Today was Saturday. Steve said it out loud, "Thaturday." Saturdays meant cartoons and where Momma would sit on the couch with him and hold his hand – when he had all of its fingers.

He found three Froot Loops on the floor, under the small table with smeary aluminum legs. Slipping them one at a time in his mouth, the yellow tasted the same as the red and blue. The Mandela Effect delivered a pair of O's opposed to the other vowels. Not understanding the difference between Froot and fruit anyway, Steve assumed that color delivered nutrition. Perhaps they weren't truly representing the color of their distinction, Steve decided. He studies the bird on the box with the over-sized bill and wondered what Toucan Sam ate to always appear so happy.

✳✳✳✳✳

"It isn't real," Brian repeated to Laki.

"But you don't know unless you try. Isn't that what you always say? The twenty grand was real. That came out of nowhere."

"Yeah, maybe that isn't real either." He reached down to pinch her butt.

She squealed, "Hey, what are you doing there?"

"Seeing if it's real."

"Ha-ha, funny. Watch it, I'll pinch you back when you're least expecting it." Laki tossed the damp dish towel over her shoulder. "It's about time to pick up the kids."

"Yeah, yeah...remember when Saturdays were ours? Filled with..." Brian let the unfinished sentence linger purposely.

"Filled with what?"

"That's just it. *Filled with what?* Nothing. No agenda." Brian fell back onto the couch. Lying there, he opened his iPad with facial recognition to check SportsCenter. The NFL playoffs were a bust for all of his teams, but still important for his business as a national chain of sporting goods stores – as a District Manager for southern California. Golf was a yawn to him, even though he had fist dibs on the 16th hole at the Waste Management Phoenix Open. March Madness was a way off. The NHL was a bit of a no-go for the island boy, so NBA was the only thing grabbing his interest at the moment. "The Clippers won, again. Yay!" he said sarcastically. Brian tossed the silvery device to the side. "It can't be real."

"You know what I think?" she said.

He answered quickly, "That I'm a hunk of brown-skinned goodness and you're *so grateful* I asked you into my life way back when??? That? Yes, I eventually felt sorry for you and took you in, I know..." Brian Kekahanamanui teased Laki whenever he could.

"Um...yeah, no – none of that. But I do believe that once upon a time, before I felt *sorry for you* because you had no charm and had to be schooled on how to treat a lady and I felt that I could use a project and took a Hawaiian boy on as a low member of my harem..."

"You lost me at *once upon a time*."

"No, seriously," Laki stopped what she was doing in the kitchen and spoke in his direction with her hands on her hips, "I wasn't always like this. It wasn't always like it is with us, now. *We weren't real.* And we made it happen. So, there it is again. Hope. Love. Fate. Something from nothing – never loses its charm." She resumed stirring the contents in a pot on the stove. "Just stealing a page from your playbook – you got to put yourself in play to score. You got to move those chains. You know?"

"It's the Aztec guys. Pranking me – I'm being punked. Not falling for it."

"Give me your phone. I'll reply," Laki shouted as she walked down the hallway taking off her top. Her bare back walked away from him and turned into their bedroom.

Brian had two options. A quickie before picking up the kids. Or, what he did instead. He reread the text messages from the solicitors:

The New York exchange text read: "*Choose Thrill over Chill. Why have a lame job or a vanilla career when you can deliver a real difference. Are you wasting your time running the circular race? Want more than the bore? Interested?*

Type Y for 'yes'. Or go back to what you were doing and type O for 'opt out'."

The next day, an 808-exchange text message supported it: "*We didn't hear from you. Surf's up! Want to catch our wave?*"

Three times the sequence repeated, with slight differences, indicating that it might not be bot generated. The last sequence included his first name and football number: "*Hey there, Brian, #16! We didn't hear from you. Surf's up! Want to catch our wave?*" That's what led Brian to think that an Aztec from San Diego State was pranking him.

Maybe Laki was right. Sort it out. Take a small chance at least to satisfy his curiosity. Time to bite on the bait, "*Who dis?*" Brian replied in a text.

In ten minutes, a response came through: "An acquaintance. Go Golden Hawks! An opportunity in leadership is emerging. Thought of you. Will be in touch soon!"

He was a little closer to solving the mystery. It was someone, likely from high school. Brian thought of family. His Aunty and late Uncle and the cousins of Nanakuli. It had been a minute since his uncle's funeral. *There's no harm in reconnecting with someone from the old west side,* Brian thought. *But, who?*

* * * * *

Ashford sat in silence waiting for the next text to come through. It had been a few minutes. When he received a reply, he'd want to take a minute or two to think things through and perhaps another minute or two to make them wait for him. The game of cat and mouse was strong.

'*Vindica te tibi*' was what Lady Barbara kept repeating. He remembered her explanation: "Emancipate yourself. Lay claim to yourself. *Vindica te tibi* - It means stop time from being stolen from you. Do not let it slip away."

Lady Barbara, the aged woman with overdone eyeliner, heavy mascara, a deep and raspy voice who saw into his heart immediately,

Ashford was thinking about her long fingernails, stroking the white smoke of incense in the still air between them. He thought about her words, what they might mean – if, they were meant for anything. "*You are strong. You are preparing for a battle.*" Then, she whispered. "*You are wise in this conquest. You will face evil spirits. You must be stronger than they, but...*" She paused. "*But not for your woman...*" Her eyes remained closed. "*For you...*"

"It isn't real," Ashford said out loud. No one was listening. He needed real things, not a fortune teller seeking desperate patrons to sink their dollars into the wooden box by the front door in their hopes of just that: hope. "It isn't real."

He did like the line, "...*emancipate yourself. Lay claim to yourself.*" He'd been enslaved since Ashley was taken. The time had finally come when he could do something, anything, one thing toward finding her.

If this didn't pan out, perhaps he'd give Lady Barbara another shot. But as seemed now, the text messages were more traction than anything the mystic provided. They were tangible, which was something his Software Engineer type of problem solving sought.

The text came through: *Okay – here's how this works. You rent a white service van. Ford, Chevrolet, or Ram. You drive it to the address we'll provide after we check you out. You arrive at 9am promptly. Promptly. Not 9:05, not ten after. You'll wait on the premises for exactly one hour. The team will arrive at 10 for a meeting. It is crucial that you arrive at 9:00am. We will be watching you. You'll need to complete a profile questionnaire in a link. Will send separately.*

Thirty seconds later, a hypertext link came through. Ashford smiled. It was their mistake, allowing him to track them through triangulation. If were merely SMS and MMS services, he would get close. With the link – causing a dynamic response – he'd identify and address which would either send him on a wild goose chase or uncover more detail than he wanted to know.

Ashford read it three times before the next text arrived: *If you do exactly as you are told, you receive $2500. If the team takes you on, there's another $2500 for you.*

He allowed a minute to pass before replying: *Copy that. Won't let you down.*

Ashford completed the brief query from the hyperlink, which included a headshot, asked for a driver's license or passport number, requested a home address, questioned for any health risks, and sought basic information he'd be able to falsely create. By embedding tails into any answer, he would be capable of seeing where and when they were opened. One of the links would arrive to an inaccessible server, notifying him of the ping's location. Unless they too were software engineers, it was as close as he'd come to someone who might human traffic with a degree of tech sophistication.

He started looking into white vans in the Fort Myers, Naples, Miami and Fort Lauderdale markets. There was plenty of availability. That wouldn't be an issue. Wherever the location might lead to, Ashford would be prepared for the potential battle which Lady Barbara mentioned.

Ashford thought that it was happening fast. Perhaps too fast. If anyone had a career with plans or an Outlook calendar chock full of meetings or a family or any responsibility – this wouldn't be happening. It was drifters. Rogue operators. Their trade was crime. These were the aggressors he was snuggling up to. Assumptions were being made that he was like them. He knew he'd have to become something that he wasn't. Acting would be required. Unreal behaviors would be called upon. He'd never taken a life before, but he was prepared to if it meant returning Ashley.

His thoughts were of how real his love and life with Ashley was before her disappearance. Now he was left with the thought of the changed man he had become. "It isn't real," he said once more hollowly – knowing that he might have to make something of the *real* and earthly choices he may need to make.

Nearly an hour after he had sent the answers to the questions he was being asked, he was able to source the location of the person opening his reply: Miami.

Ten minutes after that, he had the location of the property he was to arrive to at precisely 9 a.m. It was in Everglades City. He'd need a white van from Fort Myers or Naples. He was on NOAA searching the forecast and observing the swampy terrain minutes after booking the van. Ashford's heart was beating rapidly. He looked into Ashley's smokey eyes looking back at him from her picture on his desk.

"Soon," he said to her photo. He imagined her in his arms again, smelling the beachy coconut perfume she liked to wear. Her soft skin against his, running her fingers on his chest as she sat upon him in their bed. Hair, tossed on her shoulders as they rocked. Their secrets of intimacy were theirs and the depth of their lovemaking was intoxicating. A see-through gown was the only thing between them as Ashley would caress her soft hand on his cheek and chin. He had visited this illusion many times before. But now, now they were closer than they'd been before – reuniting the love they had together. He looked longingly into her smokey eyes.

"It isn't real – " he heard her whisper in his ears. Ashford froze. Coldness coursed through him, from the inside out, and down the back of his spine, causing him to shudder from the sensation.

He didn't think about it long enough because his cell phone rang. Answering it, "Hello?"

Ashford heard a man's voice, "Patriot?"

"That's me."

"This is Stanley. Everything checked out. I've just sent you some additional

information in an email. Read it. Delete it. Delete it from your Deleted Items folder. We good?"

"Will do, we're good." Ashford replied. He knew there was much to do in a short period of time.

"If anything changes, call this number and leave a short message. Not too much detail though." It sounded like a deep voice, a formidable force of size and strength. This 'Stanley' might not be small and easily overcome. Ashford would need to plan, as much as possible, for pivoting upon unexpected actions. The others which he expected to encounter – may not be able to be contained. He would need to go into this situation in a fluid state, able to be a chameleon and adapt to overcoming potential adversity.

For whatever reason, arriving at nine and waiting until ten felt odd and brought to Ashford an unsettling suspicion of a potential ambush.

"Okay. See you then and soon." Click. At the other end of the call, the baritone Stanley hung up. Ashford contemplated the risk, the reward, the in between which was worst of all. Not knowing was the quagmire, the quandary, the in between. He had little time to prepare for a viable battle which Lady Barbara alluded to.

*****

It was Thursday.

"Well, hello there. Don't you look quite pretty." Sydney complimented Allegra who had put in some effort into her appearance. There were curls in her hair, some dangling to the sides of her face down to the top of her chest. A silky low cut blush blouse and short and tight umber-tan skirt showed her figure nicely. She was pretty on any given day. Today, Allegra Sinclair was exceptionally well put together – looking beautiful as she sat up straight in her office chair in the United Nations meeting room. Her legs were crossed, showing her long-fit legs. A matching heel was hanging from her toe rocking it.

They were where they agreed to meet. Allegra was just several minutes early, awaiting Jacob and everyone else.

"Thanks Sydney. Just had a little extra time this morning. I like that necklace you're wearing."

"Ah yes, an old family heirloom. My..." she held her index finger to her chin, "Great Grandmother's perhaps?" It was more of a question than a reflection. Thirty seconds behind Sydney through the doorway followed Vendemer.

"Hey foxy ladies."

"Hey BenVen," Allegra said as she reached for a laptop, laying it on desk, unopened.

"Hello Benjamin," Sydney mumbled as she clicked at the keyboard, looking at him briefly, and then back to her screen.

"So, we iron out the remaining detail today." Vendemer said to the two of them.

"That we do," Allegra replied as she bobbed one leg crossed over the other. A paper cup with coffee steamed in front of her.

Ruby walked in with Adele shortly after Vendemer. Allegra watched the door for her fantasy man. But he didn't follow.

They sat around where Sydney and Allegra were positioned at the table, facing the screen at the front of the room where the missionaries would join their call.

Sydney asked the question which Allegra was dying to know buy didn't ask, in the effort to not appear infatuated, "Where's our one-percenter?" she was referring to Jacob's wealth - flirting with the top one percent of all wealth. It was unusually crass for the Brit, and only Adele seemed touched by the comment, squinting after it was said. Sydney made no mention of her Old England money – nor Ruby's indescribable sum – or of Vendemer's vast fortune from his Russian heritage. The tease was of the new-money man, missing from their presence.

Ruby needed to do the talking, "He's on a simultaneous assignment which plays to his strengths and gets guns, the wrong kind of guns, off of the streets. Jacob is in Savannah, on his way back to New York. He'll be back in Manhattan tonight and then with us in Florida on Saturday. No one seemed moved. Allegra's shoulders slumped.

As Sydney opened the bridge for the conference call, several of the Ellipsis warriors were already on the call. These were their fighters who would be onsite at the Everglades City compound where the victims were being contained. Support staff were also on the video call. There were several faces which Allegra and Adele didn't recognize, but Sydney, Vendemer, and Ruby did. They shared greetings and framed up how this mission would be different than on the outskirts of San Diego, Yuma, and McAllen.

At the previous sites which were liberated by Ellipsis, the offsite containers, hiding the young men, women, and children, were all similar – out of site, lightly guarded, and had a uniform structure of supplies, food and water, cleaning, checkpoints, and logistics. It all made Allegra and Adele angry – thoroughly disgusted that such a network existed. They were in disbelief that more wasn't actively being done to dismantle the vile system trafficking people.

"How long have you all been after these...these heinous people, buying and selling these children?" Adele asked.

"About eighteen months now," Ruby replied. "We've made five raids, small in size, before we ran across the containers which housed the victims taken and being trafficked. Once we locked on to that, we knew we had a larger issue to take on. The state and local police, the feds – they were somewhat helpful but lack tackling the larger picture in an expeditious manner. It required using, how should we say, some tools which violate privacy. We...we don't have as much respect for breaking those laws in an effort to free our victims, our people held up for sale. You need to bend some laws to break the system that these human traffickers are using. That's the problem with rules."

"That we simply don't pay too much attention to," Vendemer added.

Allegra's comment was solemn, "Wow. We're not schlepping laptops anymore, are we BenVen?" She was amazed at how well he contained all of this from her – for years.

He said nothing, looking down at his knees and then back up to the screen with the raiders all looking back at them, in the meeting room.

The tone was pensive, not as jovial as their last meeting when they were flirting with Allegra. There were six people on camera, in addition to the four mercenaries from the last call – ten total. Bing, Chuck, Jude, and Marco were joined by the other solders: Rave and Tucker. Four addition teammates, two men and two women, were on the call. They introduced themselves as Deployment Operators, or DepOps.

As the DepOps team asked Allegra questions about the drones, the bandwidth required, several of the requirements for the audio and video – they determined that instead of operating from a trailer out of Marco Island, she and Jacob would be on one of the two helicopters. Their purpose would be to keep the wrong people from storming the chopper during the siege. She agreed. Setting aside the warm feelings she had for him and may have recently been playing around with – the seriousness of the mission superseded the thought of a fantasy outing with Jacob. Adele and Sydney were to be in the other helicopter, the transport, which had the capacity to carry nine to twelve others – victims from the container.

Cameras had been set up on the Tamiami Trail, at the Carnestown junction where the evil men and woman in the white van stopped every Saturday, and at a midpoint on the small two-lane county road leading toward Everglades City.

"For a precaution, let's hope it doesn't lead to that, another camera is positioned at the bridge leading into the Everglades City peninsula." One of the DepOps women added to the staging.

"Why did you say it that way?"

"Civilians. What we do, or most of what we do – is out of the senses," Marco, one of the soldiers added.

"Out of the sense?" Adele asked.

"People don't see or smell or hear or sense us," Chuck, the oldest soldier on the call, replied. "We completely operated in the shadows. Always best if we allow the local authorities to step in and say something to the press, such as they were running a sting operation – or something like that."

Ruby piled on, "We continue to exist because we're a well-kept secret. What we do might need to be deciphered. When we draw attention to ourselves, we create a risk we just might have to manage to." As he spoke, Allegra watched the words slip through his lips. Ruby had scars. Not the kind that you see, but those which were on the inside. So did Vendemer and Sydney. Allegra and Adele were about to earn theirs. " Our pledge to do what needs to be done, our covenant, this partnership, the charter – it doesn't do well when someone wants to examine. So, we stay out of the populated areas when…well when we go in aggressively like this."

Tucker and Rave, the two which were on another mission when they spoke last, were the quietest on the call. They were also not what either Adele, or Allegra were expecting. They wouldn't have had pastel polos on, like the others did on their previous call. Thick necks, tough exteriors, they seemed to be taking notes from the DepOps teammates and agreed with much of what was being decided upon.

Sydney pulled up the map of the area and reviewed the staging points. "Okay, the DepOps IT team is in the trailer here: Marco Island, Point A. The drones will launch from here, a local airboat tour company – we bought out the operator for the day. It's Point B. they'll fly across this small stretch of the Everglades, plenty of range to the take-out target, Point X. Both helicopters take off from this location, Point C. Copeland, Florida, up the same county road as the target point. Once we have the extraction of our victims, one helicopter returns to Point C, the other deviates toward Naples where we get these kids home safely – or at least turned over to the authorities which can do that. The Naples location is Point D. Questions so far?"

Allegra asked, "Where do the backup drones, the trailers, launch from?"

"Good question, Miss Sinclair. They're already positioned to launch, if necessary, from the mangroves out here in the Ten Thousand Islands wildlife preserve. Two unarmed, and if necessary, one armed – the type you recommended. Point E. Hoping that doesn't become a thing. They'll be flying with a small payload above a small touristy town with population of, say, six hundred souls or so."

"Plus, plus the twelve unaccounted for," Adele added, thinking of the kid's held captive in the container. The blouse she wore had a broad collar. She stroked its silkiness and dropped it to her collarbone. "Plus, twelve very important, unknown and unforgettable people fearing for their lives - perhaps every moment of every day."

No one said anything right away. Sydney nodded her head, slowly and politely, out of respect to the plus twelve.

Then, it was Chuck doing the talking again, laying out the plan: "We were thinking, Adele, that you and Sydney fly in with chopper one. This will be the transport for you two and the *Plus Twelve* when we return them safely to the authorities in Naples. You will *stay on board* the helicopter until given clearance to disembark and help with the extraction. Again, Adele – *stay on board.* Allegra and Jacob – *stay on board!* I repeat, *stay on board* chopper two. Allegra – you especially – first mission, you are observing. *Stay on board.*"

She held up her hands, "Hey – I'm there. Not going anywhere."

Chuck continued, "This will be the transport for the gruff looking folks on the screen. Only if there's an emergency situation will you two even *think* of leaving the helicopter. But don't worry – that won't happen. Headcount – very important. Shit may blow up, get smoky, there may be fire, an explosion – we don't know, you just never do. If anyone gets off any helicopter for any reason. You get back on the same helicopter. Can I get an 'amen' from all of you?"

The soldiers immediately offered 'amen' acknowledgments, but everyone was looking at Adele and Allegra. Eventually, they both offered there's without as much gusto. They were both realizing that they were in for something which was potentially much more dangerous than they may have anticipated ten minutes ago.

"Adele – for you. Once given the all-clear signal, you, the woman, the mother, the most friendly face – no disrespect Allegra – you, Adele will be there to work with the women and children which we release from the container. Hopefully it goes just like south of San Diego. You get them into the transport helicopter and you, and Sydney are there to comfort them back."

Adele shook her head eagerly thinking of the moment she embraced the children in the field south of San Diego. Tears filled her eyes thinking of liberating them.

"Allegra – you, not in the cheap seats, but you'll have a front row opportunity to see how we execute an extraction. Let me add – it's very rare to have someone so new witnessing so much but BenVen and Ruby think it's your thing…"

"And I don't – sorry girlie," Sydney interrupted adding her sentiments.

He continued, "Stay the hell out of the way or get shot, you got it?"

"Got it." Allegra paused, thinking it through, "Wait, how would I get shot if I can't leave the helicopter I'm observing from?"

"Friendly fire. One of us might disable you. Don't challenge us. The less feet on the ground during an extraction like this, the better. Remember – you stay on the helicopter and return in the one which you came." He assessed his instructions by looking at his close-knit team and the team in New York. "Joking about shooting you, Allegra. We wouldn't do that." Chuck paused again, "I don't think."

"Can we review everything once more?" Adele asked earnestly.

The soldiers and DepOps teammates chuckled causing Adele to smile and hold out her hands slightly seeking some understanding on what she may have said to cause the small stir.

Chuck added, "Adele, it may get a little boring for you all at this point, but we're going to red team it. A military term. We're going to try to pick it apart by reviewing the plan a half dozen more times."

She let out a sigh, "Good. Let's do that."

"Okay everyone, buckle up. Here we go. No cockpit culture here. Let's look for holes in our plan. Finder's Fee if you uncover one." The team of vigilantes grinned. Chuck led the conversation about the deployment with the team from the start. Only occasionally, one of the teammates interrupted with a 'what if?'. The Finder's Fee meant everyone owed you a beer at the conclusion of the mission.

The meeting carried on, from the morning into the afternoon. There was a moment, mid-day and just after their working lunch, and as the sun was beginning its moment of arcing from rising to descending, when Adele and then Allegra, both excused themselves from the meeting for a run to the ladies room. They glanced at each other briefly, jockeying for the wash basin. As Adele was drying her hands,

Allegra spoke first with a statement followed by a question, "This...all of it...it isn't real. Is it?"

* * * * *

Victoria picked up the handset in the partition she was assigned to in the visitors meeting hub. An inch of glass was between herself and her lawyer. She held the black receiver end of the phone to her ear and looked at the man in the dark grey suit on the other side of the glass. Pulling the mouthpiece next to her bare lips she said, "Give me some good news."

"Good news," he said. "We have a lobbyist who knows a little more than he's supposed to know - and a guy who he knows has got something on a Senator from New York. He's being compromised right now. The NRA has a creative play involving the..."

"So, you know a guy who knows a guy who might have something on another guy..." She rolled her eyes. Even dressed in an orange jumpsuit, she was attractive. Her brunette curtain bangs framed her face. Big eyes, high cheek bones, a pert little nose, and thin neck – she still turned heads, even in prison. Victoria was far from the Park Avenue, high end stripped turned prostitute that she once was, and even further from Jacob Paisley's preference in women – but she still had game.

The lawyer watched her summarize his opening statement with disregard. He wondered what she would be like in bed. What kind of a tigress might this attractive inmate be after her stay in the slammer. He knew about her arrangement with Jacob Paisley. She admitted to him that she'd grown bored and after the money dwindled, her appetite for excitement branched out some. Being off cocaine must have been difficult for her, the lawyer layered his fantasy with means in which he might assist her. A little quid pro quo. Thinking that he could supply her with some snort and help get her on her feet, perhaps there might be a little something-something between them. He fiddled with the wedding ring on his finger as he fantasized about sex with her.

"I should have led with – we'll have you out of her in a week," the lawyer said. "How do you like me now?"

Victoria smiled and leaned forward, "Well...I like you a lot better now. Her teeth were perfect. Lips, even though they were glossed in Dior Rouge Premier Lipstick, were to be kissed. Her eye contact was irresistible to him.

He thought about it personally, but kept it professional, "It's going to cost you something though," he said – thinking personal thoughts, saying professional things, "You're going to owe them a favor."

"Of course, there's always a catch," she said, looking off into the distance. "What?" Victoria returned her look to the lawyer, "What do I need to do?"

"You'd need to set up shop again, on the island."

"That's what got me here," she spoke quietly yet pointedly.

"No, getting caught doing the wrong thing is what landed you here. You don't do it like that next time. Listen, I can get your legs under you, stand you up on your feet, but you'll need to come up with a hundred grand for the first round of funding. I don't have that kind of money just laying around. You still have some connections?"

She wasn't as cheerful at the catch she was presented with. "I burned through my money on legal fees attempting to avoid all of this. I won't have that kind of money. It'll take time."

"What? Two months? I can probably negotiate." The thought of working closely with her for a couple months gave the tainted lawyer something to look forward to.

"At least. Maybe three...unless. Unless..." she thought of Jacob. Of what they had, how she fled, the unfinished business – and how perhaps she could light a fire. He was her best pony. She thought of the others – the less desirable, diminished in net worth, perverted and smirched. Jacob. Jacob Paisley had always been her favorite play.

"What are you thinking?"

Victoria was thinking of how she might apologize and manipulate him into another amorous entanglement with her. A dalliance like that would involve artificial honesty as a centerpiece along a deep, missing, and loving longing as the mechanism of deception. No, that wasn't it. That couldn't be her play. It would involve a garden, an apple, and a snake. Forbidden fruit. The Jacob Paisley that she knew had moved on to simpler things. Maybe he needed to remember what salty and sweet tasted like together. She'd need to reassemble herself, draw out her best girlfriend experience allure, rekindling the memories of the exploits which Jacob liked best. His tastes were mischievous and indecorous as they were refined and sophisticated. It might take the damsel in distress or the girl on the rebound who just happened to help him remember his incongruous side of life while he was being a do-gooder for an old friendly friend – a memorable acquaintance.

"Yoo-hoo... Hey Victoria? Where did you go there?" the lawyer asked again.

"I think I can maybe get hands on a hundred thousand in maybe two or three months. And I'll take you up on that offer to get me on my back." Victoria made eye contact with him, a dead lock and deep stare.

He smirked, "I said I'd help get you on your feet."

"I know what you said," she hung up the phone and turned away from him, looking back once quickly and playfully to meet his glance as she walked away from the phone bank.

She missed things. Her wardrobe, the sweet perfumes which Jacob Paisley doted her with, his generous and unexpected presents, the handsels from the girlfriend experience she provided him with and the shadowy sums of money which found its way into her checking account monthly. He called it 'walking around money' – to spend as she wished. The financial windfalls arrived quarterly too. Larger sums. She blew much of it – up her nose. When his generosity came to a crawl, she cut and ran. The direction didn't bode well for her, creating her current predicament.

Victoria's thoughts were not of the flirtatious and married lawyer, who himself was imagining her in a missionary or doggie style position at a mediocre MidTown hotel at some point. Her mind was wandering elsewhere. She was in an inventive mode of her own. Thinking of some of her best sex work with Jacob – building upon one of the voids he was filling in for, she knew some of his deep and darkest thoughts might need to come into play. There was their menage a trois in the south of France, a rocking weekend on a sailboat at sea and off of the coast of Saint John in the Caribbean, and a menagerie of indiscretions which could be relived – or perhaps revealed to Adele.

The sticking point. Adele – she often was. A little intel had informed her of the relationship. A wedge would be needed. That might take some work. Jacob didn't participate in social media. He was no longer a CNBC poster boy. The financial cult following, his Paisley Pierce Capital Management traders, were disbanded. She didn't know of a best friend which he hadn't discarded following his fall from grace. But Adele, loyal Adele – the one who always seemed to come to his aid. She would be problematic for Victoria's reemergence.

Adele would somehow need to be displaced if indeed they were a thing.

Victoria's work with Jacob would need to be something which played upon his desire, his want – not what he needed. It would need, perhaps, to involve some guile and dupery. A garden, a snake, an apple, an insatiable curiosity, a ravenous desire for something. Forbidden fruit. She knew him: he'd want what he could not have.

12

My Uncle's Place

The congressmen arrived at the Bombardier Challenger 3500 early. Jacob was surprised to see them not only on time, but ahead of schedule. Seeing them climb out of the limo, he was even more alarmed - at their size. *Are we going to be able to lift off with those two bubbas on board?* he asked himself. They were two wide-bodies. Big boys. Jimmy and Bobby. *Linemen perhaps? Sumo-wrestlers? One is a republican, the other a democrat. One is from Florida, the other from Georgia. Buddies from across the aisle. They like to fly privately because they don't fit coach on a domestic jump, and don't want their constituents to see them fly first class. Okay – gametime.*

Looking up from his phone, pretending to be in the middle of something, he greeted them as they huffed up the several stairs to board the body of the jet, "Hey fellas."

Their southern draw was strong, "Hey there buddy, thanks for the lift," the first one said. He introduced himself as the Republican Congressman from the Great State of Georgia, Jimmy Gaines.

"Hey – have I seen you on TV?" The Democratic Congressman asked Jacob, "My name, by the way, is Bobby Fonteneaux – from the *Greater* State of Florida. Pleased to meet you."

"It was a while ago that I made some pit-stops on the financial news channels. I've moved on to Private Equity in the darker channels. Jacob Paisley. Nice to meet you Bobby...Jimmy."

"We like dark, don't we Bobby?" the Republican, named Jimmy added as he settled into a large white armchair across from Jacob. "Where you want us?"

"Anything goes." Jacob pointed at the wide white buttery leather seats across from him in the cabin. The door to the cockpit was closed at the moment. They both plopped into the cushiony seats, rocking the jet as they sank in. The leather or the treatment for it smelled new, rich, and clean.

In a whisper, Jimmy asked, "Hey brotha – anyone else joinin' us?"

Jacob pretended to look at his phone as if he were checking a manifest. Holding his finger up in the air, he said. "Nah, just us mother fuckers. We drinkin' all the way to the Apple, or what?"

"See, I told you – private equity gets it, and them other squeaky stiffs just don't," Jimmy said.

Not listening to his buddy, "Speaking of what you said, Mr. Paisley, what does a southern man need to do to get a drink around here?"

"Well, I'm sure libations will be plentiful and flowin' soon." Jacob tried his best to dial down the proper English and appropriateness in the effort to fit in and be welcomed. "I love Savannah. I could live here."

"We spend some time between here and Jacksonville," Bobby, the Democrat admitted. "Savannah is alright – but it ain''t Florida...so...there's that. And it's haunted."

The Republican, Jimmy, added, "Drinkin' opportunity, Bobby – I told ya that. Take me up on the offer. Haunted pub crawl, Jacob. You're invited too."

Jacob watched a small shuttle pull up and a redheaded flight attendant step down from the vehicle. He looked at the two hefty congressmen and began with the betting. "'Bout time for our flight attendant, bet she's a blond. Hundred bucks."

The two Congressmen smiled and snickered, and Jimmy said, "I'll take that bet - she's gonna' be a busty brunette."

" Awe, shit on me. Double er nothin', fuckers – that she's a redhead." Bobby chimed in, holding his beefy hands to his barrel chest, "Ya know...petite with nice hooters."

A minute passed. They were thirsty – for a revelation and their three o'clock cocktail.

"And you're off," Ruby chimed into his earpiece. "We'll help you be predictably unpredictable along the way, Have some fun, Jacob."

He didn't respond, but Jacob accidentally smiled to himself as he heard Ruby's play-by-play promise.

A stunning redhead climbed the steps to the threshold of the private jet, and as she walked into the cabin was greeted with an arousing "Ahhh" from the three men sitting. She smiled widely, knowing that she played a part in all of it too.

One was handsome. The other two, she quickly determined, were large, loud, and lawmakers of some sort. She didn't really care because she never voted. They, as in the Jimmy and Bobby, flirted with her unfailingly from SAV to JAF.

Jacob made wagers along the way, with the support of Ruby's prompts. Deliberately running behind in the count, he was a two-win, three-lose plunger in the growing stakes of the Atlantic flight. Sports Center was streaming on the monitor in the cabin. From the over under of departure, to the right or left bank of approach, to the number of pilon lights on the runway, Jacob, Jimmy and Bobby bet on nearly anything.

Ruby, listening to each discussion, coached the pilot to bank left or right, sweetening the advantages to the congressmen's advantage. Some of the wagering was nothing more than guesswork. The outcome, favorable for their armature play.

"Hey Jacob – how's your poker game?"

"Hmph..." Jacob slipped a smile into his reply, "Tomahawks before Showdown, gentlemen? You pussies from the South do like red meat, right?"

Silent to the cabin where the congressmen chatted, but alive and active in Jacob's ear, "Nice. Where do we need reservations, high roller?" Ruby asked in Jacob's earpiece. He said nothing, of course.

"Surprise us, big daddy. It's yo city, you the slicker," commented Bobby, pointing at Jacob.

Jacob pretended to be scrolling on his phone. Ruby commented in the earpiece.

Without acting surprised at the Madison Avenue exclusive establishment which usually required a 30-day advance reservation, Jacob sprung it upon the Republican and the Democrat, "Fella's. how about a table at Rocco Steakhouse before whatever mischief we can get ourselves into?"

Jimmy said to Bobby, "Remembah what I said bout New Yorkers?"

"Uh-huh, do," replied his Democratic counterpart.

"I do most respectfully take that back," said the Republican.

The remainder of the flight to JFK was filled with red meat talk, hooker preferences, voter apathy, and the problems with clean energy. As the flight approached New York, and Jimmy was up – from hundreds to thousands to nearly ten thousand dollars in gentleman bets while in flight, his smile widened.

The stretch from the airport to the steakhouse was impressive, even by Paisley standards. The service at Rocco Steakhouse was exceptional. But what happened next was a play out of Jacob's Paisley Pierce Capital Management playbook. It was similar to the Day of Decadence event which Jacob would share with only his most favored traders.

"It's called, get this," a dramatic hand slid across the space between them, "My Uncle's Place," Jimmy Gaines chuckled as he said it.

Bobby Fonteneaux slapped his knee while he elbowed Jacob. "Fuckin' brilliant. My Uncle's Place. Ya say to yer old lady, Honey – Ima' headin' on over to my uncle's place," he broke out into more laughter than it deserved, and Jacob played along in the pretentious amazement of the namesake of the poker house they were en route to.

The three of them hit it off. Jacob, acting along as a part of their tomfoolery entourage.

Ruby, listening, while having a cocktail with his son, Charlie, and friend, Sammy, leaped into action if anything was required, such as the reservations at the swanky steakhouse. But it was really the Jimmy and Bobby show at this point. Once the table betting would resume, Ruby would need to coach Jacob on what might be manipulated leveraging resources and technology.

What happened next was not a surprise to Jimmy and Bobby. But it was to Jacob Paisley, the maverick of money, monarch of multiplication, and former mariner of Manhattan mischief. To him it was – astonishing. The holding room contained one hundred people, well dressed, wearing exquisite masquerade masks. Their accessory designs were gold lace, black silk, platinum sparkles adorned some, ruby red sequins decorated others. Women wore boas of black, royal blue and crimson and feathers in their hair. Men matched a woman which they may be there with.

Immediately, they were offered their masks. Midnight black, a suede-like material with an elastic strap. The Republican, the democrat, and Jacob who referred to himself as Switzerland each slipped on the identity concealing eyepiece.

The incognito masks weren't as secretive as they could be. They were revealing. There weren't any introductions between the guests. Jacob assumed it was a thumbnail code. As if, *I'm somebody and I'm here – and you're somebody and you're here – and we're here together in this discreet and reticent place together – so...no one knows anything.* He wasn't positive, but he thought he could make out several celebrities, starpower from the sporting world, two additional congressmen, a couple C-suite members from the advertising industry, and countless women wearing just enough covering their nipples to not have the place be deemed topless.

Bob Segar's song, *Her Strut,* played loudly as the long-legged slightly dressed servers delivered cocktails and top shelf liqueurs. Boas and feathers and pearls were tops. Thongs were bottoms. Heels were stacked. Their confidence in their appearance was strong – yet they were approachable and accommodating, not arrogant. They provided what was requested. If it wasn't available, it was summoned. Nothing was off limits. This was a place of elation and debasement. *If Adele knew where I was right now...?* Jacob thought to himself. He pictured her asleep, between their crisp sheets, and questioned whether the sinful pleasures were worth the trade-off from the simple silence next to her within the bed they shared.

"How did I not know about this? Would have been at the top of the stack," Jacob said to himself. Only Ruby heard, through the earpiece.

"Am I missing out?" Ruby said, knowing only Jacob could hear him.

"Well..." was the best way to describe the sexual circus he was experiencing.

Once the holding room doors opened to the grand gambling room at ten o'clock, the buy ins were collected through crypto, credit cards, ACH wire transfers and in a few cases, a freshly printed wrapper of cash. A ten-thousand-dollar deposit granted a red wristband which was required to place table bets. It wasn't just twelve card tables. There were other tables which would place bets on the strippers and the hookers. Jacob walked the floor, first with Jimmy and Bobby, who were greeted by the dealers and women serving drinks as regulars – then by himself.

The lighting was low. The parameters were wide. The guardrails for making good choices at this point were off.

Women appeared to be the aggressors here. Commonly fondled by women, sometimes a couple of women seeking a man as a potential partner, Jacob realized the shoe, in this case a Lucite stack, was on the other foot. It was flattering to be so prized and wanted. But it was suggestive and perverted and shallow.

To observe some of the off-color bets being made, Jacob snuggled in next to a couple suits which had chips placed on green felt. The markings on the table were printed. 5. 5 ½. 6. 6 ½. 7. 7 ½. 8. 8 ½ up to twelve. The platinum blond woman smiled at the men and licked her red lips. She wore little, covering her chest and less hiding the rest of her. Taunting increased as she rolled her head and stretched her neck and tousled her hair. Four bets were on the table, nine spots of total availability. Like a circus act – a floor worker, handsome young man, approached the table and spoke loudly, "Ladies and gentlemen – meet Trixie. Isn't she pretty? Let's give it up for her seductiveness!" A small applause followed. The emcee played to the small gathering at the table and those in the surrounding area, interested in the activity by speaking much louder, "She's going to put on a show for your pleasure! Let's give her some encouragement! Ladies and Gentlemen – Trixie – who's hungry – if you know what I mean…" A louder applause followed.

Jacob looked at Trixie and she looked back at him. Several other betters laid dollars and tokens on the kelly-green felt, placing their bets. A zucchini, about eighteen inches, was brought out from under the betting table. Trixie continued to look at Jacob, opened her mouth, and stuck out her tongue as far as it could reach.

Sex club meets illegal gambling, Jacob thought to himself. He watched Trixie try to lure him in to betting on her ability to swallow the depth of the zucchini. She tickled the air with her index finger, attempting to draw him closer to a seat at the table. "I want you," she said. Her voice was rasp. "Wanna play with me?"

You might be twenty-five. Maybe. Jacob thought to himself. *You're some mother's daughter. You're some father's best work. You just don't know it.* He smiled at her and winked and walked back from the table, allowing another couple to slip into the space which he was occupying. She smelled sweet to him, a fragrance which Victoria would have chosen. An ambrosial scent that was nearly edible wafted his way as she approached him and stayed close. Jacob refrained from more.

He didn't want to know how many inches Trixie could swallow a zucchini. The seductive parlor tricks were once amusing, and perhaps a PPCM dirty-little-secret night out on the town, but to Jacob - no longer. All of the strip club-like songs played, affording no quietness to hear the moaning in the raunchy ballroom. Warrant's, *Cherry Pie*; followed by Def Leppard's, *Pour Some Sugar On Me*; chased by Motley Crue's, *Girls, Girls, Girls*, and Nelly's, *Hot In Here,* were the naughty acclaims beating loudly and caused the servers to sometimes dance erotically with those they served.

It got darker.

In the corner of the ballroom, a couple, man and woman, were completely naked. They were in the early stages of foreplay. Kissing, stroking, caressing, and occasionally groping each other for effect – the acting couple was caged from the gatherers. Many women wearing evening silky dresses watched with their jacket wearing men or other women close to them. This highbrow crowd held glasses of bourbon, or whiskies, or martinis. A server, wearing barely, a string of pearls hiding her breasts walked around the gathering crowd asking, "Glass of Fifty-Seven Bowmore? Glass of Fifty-Seven Bowmore? Glass of Fifty-Seven Bowmore?"

Jacob thought of reaching for his phone to research the significance of the fifty-seven in the rare Bowmore, then thought better of that. He assumed that it was a single malt scotch.

"It's thirty grand a glass. There are only twelve bottles, and this is one. What, you don't want one?" A honey blond asked him. She had a warm golden shade of caramel curls falling from her head to large breasts in an open dress which stopped short of her navel. She had a woman behind her reaching for her tits to caress them occasionally as she spoke to Jacob. The woman behind her looked like Victoria. He turned away and looked for Jimmy or Bobby in the scene. They weren't nearby.

Like the Trixie wager – a betting opportunity was present. How many minutes would he last before an orgasm? In a similar circus fashion, a different announcer approached the small gathering crowd and rallied the gambling. She was stunning. A small Australian redhead approached the contingent and taunted the group, "Ladies and gentlemen. I do think you know what's happening here. But how long will he last? Two minutes? Five? Ten?" She looked at the woman in the cage. "Lucky girl," she teased. "Place your bets!" she shouted. A similar table with green felt was off to the side of the cage. Women and men gathered with their tokens to fill the timeslots on the table.

Jacob looked at the woman who resembled Victoria again before he walked away to the next gathering.

"Tell me that Adele isn't listening in with you," Jacob spoke to Ruby through the earpiece when he was certain that no one was listening or suspicious.

"Are you making your way to the tables or still walking through the...festivities?" Ruby asked.

"This is..." Jacob paused. "Well, twenty years ago maybe."

"You're not there to pollute your eyes, find..."

"There they are," Jacob interrupted Ruby. He walked further and saw yet another diversion in front of him. Three willing participant couples were gathered at the card table. A dealer was in front of the sexually amenable couples of men and women. He tossed cards in front of them face up. It was a teaser for the stakes on the table in front of them. A man wearing a cream jacket and bow tie behind Jacob with a woman in a matching silk cream gown on his arm, came too close to Jacob's ear, "This is one of my favorites. Twenty thousand on the second couple."

Jacob looked at the couple sitting at station number two. They looked like they could be from Queens or Long Island. They were ordinary when compared to the other two.

"What's at stake? I'm sort of new here?"

"The couple which loses in cards – the woman and the man – they must please the winners...if you know what I mean? Ten thousand buy in...for them...and...well as they say, 'Winner Take All'."

"So, we're betting on them betting?" Jacob asked the handsome gentleman in the cream jacket.

"Hey – you look familiar. Have we met?" the woman on his arm asked Jacob.

He looked off into the distance and fibbed, "I was on an episode of the cooking channel a couple years ago. Maybe that's it?"

She frowned and replied, "Yeah, maybe so..."

Jacob turned away from the shenanigans of the couples jerking each other off and back toward the search for the Republican and the Democrat.

"Dude. You can get sucked in here. Come with me." It was Bobby rescuing Jacob from the upcoming jerkfest.

Their table was structuring. A scantily clad dealer, an Asian woman which wore a lei around her neck covering her tits was shuffling cards. Occasionally a pit boss would come up behind her and pinch one of her small nipples while the seats at the table were filling. To which she would moan, lean back and deeply kiss him with her mouth opening wide, swallowing his tongue.

Shock value, Jacob thought, as he took a seat next to Jimmy and Bobby.

She reached down between her legs with her dealing hand and rocked her head backward as if in a moan, acting as if she were touching herself. Then she licked her fingers and pretended to resume dealing a false hand - as if practicing.

"This is Ginger, Jacob. She works with us. And she knows what you represent." Ruby spoke into his earpiece and couldn't see Jacob scowl. "A Cambodian lovely, right?"

"Just when you think you've seen it all – you see more than before," Jacob said to himself, knowing Ruby was listening.

"We like the hell outta her," Jimmy said as he leaned toward his buddy, Bobby.

"First-timer. Go easy on 'im," Bobby added, looking at Ginger.

She looked at Jacob and said, "You lose, you eat me tonight. Okay? You win, I make you very happy. Okay? Good." Ginger, or whatever her real name was, looked at Jimmy and Bobby and asked, "You guys back for more?" She looked back at Jacob and winked.

Jacob found it coincidental that this club was not only on Ruby's list of secrets, but also on that of the congressmen. The two other seats filled, and the game was underway. Drinks were distributed by the nearly naked servers. Women groped the pecks and ribs of the seated players as they bounced from table to table observing, and dealers were cycled through at many of the other tables. For some reason, not theirs.

Lasting for nearly two hours, it was now two in the morning. The stakes were getting high. Screaming and shouting arose from the sex club section of the dark ballroom. The assumption was that merry-making, and the carousal of the night had reached a climax from an expected development.

My Uncle's Place was filled with moans, laughter, cheers, and proclamations of defeat as losing bets met the winning wagers. Jacob, at the instruction of Ruby and spicy Ginger the dealer, was meandering from losing hands to winning hands. Jimmy consoled Bobby, then Bobby consoled Jimmy as the server's tops diminished late into the morning. Bare-breasted, even the dealers were into it. Commenting on the sway in winning, flirting with the players and downing shots of anything with them to celebrate victory or comfort a fiddling steak of losses. Ginger's top was removed too. She looked at Jimmy and Bobby and said, "You tell him." She pointed to Jacob, referring to her small and perky breasts. What I might be lacking up here – I make up for down there."

"Or in yer mouth," another man wearing a dark green mask at the table added with a chuckle. The woman with him, licked him in the ear and nibbled his lobe.

"What'sit? Two? Three?" Bobby asked Jimmy. When we meetin' with them tomorrow?"

"Uh, hell if I remembah," Jimmy replied. "Where are we at here my sweet Ginger?"

She pointed at Paisley. "He up by forty. Me going to make him happy maybe." Ginger looked at Jacob. He knew the Cambodian cutie was in on the Rubenesque play. He added, "Might be my lucky night, fellas – if you know what I mean."

"Forty?" repeated Bobby. "How the hell did that happen?"

"You drunk, Bubbah, that's how," Jimmy replied to the inebriated question.

Ruby chimed in, "Bet the balance, the whole forty, on their upcoming vote. Do it now."

"Or what do ya say we call it even... Mix it up a little here – say and you owe me nothin'? I'm a New York City betting man." Jacob looked at Jimmy and then at Bobby. "You see. I'm a opportunist Wall Streeter. Beating the street means more to be than beating the two of you. More than forty thousand dollars. We make money when we win...capital appreciation. And we can make money when we lose, a hedge on call options. You vote against what we talked about earlier – wink, wink - and I almost double my money by options trading," he looked at Ginger, then at Jimmy and Bobby, "the things we talked about earlier."

The dealer pretended not to understand and shrugged her shoulders, looking innocent.

"To be clear," Jacob added. "What I'm saying is if I lose the next hand – the forty grand is erased you owe me is erased and you'll vote 'no' – in which case I'll know how to play the market. If I win – well, then you're going to have to pay up."

It was pure insider trading. No one acknowledged what was taking place.

Bobby and Jimmy looked at each other.

"Fuck it," the Democrat said first.

The Republican followed, "Ima' gonna piss off half my constituents anyway, what the hell. A vote, wink-wink, on the next deal." As if he were purchasing an Egg McMuffin at a McDonald's or a pack of mints at a convenience store, he acted like it was nothing.

Ginger, on cue from the instructions she was receiving in her ear-piece, the voice of Ruby coordinating the hustle, cocked her head to the left and to the right as she spun the five cards to each of them. Before she flipped the final card Jacob's way, she said to him, "Either I'm in your mouth or you're in mine, what's it going to be?" She dealt the last card to Jacob. He looked at the five cards and asked for two.

Bobby asked for one. Jimmy thought about it, looking at his hand. He also asked for two cards. Both of them smiled when they received their cards slipped across the felt from Ginger who was looking only a Jacob. "I scream. I scream loud. Just so you know."

Jacob looked at the pair of Jacks and the pair of Queens and the deuce in accompaniment. Had it been for anything other than an El-lipsis wager, he would have gone through with it, betting it all - minus the sexual trade-off with his dealer. He tossed the five cards onto the felt, face down. "Fuck it," he added.

"Beat by a pair of nines?" Jimmy proclaimed.

"And a pair of eights?" Bobby, just as excited, looked at Jimmy.

"You do realize you're voting 'no' on a gun legislature, Mr. Repub-lican, don't you?"

"Ah shit. Time to piss off somebody and piss on someone else. What else is new?" Jimmy Gaines reached over to Jacob and shook his hand. "Welcome to My Uncle's Place, Jacob. We hope to see ya 'round here again, real soon. Keep in touch now, ya hear?"

"I will fellas," Jacob said as he watched Ginger coming around the table. She grabbed him by the jacket collar and said, "You. You come with me. If you know what I mean..."

Ginger looked at Jimmy and Bobby and smiled.

"I think that Paisley is about to get poked," Bobby, the Democrat from the greater state of Florida, leaned over and told Jimmy.

"Reckon so," the Republican from the great state of Georgia agreed.

"Have a nice night, buddy," they heckled - as the two of them departed the chaos of the sex club's early morning

They walked away, Ginger dragging Jacob by his hand, from the table toward a thick purple velvet drape in the back of the ballroom near a moaning couple in a cage.

Once beyond the purple velvet drape, Ginger looked at Jacob and said, "Well past your bedtime, old man. You alright?"

He thought of the limited amount of alcohol he'd consumed. "I nursed three drinks over four hours. Junior varsity work. You, okay?"

Ginger rolled her eyes, slipping her top back on her supple small breasts. "Get the hell out of here. Tell Ruby that he owes me one. I've done a few of these stunts for him. Convincing, I know. But this isn't who I am. And I can tell you're out of your zone."

Jacob watched her walk away, his unknown and alluring Cambodian teammate-actor-dealer, into the backroom darkness of My Uncle's Place. Far from fiction, the squeals of ecstasy and clamors from the spectators continued to be heard as the late night crept into the early morning hours. He was reminded that the human imagination continued to jangle its way forward, regardless of how disentangled he chose to become from its ornamental procession.

* * * * *

Maggie added, "And check out his name. Even his name is dreamy: Sebastian Heartspark. When I showed him your picture, he tilted his head, took a deep breath, ran his fingers through his dark hair and looked at me. It was one of those, love at first sight looks."

"You know I don't believe in that crap, Mags." Allegra shook her head to herself as she spoke on the phone with Maggie.

"Maybe you should. He isn't as old as you normally go for, but I think he'll make up for it elsewhere. When you two meet, and you look into his eyes... They're a deep ocean blue – filled with want. Anyway, I'm sending you, his picture. You can thank me later."

"Oh god, what are you reading right now?"

"Nope," Maggie dug in, "That's deflection. Not going to let you do that. Did you hear me. They're an irresistible blue and blue is what you do. It's your brand of blue, Allegra."

Allegra looked out the window of her bedroom, watching the city lights of Brooklyn, spring to life. Friday. It would be much different than Saturday, in southern Florida, eight states away.

"Did you hear me?"

"Uh, yeah. Blue." Allegra was listening, but elsewhere.

"I know that tone. You're thinking about work. Your project gig. How's it going over there at the UN?" Maggie asked. But before she allowed Allegra time to make up an answer, signifying something tech related, her statement diluted the lie Allegra would have to concoct. "The UN logo is blue too. Not as deep and mysterious as Sebastian's eye's though."

Allegra had it. "Listen, this weekend is shit. But next week, Saturday or Sunday – I've got nothing."

"So, yet another weekend I get skunked on meeting my bestie for drinks? Your new gig is getting in the way a bit, don't you think?"

Allegra thought of the million-dollar signing bonus, and raised her eyebrows for herself, alone in her apartment. She mouthed a 'no', as she thought of the growing divide between where she was and where she was heading. "Tonight is just, no good. Sorry Maggie. Go be with your Mr. Marvelous…"

"He's visiting his parents in Washington," Maggie replied.

"The state or DC?"

Maggie huffed. "Outside the beltway. More like Alexandria, Virginia. Near the Potomac somewhere."

Allegra heard Maggie's enthusiasm dwindle, knowing her friend was disappointed that she wasn't invited by her boyfriend for his quick trip home.

"Don't do that to yourself."

"What?"

Allegra added, "You know what you're doing. You're giving yourself a needless case of the blues."

"You suck," Maggie pouted, "I am going to go find someone who likes appletinis almost as much as I do, buy the first three rounds, and talk shit about Allegra Sinclair."

"There you go," Allegra smiled. "I like it. Leave out the good parts." She knew the sacred secrets were safe.

"Oh, no. I'm telling all." Maggie joked. Their code would go unbroken.

"And next weekend I'm all yours. No Sebastian just yet. I'll think on it."

Maggie squealed. "Really?"

"I said I'll think about it. Who knows, maybe another mystery man will appear and sweep me off my feet."

"You don't believe in that crap," Maggie repeated.

"See...? There' hope for you yet. You're a listener." Allegra thought about how things would need to be different in her new environment. It would be tough, regulating what she divulged with Maggie and what she simply could not share. The division would be hard on her friend. Perhaps the boy-toy of hers would mitigate the difference in their close relationship. Or something else might intervene.

"Good talk, coach," Maggie said.

"Listen, sister. I've got to get ready. Another day of deep state secrets. Call you Monday to see if you're still living. Maybe Sunday, 'kay?"

"Oh...'kay," Maggie replied. "Miss you."

"Miss you too, Mags." Allegra pushed the red button on the face of the phone. She turned on the TV, listening to the financial channel as background noise while she walked into her closet.

"Let's see... Dress to impress. Tomorrow I may be wearing, don't know, camo?" She slid hanger after hanger from right to left until the clothes would no longer slide. Organized by color, heavily dependent on dark solid colors, Allegra looked at the blouses, followed by knit dresses, silky and sexy skirts, pants and summer attire tucked in the back. She settled on navy pants and a white blouse. Dropping her pajamas on the floor, Allegra faced a wall mirror. Grabbing her own breasts, while briefly imagining him standing behind her with his hands holding them – she thought that Jacob would be back and would likely have an entertaining story or two to share. *That's it. I need a story for Maggie.* Bluey-eyed, Sebastian Heartspark just may help hide Ellipsis from Maggie in the near term. *Then again, what the hell kind of name was Heartspark anyway, a made-up one?*

✳✳✳✳✳

"What if?" Victoria asked herself, "reconnecting with Jacob went a different direction?" She remembered how much fun spending his money was. Then, it changed. Her responsibility to him grew. No longer thinking of him as a sugar daddy with boatloads of resources and money – she fell for him. She liked the man – much. Those were the early days in their relationship, Victoria leading him into mischief – and he, the responsible one, looking out for her best interests while running wildly through one good time after another with her. As good as Jacob Paisley was, at least back then, he was a bad boy too.

She didn't leave him wanting anything. He wasn't the best lover, but good enough. In her eyes, he was enamored with her when they first became an exclusive thing. Then he was crazy about her adventuresome lovemaking and desirous ideas of traveling together to exotic destinations. As time moved on, their first year became a second and then another – his enrapturement became a fond respect. That's when she began to settle in for monotony. Their relationship became tame. It was hardly boring or annoying. But their time together, before the end, became dusty.

"What if my feelings for him trigger some speck of want?" She looked at herself in the metal mirror affixed to the wall in her cell. It wasn't optimal with the small bend in it, but she could see that it'd take an afternoon at Danka Panka, the salon of the celebrities to bring back the brilliant shine of her hair. Victoria wondered if her colorist was still there. Her nails, there were none – would need work. Yuki Marie's might remember her. At the end of a row of cells, a guard looked in and clinked a Billy club on the metal bars. A loud buzz rang out through the common area.

"Let's go, Victoria. Stop looking at yourself and go to work. Chop-chop, boogie-boogie. Those potatoes aren't going to peel themselves."

She said nothing, moving from the image of herself toward the rustling beginnings. Wondering when she might hear from the lawyer next, she'd need to enlist some resources to get stood up. In a Hoboken storage facility, she had a ditch bag and boxes of things that were outdated, she no longer wanted yet didn't want to throw away, and treasured trinkets – many from her travels with Jacob.

Maybe it was there, maybe it wasn't. Prepaid from an offshore cash stash account, she wasn't sure of what stability might be awaiting. And that was if, if the lawyer wanted to help her without too many tethers.

A parole officer – she knew would come along with her release. Seeking employment, getting it, not a problem in Victoria's mind. Having a babysitter – problematic if she'd need to navigate the island in free form. 'What if...' no longer clouded her thoughts. She knew she'd make out just fine on the outside. Hell, I'll fucking thrive. A smile found its way to Victoria's face as she made her way to the kitchen for the awaiting unpeeled potatoes.

"Victoria!" another guard shouted out to her. "Come here, there's someone in the visitation center that you're allowed to meet with. Case Manager and Team Leader approved it. Girl, you must know some people." She followed the corrections officer to a corridor. Then, down another, back to the area she was in yesterday. The door buzzed allowing Victoria to return to the bank of phones on the walls facing the inch thick glass. It was off-hours and highly unusual. She was the only one with a visitor. *"What if – this is a trick of some sort?"* Her intuition had served her well.

The area where they met visitors always smelled like stale vacancy. It was a nothingness odor. An inch of bulletproof glass kept the outside world scents just that – outside. There was no embrace, hosting the senses of the seasons. No flowers of spring, no fresh cut grass of summer, no rustling leaves from autumn, no cinnamon or sugar spice from winter. Just the plastic handset tethered to the wall from the previous convict.

There he was. Sitting there with a smug grin. Victoria picked up the receiver. "To what do I owe the pleasure?"

"You wanted good news. We have it. Today is your last day here, and your first day somewhere else." The lawyer was dressed much like he was any other day, ordinary, but the smile was new.

"Well, you know how to make a girl's heart leap." She had practiced being seductive as she fell asleep last night. A little rusty, working out the kinks in her timing, she tried adding, "What got you so motivated so quickly?" Victoria's eyes went as far down his torso as she could see. A table on the other side of the glass prevented her from examining anything below his belt line. "Cat got your tongue or are you saving it for..."

"It'll happen quickly. You'll meet with your PO – Manuel Vega or something like that. No coercion there, so play your part and be a good girl. They'll discharge you following processing. You won't have what you had prior to your sentence, at least I don't think you will. But you'll be out instead of in. A car will take you to a halfway house in Yonkers. These facilities range from entirely carceral to not much at all. We're trying to determine what you've been assigned to because we're not familiar with this one. Sometimes it's complete with surveillance and intense scrutiny. Other times it's a bit of an honor system, with periodic check ins. And there's this, we will need you to wear a PEM the first thirty days. Uh...Parole Electronic Monitoring. There's no getting around that in the near term. We're sorry. You step outside of one of the five borough counties; a trigger pings Vega and you're counting you first strike. Or second or last – depending."

Something changed. The personal pronouns he used the day earlier were replaced by pluralistic pronouns. She may have been a fantasy girl yesterday. Today, there was something much larger in charge. The favor. She'd need to understand what her favor owed would be – for the release.

Another female guard dressed in familiar battleship grey guard attire approached Victoria and placed a form in front of her. It was a Parole Release / Civilian Clothing Size Request form. On it were shoe size, pants, top, jacket. "Don't get too excited. It's thrift shop goods. Not Saks Fifth Avenue. I haven't seen any cocktail dresses or heels follow that form. Fill it out and hand it to the processing guard at the cage on your way on to what's next." She put her hand on Victoria's shoulder, leaned over and whispered, "Congratulations girl."

In a state of shock, Victoria looked back across the glass barrier at the lawyer. He was standing up and staring blankly at her. It wasn't a lustful look as it was the day before, but a mission accomplished look where he'd have little to do with her as she got swallowed up in a web of unknown obligations. She remembered what he said or something like it, *"You'll need to find some money of your own to stand up your project."*

Victoria watched him give her a slight wave. "We'll be in touch."

"Wait! What's next?" she asked.

She sensed that he couldn't get out of there fast enough. It seemed to her that this was his role, his due diligence, but he was also concerned about something – and drawing a line between them was apparently required. Or...he had second thoughts about her. *Nah...not that*, she whispered to herself.

He pointed at the door which buzzed in his queue. Another corrections officer allowed the lawyer to leave and looked at Victoria asking her to return to her side of the phone bank. When she did, the door buzzed, and she opened it listening to the metal clicks of the latch against the striker plate. She was escorted to a private dressing area, awaiting her street clothing and more paperwork to process her release.

As fast as things were happening, she assumed that they may move expeditiously on the outside too. She would need to accelerate her designs on meeting up with Jacob Paisley – and plead for his help.

What if...? The two little words, combined for grand gestures and small in-kind things, were weighing on her light moment. What if – he isn't interested? Then what. What if – he is? Where do we go there? What if – he simply wasn't available. She didn't know what his agenda was now that he was a free agent, without the corporate obligations of a Board of Directors or a private financial firm to manage.

Victoria thought of the other resources pre and post Paisley she had had relationships with. No one was the thoroughbred which he was. "You win with the winners, not the losers," Jacob had schooled her at The Kentucky Derby. Her big flowing hat and low-cut dress, overexposing her bare breasts made her the talk of their private suite. She remembered the horses lined up on the muddy track. He'd helped her with a sizable bet placed on the favorites. A fifty grand bet spread across the top two picks would pay out nearly seventy-five thousand dollars.

In a matter of two minutes, she made an incremental twenty-five thousand bet on two three-year-old horses, named *Something From Nothing* and *Fierce Freedom*.

Jacob Paisley taught her to pick her ponies. *You win with the winners;* she heard him speak it. *Ugh,* she thought. *Why did I leave? Was I afraid? If so, of what?*

"Victoria?" A parole officer asked her to follow him into a small office where he breezed through paperwork, expectations, the consequences of violations, and a three-strike warning system.

That was followed by worn denim jeans, a sweatshirt, a bra without an underwire, and used tennis shoes. "I know it's difficult to give up the striking orange jumpsuit, but this is what you get until you get wherever it is you're going." The woman officer saying it was joking about the trade-off of orange prison apparel.

"Well, I like the Keds," she replied. "They're a little big, but they'll do. Thank you."

"You just said that as a free woman," the officer said. "You've been processed. I'm looking forward to never seeing you here again," she smiled as she looked at Victoria. "I'll walk you out."

"The lawyer. My lawyer. He mentioned something about a PEM? A tracker?"

"Yeah sweetheart, your PO will get you set up with that."

"Like now?"

"Naw, they don't do it like that anymore. Later, when you two meet up."

Walking without anything in her hands, only a sense of wonder in her head, and no agenda in front of her – other than to make a play upon Paisley, she heard the final buzzer – the door to the outside caged area where recently released prisoners were reconnected with their families or friends or acquaintances. No one was waiting for her. She was alone. Looking up at the overcast sky of low grey clouds, she was thinking that this moment was nothing like that which she had pictured.

"You have anyone to help you out...?" the same guard asked her.

Just then a large black limo rolled up. The driver quickly opened his door and ran to open a back door for Victoria. She said nothing.

"I guess so," the guard added. "Not how it normally goes. You take care now, you hear?"

Victoria smiled at the thought of her 'what's next?', for the good graces of her exit from the prison system in a shiny mysterious black limousine, and for having a surprise of a day. She hadn't had a nice surprise in a long time. Since Jacob Paisley's doting her with them.

Then, as she climbed in, hearing the Lincoln's heavy door click shut, her smile turned into a small frown. A favor loomed. The thought of her pending indentured servitude – the catch for her early release - was an unknown arrangement she may have to concede to.

A small vanilla envelope was on the seat next to her. She reached over to open the unsealed flap. In it was a wrapped band of money and a cell phone that was a generation behind what she had when she was incarcerated. Victoria looked at the cash. It was a small bundle of worn hundreds, fifties and twenties. In the middle of what appeared to be six or seven hundred dollars was a NYC phone number, hand-written on a torn strip of lined ledger paper, slightly larger than the size of a business card. She knew class distinction and the covers for distorting gentry. This raw dog sign was not of gentility, but of either of an ignoble or covert directive. Either way, Victoria would have some unraveling to do.

"Well, at least the car's nice," she said to herself as the car began to roll away from the correctional facility toward the Rikers Island Bridge. She breathed deeply and changed her mind about the glitzy vehicle driving her from the clink. Hoping that the smell of freedom would be different than it was, Victoria wrinkled her nose at the rankness of the funk likely squirted on the floor mats, resembling a cheaper version of Pine-Sol.

* * * * *

Adele was taking Kolohe to the kennel for an overnight stay in Yorkville. Too far to walk both ways and still make it to their meeting on time, she loaded the yellow lab into the BMW and drove him, telling him what a good boy her was incessantly. She would meet up with Jacob, Ruby and the rest of the team for the final 'go' / 'no-go' meeting, reviewing any additional planning before their deployment in Everglades City, Florida.

The late morning light was reflecting off the Manhattan towers. Bouncing from building to building to building, the reproduction of brightness making its way to the streets below the skyscrapers illuminated the greyness from charcoal to coin-like colors. The shadows were growing shorter as the sun continued its climb into the sky. Jacob was walking into Ruby's apartment in Tribeca. It was his first time visiting Ruby at Ruby's place. It was the first time he'd been invited to.

Jacob rode in the bronze high-speed elevator to the thirty seventh floor. He rang the bell outside 3701. A soft ding was heard coming from the other side of the door.

Ruby opened it slowly. "Come on in." He coughed harshly, using the bend of the inside of his arm to capture his wheezing breath.

It wasn't what Jacob was expecting. Minimal amounts of furnishings were scattered. Packing boxes were stacked in one corner of what would have been a living area. Others were on the couch. "Are you okay?"

"I get like this sometimes when I wake up. Like I've got a chest cold. I'm good. Think nothing of it."

"You've got a," he paused looking over at Ruby who was slipping off his slippers and awkwardly stretching out an arm of a sweater at the same time, "big project going on here?" It began as a statement and ended as a question.

"Charlie," Ruby answered, "made a decision. Bit of a surprise to me, but MIT was in the mix. You'd think he'd tell his, I don't know, father?"

"You'd think," Jacob looked at the scattering of stuff and confusion surrounding him, "But I'm no father. So, I practice sympathy for what parents endure, not empathy."

Another cough robbed Ruby of his breath.

"Anything I can do to help here? Like..." Jacob saw a baseball glove, a jockstrap, a vinyl record of Ray Charles, two sweatshirts, and a Rubik's Cube next to an empty box. "Like put some stuff in an empty cardboard box?"

"God no. Then, it's my fault if it goes missing. Leave it, please." Ruby finally got the arm through the sweater and moved to the coffee pot which had its last glurp, glurp, glurps from percolating.

"Are you happy to see him go? Perhaps proud of his decisions and growing into himself? Does a father...?"

"You know...? Of course, you know – look at me - I had him late in life. We, we had him late in life. His mother...Sharon was her name...she wasn't around much. Problems. Addictions. Bad addictions, bad drugs. Stole her soul. It's why I asked you here. So that we had some private and uninterrupted time to ourselves to talk about some things that I've been preparing for...for a while now." Ruby pointed at the empty box consuming a cushion on the couch.

Jacob tossed it aside and sat while Ruby asked, "You take it black, right?"

"Correct. Did she leave, did you leave, did...?"

"She killed herself. Eventually she took her own life. An overdose. That, you'd think was the end, but it became a beginning."

"Ellipsis," Jacob stated.

"Ellipsis," Ruby confirmed. "One thing led to another, and I became completely obsessed with ending a drug-trafficking syndicate in South Bronx. As it turned out, I was addicted to something too. Not proud of what I tell you next, but here it is: I killed two men as a result of my findings. Set them up, verified their guilt, faced them and fired a gun into their belly's – ending their lives." Ruby's face was blank as he told the story to Jacob looking at nothingness and away from Jacob. I was sitting at a park across from Yankee stadium, thinking about ending my own life from the guilt of killing two others. Wondering how Charlie might be taken care of, a stranger sat down next to me. A man similar to me. Looked a bit like me, in an odd sort of a way."

"Was he your...?" Jacob asked but was interrupted.

"Father? No. My dad was long gone. But it was timely." Ruby looked at Jacob finally, "Just needed to hear that man's voice at that time. He said, *'They took someone from me that I love too.'* He laid a bullet on the bench next to me as said, 'This is my calling card.' I looked at him and didn't know what to think."

He stood up, placed his hand on Jacob's shoulder and walked away, into the sunlight.

"Calling card?"

Ruby approached a desk in the corner of the room where his closed laptop sat. From a dark wooden cherry drawer at the desk, he retrieved something small. Holding it tightly in his hand, Ruby returned to Jacob and handed it to him.

The copper-colored ammunition was weathered. As Jacob looked at the shell, he noticed an engraving on the metal casing, it read:

VINDICATION

"Sort of strange, right?" Ruby looked at Jacob directly, seeking his confirmation.

Jacob said nothing, rolling the round bullet through his fingertips, stopping to read the etching several times.

"What did you do?" Jacob asked.

"Well, immediately, nothing. Thought about it for a few weeks. Then, an absolution grew within me. A remission for acting upon sinful, unlawful and wicked wrongdoing grew within me and then...and then I cannot explain how it happened exactly, but pieces started falling into place."

Jacob reached over and picked up the Rubik's cube, "Like a perfect puzzle, it came together. It made sense."

Ruby shook his head, "It made sense. The world as we know it needs help. Religion alone is not solving all of our problems. Moral compass needs a navigator. Government – ugh, don't get me started with those baby-shakers."

"Just as a generalization, a little prudence might be missing there," Jacob added to Ruby's distinguished frown.

Ruby continued the political point he was making, "The fall of the Roman Empire was because of internal corruption, division, and a concern for protecting the few from rule, opposed to the rights of the many. That sound familiar in any way to what you see?"

"There's a reason I'm here. Doing what's right, rather than what's easy – it eventually finds a way. But, if it doesn't or perhaps it's too late to arrive... Well, then the Barbarian tribes raid and the instability consumes."

Ruby winced at Jacob's quick assessment. "The interaction, Ellipsis, the thing in between something happening – it tends to make the right things, the necessary, the timely, the required occur. Exoneration transpires or an acquittal comes about. And..." he held an open hand in the air in front of him, "the prosecution proceeds. It needs to. Ellipsis. Something is happening. Not sure just what all the time. Rights over wrongs. Corrections required. Sometimes, in the middle of a play – it seems like a maelstrom in a rough stretch of churning uncertainty. Then a copper bullet finds its way, a calling card. And it all makes a little more sense." He paused in his cryptic homily.

"Vindication," Jacob added. "Vindication takes place." He looked at Ruby who wasn't making eye contact just yet.

And then he did.

Ruby switched gears. "Listen. That's just a part of what we need to talk about."

"Are you alright? You? You...okay?" Jacob wouldn't look away seeking reassurance.

"I'm getting old, Jacob. We've been moving faster now, with you, for a reason. You said it the other night, that bottle of wine, Succession."

Jacob added his assessment, "Well, when compared to Allegra, we haven't moved that quickly."

"BenVen has watched her for years. We know what we've got there. Let me finish my line of thought. There will come a point when I'm out, dead, gone, unable...whatever. I want what we're doing here with our group, our work, to go on. You, Adele, Sydney, Vendemer, the young woman...Allegra, others... It takes time and work to build a team of people that seek vengeance upon wrong and wish to lift the light of the world higher so that it shines on all people."

"I'm far from leading..."

"You're not. I hope you can get a glimpse that you're not far from a small team of do-gooders. A step at a time. Start small. But there's a reason that it was you, Jacob. All along, you were one of our jewels. Well, you and Adele – a package deal. You think and she tends to fill in the gaps or help you pivot when you need to. You just needed chiseling and polishing to shine like you are beginning to. Brilliant." Ruby held his paper-thin skin on Jacob's firm hand.

Not knowing what to do with the man-to-man intimacy, Jacob handed the VINDICATION bullet back to Ruby.

"You keep that. And you didn't even have to shoot a man," Ruby mustered a chuckle before another series of coughs

Jacob tucked the cartridge deep in this pants pocket and asked, "That's not going to go off in my pants, is it? Shoot by balls off?"

Ruby smiled, then laughed which caused more coughing. They both chuckled as they made their way through the college bound debris to Ruby's door. "A shot in the nuts – sounds like a happy hour drink to me..." They both laughed lightly as they made their way to the front door.

"Something else about you that I didn't know," Jacob spoke out of the side of his mouth near Ruby.

"Well, there's another thing." Ruby held up a finger. "About a year and a half after the meeting with the man, and his words, and the bullet took place...after I killed those two thugs who had much to do with Sharon's death...a lawyer finds me. A clean-cut white dude with a briefcase shows up. He asked to take me to lunch. I had no clue what I might have done. Well, I knew, but didn't think my covert and secluded actions had anything to do with the uptown man. We met at a deli, and he quickly mentioned an inheritance."

"Seed money for Ellipsis," Jacob asked.

"No. Ellipsis already had tentacles – although we didn't call it Ellipsis when a bunch of us banded together and started doing shit that the authorities would deem the conduct of vigilantes."

"Vigilantes. They're loved and hated…"

"Often," Ruby interrupted, "misunderstood. I'd add that they're underutilized too." He sat silent for a moment. "Well, that's what I wanted to share with you today, friend. You didn't ask me how much."

"How much was the inheritance?" Jacob asked, more so to be polite than because he really needed to know.

"Thank you for asking me. It was just shy of eleven million bucks. Who gives that kind of money to a stranger?"

"Maybe you weren't really a stranger. Maybe you were groomed like I was. A mysterious person guided you, prompting your thoughts, choices, actions…" Jacob again thought of Ruby the hospital volunteer, Ruby the bartender, Ruby the faux-blind cancer victim on a sunset cruise in the Pacific. Ruby Hollins, the shaper of Jacob Paisley.

"Work to do. Let's go." Ruby picked up a small, brown, worn leather duffel which looked like it had seen the better part of his lifetime and a countless number of airports. "Where's your bag or your suitcase?" he asked.

"Adele has it." Jacob had nothing in his hands, a bullet in his pocket.

"She's still got your back, after all these years. When you going to make an honest woman of her?" Ruby turned his head to see Jacob's expression.

Jacob hesitated, "She is honest."

"You know what I meant," Ruby replied.

"I know what you meant."

The taxi to the UN building where the others were gathering would be twenty minutes along the East River. In the cab, they'd chitchat about the Knicks drought, how the NASDAQ and the S&P 500 were entering a potential bubble territory, the troubles with the current administration, or Charlie's choice in college and how pricey it might be.

The barbershop talk was recreation on their way to their meaningful connection with the others.

*****

"Well, Jacob had one hell of an interesting night," Ruby said as they sat at the table.

"What time did you get home? I didn't hear you," Adele asked.

Before he could answer, Ruby did. "I heard you on the comms, at what four? Saying goodbye to the dealer?"

Adele, Allegra, Sydney and Vendermer each had a silvery laptop opened and were reviewing briefing notes from the mercenaries.

"Something like that," Jacob finally answered while swallowing the last gulp from his fourth cup of coffee. Hoping that his tattletale friend wouldn't share too much, Jacob acted preoccupied with a bunch of nothing on his phone.

"That place – I'm surprised..." Ruby paused, "Well, look at us, a well-kept secret, at least for now..." Jacob looked at him, thinking that Tamsen was a suspicious threat weighing on Ruby's mind. "I'm surprised that that place with it's reputation hasn't drawn awareness and a police raid or something."

Adele paused typing, but didn't look up at either of them. She was told by Jacob that he was playing poker with two congressmen and wanted to assume that was that.

Allegra, who had again, placed great effort into her looks – dress, shoes, hair and makeup – asked the question Adele was wondering, while she continued to type, "Where did you end up? Which strip club, I'm assuming? Sapphire? Rick's? Pumps?" She was still looking at the notes while she said it being playful, somewhat teasing, but not expecting the answer which Ruby provided.

"My Uncle's Place - right Jacob?" Ruby wasn't there and lacked in seeing the things which Jacob couldn't un-see.

"The sex club?" Allegra snapped her head up to look at Jacob, then at Ruby, then back to Jacob.

He said nothing at first.

Adele didn't look up and pretended not to notice Allegra's quick reaction. Instead, she slowly turned her head toward Jacob who looked at her and shrugged his shoulders. Then Adele slowly turned her head toward Allegra for a brief verification glance and frowning, back to Jacob. "Hmm..." she quietly to herself.

"Shut up, Ruby," He frowned too and reached for the phone he'd set down in front of him.

Ruby had a sheepish grin on his face assuming that a doghouse conversation was looming between Adele and Jacob.

Shortly following 'The sex club?' utterance she had made, Allegra added, "or, so I've heard," attempting to brush off her carnal knowledge. That secret not only needed to remain locked away, it belonged in the back of her mind's vault.

At the same time, Adele pulled up My Uncle's Place / NYC on a browser. Nothing appeared on the top of the search page. A caterer in Memphis, a restaurant in Baton Rouge, and a bar and grill in Toledo were suggested. *Of course,* Adele thought to herself – *it's a secret. One which Allegra and Jacob share. And then there was Ruby, with a smirk on his face resembling the voyeurism listening pleasure he too shared.*

Ruby added. "For what it's worth, he did it. Jacob convinced the gentleman from Great State of Georgia, a republican, toward a vote of 'no' on a gun law. Or at least for now. Honesty among politicians isn't something which we should count on."

"Right... Less bad guns – a good thing. More bad guns – a bad thing," Sydney redirected the conversation to the big screen in front of them. "I'm going to pull them up once you boys are done talking about sex clubs, your members of parliament, and gun legislation. We good?"

Ruby nodded toward the screen, but then added looking more so to Adele than the others, "Ginger – that was the informant's name.

The resource at the club. She's here creatively we'll say. She works a unique gig. A currency of favors, we'll call it."

"So, she's compromised?" Jacob asked. "She's prone to behave a certain way?"

Ruby held his chin in his fingers for a few seconds, thinking, and continued, "Hm...certain way. Well...one way or another. Qualified or disenfranchised. Yes, one way or another. Listen, good and bad. We haven't established a ton of trust there just yet. If anything should happen to me, you know...like I win the lottery or get hit by a bus and don't show up anymore – when you come in contact with Ginger – keep her at an arm's length. The arm is part of the body, but it doesn't do the thinking. You know what I mean."

Was this some sort of foreshadowing? Jacob thought to himself. He frowned while looking at his friend.

"You asked if we good? We good." He nodded again toward the big screen and pointed with his fingers, lightly stirring the air in the direction of the front of their meeting room while Sydney began speaking. Allegra, Adele, and Jacob weren't really listening to her preamble.

Jacob wanted any conversation to take the place of Adele's curiosity about the sex club. He thought to look Adele's way, shake his head and say something such as - *Adele...it was just Day of Decadence nonsense. A boy's night out on the town* - drawing back to a time which he rewarded his top traders at PPCM with lavish parties, but he thought better of it, thinking perhaps a comment like that might be met with her squinting and disapproving eyes. That was, after all, how Victoria entered his picture.

Allegra sat silent, pretending not to be interested in either topic, My Uncle's Place or a vote taking place on gun laws. Instead, she pictured herself on Jacob's arm at a sex club, wearing the elegant lace masquerade masks to hide their identities, watching the dark acts by the willing participants in the dimly lit ballroom. Her secrets were still safely tucked away.

The next two hours were spent reviewing the final operational tactics. A small team of tech specialists were already on the ground in Florida, working in the Marco Island communications trailer. The drones were receiving their software programming to flood the scene, overloading the detection devices and crashing the servers. Two black Suburban's were on the premises at the hotel. Most importantly, the Ellipsis soldiers were buttoned up for battle. Their teasing charm was missing as they all spoke and tied out on remaining detail.

It was decided that Adele, their maternal ambassador of care and comfort, would ride with Sydney in helicopter one, "the retriever". Allegra and Jacob would ride in helicopter two, "the instigator" with the soldiers. Two drivers for the Suburban's and two additional soldiers would approach the site by vehicle. One additional driver would be in the area in a white van resembling the van which they had been observing on the county traffic cameras. The backup transportation could carry the victims if there was an unexpected situation. They had plenty of firepower to meet the merriment of six south Florida rednecks, one on-prem caretaker, and potentially a new addition to their team from the Tampa vicinity.

They rehearsed the siege two more times. Then, it was time for the New Yorkers to catch their three-hour flight to Fort Myers, followed by the short Gulf Coast drive to La Isla de San Marco.

On the way to the airport, Adele sitting next to Jacob, whispered in his ear, "You're only doing this because of me..." She turned her head to look back out the back seat window of the yellow taxi.

He looked at her, smiled and reached down to her soft hand and held it tightly. Leaning over to her ear, he returned the whisper, "There's some truth to that."

They were sharing the memory of sitting in Jacob's office, back in their Paisley Pierce Capital Management times. When wrestling with any given predicament, stressed out or cornered, in a moment of levity, as the CEO, Jacob would add, *'You're only doing this because of me.'* As the founder of PPCM, he knew that the pickles they'd gotten themselves into were often his to run his way out of. When they were solving or had solved their problems – or were on the cusp of getting a favorable outcome, Jacob would tuck his tagline into the conversation. "You're only doing this, because of me." Adele, his loyal secretary, would add her own, "There's some truth to that." The we're-in-it-together exchange between them was also used for the best of times, and occasionally the worst of times.

She reached into her bag fishing around for something. "Are we doing what we need to be doing?" she added, not in a whisper, but spoken quietly and privately. It wasn't the hesitancy she sought from him; Adele knew him too well for that – but it was his Jacob Paisley conviction, just delivered with pause.

He looked into her eyes, sparkling back at him, and shaking his head, answered, "Finally."

Adele gave her lips a touch up with the peony lipstick.

Jacob gently reached for the tube from her fingers once she was done with it. Holding it to his nose, he smiled, looking at her out of the corner of his eye. It was one of her scents. It was Adele. Simplicity and modesty, yet elegance. A mindfulness for others and for doing good – coupled with the great power of words. She was as woman that took care of her mind and body. Adele could take a compliment and knew exactly when to distribute one. Her way was to do the right things, even when no one was looking because she would know that someone might be. Strong, yet humble – she knew herself and those closest to her.

He handed the tube of lipstick back to her, after screwing it closed. Jacob hoped that he would never disappoint her.

✼✼✼✼✼

"Hey – it's late there," Tamsen said as she took Ruby's call.

"Yeah, can't sleep. I'm not there – there – New York. I'm at a JW Marriott on Marco Island." he replied, followed by a long pause of silence.

"I thought you were flying there in the morning. Florida – it's still late. Same time zone." She counted the six hours backwards from Hawaii, realizing that it was midnight.

"He's not even close to being packed and is heading out mid-next week. I'm not doing it. He'll leave half of it behind – head off to college with a toothbrush, his Xbox, two sweatshirts and a pair of jeans – I just know it."

"A worried father who seeks the best for his son, do you know how lucky he is?" She was soft with her words, "Does he know how lucky he is?"

"Well…" Ruby coughed.

"Is that getting worse?"

"Comes and goes," he answered, "We've got the gig in here at Everglades City in the morning."

"Like, later this morning – for you?"

Ruby looked at the small alarm clock next to the bed, "Uh, yeah."

"How far are you from the situation site?"

"Ah…about 40 minutes across swampland," Ruby replied.

"Going in by airboat?'

"Nah – got two choppers and a couple vehicles on the ground. We get them out and transport them to Naples. Then the cleaner shows up and does his thing, erasing our footprint. We'll keep the local authorities busy with a few harmless shenanigans during the raid."

"You're not in the field for this one, are you? I hope not!" she said rather alarmed.

"Oh, hell no. I'm with Vendemer, holed up in a communication trailer on the island here."

"Good to hear. Then you'll be off to Oahu soon after that. What will you do in the meantime? Pick and pack all the things Charlie forgot behind?"

"Yeah, probably. Say, that's actually why I'm calling. While in Hawaii, I've got a creative play we should talk about."

"Here we go... It always starts out like that." Tamsen acknowledged that the beginning of one of his projects began with the term, 'creative play'.

Ruby added, "And Honolulu is in a hot-spot strategic position."

"You really need a vacation so bad that you find a project to bring you to my island home?"

"C'mon, seriously," Ruby continued, "How do you think you're making out with the new talent?"

Tamsen hesitated. She flipped the eggs. "Damn it."

"Damn what?"

Placing a lid on the skillet she was the master of the obvious, "What is it with me and broken yolks?"

"I'm not following you," Ruby remembered looking at his own kitchen before he departed that morning with Jacob for their prep session. It was dark and emptier than ever.

"I'm frying eggs, and I think I'm about oh-for-eighteen on unbroken yolks."

He frowned to himself, "Fried eggs for dinner?"

Tamsen affirmed, "Those little cocoons of nourishment? Sure. Breakfast – check. On a plate lunch, or rice covered with gravy and topped with a slimy egg for dinner, boiled eggs as a snack – one of the healthiest things you can eat. Deviled eggs – 'so ono', uncle. I can eat eggs here or there. I can eat eggs everywhere."

"Whatever. Don't go Dr. Suess on me. Scrambled works. Listen, progress report. The surf girls? Potential, or no?"

"When you're here, we're eating green eggs, old man," She looked up at the setting sun in Oahu from her kitchen window. The girl had departed. "Yeah, it's pretty much a 'no'. I don't think so. I'm not seeking it. The spark isn't there."

"In time?" Ruby asked.

"Umm...trust issues, I think. Can't put my finger on it, but she lacks that...that compass thing you look for." Tamsen clattered the skillet and a plate on the granite counter top. "You know that lone wolf. Person with a unique vault of confidentiality. These girls I picked, their behavior style. I just don't want any loose cannons."

"That's what I told Jacob you were. Unpredictive. Maybe a little emotive." Ruby smiled thinking that she wasn't but that he was having fun pretending that she was.

"Adults are easier in predictability than impressionable young ladies with no coordinates, or a spinning compass, or I don't know...an attention span of a goldfish."

"Well, I trust you. Take your time with it. We'll need..." Ruby paused, his head on the pillow, staring at the ceiling, seeking the right words, "an influencer."

"You mean a good-looking young woman, don't you?"

"I didn't say that."

Tamsen smiled, watching two black mynah birds straddling her decking sounding her home. They were squawking and pecking at each other's beaks. Nearly pets, she'd groomed them to show up as the sun was setting for an evening snack.

"Always recruiting, aren't you?"

"Always thinking about what's next," Ruby replied.

She switched topics. "And no one knows about you? Not Sydney, not Jacob, not Adele?"

"No," Ruby contemplated the answer, "I'm...I'm still working that through my head."

"Not even Vendemer?"

"Not even BenVen," Ruby affirmed.

"Not even Charlie?'

Ruby smirked and slunk further in the bed, "Just you. You're the only one."

"Wow. Okay. Have you booked your flight yet?"

"I'll do that when I get back in the city." Ruby looked at the clock again, to see that not only on his iPhone, but he also had an alarm set for six. A small bell was illuminated on the face of the device. "I think I'll have eggs for breakfast tomorrow morning."

"You mean later this morning?" Tamsen corrected him.

"Yeah, later this morning. Scrambled, of course. Will think of you kid." Ruby listened quietly.

"Get some rest. Good night old man. Looking forward to seeing you soon."

The quiet of the night returned. He closed his eyes, hoping that the darkness would take him away. Instead, he contemplated what the next day might be like. He played it in his head - and how Ellipsis was attempting to, again, right a wrong.

13

Extraction

The morning sun was shining upon the Everglades, casting shadows from the trees, scrub and brush across the blue and brown pools of water, which was the Everglades home for over 200,000 alligators . The sky, dotted with occasional white puffy clouds, had a slight breeze. It was a perfect day for liberating victims of human trafficking.

Allegra sat snugly next to Jacob. "These look like Army helicopters," she said - not really expecting a truthful answer. It was

After a slight delay, it was confirmed that the white van was on the way

The blades whirling through the air were louder than Allegra thought they'd be. *Whomp, whomp, whomp, whomp...*they sounded as the engine to their helicopter began. Four of their soldiers were buttoned up for battle and sitting close together in the back of the chopper's body. Two others were approaching the Bell Jet Ranger. Each wore a tactical vest, carried an assault rifle, and a tight-fitting Kevlar helmet with the chin strap tightly fit on their faces. This was a morning without a lot of chatter. They had serious work to perform. Game-faces were on. The silly moniker names for Allegra shared not too long ago were far from this moment. Today she wasn't the mercenaries' Foxy, Bunny or Dreamy.

She said nothing more.

Jacob only asked if they were in the right spot to not interfere with the mission.

Chuck answered, "All good Captain." Without a smile, he looked at each of his squad and sought a thumbs up. First, it was Jade. Next to him, Bing. Rave followed with her confirmation. Tucker and Marco were simultaneously issuing their thumbs up.

He looked at Allegra, "No turning back now, sister." The friendliness was gone. Allegra looked at Jacob and sighed deeply. It wasn't going how she thought it might. She wondered, to herself, if she were up for this, but said nothing while biting her lip.

Jacob and Allegra were given olive-colored tactical vests like the soldiers. The difference was the accessories that they were missing. The camouflage Velcro to hold the rifles next to the mercenary was stripped. The pockets containing grenades or smoke bombs were gone. No carabiner to attach a backpack was necessary. Nor did they wear the avocado-green neoprene gloves which the fighters wore.

Similarly, in the other helicopter, Adele was trimmed how Jacob and Allegra were. The body armor vest, protecting the internal organs from a stray bullet. Sydney was dressed to kill – like that of the fighters on Jacob's helicopter. They made eye contact before the doors were shut and gave each other a small wave.

Allegra and Jacob were given large headsets so that they could hear all communications taking place. The pilots between the two helicopters chatted as if they'd known each other for years.

"These two guys flew together in Nam," Chuck shouted to Jacob, paying little attention to Allegra. Jacob just nodded his head, confirming he had heard. "That means, they're fuckin' crazy. Hold on to somethin' anything. Her. We're in for a treat." He smiled.

Jacob looked at Allegra.

She asked leaning into him, closer than she'd ever been to the man of her daydreams, "What did he say?"

"Might get a little choppy up there... Be prepared to brace for impact." Jacob did his best to shout into her ear as the noise from the blades grew louder. *Chop, chop, chop, chop, chop* – rapidly consumed the cabin where they sat. The 'chop' sound became a 'chip' sound as the rotors spun faster. *Chip, chip, chip, chip, chip.*

"This is your Captain speaking. Welcome to my first solo flight. Glad you volunteered to come on board." His attempt at a joke wasn't met with anything other than Allegra rolling her eyes at Jacob. "For you listening pleasure..." the captain of the helicopter looped in music.

What came across their big black bubble headsets couldn't have been what the pilot was expecting. Belinda Carlisle's, *Heaven Is A Place On Earth,* began to play loudly and crisply in their headsets. "Oh shit. Not that crap..." could be heard in the distance as the pilot punched a few buttons. "Sorry, gave the wife a lift to the Piggly Wiggly earlier this week..."

AC/DC's, *Dirty Deeds,* took the song choice place. The volume was cranked, buzzing in their headsets.

Once the second helicopter's rotor was fired up, collectively, their hearts beat faster. They no longer sat idle, waiting for the 'go' signal or the pleasant distraction of fast-paced rock music, the wheels of the whirly birds were up quickly, and like a ride at an amusement park they tipped into the wind heading south. Flying faster, picking up speed, the helicopters flew off of State Road 29, quickly approaching Tamiami Trail. To avoid alerting any ground noise they slowed, awaiting the communications crew to call the shots.

Ruby and Vendemer watched from the four screens showing the white van driving down the single road into Everglades City at 8:58am. A communications commander in the tactical trailer back in at Marco Island shared what they were seeing, "The ruffians are rolling in, guys. Choppers One and Two – stay back for now. Up and away. We have Suburban One and Two pulled over at the Carnestown junction. Albino is on the ninety, heading East." They watched their white van with a GPS dot blinking green as it approached a turn off point where it too would sit and wait.

A massive swarm of drones, launched from Ochopee, were enroute across the mangroves, waters, cypress trees hosting Spanish moss. Their speed, altitude, and navigational maneuvering were controlled from the communications trailer and from their launch point across the alligator's crib, the swampy wetlands.

The synchronization was going as planned, yet dependent upon the white van presumably filled with the traffickers. With their structure and rigor in precision, it was assumed that the contracted pimps may be of military experience. For that, it could become soldier versus soldier.

*****

Ashford had been up since three, cranked on two Mountain Dew's, a Red Bull, and three cups of coffee – he was amped and ready for this. His hands gripped the steering wheel tighter than any hands in the State of Florida ever held on to any steering wheel. Ready to attack, his eyes squinted, not from the sunlight, but for the preparation of a pending battle. Aware that the Adrenalin was in control – he attempted to manage it, knowing he'd need his wits and not just his willingness. He found comfort in the words from Lady Barbara, *Vindica Te Tibi*...or translated meant, 'claim yourself'...or 'set yourself free'.

It was happening. He slowed the white van down to slowly roll into the compound at precisely nine.

To the left of the road was a small ditch, a canal, with water in it. He assumed that it was dug and drenched as a water easement to avoid flooding of the roadway. He also assumed that it wasn't where you might want to find yourself with so many alligators and snakes in the area. Tampa felt so cosmopolitan compared to this wilderness area. *How many people who went missing...?* He stopped himself from finishing the thought in his head.

Thick wrists, bulging biceps, broad shoulders, protruding pecs, sporting a six pack – much of his fitness, strength and conditioning, was hidden under his black crew neck henley, blacker cargo pants, boots, and unmarked ball cap.

At exactly 8:59 he turned left, creeping onto the shell gravel driveway. When no one opened the gate to the complex, he opened the door to the white van he was instructed to rent and rolled across the property line. He slowly crept to the middle of what appeared to be a work yard for machine parts. A diesel engine was hoisted on a tripod, various motor parts were under dissection, and tools were scattered across several workstations. The tenting covered some of the work areas and a structured canopy built with hatch aluminum covered the master tool area where the boxes and parts were. This area would be where the mechanic who lived here would have stored expensive tools, flammables, and materials of value.

It was quiet. He thought he heard mosquitoes or locusts in the distance. Unaware of several drones encroaching on the area, Ashford continued to walk slowly on foot toward the small shanty of what appeared to be someone's home. Something smelled fowl here, like rotten eggs or musty socks from the bottom of the hamper. The swampy atmosphere was backwoods buggy and stagnant.

"Hello…" he shouted. There was no answer. "Hello. It's Aiden Ashford. Is anyone here?" Again, silence – other than what Ashford assumed were the bugs in the distance. Eerily quiet, he tried once more – "Hello, is anyone here?" He heard nothing from the area.

Steve Booth didn't recognize the stranger. It was the white van, but it wasn't Stanley the cutter of fingers or any of the crew that had been arriving each Saturday at 9:00am promptly to swap out The Product. Watching the man walk slowly from area to area, Steve was quiet and careful not to stir up noise from within him home. Momma taught him how to be quiet when people came to collect money. Momma taught him how to be quiet when he was in bible school. Momma taught him how to be quiet when going to the social services office where they would ask Momma a bunch of questions and she'd get money. He could be quiet just like that while this man in black walked around. Maybe it was the man snooping around that Staney the pinky cutter warned him of. They should be here soon. This had to be just another white van that rolled onto Steve's property at the same time the regular Saturday crew rolled in. Steve would keep quiet and hide.

Ashford knocked on the screen door. It squeaked as he did. "Hello. Anyone home?"

Steve hid in the bathroom and crouched down on the toilet. He could always hide in the bathtub which he seldom used if necessary and close the curtain. Most of the plastic was still dangling on hooks on the bar at the top.

Something wasn't right about this, Ashford thought. Why roll in at nine – see you at ten? Was he...? Could he be some sort of a...what...decoy? Unsure of how he came about this growing suspicion, maybe it was Ashley, or perhaps it was Lady Barbara, and possibly it was just a sense of how creepy the conversation felt from the communication leading to this quirky rendezvous – something felt 'off'. Ashford took a step back from the screen door and slowly returned to the van, trying not to make any additional noise. The tempered gravel under his black boots made little sound as he took soft steps. Opening the side door of the white van, he retrieved a sidearm, two of the AR-15 rifles and the M-9 tactical knife. Once he was equipped for an altercation he wanted to seek vantage points, places to hide if necessary.

In the distance was a building of some sort. He didn't notice it when he slowly drove the white van onto the property. It was covered with something, but what? He walked toward it, carrying one rifle in his hands and another strapped to his back.

Steve cowered in the bathroom, not hearing any knocking at the door, but too afraid to approach the stranger. He'd be quiet, just like Momma taught him to do. Stanley, the cutter of fingers, and the others would be here soon and at that point Steve Booth would appear as if he were expecting them and taking care of any matters at hand which might present themselves – even if one of his hands didn't have all of its fingers. And then there would be lunch. Steve and his new companions would have a bite to eat together. He thought they were probably held up at the Subway up at the Carnestown junction.

Ashford crept closer to the building which grew larger with each step. It appeared small from the middle of the gravel complex where the white van sat, doors open, but now was clearly a shipping container covered in army-netting camouflage. As he looked closer, he could even make out a number on the upper left corner of the metal container: 53'. It was the dimension of a semi-truck, railcar, or ocean-bound shipping cargo's steel container.

He stopped - in the realization that it, the container, might be perfect for hiding...people. Ashford took two more steps toward the container and realized that whether or not Ashley could be in there, someone might. Somebody's mother or father. Someone's child. Anyone's 'somebody' could be in there. What was a container like that doing in a place like this, hidden from sight and sound?

The thought of him serving as bait grew in this stomach. It hurt. Being used, a sucker, played – he felt like a lure on a hook. There was a snare in play, and he was in the net. It was time to hide. He'd wait this out, awaiting the right time. Ducking behind a workbench in the tool area and creeping off to the side area of the complex, Ashford would await the so-called Patriots while trying to sneak closer to the steel box containing who-knew-what, maybe Ashley. Hopefully Ashley.

*****

"Are you guys seeing this?" one of the communications teammates acknowledged to the others, "Conan the Barbarian?"

"Why's there just one? And just one – who doesn't seem to know what's going on, creeping around with weapons on his back?" Vendemer asked the team.

"That's John Rambo," Ruby smiled pointing at the screen which he was watching on. The man dressed in black walked softly on the grey crushed gravel attempting to mitigate sound.

"He isn't one of them. A rogue operator? He's..."

Vendermer and Ruby exchanged glances. "Your call," Vendemer said.

"Hold. Let's see how it plays out," Ruby stated.

"Where are the drones?"

"Stationary," one of the Tech's yelled. "Allegra has them sectioned off into three tranches. Roughly one thousand, followed by one thousand, and then another one thousand."

"Roughly?" Ruby asked. "Can you patch us in on an open line to Chuck and the others," he asked again.

"On it. Line is open." The Tech gave Ruby and Vendemer headsets to speak into. The black loops slid over their heads opposed to the speakerphone they were on, and they had the entire team on intercom.

"Chuck – the van appears to be either a coincidence or some sort of a...we don't know...distraction," Vendemer said.

"We see a Rambo-looking dude lurking around the compound wearing an assault rifle, carrying another. It appears he's questioning his presence and hiding."

Ruby held his hand over the mouthpiece, and said to Vendemer, "Not what we were expecting, what say you, Benjamin?"

Vendemer shrugged his shoulders, "Proceed with caution? Better one than six or seven or eight?"

Ruby watched the screen which showed no movement on the ground. The mystery man was hiding somewhere. "Let's get those kids out of there. One and Two, – go to the ground. Proceed with extreme caution. Extreme caution. Assume that there is a questionable and armed predator on the ground amidst you during retrieval."

"Roger that, One...over."

"Copy that, Two...over."

"What do you think?" Ruby asked BenVen, again with his hand covering the mic.

"Right thing to do. Let's get those women and children out of there but keep a close eye on the ground with the drones and as we touch down." Vendemer, Ruby, and the technicians in the communication trailer were observing each screen provided by a multitude of stationary hovering drones ready to crash the system on command.

"Allegra...?"

She glanced at Jacob and lifted her mouthpiece to her lips, "I'm here."

"What do you think about splitting the scale? Divide and conquer?" one of the technicians asked.

"Throw a hash-two next to the contingency build-up and add about fifty feet and the algorithm should split the factor," she shouted into the intercom.

Jacob looked at her. *How far we've come,* he thought, *from coffee and mentoring to the latitudes of human trafficking liberties and longitudes of algorithms of self-flying devices governing the wilderness.*

She looked at him and rolled her shoulders, cutely, "Maybe," she mouthed to Jacob only and winked. Wind from somewhere tossed the blond strands of her hair into his face. Allegra tucked the tendrils behind her ear, next to him.

Ruby, meanwhile, was asking one of the technicians about the mystery man on the ground at the complex, when the pilot of the first helicopter shouted, "touching down in five, four, three, two..."

The next pilot echoed the countdown, three seconds behind the count.

They were on the ground.

"Time to be expeditious, team." Ruby reminded them of the play – in and out. Make haste.

As soon as the doors of the helicopters were opened the soldiers leapt onto the gravel. Their boots were heard running across the crushed shell-like gravel to the container. The drones flew low and triggered the turrets. Bullets from the unmanned turrets flew from hidden machine guns and rifles in the cypress trees. Aimless rounds of ammunition fired in pointless directions. Ill-equipped precision had the gunfire pointing into the sky and away from the mercenaries as much as near the surface where they were. They took cover, behind the helicopter, workbenches, and rocks and stumps in the area as the short array of gunfire ceased.

"Fly ten drones lower," Allegra commanded.

Ten broke from the pack directly above and drew no more shots.

"Try another ten!"

Again, another ten drones flew lower. No more bullets fired.

"Maybe it worked?" Allegra asked instead of stated.

One of the technicians weighed in, "The power consumption from the facility has been reduced. It isn't as juiced as it was. Perhaps the server is crashed."

"Go get 'em," Ruby declared.

The extraction had begun.

"What do you think, BenVen? Drones – part of our arsenal from here on?" Ruby seemed pleased that progress was made. They were on the ground approaching the container.

The pilot looked at Jacob, "You have to stay, but I don't. I'm not missing this for nothing!" He stuck out his tongue between a smile.

The video was crystal clear. Cutting the lock on the steel metal box with a bolt cutter, Sydney grabbed Adele by the hand, ushering her to the point of extraction for the victims. Allegra and Jacob were tightly next to each other to watch the potential moment of liberation from the helicopter they were within. Saying nothing, they watched Sydney, Adele, the mercenaries guarding the door and the cutting of the lock.

It was courageous Adele, Jacob's Adele, first into the dark compartment. She escorted a young woman out of the back of the container. She was in her early teens, black, skinny, dressed in a dirty beige T-shirt, jeans and had the band with an air-tag on her ankle. The soldiers guided the young person to Adele's helicopter. A second child, younger, blond, frail, walked with Adele, holding her hand to the escort of the soldiers. Sydney was seen bringing a young boy to the open door of the container. He reached back and grabbed the hand of another. Now there were four on their way to the helicopter, with the first climbing in following the direction of a soldier.

Allegra held her hand to her mouth. Amazed at the site of the rescue, she simply said, "Oh my God, oh my God, oh my God"...as she witnessed one after another being liberated from captivity. Each of the victims appeared grungy, unkempt, and were lacking basic health and wellness as they limped or walked slowly behind each other.

"Nine to twelve," Ruby said to Vendemer, off of the intercom. Just like in the other locations.

Vendermer was attempting to size up the situation when one of the Tech's shouted.

"Two white vans just turned on State Road 29 driving very fast toward the location! Very fast. Fly Team, do you copy?"

"Five," Ruby proclaimed. "Hurry!"

"Two white vans, approaching the area in about thirty seconds..."

"Six and seven..." Hand-holding little girls of seven or eight years old stumbled to light, holding their hands above them as if it may have been the first light of day in weeks, awaiting their next and worse destinations.

"Eight, nine, and ten..." Three, what appeared to be small boys, again, encouraging each other to follow those before them which ran to the transport at the encouragement of the Ellipsis fighters.

"Turning!" one of the operational technicians shouted.

Sydney could be seen running from the container to the helicopter which had fired up the propellers in haste of departing as quickly as possible.

Adele emerged from the metal box holding hands with a small girl, who couldn't have been more than four years old. The child was pointing back to the container, crying and shaking her head violently. She was flailing as Adele attempted to pick her up. Adele summoned all of her strength to carry the child to the bed of the helicopter – to join the others. Turning back to the container for another check, running toward the metal box, out of the corner of her eye she saw fast driving vans in the roadway which was in the distance.

Jacob was looking at Allegra, losing Adele in the commotion. He watched the struggle of getting the kids onto the helicopter and was fixated on them. Their eyes were wide. They were frightened. He reached for the handle of the door.

Allegra placed her hand on his quickly, "No...Jacob. I know what you're thinking. Don't do it!" They looked at each other. He slowly withdrew his hand from the sliding green door.

It sounded like firecrackers at first. *Pop – pop, pop – pop, pop, pop!* Coming from behind them, there was a squeal, and gravel grinding noise. Then the firecracker sounds began ricocheting off items in the work yard, pinging metal and wood and plastics. Fragments of materials splintered in random places. It was when several cracks in the glass from the helicopter being struck happened, that Jacob realized the firefight and yelled, "Gunfire? Down! Get down!"

A boombox had been bumped or knocked over in the first shots. As it struck the ground, the play button was clicked. Metallica's, *Enter Sandman*, began playing loudly across the work yard. It was fitting.

Allegra scrambled to her stomach, watching Jacob do the same. They listened to the bullets hit the metal frame and bounce off the carriage. Jacob raised his head just enough to ensure that Adele was in the other helicopter with the last child. However, as he was about to, additional shots hit the helicopter. *Pop! Pop! Pop!* Retaliation – from work yard was directed at two white vans which had pulled into the complex behind the helicopters. Now there were three white vans on the property.

The soldiers serving for Ellipsis were relentless in the rounds they fought back with. *Pop! Pop! Pop! Pop! Pop! Pop!* Several additional bullets from the friendly and the foe side of the gun fight struck the helicopter. Smoke bombs exploded behind them, causing billowing white smoke to rise above the choppers.

Together, Jacob and Allegra laying on their backs, watched the white smoke on the windows above them. It was growing thicker, and they could no longer see the blue sky with white puffy clouds. As the white smoke changed to grey, and shouting took place outside of where they were, they could hear one of the vans behind them revving its engine and pulling forward. It jammed into a large workbench in the yard with a loud crash sound. Grunts were heard. Not knowing whether it was from the attackers or from one of their own, Jacob tried to sneak a peek at the chaotic disruption unfolding.

It was then that a purple ooze was shot onto the glass of helicopter.

"Oh my God, what is that? Blood?" Allegra screamed.

They watched the gel creep down the glass slowly. The violet substance streamed down the glass like molten lava finding its way to the lowest point of gravity.

"What the fuck is that?" Allegra shouted in a panic. The shots outside continued. *Pop! Pop! Pop! Pop! Pop!* Small explosions were heard in the distance, but close enough to cause Allegra to shudder and pull her head close to Jacob's shoulder.

As they looked up, at the ceiling of the helicopter, the mulberry-colored goo continued to inch its way over the glass. Several more blobs of it were lobbed on the helicopter causing the light filtering in to grow darker. With the additional splats of the dark sludge creeping down the glass, it was dimmer and more difficult to see outside of the glass. The slime stuck on the cracked windows. One drop of it found its way into a crack and seeped onto the aluminum floor bed of the cabin. The gunfire approached non-stop pops, cracks, pings and bangs. Coming from both sides, in front of them and behind them, Jacob dipped his finger on the drop and held it up to his nose.

"It's an accelerant!"

"What?" Allegra shouted.

"An accelerant. A Firestarter... I don't know. An incendiary maybe?" As he said it, the shots stopped.

"What's happening?"

"They're reloading," he said to her – speaking instead of shouting to be heard. "Never too soon for 'no' vote on bump-stocks to go through congress," he said to himself.

"Uh...Jacob?" she asked.

"Yeah, what is it?" Jacob replied.

She hesitated, "Who's flying us out of here?"

Without a thought, he faked conviction, "Our psycho pilot. He'll be back. He's like Keith Richard or cockroaches – cannot be killed, gonna' live forever."

She lay there, still, yet restless, not knowing what to do. "How can you act so calm?" Allegra, wide-eyed, rolled her head over to see him.

"Feels like the end of a quarter on Wall Street," Jacob said, quietly. "Giddy up..."

"Well... It pisses me off!"

They heard a hissing sound not too far away. It would go on for ten seconds, then ten more, then five, then five more, then a short series of bursts of hissing noise. It sounded like pressure from a garden hose beating against a Rubbermaid trashcan.

Several shots began again: *Pop! Pop! Pop!* A short pause was had. Some shouting, presumably from behind them. Neither Jacob nor Allegra recognized the voices. Pop! Pop! Pop! The shooting paused again, and he heard footsteps and rustling outside. He propped himself up, and whispered, "Stay down!" But Allegra was already propped up, trying to peer outside the window between the streams of the purple sludge. Jacob held his hand in the air between them, signaling for her to remain where she was. "I want to see," she whispered as she appeared on all fours next to him. As she did that, the fire broke out. It was some form of a homemade Molotov cocktail. It began slowly and burnt brighter as it grew.

The door to the helicopter sprung open. Sydney looked at the two of them on their knees facing her. "You, come! Now!" she grabbed Allegra's hand at the wrist. Then she looked at Jacob, "You, stay! I'll be back for you." He said nothing as he looked at them holding each other. Allegra looked back at Jacob as Sydney helped her out of the helicopter. Additional gun shots were fired. Cover. It was cover. They were couched down, running to the other helicopter where the women and children were taken. It had the same substance on it, but a fire extinguisher had been swept over the flames, charring the exterior and leaving a white powdery residue. One of the soldiers closed the sliding door to Jacob's helicopter and used the fire extinguisher on the black cloudy smoke drafting in every direction. He could no longer see Allegra or Sydney – nor did he see anyone from the other chopper with the doors shut.

More gunfire. *Pop! Pop! Pop! Pop! Pop! Pop! Pop! Pop! Pop!* Bullets hit the metal door panels and dinged as they bounced somewhere else. He heard someone shout out in pain. "Ugh! Fuuuuuck!"

"Jade?"

"I'm hit," he cried out. More pops and bangs and grunts from not only Jade, but others.

"Tango Team check in," the intercom from the pilot's chair had a squeaky and fuzzy squelch sound to it. "Chuck...check," he added.

The pilot made it back. Opening the cockpit door, panting from a run back to the helicopter, he jumped in the bucket seat, slipped on his headset and looked back at Jacob. "Well, that didn't go quite as planned."

"Bing...check."

"Jude – tagged...but...check' he grunted.

"Rave...check...hang in there Jude."

"Marco...check."

"Tucker...check."

"Uh...hello? And you're fuckin' pilot is a check...too...if you were a wonderin'?"

Silence followed.

*****

From the communications trailer on Marco Island, the scene in Everglades City appeared panicked, unorganized, off-plan, and advantageous to their hostile combatants.

Ruby and Vendemer were watching from drones and several small dashcams on the helicopters and stuck on fixtures as the team invaded the site.

Ruby shouted, "Where did John Rambo disappear to?"

"He's on top of the hatched roof of the work area, I think!" replied one of the communications specialists.

"What's he doing up there?" Ruby asked anyone willing to answer. No one spoke, paying attention to the smoke and fire and unending rounds being fired in all directions. "What are you doing up there, John?" he asked himself.

"Where's Jade? How's Jade?" shouted Vendemer, seeming troubled.

"Hit, but – he checked in as 'available'. He got grazed - or so he says," one of the communication technicians added in an intercom from a location not within the trailer they were stationed in.

Vendemer looked at the young woman wearing a headset sitting next to where he was standing, next to monitors, blinking lights servers, and networking gear.

She affirmed, "Jade is ready, willing, and able."

He shouted something in Russian which appeared to be the equivalent of *Shit*, or *Fuck*, or *Damn It* – and Ruby turned his head and frowned at his friend, more at the fact that he didn't know the Russian curse words of his friend than at the seriousness of their predicament.

"Sydney...?!" Ruby shouted into the mic.

A pregnant pause of silence followed his request for her to acknowledge. From one helicopter to the other, an on-the-ground decision was made. Allegra's ponytail of blond hair was seen from above following her from the first to the second helicopters where it was assumed that the victims and Adele were within.

It made sense: women and children, first. The Birkenhead drill was to save the vulnerable and societies most valued – the lives of women and children were to be saved first in life-threatening situations.

'Sydney...?! Check in!" Ruby requested.

There appeared to be two remaining streams of gunshots remaining from six originally. Two of their opponents could be seen lying on the gravel, an AR-15 at their side or laying nearby. Two were missing. The other two were firing shots at the Ellipsis mercenaries.

As Sydney approached one of the sources of shots, she heard Ruby's request but could not speak. She needed to maintain her silence. The firing was coming from behind a worktable under a roofed area, shielding a torn apart engine block sitting on railroad ties from receiving rain. The cast iron would serve as a safe place to fire the assault rifle from.

Creeping carefully, quietly, slowly to the side of the area she stopped. No one was there when there had been moments ago. Her gun faced forward.

She heard a metal click behind her. When she turned quickly, she saw the barrel of the gun pointing at her face, six inches from her nose. "You're in the wrong place sister," the shooter said quietly, retaining his crouch to not be seen. "Drop it!" She wasn't able to outmaneuver in such close range with her rifle facing the opposite direction. If she drew, she'd have five rounds in her head before she could pull the trigger. Sydney would have to comply. As she dropped her gun, she saw a rifle and the torso of a man appear from the canopy above.

One shot. *Bang!* The man in front of her was taken out by the man coming down from the covering.

"Who are you people?" he asked as his heals hit the ground making a small crunching sound.

"You first," Sydney asked him.

"The name's Ashford." He was big, strong, dressed in black clothing much like hers and theirs. "I have reason to believe these dipshits did something with my wife."

Sydney looked up to him towering above her. Keeping her voice quiet and just above a whisper, she commanded, "Sydney." She looked at him and without expressing gratitude for his action or questioning his motives, she nodded. "Stay low. Follow me! Five down, maybe, one to go...maybe."

Ashford listened to her British accent. He was caught off guard by the forces at play. An elite special force of some type versus the redneck traffickers. Helicopters. The coordinated gunfight. It made little sense. More gunshots were fired – this time not in their direction. *Pop! Pop! Pop!*

Marco suddenly appeared in front of both. His gun was drawn facing Sydney and Ashford, but there wasn't a clear shot at the tall man dressed in black next to Sydney

"No!" She shouted, "No Marco! He's not one of them. Stand down," Sydney continued speaking lowly, knowing they needed no more attention drawn upon them in this open area.

"What makes you so sure?" Marco asked – and as he did, a bullet struck the back of his left thigh, causing him to stumble in front of them. His gun tipped downward, and he winced from the painful shot.

"Marco is tagged, Sydney called into her earpiece." She grabbed Ashford by the hand. "If you don't stay by my side, they'll think you're one of them."

She tapped her earpiece. "That rogue *additional bandit* we identified on their communications exchanges isn't with them. He's here on his own accord, attempting to sabotage their efforts. He saved my ass; I'm bringing him in. Do not fire! Repeat, Do Not Shoot!"

The gunfire from their side eased, but it was not from the remaining shooter or two. The savages held up behind one of the white vans tasted the opportunity to kill. *Pop! Pop! Pop! Pop! Pop! Pop!*

The helicopter carrying the children rescued from the container started spinning its blades. Slowly the whine of an engine engaging became the familiar Whomp! Whomp! Whomp! Whomp! Sydney had helped bring Allegra to it, assumed Adele was comforting the small children, and had used an extinguisher to smother the fire from the paintball projectiles burning on its surface. Now she needed to get Jacob on the craft with the others. The suspicious man named Ashford crept behind her as low as he could while she moved slowly toward Jacob's chopper.

They crawled to Marco. Genuflecting, he was looking at the wound and turned his head to smile and say, "*Just nicked me*," as the next noise was a bullet hitting him in the neck. *Thunk.* He fell to the ground.

Sydney and Ashford pulled him from the line of fire, dragging him across the gravel behind two dull black barrels they hid behind.

"I think these are oil barrels. I smell it," Ashford said. He looked at Sydney, "We can't stay here."

Sydney was only thinking about the blood streaming from Marco's neck. His eyes closed immediately. She saw that the volume of blood pouring from him had likely struck an artery.

"We can't stay here!" he repeated, louder than before.

Grabbing Marco's gun, Ashford shot at the area which bullets continued to stream from. As Sydney watched Marco's breathing become shallow, and saw his final breath, she said briefly, "May God be with you, you brave and good Soldier of Fortune. You fought for what you knew was right." She said nothing more to Marco's still body or for those listening on the intercom earpiece. It was heard, but nothing was said.

He passed away quickly. Lieutenant Colonel, Roberto "Marco" Delgado lay motionless.

From the drones above, Vendemer and Ruby were fixated on the helicopters which had been on fire, then doused with the white powdery substance from the extinguishers. The tri-class dry chemical dusted the middle section of the choppers. It was premeditated and may have been intended for trucks or ground vehicles but nearly caused plans to change. Because they were in an area servicing the airboat's diesel engines, two fire extinguishers were available and visible.

Between the bursts of flames, the shots, seeking groups running and dodging a firestorm of shots – it was a chaotic scene and difficult to identify the ground level execution. All eyes were on any movement or disturbances from the uncountable number of guns, flames, noises, and jumbled disorder taking place.

*****

No one saw it. The cutter of fingers, Stanley, had entered Steve Booth's small hooch of a house as the bullets started firing. He shouted, "Steve! Steve Booth! Where the fuck are you, Steve?"

In the tub, curled up in the fetal position, hands curled over his ears to deafen the noises outside, Steve looked up only when he heard the door to the bathroom creak open.

Pulling the yellow shower curtain aside, the tall man with long hair to his bowling ball shoulders said, "Steve – what the hell are you doing down there?" He sniffed the air. A sharp chemical smell filled the air of the bathroom. "Stinks in here. I smell fear."

"The noith..." Steve cautiously pointed outside in the work yard, "the thcary noith..."

An automatic weapon was on a nylon holster which resembled a black seatbelt, wrapped around his shoulder. "Come with me," the pinky cutter commanded, helping Steve up from the hunched position. He held the barrel toward Steve face and said quiely, "Sssh. Be quiet now, Steve. Follow me. You know how to shoot, right?"

Steve nodded that he did. Reluctantly, Steve rose and waddled though the small house as he followed that man who had removed his pinky two years earlier. However, his lack of confidence did not earn him a gun. Stanley kept this sidearm to himself, thinking Steve may accidentally fire it.

They made their way quickly to the back door and quietly opened it. A hinge squeaked slightly. Stanley and Steve hid behind the container which once held The Product, their trafficked victims. The wheezing was excessive - Steve's, not Stanleys.

"Dude...back up some." Stanley looked at Steve who was reaching in his pocket for a rescue inhaler. Taking four puffs, Stanley shook his head and whispered to himself, "Whatever." *Pop! Pop! Pop! Bang! Bang!*

Slowly, they tiptoed across a small, bushed opening to the doors of the container. Stanley took short breaths, smelling the stench. As they approached the latch, he grabbed the metal locking mechanism and slowly raised it. They crept inside the darkness and remained there, motionless, listening to the inconsistent gunfire outside of the trailer between the white vans, the helicopters, and the work yard.

"Quit moving around," Stanley whispered to Steve.

He said nothing in return but was not moving.

"I said stay still!"

When Stanley looked at Steve, he saw that he wasn't moving, but something else in the container was. With the door nearly closed, only a thin inch of daylight was able to enter through the crack. Stanley reached for the Surefire flashlight on weapon. Flipping its switch into the on position, he saw the façade at the neck of the trailer. Somewhere behind the plywood wall, something was stirring. With his finger on the trigger, ready to kill, he was apt to find out who? *Shoot first, ask questions later*, was going through his thoughts. He nudged a small Tupperware tub once filled with rice aside with the nose of the gun, pointed into the darkness. Tripping the light up into the empty space he saw that he and Steve weren't alone.

Adele had her hands up, knowing that a gun and a bright light were being pointed at her and probably not by the Ellipsis mercenaries. The silhouettes of two people appeared. It looked like a tall, strong man with long hair and a short plumpy man. Too dark to know for sure, she held still, static in all action.

"That's it. You just stand there and look pretty," Stanley said to Adele. He could see her with the light at his back. It was dim, but she was certainly out of place – looking like she did in this circumstance.

She said nothing.

The pinky cutter reached into his pocket for a plastic cable tie. It was the kind they used to zip tie the air tags onto The Product. Always on the left ankle. With Adele he would bind her wrists behind her back. "Turn around, slowly. Hands behind your back. Slowly – if you want to live – slowly."

Adele, to buy time and to live, did as she was told. She knew she was out of place, here in the container, avoiding the gunfire in the metal container. Several bullets had ricocheted off the box, covered with camouflage. Laying low to avoid stray shots fired, she had dirt on her white blouse. Tears had smudged her mascara earlier, but there was no place on her cheeks for tears now. Fear filled her eyes as she squinted toward Stanley and Steve. She would need to do as told.

Stanley bound her wrists tightly. A second cable tie held her to the wall of the container on a welded loop. She had to stand on her toes to prevent the plastic from cutting into her thin wrists. He could tell that she was in pain.

"Does that hurt?"

"Yes," she said softly, "Much."

"Good. You say *anything*. I mean *anything* – you call out for help, and you die. I shoot you. I shoot you dead. Now, you going to do something like that?"

She shook her head 'no' quickly as she winced at the piercing pain from the zip ties binding her tightly. Outside, the shots continued to rain. *Pop! Pop! Pop! Bang! Bang! Pop! Pop! Pop!*

Steve watched. Not knowing what to do or how to behave he looked between Stanley and the woman they had captured and handcuffed with the plastic ties to the wall. She seemed to be hurt. His attention was on her face. She was pretty. Not like the internet girls which Steve liked to watch, but a gentle and true beauty. The expression of pleasure and pain was sometimes the same, he thought.

The gunfire continued outside the trailer. *Pop! Pop! Pop!* Three, four, five, six shot successions were what happened for ten minutes. Occasionally, undetectable shouts and grunts were heard. They listened to a British woman whisper but couldn't make out what she was saying.

Stanley was ready to fire if the doors were opened. *Shoot to kill*, he thought.

The welts on Adele's wrists began to bleed at the tightest points. Small trickles of blood ran down one of her hands to her fingertips.

Pop! Pop! Pop! Pop! Pop! Pop! Bang! Bang! Pop! Pop! Pop!

* * * * *

"Shite!" they heard from her British expletive eloquence, "The bloody wankers shot me in the Jubblies..." She allowed a moment to surpass before adding, "Fuck those fucking fuckers!!!"

The word used as verbs, a noun, an adjective, an adverb, an adjective enhancing an adverb, and as any word in a sentence such as Sydney's 'fuck those fucking fuckers...' the word of dismay, trouble, fraud, curiosity, bafflement, displeasure, difficulty, incompetence, dismissal, enjoyment, hostility, greeting, clarification, innovation, and surprise delivered a sense of urgency toward her anguish.

It was Ashford that picked up Sydney and across the work yard, munching upon the gravel, he carried her to the door of the helicopter preparing to take off. Its blades spun evenly and forcefully in the air above the warcraft machine. The sliding door opened. In it were children huddled together. A beautiful woman looked at Ashford and helped pull Sydney onboard.

"Who are you?"

Ashford looked at her and only could utter his last name as several more shots were fired in his direction, 'Ashford." He reached for the door to close it and protect those inside from a stray bullet. Crying, bewildered, in shock – the children, the young and the old, held each other as the wind from the turbines grew louder and faster. As the door latched, the trundle wheels were up, and the whirlybird was off.

Before Ashford could return to retrieve Marco's body, the white van closest to the road spun its tires loudly. Jacob peered up to see what he could in the cracks of the helicopter's window where the scorched liquid didn't discolor the glass. He saw the white van with at least fifty bullet indents squealing backwards. More shots were fired. *Pop! Pop! Pop!* As it turned around and onto the private drive back to the public roadway, Jacob said it aloud and to himself, "How is it able to drive?"

The door to the helicopter slid open. A big man carrying Marco's body, laid him on the threshold and pushed him further into the body of the aircraft. He looked at Jacob and said what he said to Allegra in the other departed helicopter, "Ashford."

Not knowing whether it was a first name, last, or designation of some sort, "Paisley, Jacob." It was all that Jacob said, looking at Marco's body. Still warm, his body heat was next to him. Blood drenched his vest and shirt. It covered the forearms of the Ashford character. He pulled the corpse further into the chopper as its rotors began to turn. The door was closed by the gruff big man.

Several footsteps were heard, and Chuck was telling Ashford to get in. Returning to the chopper were Jade with the gunshot to his backside, Bing, then Rave and Tucker. They were sweaty, had blackout on their faces smeared into their eyes, and were breathing heavy. Each of them laid their hand upon Marco's body as they entered the helicopter.

Chuck shouted into his earpiece and to their pilot, "We've got to go get that van. Take those motherfucker's out."

Jacob reached for the black headset, adjusting the big protruding bubbles over his ears so that he could hear the other side of the conversation.

Ruby shouted that the drones with the payloads were on the way. "It'll be one hell of a scene," he added.

"Yeah, fuck that Ruby – they took one of our guys – we're going to eliminate them ourselves. No drone work. It's personal. This havoc is ours to have." Chuck wasn't about to have a soulless drone take the pleasure of inflicting pain upon the heinous villains trafficking people and killing one of their soldiers.

"It's additional risk, Chuck!"

Chuck looked at each of his team members. They all took turns nodding. "Worth it. We're going after them...him...her...whatever. We're coming and hell is along for the ride." As he said that, the helicopter slowly rose into the air, and they tilted toward the roadway into Everglades City. Once their altitude climbed, they could clearly see the small county roadway. The smoke of the work yard was behind them and the scorched bird picked up speed in the chase.

"How many grenades do we have?"

"A dozen," Tucker replied.

"Fifteen," Rave corrected him.

Chuck looked at the two of them and nodded his head, "That ought to do the job." In an empty olive colored denier backpack, they collectively gathered the explosives. The lemon-shaped metal clinked together as they gently combined them.

Ashford sat watching, as astonished as Jacob was, he asked them the question he asked Sydney, "Who are you people?"

"Warriors – kind of like you." Rave looked at his shoulders and neck. "Military?"

Ashford shook his head 'no' and added, "Student of the game of war." He paused, then spoke the truth, "Call of Duty." He didn't expect them to appreciate the video game skills he had with the Activision game.

She smiled. "COD addiction – all of us." Nodding her head and circling her finger to represent their unit. Looking back at Marco's body,

Rave added, "Two TODs with him. Kabul and Bahrain." Rave's hand was placed on Marco's bloody hand, laying on top of his still chest.

"You run, but you cannot hide," they all heard the pilot say. Jacob realized that the stranger, Ashford, didn't know what was being said and handed him the bubble shaped headset which Allegra wore earlier. He slipped them on, adjusting them to fit his head, and squinted to try to see out the burnt and blackened window.

"Chuck, approaching a speeding white van. About one-hundred feet below us. Time to go fishing with dynamite?" The pilot announced the van on the ground driving recklessly at a high speed ahead and below. Should take about two seconds for one of your handhelds to drop and we'll want to drop about twenty feet forward."

"Sounds like you've done this before..."
"Gator hunting, Commander." The pilot smiled, looking back at Jacob, Ashford, Chuck and the others. "Let's light up their morning, what'd'ya say?"

"Say when..."

"Go for it!" their pilot yelled. "But expect some scatter once our presence is known." Jacob and Ashford looked at the aluminum flooring and wondered if it might withstand bullets from below if the first grenades didn't hit spot on target.

Chuck opened the door to the flying helicopter in tandem with the speeding van. He pulled the first grenade from the backpack, pulled its pin and said, "Bombs away!" as he dropped it. It bounced off of the hood of the van and exploded fifteen feet behind it. Immediately, a window was opened and gunfire from an AR-15 shot wildly in the air – not touching the helicopter.

Watching the pin being pulled from the grenades, and feeling gunshot ding the armor under the carriage of the helicopter, Jacob thought that the drones sounded like a good idea, but kept the thought to himself.

The second and third grenades were also behind the van. One hitting the top of the van with the other missing completely. Realizing that he would need to hold onto the grenades longer, Chuck pulled the pin and counted to five instead of three. The fourth grenade exploded five feet above the van, causing it to swerve wildly and nearly causing it to leave the crushed shell roadway. Again, rounds were scattered into the air missing them. The other door on the side of the hovering helicopter's body was opened so that Bing and Jude with the flesh wound could also see. Jude winced as he leaned over.

It was the fifth grenade which exploded precisely on impact and directly above the windshield. The van catapulted over itself landing in a deafening explosion and pile of fiery debris in the middle of the light grey roadway. Black plumes of smoke engulfed the area as it sat still burning fiery orange flames.

"Stay right here!" Chuck shouted out. "For Marco!" he yelled as he pulled a pin and dropped another grenade on the burning van. It exploded brilliantly, making the fire brighter and hotter and black smoke darker. An approaching pickup with an airboat on a trailer slowed far from the fire.

Chuck motioned to Bing. Bing dropped the next grenade on top of the explosion, repeating, "For Marco." It too exploded and caused the destruction to grow bigger and more intense.

They each took turns, dropping a grenade upon the wreckage, stating, "For Marco" and watching one explosion after the next.

Once all of the grenades were detonated and dropped to make an unrecognizable wreckage even more undetectable – the helicopter careened north to the location it departed from two hours earlier: Copeland. The drones with explosive payloads arrived after the helicopter left the area and finished off the unreckoned burning debris still in the middle of the roadway.

Before they touched down, Jacob asked if he could call in to check on Adele. They patched him through. He was on the public intercom. Everyone heard his conversation with the other helicopter which had landed safely in Naples to deliver their precious cargo, the victims of the container - the precious product, the children preyed upon by the most villainous people on the planet. The Product.

"Hey Sydney - how are you holding up?"

In her perfect British form, "Right... Well, the bloody bullet shot through my left teet," she held her hand lightly over her left breast which had been bandaged. "But I still have my good one. I heard that Jade got a shot in the arse? A day for getting shot in the privates, right?"

"A bullet in the butt. I'm sure that will make a good story at some point. Maybe he can tell it with some color after he can sit up straight. Hey – how are the kids and how's Adele? Can I speak with her?"

"Yeah right. She's with you, funny guy," Sydney replied. After silence, "Isn't she?"

*****

As the second helicopter departed, Stanley lifted Adele up off the metal hook which was welded to the trailer wall.

"You're a petite little thing," he said feeling her weight as he set her down.

His breath stunk. Turning her head away from his face as he sat her down, she cringed at the tight restraints around her wrists. The agitation was beginning to be numb which was better than the pang and the sting.

It had been quiet for several minutes following the van and the helicopter leaving. "Let's see what we got here..." Stanley said as he opened the door wide to let in the daylight. "Shoot, what's a refined lady like yourself doin' in a place like this? Poking your pretty little nose where it doesn't belong, are ya'?"

Adele looked at him, standing above her, drawing his face closer to his again. "Those are pretty eyes. Bet they've seen some things." She assumed things weren't going to go her way. "Maybe they'll see more – bigger things, if you know what I mean."

Steve said something as he stood in the corner.

"Steve – shut up, my friend. I'm makin' acquaintance with..." He looked at her blouse, covered with dirt and brushed it off, allowing his hands to brush slowly on her chest. "I don't even know yer name..."

She said nothing.

"Don'cha think we should be on a first name basis, little lady."

"Can't thtay here..." Steve said again.

"What's that...Steve?"

"Can't thtay here..."

Stanley paused. "You know what, Steve...? For a bit of an idiot, you're right. And I know just the place for us to go." He grabbed Adele by the elbow and wrapped the gun around his shoulder. "C'mon Steve. You come too. Time to meet yer neighbors."

Stanley, with Adele by the elbow, her wrists bound behind her, moved from the container into the work yard. He saw several of his patriots lying still on the ground. Their guns by their sides. Blood from their wounds was pooled into the gravel or smeared across their clothes.

"What a shame. Sixty-one Tributes...I salute your valiant efforts," he paused, paying little respect to the malefactors. In total, there were eight dead Tributes. He continued walking, with Adele taking double steps to keep up. She whimpered from the pain in her wrists being tugged against his strides. Steve followed the two of them toward another white van. Stanley paused, looking inside the cabin, to see if the keys were still in the ignition. They were. He opened the passenger door, lifted Adele up by her hips, and slid her into the van. Bullet holes adorned the hood, windshield, and body of the vehicle.

"Your people made one hell of a mess here. Someone's gotta be responsible for that. You?" Strands of Adele's brunette hair was in her face from being tossed into the van. He reached over and gently parted them from her eyes and cheek and tucked them behind her ears. "You know...yer going to have to tell me your name eventually. We just might become close... Get in the back, Steve." He smiled an evil, devilish grin as he struck the keys into the ignition lock cylinder. It slowly turned and eventually fired up. Before Steve could settle in, Stanley slid it into Drive and did a U-turn in the work yard gravel, bouncing Steve around in the back of the van.

"My name...is...Stanley. And you are...?" He looked at her as he sped down the road heading toward Everglades City. Adele said nothing. "Okay...playin' hard to get. Well, we'll see how that goes fer ya. You should talk while you can. Going to be hard to say much when the duct tape is wrapped around your head."

She took a deep breath, attempting to shed fear. *This was a risk worth taking.* It was Sydney's strength within her: *We take risks, yes – but through a moment of terror may come a miracle of life. When we manage the tradeoff, we triumph.* Adele's eyes were taking in as much as the moment could allow. She looked at him when he threatened her, but did not cry. She imagined the worst – but also knew that her disappearance would not go unanswered and hoped that the RFID patch she was wearing would work. The surveillance installed by Ellipsis in the area may or may not be recording or reporting the short field trip which Stanley had taken her and his accomplice, named Steve, on. More than looking around, she was listening for the sound of a returning helicopter.

It was no more than a quarter of a mile when the van slowed and turned left, like if it were pulling into Steve Booth airboat work yard. Here, however, were three cars with their hoods lifted open. Just like Steve's work yard, a canopy, tool benches, and wide crushed gravel drive was in front of a small home. This was an upgrade from Steve's place.

Adele continued to remember what Sydney had said to her – an internal battle cry of courage. The van stopped abruptly on the gravel, sliding to a stop.

Stanley, put it in park, turned the engine off, and jumped out of the van, shouting. "Yo, TJ!"

A radio was playing quietly in the background over near where car parts were neatly lined up on work benches, near the opened hoods of the cars. Music, much like Steve's, played at a low decibel level. Adele thought that she heard Billy Squier's, *In The Dark*, playing lowly from a boombox under the canopy.

A man of average build, blond hair pulled into a ponytail, wearing a white wife-beater tank top walked out of the front door from the small wood-sided home onto a covered porch. He was wiping his hands dry with a dish towel. He didn't say anything, observing the situation. Stanley walked quickly to the man and the two of them talked for several minutes. The man was shorter that Stanley. He looked over to the van, held his hands on his hips, and motioned to the work area as they finished speaking.

Steve asked Adele, "Do you have kidth?"

"I do," she said bravely. "And a grandson."

"A gwandthon?" Steve asked.

She shook her head, yes – fighting back at the thought of not seeing them again. Summoning the strength within her, "Yes," she said with conviction. "They live in New York."

"New York Thity?"

She looked back at Steve, behind her and shook her head. "Can you help me?" she whispered. Hope filled her throat, "Please?"

Steve looked at her and shook his head 'no' slightly and slowly. Then he tied on a needless compliment, looking away and making no eye contact with her, "Pwetty. You thmell like Momma."

She turned, looking out the windshield for Stanley. He was nowhere to be seen.

Her door opened suddenly. Startled, she flinched at the arm reaching for her. It was him. It was Stanley. His big mitts of dirty hands grabbed her upper arm, not as gently as before. "C'mon. Time for you to do some talkin'."

It was more of a drag, than a walk to the shaded area where the man who apparently lived their and named TJ had set up a folding chair. She was thrust into the chair, nearly tipping over. Stanley handed his handgun to TJ. Here entertain her, would you. Maybe when she talks, we'll go easy. Until then, I think Miss-What's-Her-Name? *'I don't know Stanley, she won't say'*, he mocked loudly into the air above him – until then, Miss-What's-Her-Name might like it rough. He looked at her and winked, *"If you know what I mean, you know what I mean."*

Adele watched Stanley grab a roll of silver duct tape, he approached her aluminum chair with poly webbing interwoven. It resembled chairs her grandparents sat on while drinking lemonade on a hot summer afternoon.

TJ took different poses in front of her, holding the gun like Charlie's Angels, pointing it directly at her, turning his back toward her, then spinning around pointing the weapon at her with both hands.

"What in the hell are you doing?" Stanley asked.

"Entertaining her," TJ responded.

"Give me that..." Stanley grabbed the pistol from TJ, tucking back in his holster. He found a blowtorch and striker to light it. He picked them up from a work bench and laid them on another small table near her. He then picked up a hunting knife and turned it in front of her. The reflection shone in Adele's eyes. She squinted at the light. Then Stanley sorted through a toolbox, seeking a hammer. A small ball-peen hammer, with a shiny head and oak handle, was picked up through the clanking of the other tools. Stanley looked at it, "That'll work." Finally, a hedge crimper was picked up from a canister holding yard tools.

Steve had just approached the area when Stanley retracted the pruning shears from the other tools. With both hands he slowly opened and closed the loppers used to cut small branches. Looking at Steve Booth, opening and closing the Fiskars lopper, Stanley looked at Steve who had held his hand missing a pinky behind his back. "Well, would you look at this." Steve said nothing, taking a step backwards.

"But first," Stanley said nothing, setting the yard loppers down and picking up the shiny nine-inch hunting knife. "But first, I'm wondering...maybe you are too, TJ...if this pretty little lady is wearin' a wire or somethin'?" He used the knife to slowly and gently remove button by button the front of Adele's blouse. Slice after slice, hearing her breathing as he cut away at her clothing, he finally said, "Well, I certainly wasn't expecting that."

With her blouse open, exposing expensive lingerie, Adele looked up at him. Fear was replaced by bravery. Uncertainty had been displaced with prowess. Doubt was supplanted and intrepidity took its place. Sydney's self-talk about purpose worked. Adele's immediate concerns were superseded by gallantry.

Stanley looked at Adele's chest. He used the knife to explore more, pointing the sharp shiny tip on the collars to open the white blouse further. "No, I didn't expect to see that. Mm... How about that, TJ?"

"That sure looks nice from here," he replied. "What is that, lace?"

He tossed the knife aside and with both hands ripped the rest of her blouse down around her shoulders. The corset white bra which Adele wore held her breasts high, hoisting her cleavage. "Don't see no wire, but I sure do see a sight..." He got close. Too close to her breasts, he inhaled her. "You smell rich. No dames I know smell like that. Are you some rich bitch, or what?" He backed up some, enough to look at her face and asked, "Cat got your tongue?"

"My name is Adele. I'm...with a special forces' operation...that intends to...to save those children. Which we...did." As she said it, the back of Stanley's hand struck her face. It wasn't a bone crushing blow but caused her lip to turn red and swell immediately, breaking a blood vessel. She nearly fell over in the aluminum chair from his hit.

"Special forces? Is that so...? Well... You stole from me, Adele. You took my property. You and your people robbed me of *The Product*. What makes you think..."

"What makes you think you have a right to violate them and take their freedom? What gives you the power to..." He struck her again from the other side. It hurt less than the first, but she spit blood off to the side from the strike.

He laughed at Adele and held his fists together in front of her, "This." On his fingers was the tattoo: the middle fingers showed a "6" on one side and a "1". "Sixty One Tributes, sister. A time when a man was a man – a woman was a woman – and the strong were in control. Nowadays – we're pathetically weak. We gonna fix that."

She was contemplating her next comment. *Question? -* for the sake of seeking time? *Debate? -* for the sake of seeking time? *Plead? -* for the sake of seeking time? *Talk about herself? -* for the sake of seeking time? Speaking slowly, she asked, "Why sixty-one?"

"Eighteen sixty-one...Adele. And that's all you need to know." Stanley turned his back to her and looked up at TJ standing there with his arms crossed. "I know what you're thinkin'." TJ smirked and shook his head.

"What is this place?" Adele asked.

"This...? This place...? Why...this is TJ's place of business...Miss Adele. Where old cars get fixed. It's the kind of place with, shall we say, a number of tools and resources." Stanley picked up the blow torch, held it in front of him turning it slowly, struck a spark with the igniter causing it to burn a blue and yellow flame. He watched the torches flame and listened to the noise it produced, a deep air gurgle. Then extinguishing it, he set it back down. "I could make you hot...Adele. Just sayin'." Stanley turned around to see her expression. She was bold and unafraid. It wasn't what he was expecting from a woman wearing such a fancy brassier. Her lip, swollen, protruded from her pouty mouth. "Awe, you got a boo-boo." His big hand grabbed Adele's chin, pulling

"My turn to ask a question. How did you know about Steve's complex up the road? Was it the patriot?"

"Who?"

"The Patriot. The warrior from Washington. The so-called DC-dedicated liberator," Stanley faked a made-up story about Ashford as he bent over to look closely into her eyes as she answered.

"Oh, the Patriot. Yes," she lied. Stanley smiled, knowing that it wasn't the contact with the infiltrator from Tampa, named Ashford. She was here with others somehow on their own. They had two intruders interfering in their business. One as a lone wolf operator, the other as a syndicate with extreme strength and capabilities.

He held her chin in the cusp of his hand, moving her head left and right, back and forth, indicating that he knew she was fibbing. "Do you want to try answering that question again....Adele?" Stanley asked. "Maybe...honestly, next time?"

14

The Hunger

Local medics, nurses and community social workers had been scrambled by radio to help with the mysterious choppers' delivery in a strip mall parking lot. The helicopter, scorched and experiencing some engine failure, flew low, but had arrived at a drop point. It landed safely, and ground support helped bring the children into a fifteen-passenger van to escort them safely to a processing center for their safety and well-being. A small step in the right direction.

Ellipsis. They were a divided force at this point – and at the same time, never more united to do what was right and needed to be accomplished. The rescue of the ten children strengthened their resolve. Banged and patched up Sydney, Allegra, the pilot, and ten victims which were being cared for by Collier County Child Services were in the Naples area. Following the safe transport and drop of the children, a vehicle had picked up Allegra and Sydney and was driving them to the Marco Island communications trailer where Vendemer, Ruby and their small staff were collected. It was no more than a fifteen-minute drive which they intended to make in ten or less.

Jacob, the mysterious big and tall man named Ashford, and the remaining Ellipsis fighters touched down in Copeland with their bird, scorched and a dashboard of Christmas lights indicating engine fatigue and malfunctioning systems. There was also the body of Marco.

A body bag wrapped around him was black and hid his remains from the sunlight.

And then there was Adele. Alone. Unexpectedly divided from the rest of them and under the grips of the rebels. Feeling the wrath of the remaining villain or villains, experiencing God-knows anguish and fear...he assumed she was frightened – filled with uncertainty – and was...hopefully...still alive.

"How far out are you two?" Ruby asked into the cell phone.

"We're rolling in to your parking lot now." Sydney's stamina was waning, but she had her game face on, knowing there was more ahead, and she'd need to dig deep for another fight within herself. She also had a gunnysack of guilt she was carrying and that was new for her.

"What's the hold up?" Jacob, who was patched into the call, was agitated it was taking so long. After their helicopter touched down in Copeland, and after they used the GPS to track the patch Adele was wearing below her belt-line – they knew her whereabouts.

"Hold on, Jacob," said Vendemer.

The cell phone call became a video call so that they could share what they were seeing from the few traffic cams they had installed, Adele's GPS beacon, and a Maps view of the area.

Now that they were on video, and Allegra and Sydney were in the fifty foot communications trailer with Ruby and Vendemer - it was Sydney who took blame. Unloading her sorrow, "It's on me. It's my damn fault. I'm so sorry, everyone. Jacob, I'm so very sorry. Bad judgment on my part. I didn't think things through. Not knowing that..."

"Sydney – stop it. You've put teammates first all along the way. Let's do what we need to do and do it quickly. If you can help with that..." His eyes filled with tears, but not to the point of cascading like waterfalls onto his cheeks.

Allegra watched him on video. Her bottom lip pouted, and she tipped her head to the side in her personal form of sympathy for him. She held her fingertips against the screen touching his face. Sympathy was strong for the feelings she saw from him for Adele.

Jacob used the palms of his hands to wipe away the tears ready to spill over.

Allegra had an idea. It wasn't a solution but might aid the situation in some way. "Guys…? BenVen…? Ruby…? Syd…?" She turned to look at them. Silent at first, then shaking her head slowly with what she needed to say. "What if it's another complex with other victims. A container like the others, but just a quarter of a mile down the road. What if…" She looked at Adele's beacon bleeping red on their tracking screen, "What if Adele is at the next compound? Like…there's another?"

"Oh, dear God," Ruby repeated.

"I know we're scrambling an operation, but do we have firepower to withstand something equal to what we just went through?" Vendemer asked. They all knew the answer was, 'probably not'.

Sydney and Allegra spun around in their chairs. They checked to location of the drones. The first two tranches were nearly back to their launch location. Codes were entered to halt their return.

"What about the drones? To scramble those gun turrets? If it's the same type of structure, assuming it is, won't…?"

"We've already rerouted the third tranche which hadn't landed yet," Allegra interrupted.

"And we're redeploying the first and second," Sydney added as she was feverishly clicking at keys.

A communications specialist posed a troubling question, "Will the drones have battery life for another, I don't know, another hour?"

"Let's hope it doesn't take that long and…we won't know until we know," Sydney answered the question. Clicking to see if there was a battery status indicator in the software for the Brince LEMURs and the Black Falcon drones, she tilted her head. She saw the battery status reading: 34%. By the time they were to fly back across the stretch of the Everglades National Park, they would surely be in their twenties. "Probably not," she mentioned slowly and only to Allegra sitting next to her. "Looking for good news, Miss Sinclair. Have any, my love?"

Sydney continued looking at her screen and cringed at the acute and dull pain in her bosom. She thought that the pain medicine which the medic gave her was lame. The hydro-gel second-skin dressing, and the white elastic gauze wrapped tightly around her torso was cumbersome.

"Well, the first tranche of drones will be there before we can get there. If that's not hope, the second tranche might be there as we arrive – assuming our team leaves Copeland in the next five minutes."

"We should have left five minutes ago," Jacob added. The looped line had the team on the ground north of the potential second Everglades City location listening to the open mic.

Chuck, Rave, Bing, Tucker, Jude with a bullet in the butt, and the outsider, Ashford gathered at the helicopter. The pilot shared the bad news, "Team, this bird has broken wings. As is, it might not make it – at least both ways."

"It has to..." Jacob demanded.

"We have the Suburbans and the van, Jacob. We can scramble them. It'll take all of five minutes to get them up here and then we have ten-minute drive down there." Chuck was floating options.

Ruby motioned to Vendemer. "Come here, please." They walked away from the others. Their conversation was away from the hot mics, out of earshot, being discussed with their backs to the rest of the Ellipsis team. It wasn't for anyone's ears, but theirs, which meant the most clandestine move was being considered. They talked for a minute. Only Jacob interrupted them with his vociferous request.

"For the love of God – can we make a move? Can I have the keys to the chopper? I'm going to go flag down the next car I see on the road and commandeer its use... What the..."

"Jacob – we're leaving a trail of breadcrumbs all over the place. We're exposing ourselves. Shut up and listen for one minute. Then, we'll act." Ruby wasn't negotiating. He was sharing what he and Vendemer had decided to do. Vendemer was already on his cell phone, asking for - or cashing in - a favor. Well away from the others, he spoke into the cell as he hunched over, near the blinking green lights on the servers well away from the team. "We're going to scramble a very small payload from Air Defense Command. They're on stand-by for the moment, awaiting orders. The launch site is Homestead-Miami. Surface-to-surface. Nike-Hercules, a leftover from the Cold War. Get the helicopter there – if the bird makes it. There will be no debris...when we're finished...if things go well. There will be no remnants of our presence."

"Damn." Jacob was impressed. The rest of the team was speechless. "Are the Suburbans..."

"Let's roll them. Now." Ruby's decisiveness was what Jacob wished for.

"You heard the orders. Board up." The pilot jumped in the cockpit first and flipped a toggle causing the rotors to reluctantly begin twirling again. He reached for a wad of pink bubble gum from above the visor and jammed it in his mouth. Petting the olive-colored steering harness, he spoke sweetly to the machine, "You've been a good girl. One more time." The propellers made the *whomp – whomp – whomp – whomp* sound for their final tour. Soon, the 'whomps' were replaced by the *chop – chop – chop – chop* sounds, followed by the *chip – chip – chip – chip* noise when the speed increased to a point of takeoff. For a second time, within a lapis sky, still dotted with small white puffy clouds – the chopper arose, heading south for what appeared to be battle.

Somewhat a surprise, it was Allegra which asked to speak to Jacob. He was handed the big black bubble headset. "Those drones..."

"Yeah?" he said – half listening to her.

"They are going to do their job. I don't know what it's going to be like on the ground, but in the air, I've got your back."

"Okay, good to know. Uh, will there be eyes in the sky?" he shouted to hear himself, and so that she could hear above the propellers making more noise at the moment.

"We're still working on that. I guess...I just wanted to say be fucking bold. Be fearless. Let's go get your girl."

Jacob paused and looked away into the distance as the helicopter continued to rise.

"Go get your girl," Allegra said again. Regardless of what her feelings were for the man nearly twice her age – despite her secrets and hidden thoughts – she recognized the deep seeded love between the two and in no way would jeopardize it. It was time to move on. Allegra Sinclair and Jacob Paisley – as much as she fantasized about her new acquaintance could not be a thing. She knew when to embrace and when to break from a sensation. The visible and sympathetic chord between Jacob and Adele was a touchstone which Allegra could admire and wish for, but not interfere with any longer.

*****

Stanley was disappointed in Adele's attempt at deception. He thought that he needed to frighten her – and perhaps that was simply letting her know the truth, which was what he had in mind for her.

"What am I going to do with you?" he asked. "What do you think, TJ?"

"My oh my...Mm..."

"I think maybe Adele wants a piece of me – if you know what I mean. Yeah, that's it. I'll give her a piece of me. Then, it'll be your turn, TJ." He got close to her as he searched her eyes for fear, for a reaction which might make her say more. "But some pillow-talk first," he smiled within inches of her nose.

Sweat began collecting on Adele's forehead. Where there was a slight breeze in the air earlier, there was still humid and oppressive heat building as the morning evolved. It's first drip ran down her temple and onto her cheek.

"Looks like I make you wet, Adele. Are you wet for me?" Stanley gently wiped the moisture from her cheek dripping further to her chin away from the side of her face.

Adele had thoughts racing through her head as she shook her hair from her face. *He's just someone's little boy. An ego, as fragile as his, inside a man's body, afraid to find his own way in the world – needing to adopt convictions from 1861 – he can't think for himself. He doesn't create. He doesn't build. He doesn't have his own thoughts. He doesn't feel what he should be able to feel. He doesn't know love.*

She listened for any noises which might signify an intervention. There were none. Adele needed more time. "You have a wife?"

He stood back up and looked at her, only shaking his head slowly while he gave her a small, crooked smile.

"A girlfriend?"

"You're going to be my girlfriend. After I get what I want from you, that is. How did you locate us? In California? In Texas? In Louisiana?"

Adele knew nothing about Louisiana. She'd have to think fast, for something, anything. "We were tipped off from a bunch of do-gooders working for Homeland Security. The government wanted to wash their hands of things, so they hired my small shop. A little team of ex-military covetous and insatiable fighters who will do anything for a dollar. They told us to give you a bad day and forked over your address."

"You sound like us – out to make a buck." Stanley picked up the knife again and walked over to her. He spread her legs in the chair and forced himself between them, holding the glistening blade close to her throat. "I'm going to enjoy you. So much."

She felt his big body between her legs. Another stream of sweat fell down the other side of her face. She'd need to keep talking. *Fake it,* she said to herself, *just like Jacob did each Monday in Manhattan.* His trade desk talks with the brokers on the floor of PPCM was eighty percent bullshit, he later told her. At the time, she was convinced. Everyone was. *Be like that,* she told herself.

"Cold, hard cash," she said. "It all a money-grabbing commodity – these creative plays we make. There's a dark web we work with and along comes an...I don't know...opportunity. Like what you all seem to do. I run point on Operations and am an Administrator for our little clique. Work in the field if needed. We have..."

"Shut the fuck up, you little liar!" Stanley shouted, still between her legs. He reached up to her neck with both his hands and squeezed her neck. She gasped for air one last time before his strength began choking her. Her eyes grew wide, and she looked left and right and tried to move her arms which were wrapped to the chair with the duct tape. Adele heels pushed at the ground, but Stanley's weight held the aluminum chair down. He squeezed harder and she felt a hissing noise in her throat, not knowing if it were air being squeezed in or out of her esophagus. She could feel her face, flushed with red, heating. It caused painful pressure in her eyes as they darted around seeking help.

When he finally let go, she breathed deeply, but it hurt to take in the air. "Maybe I never should have brought you here, Adele. A little too much risk. But, then again, maybe I'll keep you around. You can be my little pet." He stopped talking, raised his finger, and then called out a song playing quietly on the boombox. "Ssh...it's Jon Bon Jovi," he said. "I like this song." *Blaze Of Glory,* was beginning its composition duration. "Got a song that turns you on, Adele? A ballad that gets you all...uh, *hot and bothered*?" He squeezed her neck again, briefly, but with a strong force that made it impossible for her to swallow or gasp for any air.

He looked over at Steve Booth who was as wide-eyed as Adele was, attempting to find a breath with Stanley's big hands squeezing her neck. "What do you think, Thdeve?" Then, he let go.

Steve said nothing. Taking a step back, he steadied himself with one hand on the work bench next to the blow torch, the striker, the knife and the hedge loppers.

Stanley took another swipe at her face with the back of his hand.

She felt the metallic taste of her own blood from the gash inside her lip. Spitting it on the floor away from him.

"Awe, honey. You got another boo-boo. Let me see." Stanley pulled down her bottom lip and saw a small gathering of blood. "That's not so bad." He looked at her and winked, and leaned forward and whispered, "It's going to get worse unless you tell me the truth. I know you're still lying." Stanley stood and walked over to TJ, "TJ, you got some water, preferable cold, around here somewhere?"

Without saying much, TJ walked over to a cooler which was set up for the 61 Tributes ahead of time and grabbed a bottle of cold water from the red plastic tub. He also picked up a remote control and laid it next to the shears. "Water – and remote, for you-know-what, and if it gets weird. Reminder, this is a safe place."

"Why thank you TJ. See, Adele, TJ is helpful."

Steve Booth looked at the remote. It was like what was at his complex. The black device looked like a standard TV remote but wasn't. It was intended to engage the turrets which had guns in them. If anything moved, the turrets would detect movement and fire. Just as at Steve Booth's compound a quarter of a mile away, there were four of them and a master control.

"So, where were we? Oh, yeah, a love song. Our song. You can join the others, and maybe I'll come for visits and bring you a piece of me once in a while." He looked down at her, "Sweetheart."

Adele was taking in air, knowing that the next time might not be as brief or even more painful. She feared the answer to the question she was going to ask, "What others?" Her eyes finally filled with tears knowing what Stanley was going to say.

"There it is," Stanley smiled and leaned against the worktable happy with himself, "You're the do-gooder." He smirked and added choices to his next line of questions, "FBI? Sherif's Department? Homeland Security?" He paused, "Which is it? Or is it as simple as the Concerned Citizen's Contingent of South Florida?"

She said nothing, feeling the warmth of the tears create small streams upon her cheeks. Looking into the distance, she could barely make out a container hiding in the distance. It was covered better than the one at Steve Booth's place. It was more difficult to see because of the additional camouflage hiding it.

"Oh my God..." Stanley added dramatically. "Is it...Steve...TJ...could it be? You?... Adele, my sweetie pie...you too are a mother?" He put his hands on his hips, making fun of himself for just now realizing it. "A mommy. Well...I'll be damned. How about that?" Stanley mocked again, looking into the distance but at nothing specifically, "I'd say she's a MILF, wouldn't you TJ?"

"Indeed. Mm. Say 'when'."

She openly sobbed – not for her own predicament, but for others. "Where are they?"

He squinted in the direction behind TJ's small, stilted house. If you look *really hard,* way back there. Just like over at Steve's place...kinda' sorta'... And just like the container at Mr. Booth's humble abode...The Product..." he paused, disrespecting the children, "is held safely in that metal box covered with camo. Of course, awaiting their," he shrugged his shoulders, "beats me, final destination?" He looked at Adele, like you said, "Cold hard cash. It's a transaction. Turns out, very lucrative."

Adele and her Ellipsis team hadn't expected two locations. They only had the knowledge and suspicion of one. It was a big miss. The callousness was indescribably saddening. She continued to shed tears for the additional victims a short distance away. Her arms, tethered to the chair with the tape, were helpless. She clenched her fists in her anger at being so powerless and useless in aiding them.

Her torture from Stanley wasn't complete.

Steve Booth saw her pain worsen. Her face being struck was difficult to watch. Her defenseless position strapped in the chair with the duct tape made him uneasy. Being unarmed against Stanley's continuing pain, both psychological and physical, caused him to look away. But the fact that she was a mother and cared so much for the children she had never even met...it was an awakening. He watched more tears of sadness for the unprotected and vulnerable fall from her eyes.

Sorrow. Long lost in his chest, deeply rooted in his soul, within him but hidden from the present, Steve felt a sorrow grow within him for Adele and what she came here intending to do – to liberate the small children, the victims of a vile act which Steve had participated in. She was to save them, comfort them, and provide a safe refuge from the cruelty of the 61 Tributes.

Momma would approve of what Adele was trying to do. Momma knew best. Momma made it all better. A mother held comfort – be it from worry, or fear, or distress. Momma. He said it to himself quietly, *Momma.*

"That arrangement work for you, Adele? Since you didn't tell me the truth right away, and..." Stanley shook his head, "I still don't think that you are. We lock you away and I come for a visit and give you a piece of me every once in a while." He leaned close to her again. "Mm...that smell of you...intoxicating...I must admit." There was evil in his eyes, they revealed hell's devil and the vileness of hatred for others.

She couldn't help herself and spat on his face.

Stanley wiped the spit away and said, "Sure wish you wouldn't have done that. Now, I'm just going to have to have me a piece of you...Adele." He picked up the yard loppers and came to her. "Eeny, Meeny, Miny, Moe – which of Adele's fingers will be the first to go?"

Steve clenched his fingers into fists too, to replicate the mother in front of him. Then released them, looking at the pinky missing.

She balled her hands into fists as he approached with the shears. Stanley leaned over and asked, "Have a preference? Need this one, don't need that one?" He ran the metal blade over each one as he asked questions. He looked at her ring finger, missing jewelry and without a tan line. Awe – doesn't look like this one's being used." The blade was touched on her thumbs when he asked himself, "Which one will it be, Adele?" The lopper's arms were opened and closed quickly in front of her eyes. "No, no, no, no, no. No fists, please. I might accidentally take two. We wouldn't want that to happen, now, would we?"

She extended the fingers following what he said. Her breathing was becoming shortened, and the anxiety was overwhelming. Trying to hold herself together, she listened for helicopters or trucks. Only the sound of the slicing blades from the hedge clippers snapping was heard.

"How 'bout the fucker finger?"

Stanley looked over at TJ, who was flipping him off. "The middle finger, TJ? Oh, you are a bad boy, aren't you?"

"Yup."

Stanley sneered at Adele and said softly, "Would have been so much better for you if you would have just slept in today, Adele. Which finger would you have pushed the snooze button with? Or I'm wondering...Adele...I'm wondering..." He leaned forward so that just the two of them could hear his whisper, "Which fingers do you pleasure yourself with?" He jumped back. The wildness in his eyes, the pure evil from the excitement he found in her agony and fear, the lack of any remote respect left a loathing within her. *There's no place in our world for you. If not now, eventually – I will end you,* she thought to herself. *Lord, please give me the strength to battle through this moment and the next.*

Her fingers contracted back into fists. She couldn't resist.

"Nope. Naughty girl. Remember what was said about fingers drawn up into fists." He looked over to Steve who could not make eye contact with Stanley, and he shouted at him, "Hey yo! Steve! What happens with fingers which become fists?"

Steve Booth pointed at his mouth. Looking away, Steve added, "Eat your own fingerth." His nervousness caused Stanley to look at him and frown. "God, you're an odd dude. But right! Show Adele your hand, Steve!"

The airboat mechanic held up his hand missing the pinky. While looking at the ground, Steve was saying something to himself. His anxiousness was beyond Adele's.

Adele pictured Steve being forced to eat his own finger. For some unexplainable reason, it was all that she needed to hear. Perhaps it was prayer. Maybe her body had reached its maximum level of adrenaline. Maybe it was what true defeat caused the mind to do. She opened her fingers slowly, extending them, and looked at Stanley directly and said, "Do what you think you must do. I'll pray for your consequences - and then someday, perhaps, find forgiveness somewhere within me." If she kept talking, she was buying time, and time was what might be required of the Ellipsis fighters. "Do you want to know how I can forgive you?"

Seeing her extend her fingers willingly was enough to send Steve over the edge, "No, no, no, no, no, no..." He approached Stanley and extended his own hand, the one with the remaining pinky. Then he held out the other hand, the one with all five digits remaining. "Take my fingerth, not herth – pleathe..." Steve cried out, "My fingerth..."

Stanley wanted no part of this offering. Sacrifice was not welcomed. "This isn't about you, Stevey boy. I'm gonna' take a piece of Adele. Then, I'm going to give her a piece of me!"

On a sunny Saturday morning in southeastern Florida, at a compound which was unknown to no legal or moral authorities, in a hidden location which trafficked in women, men and children as a modern slavery business, and operated by some of the most heinous, disrespectful, and vile humans – an act so sinful took place. Stanley opened the loppers and cut off Adele's pinky at the base of the knuckle. Her finger fell to the ground below her. As the bright red blood spurted from where the pinky once was, Steve Booth rushed to stop the bleeding, grabbing a dirty rag on the work bench last used to absorb radiator fluid from a flush. Adele cried out from the excruciating pain she felt as the man who had problems with the letters C, S and Z because of small front teeth. He was her only ally – experiencing the anguish himself at some point prior.

The villainous and rotten man who had just taken her pinky on her right hand had the audacity to add an iniquitous golf proclamation, "Fore! Or...Four! I must work on my slice. That one was wicked."

Steve scrambled to hold pressure on the squirting wound. She couldn't help him and only cried from the torturous pain filling her.

He rushed to the workbench, grabbed the remainder of the roll of the silver duct tape and began wrapping the dirty rag over the

As the Jon Bon Jovi song finished playing, a song by Ozzy Osbourne followed it. But it wasn't the radio that sparked interest from Stanley, TJ, nor Adele. Low at first, then growing louder was a *chip, chip, chip, chip, chip* sound of helicopter blades.

As quickly as they began hearing the sound the chopper made, it encroached into their space with a deafening and wind blazing force.

Mama, I'm Coming Home, playing on the boombox could barely be heard. Hearing the approaching incursion, Stanley grabbed the sidearm and held it in the direction of Adele, and Steve who was caring for her wound. The bleeding was subsiding as Steve put pressure on the socket where the pinky once was. He kept uttering, "Momma...momma...momma...momma..." as he looked up to Adele, attached to the chair now above him.

TJ grabbed an assault rifle and hid behind a workbench.

"You're my ticket out of here, Adele!" Stanley shouted above the whirling blades. He faced the landing chopper but kept the sidearm pointed at her face.

Before the helicopter could touch down, Ashford leapt from the scorched body of the warbird. His feet found the gravel, he rose up and took aim. Fearless, he stood there waiting for the others. One warrior after another jumped from the helicopter onto the crushed stone below. Rave, then Bing, then Chuck, then Tucker. After the landing of the helicopter, with the wind from the blades diminishing, but not stopping completely, Jacob jumped out. Against Chuck's instructions, Jacob was weaponless and approached the front of their pyramid. He continued to walk toward Stanley, who was facing him and pointing his handgun close to Adele's face. Shouting above the quieting roar of the blades, Stanley shouted, "That's far enough. We don't want to see pretty Adele with a bullet in her forehead, do we?"

Ashford saw TJ peek up, and duck back down behind the aluminum workbench, likely filled with tools to service the cars with their hoods opened in the small yard in front of the stilted house.

No words were said by Jacob nor the Ellipsis squadron. Jacob Paisley leaned to one side to see that Adele was wrapped to a chair with a silver material which appeared to be duct tape and a mysterious small man was tending to a bloody hand. On a Monday morning in Manhattan, he'd have summoned some form of bullshit to encourage his traders to go schmooze high net worth individuals to invest with them. In a Board of Directors meeting, he'd lie through his teeth about the wellness of PPCM to appease his friends and foes, the BoD which he'd assembled to meet compliance. With Victoria, the girlfriend experience, which was his Achille's heel, he would have flaunted needless surprise charms and exotic trips and lavish shopping trips. Here was Adele – who loved him deeply, despite all of his flaws – and stood with him no matter what.

He wasn't sure which it was. Either Jacob Paisley was her misfortune – or – Adele Kirby was his enlightenment toward a life lived well. Nothing was more important than saving her from this moment. He began walking fearlessly and intentionally toward the unknown man holding a gun toward her head.

TJ rose up and fired shots in the direction of Ashford. It was a quick *Pop! Pop! Pop!* He ducked back down. Jacob changed course and began walking in that direction, not knowing who the shooter was – only knowing that he was here to mitigate this situation and soothe the anguish which Adele was involved in. And that a weapon of destruction was in that range. *Pop! Pop! Pop!* Again, misses. *These guys really aren't good at this*, Jacob thought as he marched forward toward the man hiding behind a tool bench.

When TJ arose a third time, Ashford took aim and shot him in the forehead between his eyebrows. He fell backwards and the gun was tossed aside. Jacob scooped it up the AR-15 and continued to walk to

Adele and the man holding her hostage. It felt warm in his hands. The smell of gunpowder from the weapon was present.

"You heard me, right? No further or she takes it in the face!" Stanley said it, and for the first time, had an unassertive tone in what he barked out. "I mean it! Not one more step! What are the odds she lives if you come any closer?"

Jacob stopped. He turned his back to the man looking at him from under the canopy where Adele was tied to look around him. Their guns were drawn. It was a circle of intimidation. Chuck. Bing. Tucker. Rave. The new and valiant large man named Ashford. In the body of the war-bird were the pilot and bullet-butt Jude. They all had his back.

The dauntless gleam in his eye was for her. This ended now. Jacob raised the gun and pointed it at Stanley.

"You really think I won't?" Stanley wasn't going anywhere today. He would die in this shitty place in southeastern Florida. "Listen, I have here a remote control that is going to unleash four turrets of fire-power which will tag all of you. I'm in a safe place. You, well...all of you ain't. So, your call who lives and who dies. One step, and I push it.'

He lowered the weapon and considered words for the forsaken man. Lionhearted, he raised it again and while pointing the gun at the man took small steps forward.

Stanley pressed the button on the remote and nothing happened. He did it again, and again, and again. No bullets rained down on them. "Bye-bye Adele..." While looking at Jacob, yet holding the handgun at her, trussed and cinched to a cheap lawn chair from the seventies – he thought that his last act would be an eye for an eye.

Steve leaped in front of Adele to take the three shots fired. The weight from the small man however, knocked over the chair and Adele was on her back, Steve lying next to her. He looked at her and softly cried out, "Momma..." *Mama, I'm Coming Home* played on the boombox nearby.

The music heard was the first time that Jacob listened to any sound other than the beat of Adele's heart from across the work yard as he left the cabin of the helicopter. Steve Booth closed his eyes as the blood poured from his torso.

Turning only his head to see that it was Steve that was shot, the man turned to look at Jacob Paisley approaching with valorous intent. The man's body was fired at by both Jacob and Ashford. The sharp shooters shot was the first to impact Stanley's trunk, hitting him in the ribs. As Stanley stumbled to the side from the velocity of the first shot, it was Jacob's relentless shots fired which continued to fill his body with lead. Shot after shot after shot after shot after shot - Jacob's rage, unending, continued to squeeze the trigger of the gun with the bump stock. As Stanley's body lay on the ground, continuing to take a non-stop load of ammunition, twitching from the impact of each shot fired, it was Chuck who came up from behind and whispered, "You got him. You can stop now."

Adele looked at Steve Booth, breathing his final breath. His short teeth, preventing him from speaking clearly, were no hindrance to his final word. "Momma..." he spoke softly. His eyes were open as he died. Saving Adele's life was the last and best thing that the airboat mechanic did in the years he lived. Mixed up with the wrong crowd, seeking an allegiance – a connection to anything, misunderstanding some rights from some wrongs, he was a young man who sinned just like others. In the end – as he had one last purpose in his existence – it was to save a woman resembling a mother – a Momma. His want to do no harm to a mother led him to place himself between Stanley's rage and Adele's way forward.

She looked at him, laying still next to her. His sacrifice would not be forgotten.

Jacob dropped the weapon and ran to Adele's side on the ground. "Are you..." He used a knife which tortured Adele to cut the duct tape and free her from the chair. She was able to sit up.

"Children...in the container...behind the house...get them out now," she said between the shuddering and blenching from pain. She held the dirty rag on her hand tightly, placing as much pressure as she could on the bleeding. They rushed to Adele, and also to the container to release the victims. Rave approached the area, leaned over to squint at the ground, leaned over to pick up Adele's finger. She found a water bottle on the work bench, unscrewed the cap and dropped the small member in the cold water. Rave cut the duct tape carefully away from Adele's wrists, helped her stand, and looked at her. "You're going to be alright. Tomorrow's not going to be this tough. I promise." Adele found a smile within the piercing pain. Rave hugged her.

Jacob stood next to her in shock of what he'd just taken part in. He looked at Stanley's lifeless body nearby – then scanned the grounds. The soldiers were moving toward the container. It was Rave, Adele and Jacob in this place and at this moment of reentry into reality. He placed his arm around her, and despite the excruciating pain, Adele's head found his shoulder and she leaned on him in exhaustion.

The Suburban's white van pulled onto the gravel. As the kids, once referred to as The Product, but no more, were released from the container, the soldiers asked them to turn their heads away from TJ, Stanley, and Steve who lay still on the crushed gravel. It was no more than five minutes of shuttling the nine of them from camouflage hidden shipping container to the vehicles. The air tags attached to their ankles with zip ties would be cut free while en route to the same facility in Naples as the others.

The last one standing at the opening of the container was Ashford. Tucker approached him. The bodycam which Tucker wore showed Ashford's head turned toward the empty metal housing. Nine more people with lives ahead of them were held hostage there just moments ago. As Tucker approached him, he said, "You, okay? Ashford, is it?"

Allegra looked at the camera of the man staring blankly in the 53' camo-covered container and said to himself, but for anyone listening, "I really thought she'd be here."

This was the man which carried Sydney across the gravel yard, lying her in the helicopter. Big, bold, heroic, but heartfelt – she admired his compassion for whomever he sought after. *"Who are you?"* she said softly and to herself.

Tucker, not understanding the loss or the pain, simply said, "Let's go soldier." The doors of the empty container were left open. In ten minutes, a rocket from another time period's battle would decimate this place, melting the metals, eviscerating the traces of the helicopter and any automobiles with their hoods pried open awaiting starters or solenoids or radiators. The location next to the swamp would become scorched earth, nearly the size of a football field.

As Ashford readied to take a last seat in a Suburban, he turned and looked back at the location. A small wind caught the mangroves and the tops of the small trees surrounding the complex. Eerily, it was as if Lady Barbara called out to him in his thoughts and through his soul, *Vindica Te Tibi* – 'set yourself free for your own sake'. He felt the chill, shrugged his broad shoulders, joined the others, and didn't look back.

15

⧜

Vindication

Laki relentlessly encouraged Brian to give it a shot. After all, she was the one prompting him to put himself out there. *'Be that audacious Brian Kekahanamanui that I met'*, she coaxed. *'He's in there'.* When she looked up to him and poked him in the chest, it was the impelling moment he thought of as he drove west on Oahu's H-1.

The middle of February, here, felt like a Midwest summer. Even San Diego experienced the June gloom.

It was true. Complacency had found its place within him. It first entered the wallet. Lifestyle creep kept it there. Then the productivity of the job got easier. He began mastering the process of being a people leader. As his talents and skills were honed and the operational gunk was offloaded – the job became a predictable and solid footing. Complacency – the silent venom which could consume anyone's potential – used that stable comfort-level as a loadstone to build from. Then it crept into his dreams of 'what might be'. The interests and projects and adventures had been muted. Laki was able to see it. After Complacency was a bane to his dreams, it entered the home. Date Night became re-runs of *Two and a Half Men*. Watching little Jake Harper grow up throughout the sitcom's series was enough when he came home from the road – out visiting the sporting goods stores which he served as their District Manager. And like the actor Angus T. Jones, who

405

played the part – there came a time to reassess all things and make a difficult decision to consider change. It was not that Brian had joined the Seventh-day Adventist Church or had any other spiritual awakening. It was when you know, you know. There comes a point when the slightest thing may wake a sleeping lion.

Whether it was fate or logic or randomness or an unknown force for change – Brian received the small poke.

Poke. It was an English word indicating a gentle jolt

Poke. It was a Hawaiian word, pronounced POH-keh, meaning sliced or cut or cubed and often marinated sushi grade fish – straight from the sea. Brian preferred the classic form: cubed ahi tuna in soy sauce, smothered with sesame oil, sweet onions and scallions. And he knew just where to go to get the best. "Nanakuli, here I come," he said out loud and over the radio playing island tunes loudly.

It would be much different now. Without his Uncle and Auntie who had raised him on the west side, he'd have their empty house to come back to. The memories of growing up here would surely fill him with a favor for this warm and loving island upbringing. Probate took time. He would continue to watch it run its course. Like the lifestyle could be at times here, *Hawaiian Time*, an authentic appreciate for a place and time was one thing, but an appreciation for people came first.

Aloha. It meant many different things to many different people. Brian remembered his Uncle and Auntie teaching him... *'Alo'*, meaning 'presence'. And *'Ha'*, representing 'breath of life'. Brian thought of his Uncle telling him as a small child, "Do not take Aloha lightly, young Brian. *'Alo-ha'*... *'Here we are, face to face, sharing the breath of life.'*

As Brian slowed down his rental passing the Ko Olina exit, he watched an older man behind the wheel of a navy sedan lower his driver's side window and extend his arm, catching the gusts of wind in the cusp of his hand like a seabird floating on a waft of air. It was 4pm and check-in time for the owners of time shares and hotels. He assumed someone was en-route to their 'place of joy', which is what the location was touristy location was called. He also remembered catching a morning run and becoming engaged at a young man taking swipes at his girlfriend. The hit, that tackle on the spongy lawn of the beach park, was indelible.

Laki was right. You put yourself out there and who knows what might happen.

As the congestion on the highway came to a crawl near the old electric company, and as Farrington's lanes compressed, he was able to lower his own windows, trading the air conditioning for the breezes of Nanakuli. On the left was the wild Pacific. It's deep and mysterious blues called to him. The beach park was where he had learned to swim. Past the bright green naupaka with its succulent broad leaves, and beyond the golden natural sands, was a gentle and rolling turquoise colored surf which fed into deeper hues of mesmerizing cobalt and delft blues. Eventually, and the forty fathom line, it all became a sea warrior's blue – left to the sailing machines and power vessels.

This...this was home.

He turned right on the main road and was heading into the lush Nanakuli Valley. It's towering Waianae Mountain Range enveloped the small coastal town. As beautiful as the water was, the ridges on the prominent rise in elevation surrounding the leeward side were of dark mossy, fern, and olive greens. When the low clouds dropped their mist on the fertile valley crests, the greens were muted. When the bright tropical sun shone, they became vibrant and galvanizing.

Brian turned onto their street and stopped in front of their home, a few driveways in. Here on their street, he shut off the ignition, leaving the windows down, and climbed out of the rental.

Taking it all in, with his hands on his hips, he looked at the two-story small home. The second-floor window he climbed out of as a teenager faced the street. They left it as he did. Memories would fill him even more once he entered the front door and began his mission of beginning to tie up loose ends.

"Hey stranger," she called out. Brian was hypnotized and didn't hear her. "Yo, Brian!" she tried again. Still unresponsive, he stood there looking at the home and the yard and was captive the recollections of his Hawaiian upbringing. Her car was directly behind his on the street heading out toward the main avenue in and out of the development. "Are you pretending to be deaf?!"

Brian turned and without seeing who it was, he bent over and replied with a smile on his face, "Well, that is what Nanakuli means in the Hawaiian..." His hands were on his knees as he hunched over and squinted.

"Yeah...I know."

"Tamsen?"

"That's me. Hi Brian. It's been what...I don't know...forever?"

"Too long," he said. "Wow. Are you living or visiting or?"

"I was visiting an old friend from high school. You know, small island, go Hawks, right?"

"Indeed. Go Golden Hawks," Brian repeated. Football hadn't ended up quite like he had wished it would, but one thing tended to lead to another. It led him to Laki.

"I heard about your Aunt. Well, your Uncle and then your Auntie. I'm sorry, Brian." She said, "They were beautiful people. I remember your Autie from bible school. She was so beautiful and graceful in hula too. And your Uncle, hell of an ukulele player."

"Mahalo. Thanks, Tamsen. That's...well, this is part of life. Seeing them off for a final Aloha. Remembering them. It'll take some time. I'm here for a work thing too." Brian didn't want to share too much with his old high school acquaintance. He was also mindful that there was once something there with Tamsen.

She turned her ignition off. "Work? A convention or something?"

"Something like that," Brian made short of detail, avoiding that it was a panel interview for an emerging sports conglomerate for the Pacific Rim Region. The text teases it turned out, was a headhunter building a roster of candidates for a Senior Executive and leadership position.

"I heard you were leading a surf brand here on Oahu?"

"That's right. I'm up on the North Shore now, near Pupukea. Bravado Surf. We're a little more than that. It's a small part of a larger enterprise. Yeah...so who ever thought we'd both end up in sports retail, right? ."

"Yeah – I keep allowing coincidences to surprise me for some reason," Brian shared.

"Listen, I'm not trying to catch you off guard, but I was on my way to pick up a few things. Would love to chat a little more and hear about you. You hungry? A man's got to eat," she said. "I'm thinkin' Foodland's poke."

"There it is - coincidence again. Yeah, I'm down for that. I was just thinking on the way in that some ono grindz were in order. That and the three-hour time delta."

"Nice," was all she said as she started the engine.

"Wait – don't they have a Foodland right there on the North Shore's Farrington?"

"Truth?" Tamsen asked, pausing for her fib to develop.

"Yeah – always best."

Tamsen continued, "Well – I'm starving. Like after I eat my fingernails, I may chew on yours too. And...I go to lagoon four over there at Ko Olina's beach park and listen to a couple old-timers arrive about a half hour before sunset I'm guessing almost every damn day and play their island tunes. Every time I'm back home here on the west side, I try to catch them."

Brian looked at her and smiled at the fact she was as drawn to the same old melodies and teachings in the Hawaiian music as he was. He reaffirmed, "You sure?"

"Sure. Get in," she motioned with her head as she said it.

He looked up at the sky, then jumped in with her. The windows were down, but it didn't look like there was a chance of rain. "You know, Tamsen. On the mainland you think about your zip code. Here, you just have to look up to the sky and consider the possibility of a shower."

"Physical proximity, Brian. You just never know where your next step may lead you to. Buckle up. This will be fun." Tamsen smirked, knowing a little bit about something which he did not.

Together, *as a coincidence* Brian would later call it, they drove into yet-to-be-known opportunities and unity of meaningful connections. As the sun began its slow descent toward the horizon, the Pacific's watery sparkles, like diamonds shining on the sea's surface, illuminated their way forward.

*****

"Good morning New Yorkers. We're off to a sunny start and temperatures are nearly fifteen degrees warmer than usual, but don't get used to it," the female weather forecaster in a teal top and dark skirt spoke about the approaching front with soggy conditions expected. Her dark hair fell to her shoulders and her olive-colored skin helped show off a dazzling pearly white smile. As she stood in front of the northeast region, indicating a system approaching the metro area, she included, *"bright blue skies will turn grey and dull and deliver drizzle as evening approaches and much cooler conditions as we move into tomorrow. If you...maybe think...you won't need a coat, you just might want to think twice."*

"It's so big," she said.

"That's what every guy wants to hear," Jacob replied looking toward Adele with a smirk. He used the remote to lower the volume of the television, not that he was paying attention to it anyway. It was on, but nearly on mute.

Adele slid the ring on her left hand with the right. A five carat E-color diamond was the centerpiece of the engagement ring. On the clarity scale, the internally flawless helped command the price of the piece. The Super Ideal cut quality was brilliant and in the evening light it sparkled like a raging firestorm, illuminating not only the room, but any moment. The side stones complimented the rock taking center stage. Her pinky, however, on the right hand, was sticking out straight like a small purple baby carrot.

"If there were a fifth C in selecting an engagement ring, what would it be?" Adele asked, spinning to look at him for his reaction.

"Is this a riddle, or a joke, or are you..."

"No, a legit question," Adele replied, "I have a think piece here."

Jacob thought about it for a few seconds and quickly replied, "Color, Cut, Clarity, Carat...and...Commitment."

"Oo, I like that one."

He asked, "Is this some Cosmo quiz?"

"No, but could be," she answered. "I'd say Commencement – because something is about to begin."

Jacob nodded his head slightly hearing his phone ping on the nightstand. Ignoring it, he added, "At least neither of us said Courage, right?'

She chuckled and piled on, "Or Condemned," laughing a little harder at her contribution.

"Compromise?" Jacob paused himself, looked at her and shrugged.

"Well...that very well may..."

"You look pretty," Jacob said, changing topics.

"Thanks...boss." Her exec admin role was...then. She was as much in charge...now. The comment acknowledged her rise as much as his wisdom and they both enjoyed her subtle innuendo. *"You're only here because of me"*, she whispered to herself, but loud enough for Jacob to hear.

"There's some truth to that", he whispered back. Jacob looked at the ping on his phone again – and shared it with her.

She read it seven times, then tightened her lips, "How do you want to play that?"

"I have an idea," Jacob answered, "It might depend how it goes, but an idea. And an idea that will involve you."

"Uh...yeah," Adele answered, "wouldn't want it any other way."

Jacob looked at her and smiled. He walked up to her and bear-hugged her. They were dressed and had a meeting at the UN to debrief with the Ellipsis team, including the fighters minus Marco.

"Ouch," Adele whispered while receiving a passionate and deep hug.

"Your pinky?" Jacob asked.

"No, it's the left shoulder."

"You sleep on it funny or...what?" he said, breaking away and returning to the credenza in their bedroom to gather his wallet and keys from a ceramic bowl.

"It's the weight of this rock on my left hand. So heavy. So very heavy. Really gives me a shoulder workout. The stress...the strain..." Her playful way of expressing appreciation was ongoing.

"Shut up, you punk."

Everyone had expressed an exceptional interest in the ring. Especially Allegra, who went out of her way to let Adele know how very happy she was for their future together. She made a fuss over how 'ginormous' the stone was and that it must represent the love they shared. Peculiar as that might have been, it was only Ruby's blessing she sought the most and he was 'away at the moment', as he called it in a text message. The ring...it wasn't her idea...it was Jacob's. Adele would have appreciated a cubic zirconia ring from Amazon, perhaps not as much.

To Adele, the size of the stone was unnecessary. To Jacob, it was less than he anticipated as they selected it together at Harry Winston. It checked the boxes.

"Hey..." she said in his direction as they moved from the bedroom to the kitchen.

As soon as she said it, Kolohe's ears perked up and he sat up.

"Not you, sorry boy," she said, "Hey Jacob?"

"Hmm..." He was swallowing a pill and a multi-vitamin.

"I don't want you to be upset. I don't want you to be pissed off. But…"

"Yeah?" Jacob prompted.

"Since we are about to be married…?" she lingered and paused hesitantly in her ask.

"Spit it out. I'm intrigued now. What is it?"

"Well…so…we've worked together for a very long time, and I know much about you." Adele's buildup to the question was more for herself than for Jacob. "I've always wondered…"

Jacob stopped with the busy work in the kitchen. No more clattering of dishes, drying their coffee cups, or tidying up from breakfast. He didn't say anything. His stare was enough.

"I promise you; this is curiosity only. I've always wondered…"

He approached her, face to face, and placed both hands on her shoulders.

"Have you ever had…?" She looked up at him and stalled.

"Had what?"

"Personal here," her reluctance to ask, but need to know, was floating in the slight space between them, "Well, have you ever had…a threesome?"

He was startled and showed it in a small twitch and in how he squinted his eyes yet held onto her tenderly. Shocked with the type of question, especially by Adele who was elegant, proper, congenial – things which were far from raw questions – he found her objectivity: merely her authentic concern. After all, she was a mother and a grandmother. Adele was much more than his longstanding friend, his former Executive Administrator, his fiancé. She needed to know everything she was in on, not just the surface material.

"It's a fair question. And I'll answer it. This isn't a stall. But where's that coming from?" Jacob answered the question with one of his own, trying to size up how he would tell her.

"Like I said, curiosity only. I just...I just always wondered. You lived a hard charging life as the CEO and your festivities were a little over the top at times and...just that...only curiosity."

Jacob looked into Adele's eyes, sparkling back at him. He could tell her anything, and he did by saying nothing.

"Was it with her?" Adele asked the question at first before pointing at his phone. Victoria.

He shook his head slightly and slowly in the direction of a 'yes'.

"Just once?" she asked

"Just once." He didn't take his eyes off her. Telling the truth, he added, "Just one time."

"I always assumed so, but didn't want to wonder any longer. Did you like it?"

"Not really." Jacob answered her quickly, then broke from their embrace and returned to gathering his jacket and slipped it on. "That's why it was a just once thing."

"Did Victoria like it?" Her tone was different but still reasonable. "I'm sorry, you don't need to go there. This is just confirmation bias, I guess, I think. Always thought the answer was 'yes' but left the question unasked. I'm sorry if it..."

"No, it's okay, we can talk about it. For me...it just was...I don't know...awkward? There's a lot going on and it's anything but intimate, and someone seems to be enjoying it more than the others and...I don't know how to narrate it. Some people get off on the multitude thing, but not me. If you want to see it – My Uncle's Place is where to go, I'll tell you. But if you want to experience it...well, I'm not..."

"No." She smiled, "Let me stop you right there. I just have never kissed another woman or been with two men, or any combination of sexual partners at the same time and was only wanting to get that out of my head."

"Is it out of your head now?" Jacob asked.

"It is. Answered. Sort of. So, you had a little threesome hookup with Victoria once. No big deal. No more wondering about that nonsense."

"It was her idea."

"Of course," Adele quickly added but was guarded to know more.

"We were in Marseille. Or was it Monaco? No, it was France...so, Marseille..."

"Nope. No, no thank you," she suspended any additional detail he was about to offer. Adele held her index finger of her right hand up to halt the details and the purple pinky, unintentionally as erect as her trigger finger, followed making it look like she was offering a rock 'n' roll salute.

He smiled at the hand horns she was holding up between them. "Less is best?"

"Just like I used to say when we were at PPCM, and your raunchy traders would share too much detail from their revelries."

"Bones, please. Not the meat," Jacob recited.

Adele lifted her chin and dropped it to her chest indicating a firm correctness to what he said.

"I know she'll probably always own a small space here." She lightly touched his temple. "I just don't want her to occupy a space here," Adele placed a finger on his heart. "It's a fragile place. That's where I want to be. No threesomes."

"I'll take the total extermination package and be done with it. An eradication of sorts, or maybe an exorcism..."

His phone pinged again. Jacob reached for it, read it once, and shared his screen with Adele. Together, they looked at the face of the phone. Victorias message read: *I'd LOVE to see you again. I'm in Manhattan today. You here? There's an opportunity I wanted to bounce off you – to get your opinion on.*

"Speak of the devil," Adele added.

"Let's talk on the way." Helping her slip on her black wool overcoat and a lapis blue cashmere scarf, Jacob gave her a small pat on the butt.

They walked toward the front door of their new swanky Waldorf Astoria Residences Park Avenue condo.

"Is that all you're wearing? A sports coat? You should put something on over that. You'll thank me later."

He shrugged and did so, sliding on his wool overcoat which looked much like hers but was a midnight navy blue. "You know...when you asked me what you just asked me about...well, I was worried you were going to ask me about S and M – now *that* would have been *one hell of an uncomfortable conversation,*" he teased as the door was about to close behind them leaving.

Jacob stopped the door from closing and leaned in briefly, "Bye Kolohe. See you soon buddy." The heavy door clicked shut.

A strategic conversation along a walk of seven blocks, Jacob and Adele had approached the Gift Garden, dubbed *Good Defeats Evil* on the north end of the UN. The United Nations building stood with its mossy green glass windows and flags bluffing in the breeze. This was where they were leveraging meeting rooms out of conveniences as well as a mutual and unwritten concern for the state of the world stood before them.

Before entering the building, Jacob and Adele sat in the disappearing sun on a bench in the garden. The sky appeared to be becoming more overcast than cloudy. It was there that they discussed Victoria and traded several text messages with her. It was also there where they decided that no matter what embryonic stage this next phase of communications may lead to with Victoria – they agreed on the outcome: her extinction from unanswered questions between them.

Once through security, Jacob and Adele realized that they were the first to arrive. The others came in quick succession of each other, separately but at nearly the same time. In walked prompt Sydney, then Allegra, then Vendemer.

It was a small meeting before the meeting. Only Ruby was on the Zoom screen. His background was blurred out, perhaps intentionally.

"Hey – miss you, old man." Jacob spoke. They put the room on camera too.

Ruby squinted to see who was on the call and gathered in their usual meeting room. "Jacob and Adele, and Sydney – good to see you again, Syd – and Vendemer and Miss Allegra Sinclair. Alright, the gang's all here."

"Not all here. Where are you?" Jacob asked.

"Well," he looked down at his hands and avoided the question. Ruby came back up to the laptop's camera with partial truth. "I had some reconnaissance work that needed to be done and am taking a bit of a break. We all need downtime, and I required a little more than a little. So, here I am."

"Care to share a little more?" Jacob asked, looking over at Ruby's ally, seeking a hint from Vendermer who shrugged his shoulders.

"I don't, I'm sorry. I know secrets are not something we want to do in this circle of trust... But I just need some time and as they say, we'll get the band back together soon." It killed Ruby to have to fib to Ben-Ven, Jacob, and the crew.

"Well, we look forward to that. The band needs its star triangle player."

Ruby did chortle at the significance of a triangle player, but went on with a task request, "Captain Paisley, could really use your help taking the helm of the ship while I'm on a short hiatus."

Jacob pried further, "Tamsen going dark have anything to do with your holiday?"

The old black man did his best to convince the team back in Manhattan and he simply shook his head 'no'. To off-topic the small interrogation, he added, "You know...I can play a mean cowbell too."

"A multi-instrumentalist? All this time and we didn't know... We'll go on tour when you decide to return." Jacob checked his watch. The face of the Rolex had a scratch on it, from rubbing against the helicopter in south Florida. *Scar-tissue,* Adele called it. *A badge of honor, keep it like that.*

Ruby looked at Adele as if reading Jacob's mind, "Adele, before we jump in – gotta' ask, how's the finger?"

Sydney jumped in on the answer, "She drinks tea like a refined Brit, now Ruby. The pinky points straight out."

Adele held up a cup of tea and did her best Sydney impression, "Twas a bit that I felt barmy, Ruby. Felt quite snookered. I said to myself, 'Self – bleeding hell, when might this sicky dicky begin to heal?' Was a bit lurgy. Then, got a little jammy and wangly and no whinge from me."

A small applause took place, and Sydney added, "Oh, well done. The next British Air flight to London from JFK takes off in an hour. Let's sit together, birdie."

"Well, that's cute. But...I really meant that *other* finger of yours. The shiny one?" Ruby held up his ring finger. "This one?"

Adele was glowing, "You mean this little thing?" The diamond in the middle sparkled brilliantly. It was nearly as wide as her thin finger.

"Please let me be the last to congratulate you two. You both have found that one special person to annoy for the rest of your lives. To Adele – it's not too late to change your mind. Buckle up, you might be in for a bumpy ride with that guy. And to Jacob – it's about time!" A few smiles found their faces as the team gathered around the table looked at Jacob and Adele watching Ruby's congratulatory sentiments.

To the comment about the bumpiness of being with Jacob Paisley, Adele added "I've been attending his rodeo for years, Ruby. My cowgirl status for the Saddle Bronc is strong. I can take all his bumps and bruises. One hand on the reigns and one up in the air for fun."

"Again – best wishes for you two. Have you set a date yet?"

"Not yet," Adele quickly replied, knowing Jacob had thoughts about asking Ruby to be a best man. "Where, when, how – all to be worked out. All we know is the why and who at this point."

"Fair enough. Good segue. Sydney, can you pull up the nice surprise you have for Adele, please?"

Sydney looked over to Adele and smiled as she shared three young faces on the screen which they were all looking at. "This. this is why we do what we do," she said deliberately. They saw two young girls and a young high school-looking boy in the images at the head of the meeting room. On the left was a curly haired girl wearing round glasses. Next to her was a small black child appearing no more than six or seven. An on the right was a Hispanic looking boy that was older and looked athletic.

"From our first liberation, nearly three years ago, a little follow up on twelve-year-old, Ella Spade – she just entered the State of Texas Spelling Bee, representing her district. Lives with her mom in Dallas, again. She's into photography and..." she checked her notes, "loves horses."

As she shared the updates on the children, their salvation stories caused Allegra and Vendemer to stop typing and their attention was paid to Sydney. Jacob's mouth crept open Ruby was seen smirking at the good news. Adele's eyes sparkled with admiration.

She described the next child. "Next to Ella, in the middle is Shayna Williams. Shayna and her parents are moving to El Paso where they can be close to Shayna's grandparents. A mysterious new job, thank you Mr. Ruby Hollins, came about for Shayna's father. Shayna plays the piano and signed up for gymnastics."

"And on the right is Daniel Acosta. Danny is a wide receiver on his high school football team. He's just in his freshman year but scored six touchdowns which was the most for their team. Unfortunately, his father wasn't there to see any of it. Child abduction has consequences far beyond what we can think that it does."

A moment of silence consumed them.

Vendemer, describing the ramifications of children or missing person taken, added, "Starts with the simple stuff like time and jobs and money. They're gone quickly. Then it destroys the family. From the inside out, physically, emotionally, psychologically. People stop allowing themselves to find joy so that they don't betray the missing person's memory. And as you can imagine, the other darker forces can follow."

Ruby piled on to BenVen's deep comment, "The prominence in what we do to creatively extricate the captive – it accomplishes more than we can realize. Always good to see the updates – thanks Sydney."

"The pleasure," she dropped the previous victims' pictures from the screen and only Ruby's image shown, "is all mine. It's mutual, yes, but I do enjoy so, stalking them and sharing with you all their progress and how they are thriving. All of the San Diego victims have been united either with their mothers and fathers, or caregivers in homes where they are safe and returning, ever-so-slowly, to what their lives were like before they were abducted. We're doing good work here, team. Much more to do. We have much more to do on this topic alone. I know there is a host of other agendas. This one, oversharing, is the most important to me." She looked over at Adele who was shaking her head 'yes', agreeing with everything Sydney said.

"All good. I cannot believe that I'm not a waterfall of tears – of joy – right now, but knowing that there's so much more to do on this front, maybe it's the determination to extinguish these evildo-ers...that..." She stopped speaking and did reach for a tissue before continuing, "that have no moral compass in what they do. How did money ever overcome the boundaries of right and wrong?" Her ques-tion lingered for a few seconds before Allegra attempted to answer it.

"Sadly, because it's *a lot* of money. And *a lot* of money tends to change judgment." Allegra pulled her flowing blond hair, dangling over her shoulders, back as she watched Adele recover from the brink of crying. "Adele, you're the only mother here. You have a depth of un-derstanding which we don't..."

It was an agreed upon sentiment and they each looked at her as she composed her thoughts.

"Let's do more of this. Let's continue to deliver a difference here," Adele added. "I can't think of a more meaningful connection than re-uniting loved ones."

The team shook their heads in unison. Collectively, they thanked Sydney for digging up the tidbits about several of the former held-captive victims and sharing some good news.

"Oh. I almost forgot. One more thing..." Sydney opened her laptop again and shared a segment from NewsNowNaples, from the organization's website, as she clicked on the link bookmarked on her browser, a man and woman news anchor team sat next to each other to share their lead story segment, the woman spoke, "Authorities from southwest Florida teamed together upon a sting operation rescuing women and children from a human trafficking organization. Details are still being uncovered, but an unofficial source from the Collier County Marshall's Office has indicated that the sting operation involving several agencies which have teamed together to rescue a dozen victims or more from an underground crime operation. This situation seems to have happened in the small coastal community south of Naples. The victims are being reunited with their families. As we have more information and confirmation from the State or Local authorities, we'll share that detail."

Then the man spoke, "Well, it's always nice to begin a broadcast with some good news. Great to see the families coming together. Another situation from that area not as awesome as reunification is that kids or young adults are suspected of causing a large explosions outside of Everglades City. Seen here are two areas of burnt land near the Everglades. Large explosions were heard before the fires were seen in two areas once known as an airboat and automobile mechanic shops. It's unknown if the two were related or if the vandals were acting independently. No persons have been charged with arson, a serious charge, at the time of this reporting. Residents report they heard the ground shake as the blasts occurred."

"No one was hurt?" the news anchor asked.

"Apparently no," he added, answering her question.

"Well, that is good news. Shenanigans," she quipped. "On to a disturbance which took place in Everglades City earlier that day..."

Sydney turned off the broadcast. "The trail of disaster we left behind us... Good to remain untwined here. Wouldn't you say?"

Ruby weighed in, "Less is best."

Adele slowly rolled her head toward Jacob, considering what they spoke of before walking to the UN building. He knew her eyes were upon him. Raising his eyebrows he smirked at the timely comment.

"Jacob?" Ruby, seeking a small task from the money-maker, "Before our guys jump on the call, did you sign off on their invoice so we can get them paid?"

"I did...not. How do I do that?" Jacob asked. "I saw a PDF with a fat ole number on it, but didn't know how to..."

"Just fake a name, any name, or initials, or anything. But don't use your name, please. It isn't us, it's them. All of the logistics and resources and coordination which went into the implementation. They need that. It's for their distributions, not us. Time for a little...remuneration."

Sydney, since she was already on the screen, slid her laptop over to him so that he could leave his mark of authority upon the document.

Jacob looked at the document again. Seeing at the dollar amount: $325,000.00

"Three and a quarter," Jacob said. He clicked fake initials on the invoice: W M G

"Great, thanks for getting them paid," Ruby added. "BenVen, did you pick up what I asked?"

"I did," Vendemer replied.

Ruby doubled back on Jacob's authorization, "What's W M G?"

"With Much Gratitude," Jacob replied.

"Right on," Sydney chimed in.

Vendemer reached into his coat pocket and pulled out a fifth of Van Winkle Special Reserve Bourbon. The shot glasses were plastic and slid into each other tidily.

"I shipped each of our fighters their own bottle to remember Marco and asked them to say a word or two about him." BenVen unscrewed the cap and began distributing brimming small amounts of the caramel-colored liquor. "Jade is visiting his mother in Indiana, so I needed to indicate that we were shipping him olive oil. Hopefully it made it in time..."

Just then, the soldiers started appearing on video. Jade was first, followed by Chuck, Rave, Tucker, and then Bing. As they went around the horn, sharing something special about Marco, they sipped and raised a glass or Vendemer's small plastic vessels, resembling a poly NyQuil cup.

Collectively, they took a few minutes each, said something soulful and respectful toward their fallen team member, Marco, and raised the bourbon in his name after they spoke. It was a short, but meaningful connection where they honored a life well-lived, taken too quickly, but something good happened as the result of his service to their cause. In no more than ten minutes time, they joined the call, said their piece, and just as they arrived together, departed the call together. Only Chuck stayed on.

"That was tough on them. Just so you know. Rave said, 'no rain, no rainbow' and it cheered me up when our team debriefed a few days ago. His sacrifice does not go unnoticed."

Sydney said, "Chuck, we don't take you or your team for granted. We want you to know that."

"I know you don't. We appreciate what you're all doing to stand it up and get things moving along." He wanted to switch topics and did, "Where's the big fella? Ashford? Was he invited to the call?" Chuck asked.

Allegra and Sydney had been group texting the big and tall, mysterious new member of their team. It was Allegra's place to speak after exchanging glances with Sydney, "Syd and I are meeting up with him..." she checked the time, "later today. He's landing, checking in, and is supposed to meet us for a drink or two or whatever. We're tour guides this weekend. You're all invited to join us. We hope you can."

Vendermer was first, "Count me in. Where to?"

"Library of Distilled Spirits," Allegra answered.

"There's a name," Vendermer added.

"It isn't too far away. Close to Union Square." Allegra paused. "There's a friend of mine meeting us. I owe her one. Have been putting her off for a while, she will be joining us. So, no Ellipsis talk."

"Let me guess, Maggie?" Vendemer asked.

"Maggie," Allegra confirmed.

"In that case, it's a rain check for me," Vendemer continued. "No one asks more questions or attempts to play matchmaker more than Maggie."

Allegra formed a quizzical look on her forehead and tipped her head.

Chuck saw what was happening. "Hey guys. Looks like little New York City libations talk. This good old boy from Atlanta is out. Work to do. This bottle is going to drink itself. Have fun. Talk soon, but hopefully not too soon. We could use ourselves a breather after this last one." He waved his hand, and not waiting for a reply ended his side of their video call. It bleeped as he hung up.

Vendemer continued, answering Allegra's funny look. Picking up where he left off, "Maggie. Always trying to hook me up with *Velda* in *Accounting.*"

She giggled. "That does sound like her. She's got me on the hook for someone named Heartspark. Sebastian, I think. She thinks it's her superpower, BenVen, come on. It'll be fun. You'll have a couple laughs. I'll make sure you do." Allegra was sitting next to him and gave him a small jab on the shoulder.

"There's only so much of Maggie's bracket brokering that one can handle." BenVen was actually fond of her incessant attempts to hook him up but couldn't let on his secret delight in having her fire Cupid's arrow at him.

"Bracket brokering?" Allegra questioned.

"You know, you two belong together and you two belong together and you two belong together and you two..."

"We got it. The third Velda is your safe word and you're out. Come on, you old curmudgeon. We're going to go have some laughs."

"Okay – but the third time she says 'Velda', I'm getting out of there."

"Deal." Allegra looked at Jacob and Adele, "You two? Good to go?"

Jacob spoke on behalf of them, making eye contact with Adele first, then the others, "We going to miss out. We have some place we need to be. Unfinished business that has an expiration date tied to it. Sorry we'll miss."

"We'll you'll be missed," Sydney added, closing her notebook since the call had ended.

Ruby had been thinking about what they were saying. Not about their excursion to Library Of Distilled Spirits, but about Ashford. "Listen, about Aiden Ashford," he said over the speaker to them. "It's a slow roll. We're going to take our time with him. See if the chemistry is correct. Maybe not as long as I tortured Paisley, but not too much too soon. Okay?"

They nodded as 'yes', knowing that stealth prudence was paramount.

Jacob asked, "Before we go, does anyone happen to have a Dictaphone? I doubt it, of course. Yes, it's all on our smartphones, but I don't want to leave my smartphone behind."

They all looked at him oddly. "Times Square," Allegra replied, "Those electronic shops for tourists might still sell them."

Adele queried, "They're still there?"

"Sure. Cameras, burner phones, cheap computers and all kinds of gizmos and gadgets."

Jacob looked at Allegra, smiled, and replied, "Allegra Sinclair – you are..." he looked at her holding his finger in the air between them, thinking to himself that she lit a familiar Victoria-like spark within him just weeks ago. Her eagerness and frolicsome spirit were welcomed, but they would remain cordoned off. "You are insightful, that's what you are," he concluded.

"Pit stop," Adele added tapping Jacob's forearm, and not understanding his pause in thanking Allegra. And as they briefly said their goodbye-for-now's to each other, Jacob and Adele left.

"Quick meeting. The best kind. Much unlike those prepping for Everglades City, a place which I didn't know was on the map." Vendemer said this while looking at the face of his phone.

Ruby, idle, listening to the conversation but not participating in the happy hour talk added, "I lost video, but I can still hear all of you."

Sydney spoke: "Ruby, your face froze on our end, but it's a good freeze. It's your superman pose. Looks like we're wrapped up here. Unless you have something else for us?"

"No. Like Chuck mentioned, go take a breather. We'll be back at it in a couple of weeks or so. Ruby out." He too hung up from the call.

After he did, and the faces on the video screen became blank squares, Tamsen poked her head around the corner. She only pointed at the laptop, not saying anything.

Ruby closed it and tossed it to the left of him. He reached to his right side, and on the small wicker couch facing the ocean was an ukulele. Picking it up, he strummed a few chords which fell together melodically.

"I take it the call is over?"

He didn't say anything as he looked for a complimentary sound to go along with the six chords he played in sequence.

"You're getting pretty good at that, old man." Tamsen left the porch for less than a minute while he continued to practice.

When she returned, she had a cup of tea for him. He coughed once and finally replied. "I'm going on tour with Jake Shimbirko. Gotta' practice."

She giggled. "Well, you need to get his name right first, it's Shimabukuro."

Ruby smiled as he picked at a few strings and strummed others.

"And you better get Brian's name right too. If we're going to eventually work with him."

He thought for a second, looking out at the surf, and said, "Brian Kemunumanimaha."

Giggling again, "Not even close. Say it with me."

He didn't as she proceeded. "Ke-ka-hana-ma-nui. Kekahanamanui."

"You write it down, phonetically for me, and tomorrow I'll have it all ironed out. And speaking of tomorrow..."

"I know," Tamsen smiled, "Brian's going to fall out of his chair when I walk in for the panel interview."

"Classic. Well pick him back up, we'll likely need him." Ruby was splitting his attention between the deep blue swells rolling in, his Oahu companion, and the ukulele cradled in his arms. "Does that ever get old?" he motioned with his chin toward the Pacific.

"Never." Tamsen sat down next to him. "There are some days when you look out at the sea and wonder, how could this not be perfect? And then you realize the things in between things and things over or under things which we do. The crazy little unknown details which make life just a little bit better. The tendering or rendering of things, I think of it as. Almost a remittance back to the world we live in for the fortunes we came across. Looking at the two of us, kind of accidentally. Wouldn't you say?"

Ruby found a smile, showing off some aged teeth, wrinkles around his eyes, and a chin which jutted out toward the sea. "Say, I kind of like the way you phrased that...a rendering...a remittance." He thought of the money he inherited and the divorce settlement she received – turning it all toward a benevolent cause. He considered how both he and Tamsen had accidentally found their way into Ellipsis' circle of influence. From unfamiliar and unwitting sources, the two of them, yet separately, found that the forces of good would outweigh the forces of evil. Doing something, anything, about the undone - through one's gifts was what Ellipsis was all about.

She sat with Ruby staring at the deep and mesmerizing North Shore. Panning it, left to right where Kaena Point's tip touched the horizon, the earth's curve could be seen. "Never gets old," she repeated. Then added, "When do you think they'll be on to you?"

"I've been thinking about that. Paisley..." Ruby thought about his friend. He sat the ukulele back down on the cushion next to him. "Jacob Paisley is somehow, some way, going to figure things out. And he'll likely be pissed because if there's an operation on Oahu, he's going to want in on it. I didn't think it was possible to love this place more than me, but he...?"

Ruby thought about the Aicon, *The Final Trade*, the sinking vessel from Jacob's vetting. That didn't go quite as planned but had a unexpected and pleasant outcome. "Listen, Tamsen. The next one's not going to be easy. These characters we're looking into. Well...perhaps there's nothing more corrupt than that. I can't think of anything. I'll say it again. There might not be anything more evil than this next one."

She let it sink in for a minute. "And you're sure Brian's going to be a good fit for the team?"

"I've had my eye on him for a while now. He's passing all of the subtle tests."

She looked at him with her best side eye, "Promise it isn't another test or some form of a baptism or crucible for me? Putting me through another gauntlet of some sort, are you?"

He stopped picking and using one hand slowly waved it across the space in front of him. "Do the waves always break from the left to the right, or do they sometimes switch and crash the other direction?"

"You are one cryptic old Brah. Do you know that?" Tamsen stood, then hunched over and gave Ruby a small kiss on his temple. "Macadamia nut cookies to go with your tea." In her bare feet, she walked across the covered porch with the wooden floor back into the open door of her Hale on top of the ridge facing the sea.

He thought of the next mission as he picked up the ukulele again. In his calculations, the diversities and learnings and calculations of this next ambition would be beyond what they'd previously done - and stretch them. All of them. As his friend Jacob Paisley would sometimes say to Adele, *"You're only doing this because of me."* Ruby wondered if this next ask may be too much. Afterall, they were doing good in what they had aligned. The outcomes from the victims were good stories with happy endings. Did he really need to venture beyond the horizon?

The next mission – one which wasn't even on Ruby's radar would take him into the unknown. He needed time to think, plan, assess, strategize, and build a roster of talent before he shared it with the others. It was the unknown. Like a great explorer, arcing the flatline, he had to go there. Like a young lover to a young lover, a small spark building into a great and raging fire, a great story which begins on page one – drawn from nothing becomes something, Ruby knew that the work to do would take time, and he also knew that time wasn't readily available.

*****

Jacob arrived at the Victoria meet up location intentionally early. He hadn't yet seen her. Madison Square Park was centrally located. In the middle of Manhattan, it was like the city's Switzerland – a neutral and charming location, surrounded by towering heights of significance. Nestled between Chelsea and Kips Bay, with the villages fifteen blocks to the south and the towers of the Chrysler, Rockefeller and Empire State Building's in the near distance to the north, the park was enclosed by New York City landmarks and history. Jacob was walking into the park from Madison Avenue, facing the one-way traffic. Without leaves on the trees, he could squint to see through to the iconic Flatiron building. The fountains had been shut off for the winter, and people were sparse on the park benches.

He looked up to the sky. For a day which had started off sunny and cool, it had become overcast and cooler, and now appeared that rain was approaching. The clouds were low in the sky, and it had become gloomy. It was a good decision, wearing the heavier wool coats. Adele was right and he'd thank her later.

An unwelcome sense of nervousness settled in. Jacob didn't know where it came from. He had a plan, was ready to execute, and knew what outcome he desired: the cessation of Victoria consuming real estate in his head. She no longer needed to be a deadbeat tenant who didn't pay rent. This was an eviction.

The gentle wind was blowing in a cold front. No thunder was heard, but the moisture was in the air. The yellow taxi cabs, cars and utility trucks making their tracks around the park added a bustle to the tranquility of the setting. Even though leaves didn't add greenery to the park as if it were late spring, summer, or early autumn – there was a dotting of bushes and shrubbery which held their leaves, planters hoisting small, manicured evergreens, climbing garden ivy, and even the grass was greenish in it winter hibernation. The streetlamps were old English, painted a glossy black, and rose up nine feet above the pavers where the walkways meandering through the park met the lawns.

Jacob kept walking, waiting, wondering. When he checked his watch, beyond the scratch on the face, the hands told him that she was five minutes late. *Typical Victoria*, he said to himself. *Maybe this won't even happen.*

"Hey," he heard her familiar voice. "It's me."

Jacob turned around. Yes. Yes, it was her. She was as beautiful as ever. Black leather boots with high heels approached her knees. A space above the top-line of the boot showing Victorias thighs was met with a short midnight purple pleated skirt, but she was covered with a black parka which she kept open to share herself with him. A paisley cream and purple top with an intentionally low neckline showed off her perky breasts. He glossed over her chest to look at her shiny brunette hair, blowing lightly in the breeze. The hood to the coat was trimmed with a fluffy faux fox fur which blew lightly in the breeze. This too, was left laying around her shoulders so that he could see her face and hair. Fresh from a salon, she lightly tossed her long hair and pulled a tendril from her cheek to the front of cheek to the side of her head, then behind the ear showing dangling earrings he'd bought for her years ago. Lazy curls from her long hair flowed to her breasts and the open blouse. Jacob looked at the silver earring flicker in the dimming light and winced.

She looked at him, sizing her up, as she had done for years before the break. Batting her eye lashes, she hesitated, "Hello Jacob. It's been too long. Hasn't it?"

Jacob said nothing.

"You don't look as happy to see me as I was hoping..."

"What was it that you were hoping for, Victoria?" Jacob's hands were in his pockets, thumbs exposed. What he wanted to do was to ball them up into fists but kept his cool playing his part. His overcoat was open also, showing the same thing he always wore now, an open collar dress shirt, a sports coat, dress slacks or jeans, and a complimentary soft soled pair of dress shoes. He no longer was impelled to dress his best. There wasn't a point to it. Long gone were his days of three-thousand-dollar suits and twelve-hundred-dollar leather-sole dress shoes beating a stride of confidence on a Wall Street sidewalk.

"I should begin with apologies. I'm sorry that I'm late. I know you dislike that. I had to take the subway, and it was running a little bit late. And more importantly, what you want to hear is that I'm sorry that I disappeared from you. I'm..." She looked at him, appearing sincere. Victoria's voice grew quiet, "I'm so very sorry. I was scared. A lot was happening and I...I cut and ran. I shouldn't have." She looked down, acting as if she were drawing up a deep regret and attempting to fall on the sword before her next ask.

He needed closure. Her pouty kindness wasn't going to do it. To listen to the apology was wanted. To accept the apology was not going to happen. Ellipsis had taught him and Adele many things. Among them, playing a part be it the main character or a supporting role. Jacob knew how to dial down anger. As a CEO commanding inspirational leadership; the captain of a luxury vessel on the west side of Oahu leveraging critical thinking; and now as an Ellipsis teammate pulling upon emotional intelligence – he now better knew that the current affairs could always be manipulated.

"You look good," she complimented him.

Finally, he spoke, returning to her blurb of apologies. "What's a girl like you doing taking the subway?"

She smiled. Her familiar face warmed up the chill. She began with, "Well, it's been an interesting couple of years."

"Has it?"

"Here we are." Victoria tipped her head to the side and toward him. Her hands were in her pockets for warmth, except when the breeze blew her hair back in her face. "Want to walk and talk? Or go somewhere and get a drink?" She quickly looked at him for his reaction. Without one, she added, "Or maybe a coffee?"

Jacob looked off into the distance, toward the circular walkway which surrounded the reflecting pool by the grand lawn in the middle of the park. "How about this way." He moved his chin toward the south side.

"Okay," she said cheerfully, "wherever you want to go, whatever you want to do. Anything." They walked on the stones laid tightly against each other through the park. She made little, small talk and he mostly listened to her fabricated story about taking time away from the city to find herself. Every fifty feet she would gently place her hand on his shoulder or elbow to steady herself on the stone below them. He looked at her hand on his shoulder, remaining there, then down at her boots. The thin heels were like one of the pairs he bought her.

"Christian Louboutin's?" Jacob thought of the designer two-thousand-dollar pair of black knee-high boots she wished for years ago.

"Ah...those were the good old days," she said and smiled. "Loved those and the Jimmy Choo's you bought me. I never said thank you enough. Steve Madden," she added.

He shrugged. "Times *have* changed," Jacob replied. "And you showed me, what was it...a transactional appreciation...instead of thanking me." As soon as he said it, he knew it was too soon for the trap.

"There are a lot of things that I wish I had done differently, Jacob. I can't say I'm sorry enough for ghosting out on you when you needed me."

I learned that I didn't need you, he thought to himself standing there looking at her trying to work into her point, her lusty trade-off, her seductive hustle. "Yeah, it was a tough time. But look at you – as... Well, you still look fantastic."

"Thanks Jacob. That means a lot to me." She looked into his eyes and didn't break her stare. "You sure you don't want to go get a drink?"

"Uh...this is good for now. Tell you the truth, I'm really trying to cut back on the sauce."

"You know, me too. But I remember..." She looked down at the ground and off into the distance and came back up pointing and shaking her index finger slowly, searching for his eyes, "Do you remember the extra-wild weekend in Boca where we swore off *ever* drinking again?" She giggled. "You said we pickled our livers that weekend."

Enough with the trip into the past, Jacob thought. "You know...I don't think there is a Memory Lane anywhere around here for us to travel on. Why are we here, Victoria. I know you. There's a motive or a mission or method of madness...?"

"It's the meaningful connection we had." She spun and looked at him. With the heels, nearly eye to eye, "And my proposition."

"There it is. *And your proposition.*" Jacob ridiculed her comment without overdoing it. He was more delighted and sportive than mean, to hear her say it.

"Meaningful connection, first. Then business. We had some fun, didn't we? Much fun? We can do that again." She looked at him from his shoes to his middle, pausing there, and then into his eyes, "I mean, if you want."

Jacob had the fish on the hook. He'd reel slowly so the line wouldn't break. "What do you have in mind."

She looked at him and pretended that she was brushing something off of the lapel of his overcoat. "If it starts raining, I'm buying us teas, or coffee, or a hot chocolate."

"My, how times have changed. Look at you...spending money," he razzed, knowing that was mostly of his own doing – him spending money on her for anything, everywhere, and for some reason he now struggled to validate.

"I spent money...on stuff...for you. Sometimes."

"How much?" Jacob asked.

"How much did I spend...? Well..."

"No, how much do you need? Business proposition...?" Jacob cut the chase short.

"It's not a crazy amount for you," she said, beating around the bush.

Jacob remembered the lavishness of trying to impress her in exchange for the girlfriend experience she provided him with. He grimaced and looked down to his own shoes to see hers creep closer. "It doesn't fall from the trees like it used to. There's no Paisley Pierce Capital Management wealth generator to fire up and have money flow from it. How much?" he asked.

Standing inches away from him, "It's a hundred thousand dollars."

"Guns?" he asked boldly.

"So, you know." She stated. "It's one of those X X X things you mentioned once. Quick money. Lots of opportunity. I need this...badly. I didn't know who else to go to." Victoria looked into his eyes. They were pleading for him to give her a handout.

"I know some things." He shrugged his shoulders. "And there's a lot I don't know. And there are some things I don't want to know that I do know. Guns aren't what you want to be involved in anymore. That, I know." Jacob was not only feeling taken advantage of – he was genuinely against it, knowing the harm firsthand in seeing the human traffickers leveraging firearms toward their heinous means. "Guns do bad things – especially when outside the lines of regulation."

"That isn't how you used to talk. *Anything goes*. Remember that guy?" She stayed close to him and extended her arm to his forearm. "Listen, I'm going to get it back to you quickly with a fifty percent return. A couple of turns. Maybe a couple of months. Yes, it's a business proposition, but I'll be smarter this time and steer clear of what happened last time. It's not like the guns are even being seen by me, I'm just fronting payment." Victoria face was within the proxemic space. His personal space hadn't been shared with her in years. A normal distance of about eighteen inches was down to eight. He could smell her perfume against the breeze this closely.

It felt awkward, but he hadn't landed her yet. "Can you tell me more about it?" Jacob asked.

"I could, but the less I tell you, the more you're not implicated. You really won't want to know more than the fact that guns are bought, they're sold, leave the details – the people, places, reasons - out of it and you're off the hook. Someone needs to front capital for the firearms at some point. They involved me because of the small network I've built..." She squeezed his forearm slightly. "I need some help here Jacob. I'll beg for it if you want me to. Please?" Her lashes batted as she watched for his reaction.

Victoria was needier than he had seen her. There was something she wasn't telling him, not for his own good, but for hers. He was being played – again.

You, Victoria, once my darling - no more my darling, are on my hook, Jacob thought to himself. "Hmm."

"I still know the sounds you make. I miss them. I do." When she said it, softly and seductively, nearly a whisper, she bit her lip. "Meant what I said about fun along the way too."

As he turned and took more steps along the stoned circle in the park, he played along with her. "I remember. Sure. It's up here...somewhere," Jacob pointed to his temple, just as Adele had in the morning.

She strutted her chin up into the air, looking at the darkening sky. The first drop of rain fell on her cheek. "You said I rarely bought you anything. Searching through some keepsakes... I found these." Victoria drew some handcuffs from her pocket. "Remember these?" She stopped and turned toward him.

Jacob was wondering whether he'd regret his divulgence of detail. "I do." The handcuffs reflected the dimming light from above and as they moved in her hands, the first evening lights from the towers surrounding them shimmered on the steel cuffs.

He stopped walking and turned toward her looking back to him. She saw him – much more of him than he wished she had. Jacob took a step in her direction. It was time for him to be the aggressor. Encroaching upon her personal space, she smiled a little more with each step closer to her he took. The space between them lessened. She continued to let the handcuffs dangle loosely on her manicured fingers between them. The shiny metal rocked on her middle finger as the space continued to close to inches.

"Give me those." He grabbed them from her fingers as the space between them disappeared. Jacob knew how they worked. He remembered that too. Withdrawing the key, he opened the steel cuffs.

She giggled her slow sensuous sex giggle. "Yeah, me too. Remember our European Sexcation? I'll never forget it. Impossible to forget that." Victoria was taking his memory for a little jog, referring to the use of handcuffs at some point on their trip.

He looked at her intentionally, remembering it well, but not saying anything. It was unforgettable.

"Remember boning me in Barcelona?" Victoria's eyes sparkled wildly.

"Of course."

"Remember mingling...remember mixing it up in Marseille? That was some fun,"

she giggled.

"Mm...you enjoyed that a little more than me...or she...but, yes I do...I do remember that." Jacob allowed himself to be amazed at how twice within a day a deeply buried secret had surfaced.

She took several small steps backwards, enjoying his slow pursuit of her, and bumped into the old English lamp post. As she did, it lit for the evening.

"Oh, damn. You still light me up," she teasingly added. There was no one around them. They were there alone – with exception to a woman walking slowly across the lawn.

Jacob reached for Victoria's arms. Guiding them behind her, to both sides of the lamp post. Overextended, he leaned into her and added, "I remember lots of things about us." It was a soft-spoken comment made into her ear as he continued holding her, tethered against him and the metal pole.

"I like it. A public place. How very daring. Look at you, as assertive as always." She shook a small lock of hair from her cheek. Victoria continued reminding him of the tantalizing sex-filled trek they had made, termed their 'sexcation'. "Remember screwing me in Sorrento...?" She moaned. Speaking softly. "The Hotel Bellevue Syrene...in Sorrento...?"

Jacob looked into her eyes deeply, then down to her lips and her body. Then he gazed off into the distance.

She paused, not breaking eye contact. She whispered, "Am I making you nervous? You're looking away."

"I remember," he said finally.

Standing there, nearly in a clasp of each other, chest to chest, she added one more recollection of their bawdy and wanton times together, "How about fucking me in Florence? Do you...? Remember fucking me in Florence?"

She felt the handcuffs wrap her wrist and click. "Uh..." her head fell back as if seductively with a moan and her chin jutted out close to Jacob's lips. Offering her wrists for the bonding, she gasped at his speediness with the bondage. They were inches from each other. Victoria could feel his warmth. "It's Symphony...like it?" she asked, thinking he was smelling the Louis Vuitton parfum she was wearing. He didn't answer. "I thought you might...enjoy it." She whispered in his ear, "This is the moment I'm hoping you kiss me."

Jacob was motionless against her. He leaned into her and continued to remain close to her while the metal tightened around her other wrist attaching her to the lamp, which was glowing brighter. His head was tipped to the side to avoid their face-to-face embrace. The first drips of rain had turned into a faint sprinkle.

Jacob took a small step back. Then two more. He didn't say anything, but he looked at Victoria, shackled to the pole.

Adele came from behind Victoria, where she had helped slip the cuffs on her wrists. She reached into Jacob's overcoat vest pocket and grabbed the recorder. She pressed STOP and then slid it into the inside chest pocket of Victoria's parka.

"Looks like rain," Adele said – to no one in particular - looking up into the darkening sky. She then reached into her coat and grabbed her cell phone and pressed ten digits, looking at a small piece of paper in her other hand. Tucking it back into her coat pocket when it was time to speak, calmly and collectively in gentle tone Adele spoke into her device, "Hello Parole Officer Vega. This is a concerned citizen." It appeared to be voicemail. "One of your recent parolees has some information you may want to be informed of. Victoria Santori is...well, she's standing here in Madison Square Park looking pretty and with a recorder of some, I don't know if it's incriminating information or not, but some public safety information - and she sure would love to have a conversation with you about her choices. Maybe you can send someone and...and have that talk. Oh, and a pair of keys for handcuffs. She is..." Adele looked at Victoria. Disenchanted in her thoughts that the seductress would ever change, she continued speaking, "Let's just say she has several entanglements. Thank you, officer, and thank you for keeping us safe." She ended the call and slipped the phone back in her pocket.

Adele looked at Jacob standing further back from Victoria. She approached Victoria and got as close to her as Jacob was. "I didn't hear everything that was said but will assume it isn't quite enough to send you back to that lovely island in the East River. But - it just might land you a first strike. Fuck with us and we will make sure that two and three follow expeditiously." Adele paused, "I'm sure you look better like you look now than in the color orange." Adele looked at Victoria, in her eyes, and again down to her barely-there blouse within the parka, and down to the black heeled boots. She saw Victoria moving her gaze of disbelief over toward Jacob.

Feeling hustled and betrayed, Victoria looked over to Jacob with disappointment first, then with resentment and scorn.

Stepping between them, grabbing Victoria by the lapel of her blouse Adele pulled her closer. She leaned in and kissed Victoria deeply and passionately. Adele held her lips against Victoria's mouth, moving her hand to her neck and finally lightly biting her bottom lip as she released.

Pulling away from Adele with a nod of her head, Victoria looked startled at the lip-locking move. She looked at Jacob again and back at Adele.

Adele let go of the silky paisley blouse, showing a lacy bra underneath. It fell back against Victoria's chest, as it was before the grasp. "No... Nope..." Adele shook her head slightly, shaking her own long brunette hair lightly. "Just...not feeling it. You know...I thought there would be fireworks. But I didn't even get the thrill of sparklers from that. Well...like Jacob said, sometimes it really is better how you play it in your head than in real life. Sorry." She backed up from the intimate embrace and added a comment. "So...so...so very unlike me. Doing that. But things are changing. Aren't they? And with the changes, we tend to go places which we didn't think we'd go. Right?" She gave Victoria a pat just below her shoulder and turned away from the woman she had just kissed, the one whom likely had kissed Jacob more than Adele herself yet had. Jacob wrapped his arm around Adele as she retreated and approached his side and looked back at Victoria one last time.

Together they turned away from her, away from Victoria who was shackled to the lamp post, and they placed their arms around each other pausing for a small moment with their backs to her.

Victoria wiggled, feeling the handcuffs restraining her wrists against the thick metal pole. "It's...it's starting to rain." She tried to pry the restraints. Useless, Victoria spoke loudly attempting to persuade them, "Okay – you got the best of me. Point made." It was futile and caused no reaction. Jacob and Adele took a couple steps away from her. "C'mon guys...uncuff me."

They ignored her and took a few more steps on the brick pavers, toward the dimming park. There was no turning back.

"Hey Jacob!" Victoria cried out. They paused, not turning around to see the seductresses wail, but only to hear it. "Did you tell her about that time I gave you an amazing after-hours blowjob on her desk outside of your office?"

Adele looked up to meet his glance and leaned into Jacob shoulder, wrapping her left arm around his back. Against the dark navy wool overcoat, Victoria could see from the light pole she was reined against and the fleeting daylight, Adele's light small hand embracing Jacob's lower back. It was Adele's left hand with the engagement ring, glistening brilliantly. It was perhaps the largest stone she had seen. In an act of defiance, opposed to the middle finger, and with her thumb tethering the other fingers, Adele extended only her ring finger for Victoria to see, showcasing its prominence.

For some, the engagement ring's sparkle would represent the luminous anticipation of things to come. For Victoria, it revealed an absence.

The guileful siren was left alone, wanting.

Jacob thought about asking Adele, *"What just happened there?"*, but he refrained from the question and squeezed her a little tighter.

Adele's question was building in her mouth, *"Who do you think was more surprised? You? Her? Or me? – shocking myself?"*, but she tabled it, appreciating his tighter embrace as a light rain began.

Slowly they walked through the park which was becoming darker as the approaching evening swallowed the light of day. The light rain began falling harder. Together, arm in arm, it was perhaps away from what they most needed to leave in the past. A past – comprised of a host of self-centric motives. The way forward was a step from the prosaic and prideful treadmill and a leap and reach toward mercy, grace, and sacrifices for unknown souls. Their unspoken words in this moment, and resolving to go forward to deliver a difference, were all that were needed for the meaningful connection between them.

*****

It didn't look like much from the outside. A white and arching awning extended around the corner location pitting it next to a Hyatt hotel near Union Square. It appeared clean and modern as Sydney and Allegra approached the meet up location. The city lights had overcome the daylight once again, and the light rain had displaced what was once a sunny then overcast day. Their destination, Library of Distilled Spirits, was much different on the inside.

Once inside, Sydney looked up to the high ceiling and the chandelier, "Nice. I like it. Secret little place you and your birdie friend would sneak off to?"

"I'm a first timer. She's a got a boyfriend so this might be one of their doings." Allegra looked at the bar with several patrons, making a fuss over smoking Old Fashions which had just been crafted by the bartender. Low lighting caused the hundreds of bottles of different alcohols and liquors to shimmer and warm the spirit. . A brass canopy hoisted above the bar area cradled wine glasses and other liquid concoctions.

Several of the small two-seater tabletops were taken and the largest communal table hosting seating for ten had a RESERVED sign upon it. Above the dark wooden table like one might find in an old library was a three-tiered chandelier fitted with twenty bulbous glass sconces. At the end of the bar, under the twenty-five-foot ceiling showcased lowly lit bottles of special reserves well-beyond reach, were available tables. Sydney and Allegra walked down there. Down-lighting made it appear brighter than it did from the other side of the bar. The glowing floor-to-ceiling library shelves were lit with warm Edison bulb lighting.

But again, once there, there was signage calling for reserved seating.

Maggie walked in on her man's, Chris's, arm. She spoke to a hostess briefly. And collectively they were heading toward Allegra's direction before noticing her.

"They're all reserved," Allegra pouted, looking at her friend.

"For us," Maggie added.

"Oh. Yes, of course. This is one of your job functions and you're good at it."

"And hello, stranger...remember me? Maggie?" Maggie gave Allegra a big hug and whispered, "I'm never letting go."

"Well, eventually you'll need to," Allegra contributed, "We'll want to drink and then have to go pee."

Maggie released her, and introduced her tall boyfriend, "Chris, finally...finally meet Allegra and...?"

Sydney spoke with her British affection, "Sydney... The name is Sydney. So nice to meet you. Maggie, right? And you too sir."

"Oh...English. You must have met up at the United Nations." As they were about to sit, while taking off their overcoats, Allegra, across from Sydney and next to Maggie, rolled her eyes for Sydney to see. Her secrets were coming together for a meeting, some of them.

Maggie repeated their names while pointing at them to finish with the introductions, "Allegra...my long-lost work wife, Sydney, Chris and me. Maggie."

Cowhide bar-stools, leather bench seating near the frosted windows facing the city lights outside, and marble round tabletops between the couples seating areas with a hardwood floor and area rugs made the establishment appear kitschy and trendy yet inviting. The one area seeming to be out of the color palette was the admiral blue velvet buttoned couch they were gathering at.

As they settled in, craft cocktail orders of authors names were taken, mixed and quickly distributed. Collectively they ordered an Edgar
Allen Poe, an F. Scott Fitzgerald, a Jack Kerouac, and a Truman Capote. The colors were as varied as the writers whose work dotted the establishment, tucked on a shelf or found leaning against a bottle liquor.

"You called ahead?" Allegra asked Maggie.

She pointed to her lengthy boyfriend with her thumb. "Chris's idea, but it's alright, right?" Maggie squeezed Allegra's forearm. "It's so good to be with you again. Let's *catch up* drink. Who are we waiting for?"

"BenVen and a new guy we're going to begin working with, Ashford. That is - if he can find his way here...Ashford. Out of towner. From Florida. Tampa. Big dude. You'll see."

"Benjamin Vendemer is on his way but running behind. He says something came up, an errand, and he needs to attend to that first, but to get the party started. In a text that is," Sydney pointed out, reading the face of her phone.

"Sounds like BenVen," Maggie added. She wondered how Sydney fit into Allegra's and Vendemer's work with the UN. *Did she work there?* So, she asked, "Does Sydney work in the UN's IT department or something?"

"Umm, she's a contractor, just like us." Allegra fibbed, thinking that the story they concocted back in the United Nation's meeting room shouldn't be tested too much more than that, tonight anyway. This was about fun. She wondered how Benjamin Vendemer had kept his secret life from her for so long. The thought of it sent her down a track of thoughts. In her mind, *click-click, click-click, click-click, click-click,* the wheels which resembled her memories, ran along the parallel steel tracks.

Allegra thought of how quickly an impression could be changed – remembering how he pulled her aside, her longstanding boss and the college professor looking man named Vendemer, and offered a new role of more responsibility, how he wanted to meet with her for drinks, how he coaxed her into venturing in a different direction and for a deeper cause, drew her into a clandestine organization for her technical prowess, then divulged that he too had been running a double life serving the secretive association: Ellipsis. She was lost in thought about how she had ascended into a completely changed woman in such a flash of time. It wasn't just the time and the change – it was more. It was a deeper and more soulful well-meaning alignment she had with her purpose and intentions. She pictured the transformation in her thoughts.

It was a meaningful connection...

"Hello...Allegra..." Maggie spoke. "Earth to Allegra..." was said a little louder. Maggie was fun but could be abrupt too. "They fry your brains over there on your work assignment at the UN?"

"Something like that," Allegra answered, seeing that Sydney was answering questions about her home location in London with Chris.

Maggie looked in the direction of her beau, Chris, and Sydney striking up a conversation about life across the pond and other common denominators. They both heard Sydney mention Leadenhall Market. "Okay – so they're hitting it off. Which brings me back to Sebastian Heartspark...he's Swedish, blond, a little short," Maggie looked at Allegra, "maybe a little shorter than you, talks like he's from..."

"No!" Allegra continued, "No more bracket brokering."

"Bracket broke..."

"I got a guy for you to meet up with...and I just found your future husband...and what are you doing Saturday night because I know a dude you'd hit it off with...and if we were going to buy four seats instead of three seats and so-and-so just happened to show up...Ugh! Maggie, it's exhausting." Allegra spoke with her hands cutting through the air up and down in front of her.

Maggie's shoulders slumped. She pouted, "I thought I was helping."

"You were. You were helping me realize that when the sparks fly, they'll fly. When it happens, it'll happen. But for me, Maggie...for me it's just got to be when I'm ready. Not when you, my friend, are ready."

"You went along with my charades for such a long time, though?"

"It was fun. It was recreation – for a while." She said it in the form of a question the second time scrunching her nose, "For a while? Then...then...I just played along, as your friend. And then it became a chore. And then..." Allegra was trying to make her point about the hookup hoard of men that Maggie was determined to pair her with was well beyond it confines, while easing into the fact that she wanted her friend to be happy with her own dude and not spend time on her part-time task of playing Allegra's advocator.

"I'm sorry." Maggie looked at Sydney and Chris enjoying their talk about favorite locations for a spot of tea and best watering holes to get sloshed and top joints for bangers and mash. London hacks talk.

"There's no sorry needed. I just, maybe should have said something about a year ago?"

"Ugh...I'm the worst."

"Well, you didn't find me a guy...so, you weren't really good at playing matchmaker anyway." They giggled. "Sebastian. Heartspark. Give - me - a - break. You find him on Tinder or what? There is no such surname by the way..." Allegra loved a good call-out, especially one delivered in tandem, lovingly and with a gentle left hook.

"Well, at least you looked it up," Maggie said defeatedly.

Their giggle broke out into a laugh as they continued speaking about guys and Maggie's new role and other office gossip which Allegra had been missing out on. Sydney and Chris kept talking about London and travel and somehow got on the topic of castle touring of the English countryside.

Unaware of the bar-goers continuing to arrive at Library of Distilled Spirits, their once cozy setting had grown busy the more that they all talked. The lights were dimmed, and the music was turned louder. Story-telling songs and folk music, yet not performed by the original artist, instead by local musicians, were played. The covers were with a slight deviation which made it their own. Someone sounding much like Carly Simon sang her *Anticipation*. Another artist resembling James Taylor, produced a swampy rendition of *Fire and Rain*. A guitar playing trio akin to Peter, Paul, and Mary asked about where the flowers went with a choir joining in on their question. Soulful music was enough of a reason to visit the establishment, but it was not what they were here for.

On the admiral and velvet blue cushion sat Allegra and Maggie. Vendemer arrived and pulled up the one remaining available chair near them and across from Allegra. As soon as he sat down, raindrops still dotting the shoulders of his jacket, he looked at them and said a quick hello, but then reached for the phone in his pocket, stood back up and walked toward the zinc-top bar. They watched their college-professor-looking boss move away with the phone next to his face.

"Look at you, you've got mizzle on you," Sydney declared, seeing the raindrop spots.

"What's that?" Maggie asked.

"Misty drizzle. Mizzle," Sydney added.

A small smile found its way to Maggie's face, admiring the British accent, and she whispered to Allegra, "She fun to talk with, isn't she?"

"Affable," Allegra nodded her head and whispered back. "You have no idea."

"Always working some deal," Allegra said aloud, acknowledging BenVen's arrival. She was wondering if it were an Ellipsis conversation or something for his veneer career, the façade, which he showed Maggie. The semblance gig was somewhat on a cruise control, allowing him to navigate the pieces and parts of Ellipsis as needed.

Sydney and Chris were deep in it: their reverence for English history.

"Great, now I've lost him to Sydney – go figure," Maggie teasingly said it out loud just to see if her suitor, Chris, would pick up on her voice. He did not and words about castles and graveyards and iconic landmarks continued to consume them.

They listened to them talk for a minute.

"She's pretty, isn't she?" Allegra asked Maggie.

"Not only is she an English fox, but she got that dry British humor. You know, where us crazy Americano's need to think about it – whether it was a joke at us, with us or for us?"

"No idea what you're talking about. All I know is she's sweepin' your dude off his feet right about now," Allegra teased.

"Eh...good riddance...goodbye Chris," Maggie waved her hand in the air, teasing back.

Small plates of soy-gingered crispy chicken, tomato-braised meatballs, slippery scallop sliders and garlic fries found their way to the table, and they munched and cruched as they chattered and nattered about nothing. The smells of the foods drifted between them as they distributed the tasty bites on napkins, resembling drawers from the Dewey Decimal System, next to their drinks.

Vendemer returned from the bar with a blood-red looking concoction. It had a garnish of basil and two black olives adorning the rim of the carnage-casted cocktail.

"What the hell is that?" Maggie asked as he set the heavy bottomed cocktail tumbler glass down. "Looks like something was butchered or died in your drink."

"A Stephen King," he answered. "Beet-infused Angel's Envy bourbon."

They giggled and Allegra added, "Of course..."

She wasn't paying attention to the murderous libation in Vendemer's glass. "Well, well – welcome to Gotham City," Allegra rose to greet Ashford with a small hug as he approached them at the end of the bar. "You found us finally."

"I found you finally," Ashford repeated. He, too, had raindrops on his shoulders, more so than Vendemer. "It's a little soggy out there," he said as he removed a brown bomber jacket from his broad shoulders. "Jesus," Maggie said, admiring his chest and the size of him. "A big, big boy."

"Not Jesus, it's Ashford. Nice to meet you. Are you Maggie?" Towering above, he held out a man's hand across the table. "I already know this guy, Sydney, and this lovely lady." Ashford nodded and winked at Allegra as Maggie, looking up, placed her small hand within his.

Then she used them both, clasping and pulling at him. "I'll scooch over, you sit in between us, Allegra and me." Vendemer was sitting across from Allegra. Ashford had been tugged to the blue velvet bench seating between the two of them, across from Sydney and Chris on the end finishing a sentence about Stonehenge.

Before they sat, Maggie and Allegra looked at each other briefly. Maggie's eyes were especially wide, code for her *oh my goodness* – approval at Ashford's presence. She mouthed, 'hell yes" to her friend.

"Yay. The gang's all here!" Maggie proclaimed.

"Don't you think?" Chris asked.

"Think what?" Maggie replied, spinning her head in his direction quickly and not knowing what he and Sydney were talking about – listening only to bits and quips of what they were discussing which was places like Cotswolds and Highlands and something of the Peak District.

"Don't you think a trip to England would be fun? Maybe catch Wales, Ireland, Scotland?"

Maggie didn't know if it was a legitimate offer to travel abroad with her Chris, but didn't hesitate, "I do!" She looked at Sydney with half of her cocktail between her hands. As they all talked about a disconnected series of topics, the folk music continued playing from local performers covering the tale-telling songs of old. A man sounding much like Harry Chapin sang a close version of *Cat's In The Cradle*; a woman who sounding nothing like John Denver performed *Annie's Song* likely for her lover; and an up-tempo version of Paul Simon's anthem to capturing human memory in vivid colors to help prevent faulty recollections. The lyrics to the tune, *Kodachrome*, found light in a world inching toward darkness and also depicted the distortion of reality

As a second round of drinks ascended into a third, Maggie's superpower took over, despite Allegra's honesty divulged earlier. Turning to her left, she asked Ashford, "So software – that's your thing?"

He nodded, "That's my thing. Engineer, developer, coder, creator, consultant. From Java to C++, Python to SQL."

"Hm...and Allegra's deal is hardware," she said looking at Allegra. "Seems like you two should pair together nicely." Allegra looked at Ashford, and he quickly glanced at her seeing her eyes peak in his direction through the strands of the soft curls of her long blond hair. They knew what Maggie was doing. It wasn't needed though. There was already a constructive curiosity in progress.

To Ashford – Allegra was an emerging interest. She was something he couldn't yet put his finger upon. His first impressions of her were of a woman with an unexplained depth – mysterious and in a pursuit of something not even she knew of. In their first few interactions, his takeaway was merely, *"There's something there. Not sure what it is, but a familiarity which is warm – comforting – yet also obscure."* But there was another reality taking center stage: Ashley. Whatever this ember might become – it would not be without time, and not completely letting go of Ashley.

To Allegra – Ashford was an emerging interest. He was damaged by his wife's disappearance. Perhaps he would never become anything more than hurt, half, and eternally hindered from moving forward. However, his depth was also alluring. There was something about him which was different. She thought of him as a puzzle which just may need to be solved. There was a familiarity in him, and she was trying to determine what it might be. Nevertheless – his interest in Ashley was part of this equation.

To Maggie – she was finding common denominators.

Sydney and Chris spoke more about travel other than England. Vendemer was studying the works from authors tucked in between bottles of colorful spirits and liquors. He slipped the waitress his card to cover the tab and to keep the drinks flowing. Occasionally he contributed to the conversation but was there for the music as much as anything else. The tale-bearing songs from the local artists continued playing. A quartet soulfully sang *Teach Your Children Well* in a Capella in homage to Crosby, Stills, Nash and Young; a woman sounding similar to Carole King played a piano while singing *You've Got a Friend*; and before Vendemer tossed back his final swallows of his third and final Steven King, the drink, a song of hope and optimism played. It didn't pair with the darkness of his drink, but BenVen liked the song. Yusuf Islam, the artist formerly known as Cat Stevens, wrote a song titled *Moonshadow*. Released in 1971 on the album *Teaser and the Firecat*, Yusuf acknowledged that the purpose of the song was of aspiration and confidence in a plan goodness: whatever happens to you...there's always something to look forward to. The rightfulness within the darkness was Ellipsis' ideal. To make the wrongs of the world more right without cognizance or mindfulness was the grand gesture and immersion.

The Library of Distilled Spirits was busy with new patrons now standing and gathering in small huddles.

He stood, indicating he was a short timer.

"Last to arrive, first to depart. Some things never change," Allegra said to him as Vendemer stood up and slipped his coat on.

"Time to call it a night for me." As Vendemer said his goodbyes, embracing each of them in some small way, and vacated his seat, it was snatched for a neighboring table. Only matchmaker Maggie, her swain, Chris, Sydney, Ashford and Allegra remained. As they adjusted to form more of a circle than in the bench style seating configuration with Vendemer, it was a three to two ratio. Maggie and Chris remained completely unaware of Ellipsis.

This meaningful connection was an important cover. Maintaining relationships with previous friends and acquaintances was normal behavior. Sudden and abrupt breakaways would be conspicuous. But there was an artfulness and proficiency required in enough and not too much information being shared. The conversation may have been good practice for that, with Ashford being coached and new.

However, Maggie's persistence was unrelenting. Her questions were steadfast and obsessive. Sydney and Allegra were ready to run interference if needed, but Allegra was learning things about the man she felt some odd familiarity with.

"So, I thought that Ashford was your first name. No? It's Aiden?"

There was no need to hide. Aiden Ashford replied with honesty, "That's correct. Aiden was the name I was born with, but out of respect for my parents who adopted me, I just began calling myself by their name opposed to the name my birth mother who gave me away called me. Ashford, instead of Aiden."

"Do you know what your birth surname is?"

"I do. It's Brand."

Allegra, interested in what might come next, had a soft smile while listening to Aiden Ashford speak. "Okay, Aiden Brand of Albuquerque. Ever been to New York?"

"Several times. But Albuquerque wasn't really where I was born either. It was a small town in Arizona." Aiden answered Allegra, then looked around the table at the others looking at the two of them with Maggie sitting in between them.

"Aiden Brand of Somewhere, Arizona. Where Phoenix? Tucson? Flagstaff?" Allegra asked. "Maybe Winslow or Sedona?"

"Blue. Small town in the White Mountains near the New Mexico border." Aiden Brand, originally of Blue, Arizona didn't realize the sparkle which he started.

"Blue?" Allegra reached for her phone. She spoke into it softly so that only the phone heard her speak. Scrolling quickly, she confirmed, "No shit. Blue, Arizona. Population...forty-six."

Within Maggie's twosome talent, her twain desire to couplet Allegra with anyone suitable, even with her slight scolding earlier, had just received a jewel for its crown. Her chin jutted out and she looked between them several times before saying it. She looked at Sydney and Chris and listened to a man strumming a guitar trying to pick up on the song he was about to sing. Tom Petty's, *Wildfowers*, sprung to life – illuminating the bright moment even more.

"Aiden Brand, of Blue, Arizona. Hm...how about that...? Allegra. Brand of Blue. That's what you do." She first looked at Allegra, then at the once Aiden Brand, and back at Allegra. The lyrics spoke of running away and finding a lover and falling within seeking respite from troubles and worries.

To make Maggie's awareness of Allegra's affinity to brands of blues less uncomfortable, Allegra quickly aided the moment by explaining the career choices she had made through the years.

However, Maggie's observation was flavored when Ashford Brand - of Blue, Arizona - salted the burbling with a long look at Allegra and a deep-seeded reflection, "You know, the first time I saw you, I said to myself, '*Self – where do you know her from?*' and felt that we had met at some point or time."

"Yeah, I know what you mean. A familiarity of some kind. Right?" Allegra gave him a kind quick frown attempting to draw a reason for it.

"Exactly. There's something about you that is...that is so unusually common, but not common like in regular. Prevailing maybe. Comfortable? A good comfort. Comfortable in a good way." His tongue stumbling only helped him.

Everyone had their own feelings and thoughts, yet there was a commonality which they shared too.

Allegra felt something she'd been seeking. A kindred spirit. Maybe it would evolve into another soul to share some of her secrets with, maybe all of them. It was new. Someone, perhaps, to confide in and with and completely. So far, the need to seek chemistry – as in an experiment, which Ruby had mentioned earlier was a stir of interest for her. Even Maggie couldn't know her new secrets, the Ellipsis kind. She watched his eyes twinkle as he spoke.

Maggie felt vindicated. Her pandering and matchmaking talent was exonerated. She knew it. Miss Sinclair would thank her for mastering the obvious later, sparking the long-sought relationship. Even though she wasn't the responsible broker of the bracket – the little things, the right word at the right time, were what made the something from nothing tend to happen. That and patience and persistence. Maggie, like a butterfly clumsily pouncing from petal to precious petal in a flowering garden, just required patience and a persistence to eventually get to the nectar.

Chris and Sydney felt a sense of affiliated interests as restless spirits, parallel travelers to distant lands. They infused each other with the wander and wonder of exploration.

Ashford felt that Lady Barbara had perhaps, in some small way, helped him find a form of freedom. Not the comprehensive liberation he was seeking, but a new horizon for him to explore and deliverance from the confinement he'd placed himself in. The psychic's words in Latin were akin to his needs, *'Set yourself free, for your own sake.'* He knew in that moment that the way forward may not need to be quite as bleak as the past - and that the potential of living brightly was a choice he would allow himself to make. He looked at each of them, knowing that they too had stories, like the tapestry woven from the lyrics of the songs playing.

A small flash of light and pearl of thunder rolled outside in the rainy streets. But that didn't matter. They complimented each other and imbued each other with something which was missing: a calm and cozy moment cocooned away from the world outside with its challenges and problems.

Sydney noticed Allegra and Ashford exchanging flashing fervent glances across Maggie who was brokering their coy coupling. It warmed her to see the emergence of something from nothing. Allegra's bright smile filled her face.

Together, the meaningful connection between them was like boarding a boat, destined to arc the flat line of the sea's horizon. It whispered that it may be taking them to new places of exciting possibilities, unexpected outcomes, and perhaps even to the greatest destination of all – a place of hope, of peace, and of freedom - for themselves and others. As an Ellipsis navigator might proclaim, when their vessel reached its destination: "Burn the boat!" The captain's commanding shout chosen would eliminate their return to what was - and forge a way forward.

Maggie and Chris traded lusty looks, and they stood to bid their farewells. Chris quickly asked Sydney for her number to keep in touch on their wanderlust conversation. While they were doing that, Maggie made sure she said something to Ashford which was loud enough for Allegra to hear. "Well, enjoy your time in the Big Apple. Be sure Eve here, gets you back to your hotel safely through our garden."

Like a touch and go, a small frown arrived and departed from forehead as she grabbed him for a quick hug. A handshake when they met. Hugging when they departed.

Maggie grabbed her friend who knew what she'd done. She whispered into Allegra's ear, "Sorry. Couldn't help myself." In a flash, they slipped on coats and were gone into the light sprinkles and the wet city streets.

Only the vigilantes remained. Fiddling with her phone, then downing her drink, Sydney added, "You know – I'm also calling it a night. Can't believe we've been here for hours. Feels like minutes, dears. Uber is three minutes away." She, too, slipped on her dress coat and made her way to the lady's room before she departed, not leaving with the lively lovers – knowing a bonding moment when one presented itself. Sydney slipped out the entrance with a small wave which they didn't notice.

The table where they sat was cleared and taken in minutes. Not too late, but no longer happy hour – the music filled the atmosphere while they sipped their author-influenced final libation.

"And then...it was just us," Allegra Sinclair of Brooklyn said to Ashford of Tampa or Aiden Brand of Blue, depending upon the moment. Crossing her legs, she scooted a little closer to him, close enough to almost feel the warmth of another person, this mighty man. She tucked a soft curly tendril behind her ear closest to him with two fingers, looking at him. He appeared slightly nervous to her, and she had an idea why. He looked at her quickly and turned his head to see the eatery and bar buzzing with life before looking at her again, longingly.

Out of the dating game a long time ago, he took a small sip of the half-consumed beverage, not wanting the moment to end and not certain whether she was game for another drink or if this was the last. He took it slow – wanting to absorb the sensation of this unfettered feeling. Knowing it might not last, Ashford allowed the twinkle of time he was enjoying with her to linger longer. Lady Barbara's words, '*set yourself free...for you own sake*'...and their intuited motive was sinking in and soothing his incessant sorrow.

In an uncanny song choice, following Maggie's farewell, and as if playing the part of fruitful fate – or of limp logic – or a riddled randomness had selected the next tune, a group sounding much like Jethro Tull began playing an intelligent song from the same artists about a clumsy trek through a lush wilderness – relating mankind as animals. The singers and musicians for the cover, including a flute, two guitars, and bongo drums were convincing in their story told within the melody. They sat in silence, listening to the music and its meanings, looking out at the liveliness of the less informed. Come what may – problems needing attention, solutions to serve, opportunities to leap and reach for – even new at this, they knew they had something greater than themselves to solve for. Whether it was through the Everglades, or New York City, or some yet unknown elsewhere; bungling through a swampy quagmire or concrete jungle, they were willing to play the part of a tiger.

Author's Note

There are no words which can properly describe the loss of a loved one by means of human trafficking. Losing a child, a partner, a wife or husband, a best friend, a neighbor, a member of the community...someone...anyone loved...it is one of the greatest defeats we endure as creatures. Modern slavery, human trafficking, is real. With estimated annual global profits of $150 billion USD, victimizing an estimated 25 million people worldwide (80% forced labor / 20% sex trafficking), human traffickers are in it for the money. For those impacted and those left behind, unknowing...there are times when the pain becomes too unbearable, when the suffering from loss cannot be comforted, when worse becomes the worst. If you think that you have come in contact with a victim of human trafficking, please call the National Human Trafficking Hotline at 888-373-7888. Learn more about missing and exploited children by visiting www.missingkids.org/home - or - by leveraging one of the resources available through the United Nations: www.unodc.org/unodc/en/human-trafficking/index.html

Afterword

BENDING THE ENDING

THE FUNDAMENTALS FOR

BRAND OF BLUE

- A MEANINGFUL CONNECTION FABLE -

But why? I asked myself... "Self, why go on? Why not just do your best to write a story and be done with it?"

There are several points and counterpoints taking place within my meaningful connection fable, Brand of Blue. This is an attempt to overshare why I wished to advocate for them.

Most importantly, the centerpiece: Human Trafficking. Modern slavery was brought to my attention as I worked upon an ESG (Environmental, Social, Governance) project. Understanding sustainability is a component in my career which I never imagined taking on or holding an interest in. Until, of course, it happened.

When the environmental piece spilled over into understanding what the United Nations does – my interest grew. The UN is a diplomatic international organization created for the intent and purpose of maintaining peace, securing friendly relations among nations, and seeking prosperity for all people while protecting the planet. Simple stuff – hardly. Founded in 1945, 193 member states (countries) and 2 non-member observer states comprise the unity of the UN. As outlined in their charter, the UN protects human rights, delivers humanitarian aid, promotes sustainable development, and upholds international law. Please visit www.un.org to understand the structure of the six principal operational organizations further.

Apart from learning from social communities, reading hundreds of articles on the topics, listening to podcasts and videos about all-things ESG and Sustainability, and seeking to understand how we've damaged ourselves – there are a few overarching and underlying points which jumped out at me.

The first is on the topic of the Environment, reducing greenhouse gas emissions and measuring our overall carbon footprint. Not to delve heavily into Scope 1 (buy), Scope 2 (burn), or Scope 3 (beyond) categories, but to simplify things, there's something to be said. It's simply this: We've been working upon reducing pollution for some time now. Bring on the acronyms: ESG specialists seek GHG data for the CDP and to understand CO_2 reductions along with LEED and ES improvements; support DEI analytics for the UN's 17 SDGs. There could be a lot to unpack there. We won't do that.

In the early 1400's mankind realized that we had waste and sanitation complications in urban areas. There were plagues and contaminations and diseases to manage to. In the 1800's we started treating wastewater. Water, land, and air pollution continued to increase well into the 20th century. Along comes the automobile, the industrial revolution, and population acceleration. In Ohio, where I'm from – the Cuyahoga River and Lake Erie erupted into flames for the first time in 1936. Legislation helped, some, with cleaning up the water and the air. But other things, other problems – as a result of our growth and other known and unknown complications took the place of the burning river and lake. There are hundreds of other examples to share, and it can get heavy quickly. To simply add levity to this, along comes a book by Theodor Geisel (a.k.a. Dr. Suess) in 1971: The Lorax.

This children's book tells a story of sustainable business in simple rhyme. It explains the concept of the circular economy in terms which primary school children can understand. The Lorax is the main character, who 'speaks for the trees'. He confronts the 'Onceler', a business which destroys trees for selfish gains. The book includes the well-known line, a rhyme" "Unless someone like you cares a whole awful lot, nothing is going to get better. It's not." The applies to many things: politics, business, the sporting world, relationships, and many emerging topics, such as sustainability. Dr. Suess, Theodor Geisel, admits – he didn't necessarily write books and colorful comic-inspired stories for children. He wrote them for adults to read and understand, and to read to children.

The second letter from the acronym is about covering social aspects.

Things are not as they should be. Her name is Elsa. She began her LinkedIn profile with a statement that said as much: *Let's face it, the world is not as it should be...* It stuck with me, obviously, because it was so on point for how things appear to be. I cannot say that we're as divided as we've ever been because I have but a glimpse at how things have always been. But I will venture into the statement that life is imitating sport. There's a defense and an offense at work against itself. Nationally and internationally, we're largely at odds with each other. Sure, there are unifications of sorts, but by and large – we have work to do. Against each other – we're far from what we could be accomplishing.

DEI – or diversity, equity, and inclusion is a hot topic in boardrooms and throughout government, business, sports, social media and more. Companies are making strides for a well-rounded workforce, while others may deem that they may have gone too far and are choosing to walk back some of their decisions.

Enter the UN's SDGs – the United Nations important. The United Nations (UNs) Sustainable Development Goals (SDGs) area call for action be all countries to promote human prosperity and protections while protecting our planet's best interests. There are 17 goals outlined to transform our world. From Health to Hunger to Education to Diversity to Resources such as Water and Air to Human Rights – the

SDGs seek peace, justice, and partnerships for equality and the advancement of all peoples.

The third letter of the acronym within ESG, is for Governance. Europe's CSRD (Corporate Sustainability Reporting Directive) and the United States' SEC (Securities and Exchange Commission) offer regulations, respectively, for sustainability reporting and to prevent public company market manipulation. They provide narrow scopes, which is boosted by another narrow scope from state legislation. Narrow? Either public in reporting or sizeable in revenue generation. This leaves a gap between what's measured and what's not. This is another day's problem. One step at a time. The first step is that you measure what you treasure and must start somewhere.

Beyond the themes listed above – there is a manner, a way, in which things happen. With 9 billion of us on the earth's surface, we're not all going to get along. So, the advancement of some with always outweigh the progress of all.

Why? Why does equality feel so imbalanced? Part of the answer to the question is...well, it's timing.

Empires rise. Empires fall. An empire thrives, hangs on, and perishes, on average, 250 years. Some last much longer, others are brief. Durations range wildly. The average: 250 years. From the Persian to the Carthaginian to the Aztec to the Russian to the British...and let's not omit the Roman empire (422 years)...the lifespan of an empire is limited. There are fiascos, wars, coups, rebellions, and unexpected ecological catastrophes which have brought empires to their knees, bowing down to the next.

In the year 2026, the United States of America, founded in 1776, will celebrate its 250th anniversary. In the words of Marshall Goldsmith: *What got you here won't get you there.* His expertise in helping global leaders overcome challenges and attain higher levels of success applies to not only what's happening at any given time in the United States, but throughout the world. In short, when we become obsessed with changing, challenging, and moving forward – we tend to thrive and progress. When we choose to maintain and deflect from making the tough decisions which are required to be made or work backwards, we often are distancing ourselves from our potential.

*****

FATE

When the best man finished his speech for the newly-wedded couple, those attending the ceremony found favor in his words. Cheering, reaching for a napkin to blot their eyes, or looking at the beaming and smiling faces of those they were seated with – those attending the wedding reception were moved by his comments which were about the new mister and misses, about their togetherness, about how they once met. It was about a little thing called fate.

There it is. The four-letter F word: fate.

Destiny – chance – predestination – luck – happenstance – kismet – lot in life – fortune... Fate takes several paths to reach its result: a state or end result that seemingly has been decided beforehand. The conclusion of fate? Generally favorable, but not always.

Hollywood, the movie and broader entertainment industry, rallies around fate. There are countless books and films featuring the concept. Turns out, betting and banking and brokering fate is big business. The publishing industry is as wealthy.

From The Butterfly Effect to Serendipity to The Adjustment Bureau and beyond, the entertainment industry plays host to dozens of flicks about the will or determining cause by which people and events are believed to come together or happen.

Wait just a minute. There's more than one fate? Fates. Plural?

From Norse mythology to Celtic Matres and Matrones to Lithuanian and other Balitic mythologies to Egyptian religion to the literature of the Mandaeans to British folklore and well beyond are the personifications of the fates. They take on namesakes of Truth and Righteousness, cosmic and natural order, and of judgment. Heavy? No heavenly – or supposedly.

So, this fate thing isn't new. It's been around a while.

In the ancient Greek religion and mythology, we find the Moirai, known in English as the Fates which were personified by Clotho (the spinner), Lachesis (the allotter), and gulp...the inevitable: death...also known as Atropos. The role of the three, the Moirai, was to see that every being lived out their destinies which were assigned to them. The Moirai either spun the thread of life, measured the thread of life, or cut the thread of life.

Otherworldly? Perhaps. Explaining the cosmos is...well, currently - impossible. It's better, or easier, or more practical to assign a divine being as the creator. Not to get into philosophical or religious opinions, but to advocate for something happening well beyond our current ability to rationalize its occurrence – we call our existence miraculously our happenchance. Again, fate isn't the fruit of our labor – but of a higher power or a pre-written script.

Our glimpse at the character, Lady Barbara, who leveraged fate as her profession as a psychic, one who had the ability to speak to those beyond, flirts with fate. Or did she truly have a gift of seeing things beyond what they are? What's to come is as cryptic as it can be embedded in what we choose to believe.

Late author, Terry Pratchett, described fate like this:

"Most of the Gods throw the dice, but Fate plays chess, and you don't find out till too late that he's been playing with two queens all along." Sir Terrence David John Pratchett, was an English author, humorist, and satirist, best known for the Discworld series. You don't bring a butter knife to a gun fight, do you?

I met my wife on our first day of eleventh grade. As a new Junior in her high school, we met outside of the chemistry classroom. Fate? Maybe. Maybe not. We'll get there. Someone introduced us. I looked at her and remembered thinking: Hmm... *There's something there*. But it turned out that she had a boyfriend, and I went on to have girlfriends and that was that. Wrong. We became friends. Working at McDonald's, not the same location we looked forward to every other Friday. Payday. Our high school was a closed campus, which meant no leaving the premises for lunch or any other reasons without consent. Did that stop a junior or senior from a cut and run opportunity. No. The rebels we were, we crept out nearly every other Friday to pick up her check, then travel for mine.

Prom season was approaching. She asked me who I was going with. Not yet working up the courage to ask Julie Tucker, I said that I didn't know if I was going to go.

"We should go together, then," she said. "It'll be great, we'll have fun."

"Well...actually...I was going to ask Julie Tucker," I replied with some hesitation, sharing my secret.

As we rolled over some railroad tracks on the way back to school, I looked over and saw her eyes welling up with the beginning of tears. The rest of the short drive was quiet. I had a crush on her. She had broken up with her longstanding boyfriend and was...available.

"What was I thinking?" was an epiphany over the weekend. *"Of course, I want to go to the prom with Millie Akins."*

Monday morning came and I made my play: "Hey Mil, I have something I want to ask you." Acting ever-so-cooly, I know that I was nervous.

"Can it wait? I'm late...for something." She either was playing coy or was truly pressed for time. I believed it may have been the latter.

"Sure..." I said it, but didn't want to. When the time was right, which was later, I asked her if she was still available, and she replied that she was because she just turned someone down...since I mentioned that I had something I wanted to ask her.

As often happens, friends became something much more. Fate? Perhaps. Here we are, at the time of this writing, wed for forty-three years. Not because I'm an awesome dude, but because she's a remarkable woman. You see, she's a better person than I am. She's a better human. Her heart is filled with compassion and forgiveness, her mind with wonder and potential, her soul with reverence and the essence of living life fully.

Everything happens for a reason...right? Maybe.

Fate isn't always fierce. It's sometimes playful. Mysterious, inexplainable, timely, and occasionally hope-filled. It's fuzzy.

LOGIC

Not nearly as fuzzy as the 4-letter F word, Fate's kissing cousin - Logic - also leads to outcomes: results, reactions, conclusions, corollaries, consequences, an aftermath, an implication, blow-backs, ramifications, side effects, upshots, fallout, and issues.

Logic is my go-to. It's science, mathematics, engineering, and technology. It comprises of what can be explained. It seeks validity and the principles of reasoning, inference and demonstration. The dollars and the numbers, the dissection of the obscure, the loathing for ambiguity – logic is all about something happening BECAUSE of something. A series of events led to a peculiar or completely explainable occurrence. If this is the world you reside in – you know that there are probabilities and odds and accuracies and fastidious facts which guide our outcomes.

As I review a candidate's resume, the first thing I seek is the dollars and the numbers. They'll spend the next hour or so bullshitting me in their rehearsed answers to my questions, sometimes sparking my excitement in their reply and other times causing me to skip questions drawing a quick close to our interview. Show me the money. Where are the substantiating metrics, the key performance indicators, to showcase the delivery of your work?

My family history states that I'm primarily English, French, and German. At least that's what my grandmother's handwriting noted from the Wood County registry and as it was passed down from generation to generation to generation. My parents remind me that our family owned a small parcel of land where the white house sits today and that my ancestor, David Byrnes and George Washington exchanged frosty glances while negotiating the acreage for the structure of the nation's capital. You see, it had yield – corn to reap – and following the autumn harvest, he would bequeath it to the country. Although President Washington oversaw the construction of the house, he never lived in it. It wasn't until 1800, when it was nearly complete, that President John Adams and his wife, Abigail, moved in.

Out of the other side of my mouth, I always thought of myself as a little bit American Indian. A smidge perhaps? My grandmother's handwriting also said as much. Proudfoot was among other names, Anglo-Saxan surnames, such as Webb, Pierce, Brandeberry, and Burnes. That explained my brow, I thought. I'm part Indian. Only the last name was provided: Proudfoot – like an American Indian might use. That justified some things. Perhaps it's why I love the sun, don't mind the heat, have an ability to tell time by the shadows, hold a good sense of direction. That 'perhaps' turned out to be a 'not at all'.

Come to find out - it was incorrectly written. For nearly forty years, I thought Proudfoot was a part of my heritage, only to learn it was incorrectly written. Profit. Profit was the surname which was part of our family history. Profit – or Proffit - chiefly Scottish and English, not chiefly American Indian.

Logic takes turns. Being made accurate, disproved, altered, edited, and taken out of context – what we think we now know has taken its turns along our timelines. As one generation learns and passes its wisdom to the next, alternative facts and new information and dis-covered data has a manner of changing our opinions and knowledge – causing our logic to evolve.

Logic. It's tough, truly difficult, to gather any logic from certain events or circumstances or happenings while they're taking place. Time and history help us see somewhat better. Not clearly, but clearer. It was 2001 – following the terrorist attacks of September 11th.

9/11/01 – If you were born, alive, remembering it - it's one of those dates we can draw from: *'Where were you when the towers were struck?'*

Was it Tower One or Tower Two? Building One, of the North Tower, I thought. That was where Windows on the World was located. The 106th and 107th floors. The fine-dining restaurant and entertainment venue was where I had gathered with other leaders for a company business meeting and to celebrate my Manager Trainer, Jon DuLong with my District Manager, John Elliott. You see, Jon, had just received one of our most prestigious awards, Trainer of the Year. He was the consummate professional I wanted to be as I progressed in my career. As for Mr. Elliott – he was the fun-loving, party-animal, resourceful, serious-if-necessary, ideal boss. I'd never reach his level of coolness.

High above the hustle and bustle of Manhattan, Jon had received the good news. We laughed, ate much, drank more and then a serious look found his face, "I have to call Dorothy!" he shouted. Dorothy, his wife, back in Toledo, Ohio. The bank of phones tethered to the wall in the lobby was where he called her to share the good news. Our celebrating didn't stop there. I can remember hailing a cab and making a trek to the once seedy and risqué Times Square area to waste the rest of our night. Giuliani led a team effort to clean up the touristy area in the mid-90s, running out the pornographic theatres, strip clubs, and other neon-lighted crime-infested rowdy public forum. Rudi Giuliani received much of the credit. It was Edward Kock's fourteen years of toil which set the stage.

Windows on the World. It was Building One, the North Tower. That's where we were years ago.

Reaching for a new clam-shell flip phone, I called Millie as I was on the way to work. "Hey – turn on the TV. I'm listening to the radio, and they said a plane just struck one of the twin towers."

"Oh my God..." she said.

Everything changed following that morning's moments.

Al-Qaeda had hoped - that in taking down the twin towers in New York City, attacking our Pentagon, and another flight destined for the nation's capital – which was crashed in Shanksville, Pennsylvania – that they would weaken the United States' standing in the world and support their political and religious goals in the Middle East and Muslim world. We all loathe the logic in that – as if there were any.

The thing about logic is that it can accompany unintended consequences.

Back to the terrible Tuesday in September of 2001:

Joseph Lott returned to his hotel room to iron a white shirt. He was wearing a green shirt that morning for an early breakfast. A work associate and friend presented him with a gift – an artsy necktie. So thrilled with it, blue and red in color, he decided to wear it for the presentation until she said, "Not with a green shirt." He was to give a presentation ay Windows On The World atop the World Trade Center. He quickly returned to his hotel room in the Marriott to iron a white shirt. At the elevator bank, awaiting his ride, returning him to the venue atop the top floors – the tower was struck.

James Stefurak had a morning commute and routine which took him from the subway through the World Trade Center for a coffee on his way to the Trinity Building. His calendar was unusually slow on September 11th, 2001, so he took his time and was running 20 minutes behind what would be his normal weekday schedule and avoiding the catastrophe.

George Keith had car troubles with his brand-new BMW. A scheduled visit to the service department for a three-minute repair took an hour. The mechanic needed to adjust the gear control with a simple fix. Running late, sitting on the expressway, he watched the calamity.

Greer Epstein took a cigarette break with a co-worker. She was in a strategy planning session, and they left their floor, descending downward. As the elevator arrived at its destination, the ground floor, it jumped, bounced, and rattled. Through windows she looked outside to see the people running, taking cover, and ducking the raining debris and flames. Outside, she saw a man taking cover next to a planter, using his briefcase to cover his head. Shortly after that, as they were leaving the building she could see people falling from the tower above her - and later, the second plane striking the second tower.

Laura Sorokoff Gelman was laid off on Friday, September 7th. A normal commute on the Port Authority subway would put her into the World Trade Center station at the time of the tragic event on the weekdays. She was planning on making the trip to the unemployment office next to the towers on that terrifying Tuesday but was waiting for the rush hour traffic to subside.

What does a wardrobe change, a slower than usual morning schedule, a car repair, a cigarette break, and a layoff have in common? Those events spared the lives of these people attached to the timelines, happenings, and choices made. It does not go without saying that they were victims and impacted in other painful and unimaginable manners. But it points out the timeliness within each moment. Be it math, logic, behavioral conduct, or unintended consequential incidents – one thing led to another. Was it fate, or logic, or something else which intervened in an action which led to an outcome?

What do you think?

What do you believe?

What will you choose to do with the unknown actions impacting you - which might just have been worse, unknown at the moment or in the time and space of your awareness?

* * * * *

RANDOMNESS

Pray for rain. Precipitation can be quite random. Right? I'm jumping ahead of myself here. I'll get to this story about randomness on the next page.

Randomness. Our lives are ruled by it. In his 2008 book, The Drunkard's Walk – How Randomness Rules Our Lives, the author Leonard Mlodinow masterfully challenges our perceptions and perspectives upon the science of probability. How the world works is a entertaining and enlightening as it can be intelligent. Mlodinow encourages the reader to consider the explanations and arguments made about logic, and to entertain the fact that 'we don't know what we don't know' as valid and nearly as valued as our reliable data toward decision-making.

Mlodinow goes on to explain that much of what happens to us in our lives, careers, investments, life decisions – is as much the result of random factors as it is our talents and skills, hard work and preparation. There are unforeseeable and fluctuating forces which can both increase our chances of success as well as quash our pursuits of our potential. Ability does matter, it is one of the factors that increase the chance of success but shouldn't be considered a sole source of our outcomes. It's quite seductive to assume that our results are ours alone.

After all, we've likely made it to the point we are, riding on someone's coattails. Those before us, paving our way, have made it easier for us to forge our way in many cases. Just as well, you'll hear about the 'good old days' when things were easier. But they probably weren't, just more familiar and comfortable to the old soul fondly remembering the past. Yes, the pace of change has changed pace – and what got you here won't get you there. Anyone living today must be grateful for the sacrifices made by the prior generations. Those coattails which we rode in on were tough: thinking steel-belted radial or Kevlar

When logic goes on holiday, takes a vacation from its intentioned reasoning, we might laugh at its fortunes and misfortunes. The Harvard Business Review points out in an article from Michael Mauboussin in February of 2011 that skill and luck combine forces in, you guessed it, randomness. Spain hosts an enormously popular Christmas lottery. In the mid-1970s, a man purchased a ticket which ended in the number 48. He found the ticket, bought it, and won the lottery. When he was asked why he was so adamant on "48", he simply explained that he dreamed of the number 7 for 7 nights and that seven times seven was 48. Well...

We may measure our successes as inaccurately as we measure our failures. Quantifying our skillsets and talents within our wins and losses factors into all of our conquests: business, investing, gambling, sports, relationships, and may lead to strong confirmations and confirmation biases as we age. Beta-checking results is a means for business professionals to compare outcomes. Think of Moneyball – Billy Beane's sabermetrics in Oakland A's baseball organization. Michael Lewis wrote the book because he fell in love with the story of undervalued MLB players and an organization better than it knew it could be. Mining the possibilities of winning, Billy Beane and Paul DePodesta hit their jackpot amidst criticism and scouting skepticism. A new look – or randomness. You choose.

It's human nature to seek out patterns and assign them to our living situations. We wish, though both our conclusive and unexplained research, that there's either a mysterious answer or stoic logic which can be entrusted to the inexplicable. Randomness sometimes produces repetition. And if it's repeatable, consistent with a pattern of any sort, it's logical, coherent, and reasonable. The problem with this is that there are patterns of illusions and illusions of patterns. We seek control when it isn't ours to host. The same is true of DUI and turbulence. We might think nothing of it to consume alcohol and get behind the wheel (hopefully not) while a little turbulence in a flight can be terrifying due to our lack of controlling the situation.

The random situations which could lead to terrible outcomes in the driving situation far outweigh the burst of air creating an eddy motion within the atmosphere. It's unlikely that turbulence will ever destroy an aircraft. Each day, about 37 people die in a drunk-driving crash in the United States. That's about 13,500 people per year. In the automobile, we believe we are in more control. Buckled in at 30,000 feet, not so much.

Random isn't so random in some situations, yet it still rules our lives. We try to explain it away with probability equations such as Time Series Forecasting, Confidence Intervals, Bayes' Theorem, Markov Chains, and Decision Trees which are a machine learning method which uses tree-like structures to model decisions based upon input features.

Pray for rain. Precipitation can be quite random. Right? A 50% chance of showers becomes an all-day drencher. Meteorologists occasionally get that forecast wrong. Back to rain - and the randomness of it from the previous page...

In 1991 I was fortunate enough to manage and operate one of the largest Champs Sports stores in their chain. Foot Locker is the parent company – purchasing Champs and Robby's Sports – melding the two together in the late '80s to scale Champs Sports. The growth for the mall-based retail chain was amazing – incredible - extraordinary - that was for most stores.

My district manager believed in me, and I believed in his vision. Thank you, Brian Bryant, for the opportunity. He reassigned the store manager before me due to the below average performance and explained to me that he needed a turnaround situation to happen. It would be difficult to do with the staff which I inherited. The six P's or the six pillars of commerce: People, Product, Plan, Procedure, Presentation, and Profit. I was tasked with tearing it apart and quickly putting it back together to restore the potential of what the high-volume store was capable of. All things began with the team – the people. Enter competition. The first thing was to make winning fun – through the people.

Baton Rouge, Louisiana was an hour's drive via Interstate 10 to New Orleans. The I-10 was primarily on peers through the Bayous filled with all kinds of critters. The Mississippi River was to the south, Lakes Maurepas and Pontchartrain were to the north as great Mississippi meandered through the wetlands toward the delta. I worked all the time. Cortana Mall was a mighty hub of discretionary spending, and we had the goods: from Air Jordans to Starter Jackets to surfboards to ball gloves, tennis racquets, pool cues, and golf clubs. It was a remarkable time to be in sports retail.

It rained a lot. Slight correction here: it rained all - the - damn - time. When it would dry up just enough to dash home quickly to mow the lawn, Millie would remind me to point the mouth of the mower away from the windows of our small home. The crawdads (mudbugs) would build their small domes outside of their burrows in the yard. Their mud teepees were two or three inches above the thick-bladed grass. We were twelve feet above sea level. The trashcans and garbage pails would often float down the street because there wasn't a place for the torrential rains to drain to quickly enough.

Business. Expeditiously engaging the people, filling holes in the lineup, seeking assertive and team members with service skills – things came together quite quickly. The home office was filling the shelves with the right stuff. Revenue, selling costs, add-on sales (accessories), shrink, overall profitability – all things get better when you have the right people. Yet I had a small problem: inventory turn. There were too many old goods choking turn. In retail, the bad word is FIFO. First in, first out. The idea was to not have old goods bog down inventory – whether it was dollars or units. The quantity of old goods was as important as the overall list price value.

As such, contests were created to push old goods. In looking at inventory reporting, there were several stock keeping units (SKUs) which were suffocating me. As it turned out, a rain poncho with a list price of $9.00 was a major culprit. "How in the hell do we have 3,000 of these?" The staff was without answers. Bought by a buyer and assigned by a merchandiser – where else in the U.S. was a Louisiana State University rain poncho going to sell? And why so many? The bright yellow piece of plastic folded in a purple wrapper wasn't going to jump off the endcap of the gondola folded so neatly. It didn't look like much. And it looked even uglier out of tidy purple wrapper. I wasn't permitted to ship it to one of the consolidation stores. An LSU rain poncho belonged in Baton Rouge.

Limping along through the year, we sold...like twenty. As the close to the year approached, an annual incentive contest – a trip to the Bahamas was announced. Millie and I had been fortunate enough to win one of those trips several years earlier. It was a cruise on Royal Caribbean's Song of America. You wanted to win those extravagant boondoggle company-paid trips.

Sales were especially strong, profits were awesome, accessory sales were looking great – the team I'd been fortunate to assemble were thriving. The chance of winning the Bahamas trip came down to selling FIFOs. The damn ponchos. They were my Achilles heel. It least throughout the year the price was reduced to $5, then down to $3. We may have sold another dozen. Great...only 2,988 more to go. If I lose the Bahamas trip, it'll be because of the damn $3 rain slickers. Forget the million-dollar sales increase. Hamstrung by a poncho.

Then, on a late November Friday afternoon a cold rain approached East and West Baton Rouge Parishes. Rain could be a deterrent – or it could drive people to the mall to shop.

Darryl was a tall, black, charming team member. He worked part-time. His smile was wide and infectious. We loved him, asking him to be our ambassador, welcoming people into the store asking them what they might be looking for to route their direction through the 15,000 square foot store.

"Hey Darryl – what do you think about wearing this poncho? It's raining -supposed to rain outside. Maybe sell twenty and I'll buy you a cheeseburger?"

"For reals? You'll buy me lunch if I can sell twenty of these?"

"Deal, Darryl?"

"It's a deal," he replied.

Standing at the store's lease line, he shook hands and smiled and directed traffic - all while several customers asked about the big yellow slicker he was wearing. Darryl sold several. Then came the rain, the hard relentless Louisiana rains, an unyielding deluge of rainfall settled in. It was dinner hour. He sold several more, primarily to customer's returning from the mall's exits – remembering the handsome black man back at Champs Sports wearing the LSU rain slicker.

"Darryl – you might just be in the wrong location. Here, take this cardboard box of two hundred, head to the exit, and sell as many as you can.

"Hey, I'm going to get one," said one of my cashiers. "They're only ringing up for dollar."

"Whaaaat...?" I may have asked, astonished that we'd missed a markdown.

"Darryl, try bundling them, five for five, ten for ten."

"What if they just want one?"

"Then it's one they get. Lead with the bundle and try to get rid of all of them if you can. Cash only. I'll eat the sales tax."

It was about seventeen minutes later that he returned, empty handed. "Where's the box? Where's your poncho?" I was confused by his blank stare. He pulled two hundred dollars in ones, fives and tens from his pants pocket. Two hundred and one dollars. He had sold his demo too.

Throughout the soggy weekend, we had staff at each exit – liquidating 80% of the ponchos. Throughout December, I prayed for rain. The prayers were answered.

Millie and I enjoyed the Bahamas a few months later. But it was nearly six months later, as I was promoted to be a district manager for the Phoenix, Arizona market that I deplaned. Mike Marchetti, my Regional Vice President and man which had promoted me, said as I greeted him, "There's someone we need to call. After he said his hello, 'He's here', Mike handed the phone tethered to the wall to me. Her name was Rebecca Harvey. She was our Vice President Sales Administrator. In other words, she had much to do with running our company. Following several words of congratulations and the importance of my new role, she added a question, "Remember that conversation which we had in the Bahamas?"

"I do. At the bar..."

"Yeah, that one. If anyone should ask, that was your interview toward becoming a District Manager." It wasn't always so easy. It didn't always rain when I needed it to. In fact, it was quite the opposite in the Valley of the Sun. The mall is long gone. Retail has changed dramatically over the years. It's an Amazon distribution center now. Go figure. But I'll never forget the reign of acting upon the rainy randomness in Baton Rouge. Go Tigers!

Leonard Mlodinow, American theoretical physicist and best-seller author is right – randomness rules our lives. I like the blurb which Fortune magazine describes his work by: *Mlodinow thinks in equations but explains in anecdote, simile, and occasional bursts of neon.*

When you see it, randomness, at work with your life – I hope you feel small and in awe of its power. It's quite exceptional that an unexpected, unexplained, unanticipated, unknown, unaffiliated, underappreciated, unbalanced, unbelievable, unbridled, unchanneled, and unapologetic action influenced you – like it or not.

*****

ELLIPSIS

Ellipsis – it's the 'something' which is happening behind the scenes of the present moment causing a leap from one topic to another - or one outcome to different one. The ellipsis, as in a grammatical tool, the punctuation mark of three dots (dot-dot-dot) which is indicative of an omission of words – suggests that something is left unsaid.

It's a garniture of sorts. The ellipsis is something which can decorate or beautify. An ornamentation or adornment or embellishment which highlights and showcases the fringe. What is happening in the border, the margins, the unwritten space on the page – it is often as required as the blazonry and the crux of the matter.

While trying to explain judgment – using a faith-based system of an eye-for-an-eye, or by seeking to understand how a loving God could allow bad things to happen to good people, we're limiting ourselves by thinking that an all-powerful being which laid out codes of conduct, an almighty creator of all-things, an eternal and omnipotent deity operates on our timeline. Our understanding of what is actually happening is minuscule. It's growing but is quite small and insignificant and evolving ever-so slowly. An immortal and immutable, merciful and compassionate Father would not need mankind's timeline to love, lead, judge. The justice of a omniscience creature would govern, preside, and steward the actions of man in an unimaginable thread of time. The linear chronology of time as we understand it is as faith-based as the beliefs and convictions which we conceive, borrow, and discard.

I've had the good fortune of working with large companies in the sports retail and technology industries over a long period of time. Corporate and motivational speakers are common at sales rallies, partner conferences, leadership events and seminars. From the late Bill Walton to Kurt Warner, Mike Ditka to Danica Patrick, Lou Holtz to Magic Johnson – they were great. I admired hearing about attempting to reach our potential from Molly Fletcher, the female "Jerry Maguire". Robert Herjavec, from *Shark Tank*, was fascinating to listen to – sharing his will to win secrets and hard-won wisdom in his simple yet sage advice.

But one speaker stands out. Not for a mouthful of distinguished words or stage presence charm or for think-piece material – but for his commonsense material. He's rather humble, crediting his school-teacher mother for much of the discipline and direction in his life.

Fred Falker is his name. He's a thought leader on "difference to distance" learnings. Attempting not to steal too much of Fred's material (you can find him on TED Talks) he shares with us his thoughts about our connections. Our meaningful connections with each other. You see, Fred Falker is an elder black man which has lived an experience we all wish to live: a human being which was struggling was helped by another human being. A Professor in his freshman year of college took him aside, across barriers to help him thrive.

There are lines of difference which we see. What we choose to do with the lines defines us. From distancing ourselves to maintaining those differences to closing the gaps in between – we choose the lines. We are the line drawers. We coach, teach and demand difference. When we intentionally and unnaturally connect with each other, we are building trust and erasing the us-versus-them approach. True, the lines we see, and draw can protect us - but not as much as they prevent us from our potential. When the lines we choose to draw are not about money and power – they can be about love and hope. Most people, when they seek the why, what, where, when, and how of line drawing are attempting to deliver a difference. The ability to connect with one another, to foster a meaningful connection, is about ability. Fred Falker points out that our decision to close the gap of differences is unity in humanity.

All of us have the ability, at all times, to create a more connected world by closing the distances which separate us.

Is taking resolution into our own hands the most appropriate course of action? Are vigilantes actions the answer to the unaccounted-for crimes of loathsome syndicates, vile clans, and heinous cabals. No. Well...probably not. A superhero didn't become the exemplification of equity with a cape alone. The guise and the pretense do not create the persona of a liberator. It required action, a vindication, redemption, and virtue of balance. The scales of justice are tied to the Roman pantheon. Justitia, or Lady Justice, is often found with a scale suspended from one hand, a sword which firmly grasped in the other, and usually a blindfold upon her eyes. She can be found on and within courthouses, law offices, palaces, town halls, educational institutions, and museums. On currency and in art – she holds the significance of law and order in her representation. Her presence on each continent is likened to impartiality and power.

This goddess of justice within Roman mythology, Justitia, is not always at the forefront of decisions made. However, she stands ever-present. Justitia holds a balanced scale, representing both sides of a dispute. Wearing a draping toga, behind her blindfold, within her mindfulness and stoic moral understanding – she also grips her sword. Coupled together her tools guide many of the corrections required. She can be diligent and rigorous - as well as swift and final.

Justitia is tireless in her pursuit of objectiveness and impartiality as well as righteousness and equity. She can be seen out in front and leading – as well as from behind and watching. Hers is also the path of the ellipsis – the unspoken word yet the 'something' which is happening behind the scenes of the moment causing a leap and reach from one to another. The intertwining between right and wrong - from the lines of difference to a closer proximity of distance – and from an un-knowing action to a knowledgeable consequence - act as her latitudes and longitudes in helping us reach our destinations. The laws may not always dictate righteousness because what may be legal might not be moral. Yet, her elliptical presence, constantly understanding matters of course, are our unspoken meaningful connections to our sapience and our brilliance.

Cover Design

The artwork for the cover of this book was created exclusively for Michael Woodruff. It is an original watercolor that was painted by Beth Stephano, a professional watercolor artist living on the island of Oahu. bethstephano.com

Beth Stephano

As they say, the journey of a thousand miles begins with a single footstep...

Originally from Erie, Pennsylvania, following a fine arts training both through grade and high school at the Erie County Vocational School and with private teachers and at the Erie Arts Center. Beth earned a scholarship and attended the Governor's School for the Arts at Bucknell University in the summer between her junior and senior years of high school.

She attended and graduated from the Art Institute of Pittsburgh. Her art courses were both commercial and fine art-based. After graduation, Beth relocated to Philadelphia to begin a career in advertising as a creative on the art side and later, arriving in New York City and working with many top advertising agencies.

As a painter in oils, Beth participated in First Fridays in Old City, Philadelphia and exhibited in different galleries. Also, she has exhibited in many artist shows and craft shows over the years.

Beth is known for her florals in oils which she has been painting for many years. Each has a unique perspective and fades into the dark field of the background in one place and differs in each work. It is always the game that she plays, not knowing where the point will be that fades into the background till she starts working.

Her watercolors are studies of the ocean and the cloud banks which travel across the horizon in many different variations of color, time of day and light. Trade wind clouds raining into the ocean at the horizon or into the ocean at night with white clouds passing by. Different iconic landmarks on Oahu are also a new interest. Recently, she has started painting on silk.

Currently: Living on Oʻahu, Hawaiʻi A member of the Hawaiʻi Watercolor Society and has participated in members show at the DAC Center. Featured pieces in the Members Show 2023 and currently 2024.

www.hawaiiwatercolorsociety.org

Beth was selected as one of the Top 10 Artists in Hawaiʻi at the Park West Competition 2022.

www.parkwestgallery.com/made-in-hawaii-2022-top-ten

Surrounded by beauty, inspiration is all around her. She pulls her visuals from her experiences on Oʻahu. It is her work every day to create her best piece next - hoping that her artwork brings happiness to someone else - in their home and life.